THE GRIM REAPER

Sobbing wildly, he rose above the grain and hewed to left and right over and over and over! He sliced out huge scars in green wheat and ripe wheat, with no selection and no care, cursing, swearing, the blade swinging up in the sun and falling with a singing whistle!

Bombs shattered London, Moscow, and Tokyo. The kilns of Belsen and Buchenwald took fire.

The blade sang, crimson wet.

Mushrooms vomited out blind suns at Hiroshima and Nagasaki. The grain wept in a green rain, falling.

Korea, Indo-China, Egypt, India trembled; Asia stirred, Africa woke in the night . . .

And the blade went on rising, crashing, severing, with the fury and rage of a man who has lost and lost so much that he no longer cares what he does to the world.

BY RAY BRADBURY
PUBLISHED BY BALLANTINE BOOKS

THE COMPLETE POEMS OF RAY BRADBURY
THE OCTOBER COUNTRY

THE OCTOBER
COUNTRY

Ray Bradbury

ILLUSTRATED BY JOE MUGNAINI

BALLANTINE BOOKS   **NEW YORK**

A Del Rey® Book
Published by The Random House Publishing Group

Introduction copyright © 1996 by Ray Bradbury
Copyright © 1943, 1944, 1945, 1946, 1947, 1954, 1955 by Ray Bradbury

Published in the United States by Del Rey Books, an imprint of The Random House Publishing Group, a division of Random House, Inc., New York, and simultaneously in Canada by Random House of Canada Limited, Toronto.

"Homecoming" and "Cistern" were copyrighted 1946 and 1947 respectively by Street & Smith Publications, Inc., reprinted by permission of Mademoiselle; "The Wonderful Death of Dudley Stone" was copyrighted 1954 by Street & Smith Publications, Inc.; "The Man Upstairs" was copyrighted 1947 by Harper & Brothers; "The Watchful Poker Chip of H. Matisse" was copyrighted by Galaxy Publishing Corporation; "The Dwarf" was copyrighted 1953 by Ziff-Davis Publishing Company; "Touched With Fire" was published originally under the title "Shopping for Death."

Del Rey and is a registered trademark and the Del Rey colophon is a trademark of Random House, Inc.

www.delreybooks.com

Library of Congress Catalog Card Number: 96-96537

ISBN: 978-0-345-40785-6

Manufactured in the United States of America

OR WHO ELSE BUT
AUGUST DERLETH

MAY I DIE BEFORE MY VOICES ‖‖

N ow, what in blazes does the above title mean?

It means that voices have been talking to me on early morns since I was about twenty-two or twenty-three. I call them my Theater of Morning Voices, and I lie quietly and let them speak in the echochamber between my ears. At a certain moment when the voices are raised high in argument or passionate declaration or are like rapiers' ends, I jump up (slowly) and get to my typewriter before the echoes die. By noon I have finished another story, or poem, or an act of a play, or a new chapter for a novel.

It was not always thus.

When I was twelve and began to write, I was busy loving and imitating Edgar Rice Burrough's *Tarzan*, L. Frank Baum's *Wizard*, or Jules Verne's *Nemo*; if the morning voices spoke, they went unheard.

So the first ten of my writing years were dumb stuff, hardly worth filing away as proof of my blind attempts to be something I could never be. Imitation was my way of life, so true creation couldn't raise its fine head.

To put it another way, there was an Undiscovered Country behind my medulla oblongata, but I never traveled there.

Shakespeare's Undiscovered Country was Death itself. Mine, when I finally charted it, led by my voices, was the territory of ideas, concepts, notions, conceits, all immensely personal, nowhere to be found in Burroughs, Baum, and Verne. I had to learn to reject them as models, keep them as loves, yes, but stop trying to live like John Carter, Tik-Tok, or the *Nautilus's* mad captain.

I came close to a breakthrough in high school. I remembered a dark place in my hometown and wrote a story titled "The Ravine," filled with terror and possible death. I was still too young to realize I had written my first original tale, something fresh from my nerve ending and ganglion. I put that story aside and went back on the road to Oz and Barsoom, which meant another five or six years delay in becoming myself.

I fell into becoming halfway excellent by the sheerest of word-association accidents. When I was twenty-two, I began to make lists of nouns to try to jar my subconscious into sitting up to beg for delivery. It didn't work until one hot noon, when, sitting in the sun with my portable typewriter, I wrote this: "The Lake." And suddenly I recalled the summer when I was seven and a blond girl companion busy building a sand castle ran into the lake and never came back. Death and drowning, drowning and death; what a mystery!

Swiftly, I set about remembering that day with my typewriter. By late afternoon, "The Lake" was finished and I was in tears. I knew that at long last, after years of dumb obfuscation, I had turned inward, discovered whatever might be original in my head, and caught it on paper. "The Lake," published in *Weird Tales* some months later, has never been out of print and has been anthologized dozens of times.

From that day on I began to pay attention to the right,

left, or perhaps lop side of my brain. I found that I could provoke memories of odd notions or strange metaphors by listing my favorite nouns, though I didn't know *why* they were favorites. Some of my first lists ran like this:

THE NIGHT, THE ATTIC, THE RAVINE, DANDELIONS, MIDNIGHT TRAIN WHISTLES, TENNIS SHOES, BASEMENTS, FRONT PORCHES, CAROUSELS, DAWN ARRIVAL OF CIRCUSES.

Then, over a period of months or years, I grabbed those words, turned them over, filed them behind my face, and waited for my new dawn voices to give them shape, rouse them, and drive me to my Underwood.

I soon learned that while I had imagined at age twelve, sixteen, eighteen, and twenty that I wanted to be a science fiction writer, I was for better or worse the illegitimate son of the Opera Phantom, Dracula, and the Bat. My proper home was Usher, my aunts and uncles descended from Poe. I wrote and sold most of the stories in *The October Country* to *Weird Tales* in the following years for a half cent or a penny a word, fighting off the editors' warnings that my stories were really not weird or ghost stories. Could I write something more, ah, traditional?

I could not and sent them "Skeleton" and "The Crowd."

I blundered into "Skeleton" through the kind services of my family doctor, who, when I complained of a strangely sore larynx, said, "That's all perfectly normal. You've just never bothered to feel the tissues, muscles, or tendons in your neck or, for that matter, your body. Consider the medulla oblongata."

Consider the medulla oblongata! Migawd, I could hardly pronounce it! I went home feeling my bones—my kneecaps, my floating ribs, my elbows, all those hidden Gothic symbols of darkness—and wrote "Skeleton." It's been around ever since.

About the same time my morning voices turned nightmare, I recalled a car crash I had witnessed when I was fifteen in which five people had been torn and killed. A crowd had appeared from nowhere, it seemed, in a few moments. The accident had happened outside the gates of a local cemetery. I wondered if . . . ? and wrote "The Crowd."

For some few years I appeared in almost every issue of *Weird Tales*, learning from these intuitive stories how I might write science fiction if I ever dared go back to that genre. The result was, of course, *The Martian Chronicles*, which is five percent science fiction and ninety-five percent fantasy. Purists have hated me since, for I dared to put an atmosphere on airless Mars so that my eccentrics could walk around, breathe, and live without all those damned airpacks.

"Homecoming" derived from my grandparents' next door house on those Halloweens when, as a boy, I rode out to the country with my Aunt Neva to bring home corn shocks and pumpkins to redecorate the house and stashed myself in the attic, made up as a wax-nosed, wart-chinned witch, to terrify relatives and neighbors. The names of the Homecoming Family are the names of my aunts and uncles. "Uncle Einar" is the name of my favorite loud-singing Swedish uncle, who was so much loved, I gifted him with wings and let him soar.

"The Next in Line," finally, resulted from my being foolish enough to descend into the graveyard catacomb in Guanajuato, Mexico. I walked between twin rows of mummies, men, women, and babies wired to the women's wrists, evicted from their graves for nonpayment of rent and stashed in the tomb hall, stricken and silently raving, against the walls. Once in the catacomb, I found it almost impossible to get the hell out. The mummies pursued me until I buried them in "The Next in Line."

So it went, story after story, once I opened the valves and acted out what Gerard Manley Hopkins once said: "What I do is *me*, for *that* I came." I tried to *stay* me from that time on.

The October Country was first published under the title *Dark Carnival*. The title story was not finished in time to go into the book. It hung around, collected midnights and funeral trains, and was finally published as a novel, *Something Wicked This Way Comes*, in 1962.

Which brings us the long way around again to the title of this foreword: "May I Die Before My Voices." My voices are still speaking, and I am still listening and taking their wild advice. If some morning in the future I wake and there is silence, I'll know my life is over. With luck, on my last day, the voices will still be busy and I will still be happy.

RAY BRADBURY
Los Angeles, California
April 24, 1996

OCTOBER COUNTRY

. . . that country where it is always turning late in the year. That country where the hills are fog and the rivers are mist; where noons go quickly, dusks and twilights linger, and midnights stay. That country composed in the main of cellars, sub-cellars, coal-bins, closets, attics, and pantries faced away from the sun. That country whose people are autumn people, thinking only autumn thoughts. Whose people passing at night on the empty walks sound like rain. . . .

THE DWARF

imee watched the sky, quietly.

Tonight was one of those motionless hot summer nights. The concrete pier empty, the strung red, white, yellow bulbs burning like insects in the air above the wooden emptiness. The managers of the various carnival pitches stood, like melting wax dummies, eyes staring blindly, not talking, all down the line.

Two customers had passed through an hour before. Those two lonely people were now in the roller coaster, screaming murderously as it plummeted down the blazing night, around one emptiness after another.

Aimee moved slowly across the strand, a few worn wooden hoopla rings sticking to her wet hands. She stopped behind the ticket booth that fronted the MIRROR MAZE. She saw herself grossly misrepresented in three rippled mirrors outside the Maze. A thousand tired replicas of herself dissolved in the corridor beyond, hot images among so much clear coolness.

She stepped inside the ticket booth and stood looking a long while at Ralph Banghart's thin neck. He clenched an unlit cigar between his long uneven yellow teeth as he laid out a battered game of solitaire on the ticket shelf.

3

When the roller coaster wailed and fell in its terrible avalanche again, she was reminded to speak.

"What kind of people go up in roller coasters?"

Ralph Banghart worked his cigar a full thirty seconds. "People wanna die. That rollie coaster's the handiest thing to dying there is." He sat listening to the faint sound of rifle shots from the shooting gallery. "This whole damn carny business's crazy. For instance, that dwarf. You seen him? Every night, pays his dime, runs in the Mirror Maze all the way back through to Screwy Louie's Room. You should see this little runt head back there. My God!"

"Oh, yes," said Aimee, remembering. "I always wonder what it's like to be a dwarf. I always feel sorry when I see him."

"I could play him like an accordion."

"Don't say that!"

"My Lord." Ralph patted her thigh with a free hand. "The way you carry on about guys you never even met." He shook his head and chuckled. "Him and his secret. Only he don't know I know, see? Boy howdy!"

"It's a hot night." She twitched the large wooden hoops nervously on her damp fingers.

"Don't change the subject. He'll be here, rain or shine."

Aimee shifted her weight.

Ralph seized her elbow. "Hey! You ain't mad? You wanna see that dwarf, don't you? Sh!" Ralph turned. "Here he comes now!"

The Dwarf's hand, hairy and dark, appeared all by itself reaching up into the booth window with a silver dime. An invisible person called, "One!" in a high, child's voice.

Involuntarily, Aimee bent forward.

The Dwarf looked up at her, resembling nothing more

than a dark-eyed, dark-haired, ugly man who has been locked in a winepress, squeezed and wadded down and down, fold on fold, agony on agony, until a bleached, outraged mass is left, the face bloated shapelessly, a face you know must stare wide-eyed and awake at two and three and four o'clock in the morning, lying flat in bed, only the body asleep.

Ralph tore a yellow ticket in half. "One!"

The Dwarf, as if frightened by an approaching storm, pulled his black coat-lapels tightly about his throat and waddled swiftly. A moment later, ten thousand lost and wandering dwarfs wriggled between the mirror flats, like frantic dark beetles, and vanished.

"Quick!"

Ralph squeezed Aimee along a dark passage behind the mirrors. She felt him pat her all the way back through the tunnel to a thin partition with a peekhole.

"This is rich," he chuckled. "Go on—look."

Aimee hesitated, then put her face to the partition.

"You *see* him?" Ralph whispered.

Aimee felt her heart beating. A full minute passed.

There stood the Dwarf in the middle of the small blue room. His eyes were shut. He wasn't ready to open them yet. Now, now he opened his eyelids and looked at a large mirror set before him. And what he saw in the mirror made him smile. He winked, he pirouetted, he stood sidewise, he waved, he bowed, he did a little clumsy dance.

And the mirror repeated each motion with long, thin arms, with a tall, tall body, with a huge wink and an enormous repetition of the dance, ending in a gigantic bow!

"Every night the same thing," whispered Ralph in Aimee's ear. "Ain't that rich?"

Aimee turned her head and looked at Ralph steadily out of her motionless face, for a long time, and she said nothing. Then, as if she could not help herself, she moved her head slowly and very slowly back to stare once more through the opening. She held her breath. She felt her eyes begin to water.

Ralph nudged her, whispering.

"Hey, what's the little gink doin' *now?*"

They were drinking coffee and not looking at each other in the ticket booth half an hour later, when the Dwarf came out of the mirrors. He took his hat off and started to approach the booth, when he saw Aimee and hurried away.

"He wanted something," said Aimee.

"Yeah." Ralph squashed out his cigarette, idly. "I know what, too. But he hasn't got the nerve to ask. One night in this squeaky little voice he says, 'I bet those mirrors are expensive.' Well, I played dumb. I said yeah they were. He sort of looked at me, waiting, and when I didn't say any more, he went home, but next night he said, 'I bet those mirrors cost fifty, a hundred bucks.' I bet they do, I said. I laid me out a hand of solitaire."

"Ralph," she said.

He glanced up. "Why you look at me that way?"

"Ralph," she said, "why don't you sell him one of your extra ones?"

"Look, Aimee, do I tell you how to run your hoop circus?"

"How much do those mirrors cost?"

"I can get 'em secondhand for thirty-five bucks."

"Why don't you tell him where he can buy one, then?"

"Aimee, you're not smart." He laid his hand on her knee. She moved her knee away. "Even if I told him where to go, you think he'd buy one? Not on your life. And why? He's self-conscious. Why, if he even knew I knew he was flirtin' around in front of that mirror in Screwy Louie's Room, he'd never come back. He plays like he's goin' through the Maze to get lost, like everybody else. Pretends like he don't care about that special room. Always waits for business to turn bad, late nights, so he has that room to himself. What he does for entertainment on nights when business is good, God knows. No, sir, he wouldn't dare go buy a mirror anywhere. He ain't got no friends, and even if he did he couldn't ask them to buy him a thing like that. Pride, by God, pride. Only reason he even mentioned it to me is I'm practically the only guy he knows. Besides, look at him—he ain't got enough to buy a mirror like those. He might be savin' up, but where in hell in the world today can a dwarf work? Dime a dozen, drug on the market, outside of circuses."

"I feel awful. I feel sad." Aimee sat staring at the empty boardwalk. "Where does he live?"

"Flytrap down on the waterfront. The Ganghes Arms. Why?"

"I'm madly in love with him, if you must know."

He grinned around his cigar. "Aimee," he said. "You and your very funny jokes.

A warm night, a hot morning, and a blazing noon. The sea was a sheet of burning tinsel and glass.

Aimee came walking, in the locked-up carnival alleys out over the warm sea, keeping in the shade, half a dozen sun-bleached magazines under her arm. She opened a flaking door and called into hot darkness. "Ralph?" She picked her way through the black hall behind the mirrors, her heels tacking the wooden floor. "Ralph?"

Someone stirred sluggishly on the canvas cot. "Aimee?"

He sat up and screwed a dim light bulb into the dressing table socket. He squinted at her, half blinded. "Hey, you look like the cat swallowed a canary."

"Ralph, I came about the midget!"

"Dwarf, Aimee honey, dwarf. A midget is in the cells, born that way. A dwarf is in the glands. . . ."

"Ralph! I just found out the most wonderful thing about him!"

"Honest to God," he said to his hands, holding them out as witnesses to his disbelief. "This woman! Who in hell gives two cents for some ugly little—"

"Ralph!" She held out the magazines, her eyes shining. "He's a writer! Think of that!"

"It's a pretty hot day for thinking." He lay back and examined her, smiling faintly.

"I just happened to pass the Ganghes Arms, and saw Mr. Greeley, the manager. He says the typewriter runs all night in Mr. Big's room!"

"Is *that* his name?" Ralph began to roar with laughter.

"Writes just enough pulp detective stories to live. I found one of his stories in the secondhand magazine place, and, Ralph, guess what?"

"I'm tired, Aimee."

"This little guy's got a soul as big as all outdoors; he's got *everything* in his head!"

"Why ain't he writin' for the big magazines, then, I ask you?"

"Because maybe he's afraid—maybe he doesn't know he

8

can do it. That happens. People don't believe in themselves. But if he only tried, I bet he could sell stories anywhere in the world."

"Why ain't he rich, I wonder?"

"Maybe because ideas come slow because he's down in the dumps. Who wouldn't be? So small that way? I bet it's hard to think of anything except being so small and living in a one-room cheap apartment."

"Hell!" snorted Ralph. "You talk like Florence Nightingale's grandma."

She held up the magazine. "I'll read you part of his crime story. It's got all the guns and tough people, but it's told by a dwarf. I bet the editors never guessed the author knew what he was writing about. Oh, please don't sit there like that, Ralph! Listen."

And she began to read aloud.

"I am a dwarf and I am a murderer. The two things cannot be separated. One is the cause of the other.

"The man I murdered used to stop me on the street when I was twenty-one, pick me up in his arms, kiss my brow, croon wildly to me, sing Rock-a-bye Baby, haul me into meat markets, toss me on the scales and cry, 'Watch it. Don't weigh your thumb, there, butcher!'

"Do you see how our lives moved toward murder? This fool, this persecutor of my flesh and soul!

"As for my childhood: my parents were small people, not quite dwarfs, not quite. My father's inheritance kept us in a doll's house, an amazing thing like a white-scrolled wedding cake—little rooms, little chairs, miniature paintings, cameos, ambers with insects caught inside, everything tiny, tiny, tiny! The world of Giants far away, an ugly rumor beyond the garden wall. Poor mama, papa! They meant only the best for me. They kept me, like a porcelain vase, small and treasured, to themselves, in our ant world, our beehive rooms, our microscopic library, our land of beetle-sized doors and moth windows. Only now do I see the magnificent size of my parents' psychosis! They must have dreamed they would live forever, keeping me like a butterfly under glass. But first father died, and then fire ate up the little house, the wasp's nest, and every postage-stamp mirror and saltcellar closet within. Mama, too, gone! And myself alone, watching the fallen embers, tossed out into a world of Monsters and Titans, caught in a landslide of reality, rushed, rolled, and smashed to the bottom of the cliff!

"It took me a year to adjust. A job with a sideshow was unthinkable. There seemed no place for me in the world. And then, a month ago, the Persecutor came into my life, clapped a bonnet on my unsuspecting head, and cried to friends, 'I want you to meet the little woman!' "

Aimee stopped reading. Her eyes were unsteady and the magazine shook as she handed it to Ralph. "You finish it. The rest is a murder story. It's all right. But don't you see? That little man. That little man."

Ralph tossed the magazine aside and lit a cigarette lazily. "I like Westerns better."

"Ralph, you got to read it. He needs someone to tell him how good he is and keep him writing."

Ralph looked at her, his head to one side. "And guess who's going to do it? Well, well, ain't we just the Saviour's right hand?"

"I won't listen!"

"Use your head, damn it! You go busting in on him he'll

think you're handing him pity. He'll chase you screamin' outa his room."

She sat down, thinking about it slowly, trying to turn it over and see it from every side. "I don't know. Maybe you're right. Oh, it's not just pity, Ralph, honest. But maybe it'd look like it to him. I've got to be awful careful."

He shook her shoulder back and forth, pinching softly, with his fingers. "Hell, hell, lay off him, is all I ask; you'll get nothing but trouble for your dough. God, Aimee, I never *seen* you so hepped on anything. Look, you and me, let's make it a day, take a lunch, get us some gas, and just drive on down the coast as far as we can drive; swim, have supper, see a good show in some little town—to hell with the carnival, how about it? A damn nice day and no worries. I been savin' a coupla bucks."

"It's because I know he's different," she said, looking off into darkness. "It's because he's something we can never be— you and me and all the rest of us here on the pier. It's so funny, so funny. Life fixed him so he's good for nothing but carny shows, yet there he is on the land. And life made us so we wouldn't have to work in the carny shows, but here we are, anyway, way out here at sea on the pier. Sometimes it seems a million miles to shore. How come, Ralph, that we got the bodies, but he's got the brains and can think things we'll never even guess?"

"You haven't even been listening to me!" said Ralph.

She sat with him standing over her, his voice far away. Her eyes were half shut and her hands were in her lap, twitching.

"I don't like that shrewd look you're getting on," he said, finally.

She opened her purse slowly and took out a small roll of

bills and started counting. "Thirty-five, forty dollars. There. I'm going to phone Billie Fine and have him send out one of those tall-type mirrors to Mr. Bigelow at the Ganghes Arms. Yes, I am!"

"What!"

"Think how wonderful for him, Ralph, having one in his own room any time he wants it. Can I use your phone?"

"Go ahead, *be* nutty."

Ralph turned quickly and walked off down the tunnel. A door slammed.

Aimee waited, then after a while put her hands to the phone and began to dial, with painful slowness. She paused between numbers, holding her breath, shutting her eyes, thinking how it might seem to be small in the world, and then one day someone sends a special mirror by. A mirror for your room where you can hide away with the big reflection of yourself, shining, and write stories and stories, never going out into the world unless you had to. How might it be then, alone, with the wonderful illusion all in one piece in the room. Would it make you happy or sad, would it help your writing or hurt it? She shook her head back and forth, back and forth. At least this way there would be no one to look down at you. Night after night, perhaps rising secretly at three in the cold morning, you could wink and dance around and smile and wave at yourself, so tall, so tall, so very fine and tall in the bright looking-glass.

A telephone voice said, "Billie Fine's."

"Oh, *Billie!*" she cried.

Night came in over the pier. The ocean lay dark and loud under the planks. Ralph sat cold and waxen in his glass coffin, laying out the cards, his eyes fixed, his mouth stiff. At his elbow, a growing pyramid of burnt cigarette butts grew larger. When Aimee walked along under the hot red and blue bulbs, smiling, waving, he did not stop setting the cards down slow and very slow. "Hi, Ralph!" she said.

"How's the love affair?" he asked, drinking from a dirty glass of iced water. "How's Charlie Boyer, or is it Cary Grant?"

"I just went and bought me a new hat," she said, smiling. "Gosh, I feel *good!* You know why? Billie Fine's sending a mirror out tomorrow! Can't you just see the nice little guy's face?"

"I'm not so hot at imagining."

"Oh, Lord, you'd think I was going to marry him or something."

"Why not? Carry him around in a suitcase. People say, Where's your husband? All you do is open your bag, yell, Here he is! Like a silver cornet. Take him outa his case any old hour, play a tune, stash him away. Keep a little sandbox for him on the back porch."

"I was feeling so good," she said.

"Benevolent is the word." Ralph did not look at her, his mouth tight. "Ben-ev-o-*lent.* I suppose this all comes from me watching him through that knothole, getting my kicks? That why you sent the mirror? People like you run around with tambourines, taking the joy out of my life."

"Remind me not to come to your place for drinks any more. I'd rather go with no people at all than mean people."

Ralph exhaled a deep breath. "Aimee, Aimee. Don't you know you can't help that guy? He's bats. And this crazy thing of yours is like saying, Go ahead, *be* batty, I'll help you, pal."

"Once in a lifetime anyway, it's nice to make a mistake if you think it'll do somebody some good," she said.

"God deliver me from do-gooders, Aimee."

"Shut up, shut up!" she cried, and then said nothing more.

He let the silence lie awhile, and then got up, putting his finger-printed glass aside. "Mind the booth for me?"

"Sure. Why?"

She saw ten thousand cold white images of him stalking down the glassy corridors, between mirrors, his mouth straight and his fingers working themselves.

She sat in the booth for a full minute and then suddenly shivered. A small clock ticked in the booth and she turned the deck of cards over, one by one, waiting. She heard a hammer pounding and knocking and pounding again, far away inside the Maze; a silence, more waiting, and then ten thousand images folding and refolding and dissolving, Ralph striding, looking out at ten thousand images of her in the booth. She heard his quiet laughter as he came down the ramp.

"Well, what's put you in such a good mood?" she asked, suspiciously.

"Aimee," he said, carelessly, "we shouldn't quarrel. You say tomorrow Billie's sending that mirror to Mr. Big's?"

"You're not going to try anything funny?"

"Me?" He moved her out of the booth and took over the cards, humming, his eyes bright. "Not me, oh no, not me." He did not look at her, but started quickly to slap out the cards. She stood behind him. Her right eye began to twitch a little. She folded and unfolded her arms. A minute ticked by. The only sound was the ocean under the night pier, Ralph breathing in the heat, the soft ruffle of the cards. The sky over the pier was hot and thick with clouds. Out at sea, faint glows of lightning were beginning to show.

"Ralph," she said at last.

"Relax, Aimee," he said.

"About that trip you wanted to take down the coast—"

"Tomorrow," he said. "Maybe next month. Maybe next year. Old Ralph Banghart's a patient guy. I'm not worried, Aimee. Look." He held up a hand. "I'm calm."

She waited for a roll of thunder at sea to fade away.

"I just don't want you mad, is all. I just don't want anything bad to happen, promise me."

The wind, now warm, now cool, blew along the pier. There was a smell of rain in the wind. The clock ticked. Aimee began to perspire heavily, watching the cards move and move. Distantly, you could hear targets being hit and the sound of the pistols at the shooting gallery.

And then, there he was.

Waddling along the lonely concourse, under the insect bulbs, his face twisted and dark, every movement an effort. From a long way down the pier he came, with Aimee watching. She wanted to say to him, This is your last night, the last time you'll have to embarrass yourself by coming here, the last time you'll have to put up with being watched by Ralph, even in secret. She wished she could cry out and laugh and say it right in front of Ralph. But she said nothing.

"Hello, hello!" shouted Ralph. "It's free, on the house, tonight! Special for old customers!"

The Dwarf looked up, startled, his little black eyes darting and swimming in confusion. His mouth formed the word thanks and he turned, one hand to his neck, pulling his tiny lapels tight up about his convulsing throat, the other hand clenching the silver dime secretly. Looking back, he gave a little nod, and then scores of dozens of compressed and tortured faces, burnt a strange dark color by the lights, wandered in the glass corridors.

"Ralph," Aimee took his elbow. "What's going on?"

He grinned. "I'm being benevolent, Aimee, benevolent."

"Ralph," she said.

"Sh," he said. "*Listen.*"

They waited in the booth in the long warm silence.

Then, a long way off, muffled, there was a scream.

"Ralph!" said Aimee.

"Listen, listen!" he said.

There was another scream, and another and still another, and a threshing and a pounding and a breaking, a rushing around and through the maze. There, there, wildly colliding and ricocheting, from mirror to mirror, shrieking hysterically and sobbing, tears on his face, mouth gasped open, came Mr. Bigelow. He fell out in the blazing night air, glanced about wildly, wailed, and ran off down the pier.

"Ralph, what happened?"

Ralph sat laughing and slapping at his thighs.

She slapped his face. "What'd you *do?*"

He didn't quite stop laughing. "Come on. I'll show you!"

And then she was in the maze, rushed from white-hot mirror to mirror, seeing her lipstick all red fire a thousand times repeated on down a burning silver cavern where strange hysterical women much like herself followed a quick-moving, smiling man. "Come on!" he cried. And they broke free into a dust-smelling tiny room.

"Ralph!" she said.

They both stood on the threshold of the little room where the Dwarf had come every night for a year. They both stood where the Dwarf had stood each night, before opening his eyes to see the miraculous image in front of him.

Aimee shuffled slowly, one hand out, into the dim room.

The mirror had been changed.

This new mirror made even normal people small, small, small; it made even tall people little and dark and twisted smaller as you moved forward.

And Aimee stood before it thinking and thinking that if it made big people small, standing here, God, what would it do to a dwarf, a tiny dwarf, a dark dwarf, a startled and lonely dwarf?

She turned and almost fell. Ralph stood looking at her. "Ralph," she said. "God, why did you do it?"

"Aimee, come back!"

She ran out through the mirrors, crying. Staring with blurred eyes, it was hard to find the way, but she found it. She stood blinking at the empty pier, started to run one way, then another, then still another, then stopped. Ralph came up behind her, talking, but it was like a voice heard behind a wall late at night, remote and foreign.

"Don't talk to me," she said.

Someone came running up the pier. It was Mr. Kelly from the shooting gallery. "Hey, any you see a little guy just now? Little stiff swiped a pistol from my place, loaded, run off before I'd get a hand on him! You help me find him?"

And Kelly was gone, sprinting, turning his head to search between all the canvas sheds, on away under the hot blue and red and yellow strung bulbs.

Aimee rocked back and forth and took a step.

"Aimee, where you going?"

She looked at Ralph as if they had just turned a corner, strangers passing, and bumped into each other. "I guess," she said, "I'm going to help search."

"You won't be able to do nothing."

"I got to try, anyway. Oh God, Ralph, this is all my fault! I shouldn't have phoned Billie Fine! I shouldn't've ordered a mirror and got you so mad you did this! It's *me* should've gone to Mr. Big, not a crazy thing like I bought! I'm going to find him if it's the last thing I ever do in my life."

Swinging about slowly, her cheeks wet, she saw the quivery mirrors that stood in front of the Maze, Ralph's reflection was in one of them. She could not take her eyes away from the image; it held her in a cool and trembling fascination, with her mouth open.

"Aimee, what's wrong? What're you—"

He sensed where she was looking and twisted about to see what was going on. His eyes widened.

He scowled at the blazing mirror.

A horrid, ugly little man, two feet high, with a pale, squashed face under an ancient straw hat, scowled back at him. Ralph stood there glaring at himself, his hands at his sides.

Aimee walked slowly and then began to walk fast and then began to run. She ran down the empty pier and the wind blew warm and it blew large drops of hot rain out of the sky on her all the time she was running.

THE NEXT IN LINE

I t was a little caricature of a town square. In it were the following fresh ingredients: a candy-box of a bandstand where men stood on Thursday and Sunday nights exploding music; fine, green-patinated bronze-copper benches all scrolled and flourished; fine blue and pink tiled walks—blue as women's newly lacquered eyes, pink as women's hidden wonders; and fine French-clipped trees in the shapes of exact hatboxes. The whole, from your hotel window, had the fresh ingratiation and unbelievable fantasy one might expect of a French villa in the nineties. But no, this was Mexico! and this a plaza in a small colonial Mexican town, with a fine State Opera House (in which movies were shown for two pesos admission: *Rasputin and the Empress*, *The Big House*, *Madame Curie*, *Love Affair*, *Mama Loves Papa*).

Joseph came out on the sun-heated balcony in the morning and knelt by the grille, pointing his little box Brownie. Behind him, in the bath, the water was running and Marie's voice came out:

"What're you doing?"

He muttered "—a picture." She asked again. He clicked

the shutter, stood up, wound the spool inside, squinting, and said, "Took a picture of the town square. God, didn't those men shout last night? I didn't sleep until two-thirty. We would have to arrive when the local Rotary's having its whingding."

"What're our plans for today?" she asked.

"We're going to see the mummies," he said.

"Oh," she said. There was a long silence.

He came in, set the camera down, and lit himself a cigarette.

"I'll go up and see them alone," he said, "if you'd rather."

"No," she said, not very loud. "I'll go along. But I wish we could forget the whole thing. It's such a lovely little town."

"Look here!" he cried, catching a movement from the corner of his eyes. He hurried to the balcony, stood there, his cigarette smoking and forgotten in his fingers. "Come quick, Marie!"

"I'm drying myself," she said.

"Please, hurry," he said, fascinated, looking down into the street.

There was movement behind him, and then the odor of soap and water-rinsed flesh, wet towel, fresh cologne; Marie was at his elbow. "Stay right there," she cautioned him, "so I can look without exposing myself. I'm stark. What *is* it?"

"Look!" he cried.

A procession traveled along the street. One man led it, with a package on his head. Behind him came women in black rebozos, chewing away the peels of oranges and spitting them on the cobbles; little children at their elbows, men ahead of them. Some ate sugar cane, gnawing away at the outer bark until it split down and they pulled it off in great hunks to get at the succulent pulp, and the juicy sinews on which to suck. In all, there were fifty people.

"Joe," said Marie behind him, holding his arm.

It was no ordinary package the first man in the procession carried on his head, balanced delicately as a chicken-plume. It was covered with silver satin and silver fringe and silver rosettes. And he held it gently with one brown hand, the other hand swinging free.

This was a funeral and the little package was a coffin.

Joseph glanced at his wife.

She was the color of fine, fresh milk. The pink color of the bath was gone. Her heart had sucked it all down to some hidden vacuum in her. She held fast to the french doorway and watched the traveling people go, watched them eat fruit, heard them talk gently, laugh gently. She forgot she was naked.

He said, "Some little girl or boy gone to a happier place."

"Where are they taking—her?"

She did not think it unusual, her choice of the feminine pronoun. Already she had identified herself with that tiny fragment parceled like an unripe variety of fruit. Now, in this moment, she was being carried up the hill within compressing darkness, a stone in a peach, silent and terrified, the touch of the father against the coffin material outside; gentle and noiseless and firm inside.

"To the graveyard, naturally; that's where they're taking her," he said, the cigarette making a filter of smoke across his casual face.

"Not *the* graveyard?"

"There's only one cemetery in these towns, you know that. They usually hurry it. That little girl had probably been dead only a few hours."

"A few hours—"

She turned away, quite ridiculous, quite naked, with only

the towel supported by her limp, untrying hands. She walked toward the bed. "A few hours ago she was alive, and now—"

He went on, "Now they're hurrying her up the hill. The climate isn't kind to the dead. It's hot, there's no embalming. They have to finish it quickly."

"But to *that* graveyard, that horrible place," she said, with a voice from a dream.

"Oh, the mummies," he said. "Don't let that bother you."

She sat on the bed, again and again stroking the towel laid across her lap. Her eyes were blind as the brown paps of her breasts. She did not see him or the room. She knew that if he snapped his fingers or coughed, she wouldn't even look up.

"They were eating fruit at her funeral, and laughing," she said.

"It's a long climb to the cemetery."

She shuddered, a convulsive motion, like a fish trying to free itself from a deep-swallowed hook. She lay back and he looked at her as one examines a poor sculpture; all criticism, all quiet and easy and uncaring. She wondered idly just how much his hands had had to do with the broadening and flattening and changement of her body. Certainly this was not the body he'd started with. It was past saving now. Like clay which the sculptor has carelessly impregnated with water, it was impossible to shape again. In order to shape clay you warm it with your hands, evaporate the moisture with heat. But there was no more of that fine summer weather between them. There was no warmth to bake away the aging moisture that collected and made pendant now her breasts and body. When the heat is gone, it is marvelous and unsettling to see how quickly a vessel stores self-destroying water in its cells.

"I don't feel well," she said. She lay there, thinking it

over. "I don't feel well," she said again, when he made no response. After another minute or two she lifted herself. "Let's
not stay here another night, Joe."

"But it's a wonderful town."

"Yes, but we've seen everything." She got up. She knew
what came next. Gayness, blitheness, encouragement, everything quite false and hopeful. "We could go on to Patzcuaro.
Make it in no time. You won't have to pack, I'll do it all myself,
darling! We can get a room at the Don Posada there. They say
it's a beautiful little town—"

"This," he remarked, "is a beautiful little town."

"Bougainvillea climb all over the buildings—" she said.

"These—" he pointed to some flowers at the window
"—are bougainvillea."

"—and we'd fish, you like fishing," she said in bright
haste. "And I'd fish, too, I'd learn, yes I would, I've always
wanted to learn! And they say the Tarascan Indians there are
almost Mongoloid in feature, and don't speak much Spanish,
and from there we could go to Paracutin, that's near Uruapan,
and they have some of the finest lacquered boxes there, oh, it'll
be fun, Joe. I'll pack. You just take it easy, and—"

"Marie."

He stopped her with one word as she ran to the bathroom door.

"Yes?"

"I thought you said you didn't feel well?"

"I didn't. I don't. But, thinking of all those swell places—"

"We haven't seen one-tenth of this town," he explained
logically. "There's that statue of Morelos on the hill, I want a shot
of that, and some of that French architecture up the street . . .
we've traveled three hundred miles and we've been here one

day and now you want to rush off somewhere else. I've already paid the rent for another night. . . ."

"You can get it back," she said.

"Why do you want to run away?" he said, looking at her with an attentive simplicity. "Don't you like the town?"

"I simply adore it," she said, her cheeks white, smiling. "It's so green and pretty."

"Well, then," he said. "Another day. You'll love it. That's settled."

She started to speak.

"Yes?" he asked.

"Nothing."

She closed the bathroom door. Behind it she rattled open a medicine box. Water rushed into a tumbler. She was taking something for her stomach.

He came to the bathroom door.

"Marie, the mummies don't bother you, do they?"

"Unh-unh," she said.

"Was it the funeral, then?"

"Unh."

"Because, if you were really afraid, I'd pack in a moment, you know that, darling."

He waited.

"No, I'm not afraid," she said.

"Good girl," he said.

The graveyard was enclosed by a thick adobe wall, and at its four corners small stone angels tilted out on stony wings, their grimy heads capped with bird droppings, their hands gifted with amulets of the same substance, their faces unquestionably freckled.

In the warm smooth flow of sunlight which was like a depthless, tideless river, Joseph and Marie climbed up the hill, their shadows slanting blue behind them. Helping one another, they made the cemetery gate, swung back the Spanish blue iron grille and entered.

It was several mornings after the celebratory fiesta of El Dia de Muerte, the Day of the Dead, and ribbons and ravels of tissue and sparkle-tape still clung like insane hair to the raised stones, to the hand-carved, love-polished crucifixes, and to the above-ground tombs which resembled marble jewel-cases. There were statues frozen in angelic postures over gravel mounds, and intricately carved stones tall as men with angels spilling all down their rims, and tombs as big and ridiculous as beds put out to dry in the sun after some nocturnal accident. And within the four walls of the yard, inserted into square mouths and slots, were coffins, walled in, plated in by marble plates and plaster, upon which names were struck and upon which hung tin pictures, cheap peso portraits of the inserted dead. Thumb-tacked to the different pictures were trinkets they'd loved in life, silver charms, silver arms, legs, bodies, silver cups, silver dogs, silver church medallions, bits of red crape and blue ribbon. On some places were painted slats of tin showing the dead rising to heaven in oil-tinted angels' arms.

Looking at the graves again, they saw the remnants of the death fiesta. The little tablets of tallow splashed over the stones by the lighted festive candles, the wilted orchid blossoms lying like crushed red-purple tarantulas against the milky stones, some of them looking horridly sexual, limp and withered. There were loop-frames of cactus leaves, bamboo, reeds, and wild, dead morning-glories. There were circles of gardenias and sprigs of bougainvillea, desiccated. The entire floor of the yard seemed a ballroom after a wild dancing, from which the participants have fled; the tables askew, confetti, candles, ribbons and deep dreams left behind.

They stood, Marie and Joseph, in the warm silent yard, among the stones, between the walls. Far over in one corner a little man with high cheekbones, the milk color of the Spanish infiltration, thick glasses, a black coat, a gray hat and gray, unpressed pants and neatly laced shoes, moved about among the stones, supervising something or other that another man in overalls was doing to a grave with a shovel. The little man with glasses carried a thrice folded newspaper under his left arm and had his hands in his pockets.

"*Buenos diaz, senora y senor!*" he said, when he finally noticed Joseph and Marie and came to see them.

"Is this the place of *las mommias?*" asked Joseph. "They do exist, do they not?"

"*Si,* the mummies," said the man. "They exist and are here. In the catacombs."

"*Por favor,*" said Joseph. "*Yo quiero veo las mommias, si?*"

"*Si, senor.*"

"*Me Espanol es mucho estupido, es muy malo,*" apologized Joseph.

"No, no, *senor.* You speak well! This way, please."

He led between the flowered stones to a tomb near the wall shadows. It was a large flat tomb, flush with the gravel, with a thin kindling door flat on it, padlocked. It was unlocked and the wooden door flung back rattling to one side. Revealed was a round hole the circled interior of which contained steps which screwed into the earth.

Before Joseph could move, his wife had set her foot on the first step. "Here," he said. "Me first."

"No. That's all right," she said, and went down and around in a darkening spiral until the earth vanished her. She moved carefully, for the steps were hardly enough to contain a child's feet. It got dark and she heard the caretaker stepping after her, at her ears, and then it got light again. They stepped out into a long whitewashed hall twenty feet under the earth, dimly lit by a few small gothic windows high in the arched ceiling. The hall was fifty yards long, ending on the left in a double door in which were set tall crystal panes and a sign forbidding entrance. On the right end of the hall was a large stack of white rods and round white stones.

"The soldiers who fought for Father Morelos," said the caretaker.

They walked to the vast pile. They were neatly put in place, bone on bone, like firewood, and on top was a mound of a thousand dry skulls.

"I don't mind skulls and bones," said Marie. "There's nothing even vaguely human to them. I'm not scared of skulls and bones. They're like something insectile. If a child was raised and didn't know he had a skeleton in him, he wouldn't think anything of bones, would he? That's how it is with me. Everything human has been scraped off *these*. There's nothing familiar left to be horrible. In order for a thing to be horrible it has to suffer a change you can recognize. This isn't changed. They're still skeletons, like they always were. The part that changed is gone, and so there's nothing to show for it. Isn't that interesting?"

Joseph nodded.

She was quite brave now.

"Well," she said, "let's see the mummies."

"Here, *senora*," said the caretaker.

He took them far down the hall away from the stack of bones and when Joseph paid him a peso he unlocked the forbidden crystal doors and opened them wide and they looked into an even longer, dimly lighted hall in which stood the people.

They waited inside the door in a long line under the arch-roofed ceiling, fifty-five of them against one wall, on the left, fifty-five of them against the right wall, and five of them way down at the very end.

"Mister Interlocutor!" said Joseph, briskly.

They resembled nothing more than those preliminary erections of a sculptor, the wire frame, the first tendons of clay, the muscles, and a thin lacquer of skin. They were unfinished, all one hundred and fifteen of them.

They were parchment-colored and the skin was stretched as if to dry, from bone to bone. The bodies were intact, only the watery humors had evaporated from them.

"The climate," said the caretaker. "It preserves them. Very dry."

"How long have they been here?" asked Joseph.

"Some one year, some five, *senor*, some ten, some seventy."

There was an embarrassment of horror. You started with the first man on your right, hooked and wired upright against the wall, and he was not good to look upon, and you went on to the woman next to him who was unbelievable and then to a man who was horrendous and then to a woman who was very sorry she was dead and in such a place as this.

"What are they doing here?" said Joseph.

"Their relatives did not pay the rent upon their graves."

"Is there a rent?"

"*Si, senor*. Twenty pesos a year. Or, if they desire the permanent interment, one hundred seventy pesos. But our people, they are very poor, as you must know, and one hundred seventy pesos is as much as many of them make in two years. So they carry their dead here and place them into the earth for one year, and the twenty pesos are paid, with fine intentions of paying each year and each year, but each year and each year after the first year they have a burro to buy or a new mouth to feed, or maybe three new mouths, and the dead, after all, are not hungry, and the dead, after all, can pull no ploughs; or there is a new wife or there is a roof in need of mending, and the dead, remember, can be in no beds with a man, and the dead, you understand, can keep no rain off one, and so it is that the dead are not paid up upon their rent."

"*Then* what happens? Are you listening, Marie?" said Joseph.

Marie counted the bodies. One, two, three, four, five, six, seven, eight. "What?" she said, quietly.

"Are you listening?"

"I think so. What? Oh, yes! I'm listening."

Eight, nine, ten, eleven, twelve, thirteen.

"Well, then," said the little man. "I call a *trabajando* and with his delicate shovel at the end of the first year he does dig and dig and dig down. How deep do you think we dig, *senor*?"

"Six feet. That's the usual depth."

"Ah, no, ah, no. There, senor, you would be wrong.

Knowing that after the first year the rent is liable not to be paid, we bury the poorest two feet down. It is less work, you understand? Of course, we must judge by the family who own a body. Some of them we bury sometimes three, sometimes four feet deep, sometimes five, sometimes six, depending on how rich the family is, depending on what the chances are we won't have to dig him from out his place a year later. And, let me tell you, *senor*, when we bury a man the whole six feet deep we are very certain of his staying. We have never dug up a six-foot-buried one yet, that is the accuracy with which we know the money of the people."

Twenty-one, twenty-two, twenty-three. Marie's lips moved with a small whisper.

"And the bodies which are dug up are placed down here against the wall, with the other *compañeros*."

"Do the relatives know the bodies are here?"

"*Si*." The small man pointed. "This one, *yo veo?*" It is new. It has been here but one year. His *madre y padre* know him to be here. But have they money? Ah, no."

"Isn't that rather gruesome for his parents?"

The little man was earnest. "They never think of it," he said.

"Did you hear that, Marie?"

"What?" Thirty, thirty-one, thirty-two, thirty-three, thirty-four. "Yes. They never think of it."

"What if the rent is paid again, after a lapse?" inquired Joseph.

"In that time," said the caretaker, "the bodies are reburied for as many years as are paid."

"Sounds like blackmail," said Joseph.

The little man shrugged, hands in pockets. "We must live."

"You are certain no one can pay the one hundred seventy pesos all at once," said Joseph. "So in this way you get them for twenty pesos a year, year after year, for maybe thirty years. If they don't pay, you threaten to stand *mamacita* or little *nino* in the catacomb."

"We must live," said the little man.

Fifty-one, fifty-two, fifty-three.

Marie counted in the center of the long corridor, the standing dead on all sides of her.

They were screaming.

They looked as if they had leaped, snapped upright in their graves, clutched hands over their shriveled bosoms and screamed, jaws wide, tongues out, nostrils flared.

And been frozen that way.

All of them had open mouths. Theirs was a perpetual screaming. They were dead and they knew it. In every raw fiber and evaporated organ they knew it.

She stood listening to them scream.

They say dogs hear sounds humans never hear, sounds so many decibels higher than normal hearing that they seem nonexistent.

The corridor swarmed with screams. Screams poured from terror-yawned lips and dry tongues, screams you couldn't hear because they were so high.

Joseph walked up to one standing body.

"Say 'ah,' " he said.

Sixty-five, sixty-six, sixty-seven, counted Marie, among the screams.

"Here is an interesting one," said the proprietor.

They saw a woman with arms flung to her head, mouth wide, teeth intact, whose hair was wildly flourished, long and shimmery on her head. Her eyes were small pale white-blue eggs in her skull.

"Sometimes, this happens. This woman, she is a cataleptic. One day she falls down upon the earth, but is really not dead, for, deep in her, the little drum of her heart beats and beats, so dim one cannot hear. So she was buried in the grave-yard in a fine inexpensive box. . . ."

"Didn't you know she was cataleptic?"

"Her sisters knew. But this time they thought her at last dead. And funerals are hasty things in this warm town."

"She was buried a few hours after her 'death?' "

"*Si*, the same. All of this, as you see her here, we would never have known, if a year later her sisters, having other things to buy, had not refused the rent on her burial. So we dug very quietly down and loosed the box and took it up and opened the top of her box and laid it aside and looked in upon her—"

Marie stared.

This woman had wakened under the earth. She had torn, shrieked, clubbed at the box-lid with fists, died of suffoca-tion, in this attitude, hands flung over her gaping face, horror-eyed, hair wild.

"Be pleased, *senor*, to find that difference between *her* hands and these other ones," said the caretaker. "Their peace-ful fingers at their hips, quiet as little roses. Hers? Ah, hers! are jumped up, very wildly, as if to pound the lid free!"

"Couldn't rigor mortis do that?"

"Believe me, *senor*, rigor mortis pounds upon no lids. Rigor mortis screams not like this, nor twists nor wrestles to rip free nails, *senor*, or prise boards loose hunting for air, *senor*. All these others are open of mouth, *si*, because they were not injected with the fluids of embalming, but theirs is a simple screaming of muscles, *senor*. This *senorita*, here, hers is the *muerte horrible*."

Marie walked, scuffling her shoes, turning first this way, then that. Naked bodies. Long ago the clothes had whispered away. The fat women's breasts were lumps of yeasty dough left in the dust. The men's loins were indrawn, withered orchids.

"Mr. Grimace and Mr. Gape," said Joseph.

He pointed his camera at two men who seemed in conversation, mouths in mid-sentence, hands gesticulant and stiffened over some long-dissolved gossip.

Joseph clicked the shutter, rolled the film, focused the camera on another body, clicked the shutter, rolled the film, walked on to another.

Eighty-one, eighty-two, eighty-three. Jaws down, tongues out like jeering children, eyes pale brown-irised in upclenched sockets. Hairs, waxed and prickled by sunlight, each sharp as quills embedded on the lips, the cheeks, the eyelids, the brows. Little beards on chins and bosoms and loins. Flesh like drumheads and manuscripts and crisp bread dough. The women, huge ill-shaped tallow things, death-melted. The insane hair of them, like nests made and unmade and remade. Teeth, each single, each fine, each perfect, in jaw. Eighty-six, eighty-seven, eighty-eight. A rushing of Marie's eyes. Down the corridor, flicking. Counting, rushing, never stopping. On! Quick! Ninety-one, ninety-two, ninety-three! Here was a man, his stomach open, like a tree hollow where you dropped your child love letters when you were eleven! Her eyes entered the hole in the space under his ribs. She peeked in. He looked like an Erector set inside. The spine, the pelvic plates. The rest was tendon, parchment, bone, eye, beardy jaw, ear, stupefied nostril. And this ragged eaten cincture in his navel into which a pudding might be spooned. Ninety-seven, ninety-eight! Names, places, dates, things!

"This woman died in childbirth!"

Like a little hungry doll, the prematurely born child was wired, dangling, to her wrist.

"This was a soldier. His uniform still half on him—"

Marie's eyes slammed the furthest wall after a back-forth, back-forth swinging from horror to horror, from skull to skull, beating from rib to rib, staring with hypnotic fascination at paralyzed, loveless, fleshless loins, at men made into women by evaporation, at women made into dugged swine. The fearful ricochet of vision, growing, growing, taking impetus from swollen breast to raving mouth, wall to wall, wall to wall, again, again, like a ball hurled in a game, caught in the incredible teeth, spat in a scream across the corridor to be caught in claws, lodged between thin teats, the whole standing chorus invisibly chanting the game on, on, the wild game of sight recoiling, rebounding, reshuttling on down the inconceivable procession, through a montage of erected horrors that ended finally and for all time when vision crashed against the corridor ending with one last scream from all present!

Marie turned and shot her vision far down to where the spiral steps walked up into sunlight. How talented was death. How many expressions and manipulations of hand, face, body, no two alike. They stood like the naked pipes of a vast derelict calliope, their mouths cut into frantic vents. And now the great hand of mania descended upon all keys at once, and the long calliope screamed upon one hundred-throated, unending scream.

Click went the camera and Joseph rolled the film. Click went the camera and Joseph rolled the film.

Moreno, Morelos, Cantine, Gomez, Gutierrez, Villanou-
sul, Ureta, Licon, Navarro, Iturbi; Jorge, Filomena, Nena,
Manuel, Jose, Tomas, Ramona. This man walked and this man
sang and this man had three wives; and this man died of this,
and that of that, and the third from another thing, and the
fourth was shot, and the fifth was stabbed and the sixth fell
straight down dead; and the seventh drank deep and died
dead, and the eighth died in love, and the ninth fell from his
horse, and the tenth coughed blood, and the eleventh stopped
his heart, and the twelfth used to laugh much, and the thir-
teenth was a dancing one, and the fourteenth was most beautiful of all, the fifteenth had ten children and the sixteenth is
one of those children as is the seventeenth; and the eighteenth
was Tomas and did well with his guitar; the next three cut
maize in their fields, had three lovers each; the twenty-second
was never loved; the twenty-third sold tortillas, patting and
shaping them each at the curb before the Opera House with
her little charcoal stove; and the twenty-fourth beat his wife
and now she walks proudly in the town and is merry with new
men and here he stands bewildered by this unfair thing, and
the twenty-fifth drank several quarts of river with his lungs
and was pulled forth in a net, and the twenty-sixth was a great
thinker and his brain now sleeps like a burnt plum in his skull.

"I'd like a color shot of each, and his or her name and how
he or she died," said Joseph. "It would be an amazing, an ironi-
cal book to publish. The more you think, the more it grows on
you. Their life histories and then a picture of each of them
standing here."

He tapped each chest, softly. They gave off hollow sounds,
like someone rapping on a door.

Marie pushed her way through screams that hung netwise

across her path. She walked evenly, in the corridor center, not slow, but not too fast, toward the spiral stair, not looking to either side. Click went the camera behind her.

"You have room down here for more?" said Joseph.

"Si, senor. Many more."

"Wouldn't want to be next in line, next on your waiting list."

"Ah, no, senor, one would not wish to be next."

"How are chances of buying one of these?"

"Oh, no, no, senor. Oh, no, no. Oh no, senor."

"I'll pay you fifty pesos."

"Oh, no, senor, no, no, senor."

In the market, the remainder of candy skulls from the Death Fiesta were sold from flimsy little tables. Women hung with black rebozos sat quietly, now and then speaking one word to each other, the sweet sugar skeletons, the saccharine corpses and white candy skulls at their elbows. Each skull had a name on top in gold candy curlicue; Jose or Carmen or Ramon or Tena or Guiermo or Rosa. They sold cheap. The Death Festival was gone. Joseph paid a peso and got two candy skulls.

Marie stood in the narrow street. She saw the candy skulls and Joseph and the dark ladies who put the skulls in a bag.

"Not really," said Marie.

"Why not?" said Joseph.

"Not after just now," she said.

"In the catacombs?"

She nodded.

He said, "But these are good."

"They look poisonous."

36

"Just because they're skull-shaped?"

"No. The sugar itself looks raw, how do you know what kind of people made them, they might have the colic."

"My dear Marie, all people in Mexico have colic," he said.

"You can eat them both," she said.

"Alas, poor Yorick," he said, peeking into the bag.

They walked along a street that was held between high buildings in which were yellow window frames and pink iron grilles and the smell of tamales came from them and the sound of lost fountains splashing on hidden tiles and little birds clustering and peeping in bamboo cages and someone playing Chopin on a piano.

"Chopin, here," said Joseph. "How strange and swell." He looked up. "I like that bridge. Hold this." He handed her the candy bag while he clicked a picture of a red bridge spanning two white buildings with a man walking on it, a red serape on his shoulder. "Fine," said Joseph.

Marie walked looking at Joseph, looking away from him and then back at him, her lips moving but not speaking, her eyes fluttering, a little neck muscle under her chin like a wire, a little nerve in her brow ticking. She passed the candy bag from one hand to the other. She stepped up a curb, leaned back somehow, gestured, said something to restore balance, and dropped the bag.

"For Christ's sake." Joseph snatched up the bag. "Look what you've done! Clumsy!"

"I should have broken my ankle," she said, "I suppose."

"These were the best skulls; both of them smashed; I wanted to save them for friends up home."

"I'm sorry," she said, vaguely.

"For God's sake, oh, damn it to hell." He scowled into the

bag. "I might not find any more good as these. Oh, I don't know, I give up!"

The wind blew and they were alone in the street, he staring down into the shattered debris in the bag, she with the street shadows all around her, sun on the other side of the street, nobody about, and the world far away, the two of them alone, two thousand miles from anywhere, on a street in a false town behind which was nothing and around which was nothing but blank desert and circled hawks. On top the State Opera House, a block down, the golden Greek statues stood sunbright and high, and in a beer place a shouting phonograph cried AY, MARIMBA . . . *corazon* . . . and all kinds of alien words which the wind stirred away.

Joseph twisted the bag shut, stuck it furiously in his pocket.

They walked back to the two-thirty lunch at the hotel.

He sat at the table with Marie, sipping Albondigas soup from his moving spoon, silently. Twice she commented cheerfully upon the wall murals and he looked at her steadily and sipped. The bag of cracked skulls lay on the table. . . .

"*Senora* . . ."

The soup plates were cleared by a brown hand. A large plate of *enchiladas* was set down.

Marie looked at the plate.

There were sixteen *enchiladas*.

She put her fork and knife out to take one and stopped. She put her fork and knife down at each side of her plate. She glanced at the walls and then at her husband and then at the sixteen *enchiladas*.

Sixteen. One by one. A long row of them, crowded together.

38

She counted them.

One, two, three, four, five, six.

Joseph took one on his plate and ate it.

Six, seven, eight, nine, ten, eleven.

She put her hands on her lap.

Twelve, thirteen, fourteen, fifteen, sixteen. She finished counting.

"I'm not hungry," she said.

He placed another *enchilada* before himself. It had an interior clothed in a papyrus of corn *tortilla*. It was slender and it was one of many he cut and placed in his mouth and she chewed it for him in her mind's mouth, and squeezed her eyes tight.

"Eh?" he asked.

"Nothing," she said.

Thirteen *enchiladas* remained, like tiny bundles, like scrolls.

He ate five more.

"I don't feel well," she said.

"Feel better if you ate," he said.

"No."

He finished, then opened the sack and took out one of the half-demolished skulls.

"Not *here*?" she said.

"Why not?" And he put one sugar socket to his lips, chewing. "Not bad," he said, thinking the taste. He popped in another section of skull. "Not bad at all."

She looked at the name on the skull he was eating.

Marie, it said.

It was tremendous, the way she helped him pack. In those newsreels you see men leap off diving-boards into pools, only, a moment later when the reel is reversed, to jump back up in airy fantasy to alight once more safe on the diving-board. Now, as Joseph watched, the suits and dresses flew into their boxes and cases, the hats were like birds darting, clapped into round, bright hatboxes, the shoes seemed to run across the floor like mice to leap into valises. The suitcases banged shut, the hasps clicked, the keys turned.

"There!" she cried. "All packed! Oh, Joe, I'm so glad you let me change your mind."

She started for the door.

"Here, let me help," he said.

"They're not heavy," she said.

"But you never carry suitcases. You never have. I'll call a boy."

"Nonsense," she said, breathless with the weight of the valises.

A boy seized the cases outside the door. "*Senora, por favor!*"

"Have we forgotten anything?" He looked under the two beds, he went out on the balcony and gazed at the plaza, came in, went to the bathroom, looked in the cabinet and on the washbowl. "Here," he said, coming out and handing her something. "You forgot your wrist watch."

"Did I?" She put it on and went out the door.

"I don't know," he said. "It's damn late in the day to be moving out."

"It's only three-thirty," she said. "Only three-thirty."

"I don't know," he said, doubtfully.

He looked around the room, stepped out, closed the door, locked it, went downstairs, jingling the keys.

She was outside in the car already, settled in, her coat folded on her lap, her gloved hands folded on the coat. He came out, supervised the loading of what luggage remained into the trunk receptacle, came to the front door and tapped on the window. She unlocked it and let him in.

"Well, here we *go!*" she cried with a laugh, her face rosy, her eyes frantically bright. She was leaning forward as if by this movement she might set the car rolling merrily down the hill. "Thank you, darling, for letting me get the refund on the money you paid for our room tonight. I'm sure we'll like it much better in Guadalajara tonight. Thank you!"

"Yeah," he said.

Inserting the ignition keys he stepped on the starter.

Nothing happened.

He stepped on the starter again. Her mouth twitched.

"It needs warming," she said. "It was a cold night last night."

He tried it again. Nothing.

Marie's hands tumbled on her lap.

He tried it six more times. "Well," he said, lying back, ceasing.

"Try it again, next time it'll work," she said.

"It's no use," he said. "Something's wrong."

"Well, you've got to try it once more."

He tried it once more.

"It'll work, I'm sure," she said. "Is the ignition on?"

"Is the ignition on," he said. "Yes, it's *on.*"

"It doesn't look like it's on," she said.

"It's on." He showed her by twisting the key.

"*Now*, try it," she said.

"There," he said, when nothing happened. "I *told* you."

"You're not doing it right; it almost caught that time," she cried.

"I'll wear out the battery, and God knows where you can buy a battery here."

"Wear it out, then. I'm sure it'll start next time!"

"Well, if you're so good, you try it." He slipped from the car and beckoned her over behind the wheel. "Go ahead!"

She bit her lips and settled behind the wheel. She did things with her hands that were like a little mystic ceremony; with moves of hands and body she was trying to overcome gravity, friction and every other natural law. She patted the starter with her toeless shoe. The car remained solemnly quiet. A little squeak came out of Marie's tightened lips. She rammed the starter home and there was a clear smell in the air as she fluttered the choke.

"You've flooded it," he said. "Fine! Get back over on your side, will you?"

He got three boys to push and they started the car downhill. He jumped in to steer. The car rolled swiftly, bumping and rattling. Marie's face glowed expectantly. "This'll start it!" she said.

Nothing started. They rolled quietly into the filling station at the bottom of the hill, bumping softly on the cobbles, and stopped by the tanks.

She sat there, saying nothing, and when the attendant came from the station her door was locked, the window up, and he had to come around on the husband's side to make his query.

The mechanic arose from the car engine, scowled at Joseph and they spoke together in Spanish, quietly.

She rolled the window down and listened.

"What's he say?" she demanded.

The two men talked on.

"What does he say?" she asked.

The dark mechanic waved at the engine. Joseph nodded and they conversed.

"What's wrong?" Marie wanted to know.

Joseph frowned over at her. "Wait a moment, will you? I can't listen to both of you."

The mechanic took Joseph's elbow. They said many words.

"What's he saying now?" she asked.

"He says—" said Joseph, and was lost as the Mexican took him over to the engine and bent him down in earnest discovery.

"How much will it cost?" she cried, out the window, around at their bent backs.

The mechanic spoke to Joseph.

"Fifty pesos," said Joseph.

"How long will it take?" cried his wife.

Joseph asked the mechanic. The man shrugged and they argued for five minutes.

"How long will it take?" said Marie.

The discussion continued.

The sun went down the sky. She looked at the sun upon the trees that stood high by the cemetery yard. The shadows rose and rose until the valley was enclosed and only the sky was clear and untouched and blue.

"Two days, maybe three," said Joseph, turning to Marie.

"Two days! Can't he fix it so we can just go on to the next town and have the rest done there?"

Joseph asked the man. The man replied.

Joseph said to his wife. "No, he'll have to do the entire job."

"Why, that's silly, it's so silly, he doesn't either, he doesn't really have to do it all, you tell him that, Joe, tell him that, he can hurry and fix it—"

The two men ignored her. They were talking earnestly again.

This time it was all in very slow motion. The unpacking of the suitcases. He did his own, she left hers by the door.

"I don't need anything," she said, leaving it locked.

"You'll need your nightgown," he said.

"I'll sleep naked," she said.

"Well, it isn't my fault," he said. "That damned car."

"You can go down and watch them work on it, later," she said. She sat on the edge of the bed. They were in a new room. She had refused to return to their old room. She said she couldn't stand it. She wanted a new room so it would seem they were in a new hotel in a new city. So this was a new room, with a view of the alley and the sewer system instead of the plaza and the drum-box trees. "You go down and supervise the work, Joe. If you don't, you know they'll take weeks!" She looked at him. "You should be down there now, instead of standing around."

"I'll go down," he said.

"I'll go down with you. I want to buy some magazines."

"You won't find any American magazines in a town like this."

"I can look, can't I?"

"Besides, we haven't much money," he said. "I don't want to have to wire my bank. It takes a god-awful time and it's not worth the bother."

"I can at least have my magazines," she said.

"Maybe one or two," he said.

"As many as I want," she said, feverishly, on the bed.

"For God's sake, you've got a million magazines in the car now, *Posts, Collier's, Mercury, Atlantic Monthlys, Barnaby, Superman*! You haven't read half of the articles."

"But they're not new," she said. "They're not new, I've *looked* at them and after you've looked at a thing, I don't know—"

"Try reading them instead of looking at them," he said.

As they came downstairs night was in the plaza.

"Give me a few pesos," she said, and he gave her some. "Teach me to say about magazines in Spanish," she said.

"*Quiero una publicacion Americano,*" he said, walking swiftly.

She repeated it, stumblingly, and laughed. "Thanks."

He went on ahead to the mechanic's shop, and she turned in at the nearest *Farmacia Botica*, and all the magazines racked before her there were alien colors and alien names. She read the titles with swift moves of her eyes and looked at the old man behind the counter. "Do you have American magazines?" she asked in English, embarrassed to use the Spanish words.

The old man stared at her.

"*Habla Ingles?*" she asked.

"No, *senorita.*"

She tried to think of the right words. "*Quiero*—no!" She stopped. She started again. "*Americano—uh—magg-ah-zeen-as?*"

"Oh, no, *senorita!*"

Her hands opened wide at her waist, then closed, like mouths. Her mouth opened and closed. The shop had a veil over it, in her eyes. Here she was and here were these small baked adobe people to whom she could say nothing and from whom she could get no words she understood, and she was in a town of people who said no words to her and she said no words to them except in blushing confusion and bewilderment. And the town was circled by desert and time, and home was far away, far away in another life.

She whirled and fled.

Shop following shop she found no magazines save those giving bullfights in blood on their covers or murdered people or lace-confection priests. But at last three poor copies of the *Post* were bought with much display and loud laughter and she gave the vendor of this small shop a handsome tip.

Rushing out with the *Posts* eagerly on her bosom in both hands she hurried along the narrow walk, took a skip over the gutter, ran across the street, sang la-la, jumped onto the further walk, made another little scamper with her feet, smiled an in-side smile, moving along swiftly, pressing the magazines tightly to her, half-closing her eyes, breathing the charcoal evening air, feeling the wind watering past her ears.

Starlight tinkled in golden nuclei off the highly perched Greek figures atop the State theatre. A man shambled by in the shadow, balancing upon his head a basket. The basket contained bread loaves.

She saw the man and the balanced basket and suddenly she did not move and there was no inside smile, nor did her hands clasp tight the magazines. She watched the man walk, with one hand of his gently poised up to tap the basket any time it unbalanced, and down the street he dwindled, while the magazines slipped from Marie's fingers and scattered on the walk.

Snatching them up, she ran into the hotel and almost fell going upstairs.

She sat in the room. The magazines were piled on each side of her and in a circle at her feet. She had made a little castle with portcullises of words and into this she was withdrawn. All about her were the magazines she had bought and bought and looked at and looked at on other days, and these were the outer barrier, and upon the inside of the barrier, upon her lap, as yet unopened, but her hands were trembling to open them and read and read and read again with hungry eyes, were the three battered *Post* magazines. She opened the first page. She would go through them page by page, line by line, she decided. Not a line would go unnoticed, a comma unread, every little ad and every color would be fixed by her. And—she smiled with discovery—in those other magazines at her feet were still advertisements and cartoons she had neglected there would be little morsels of stuff for her to reclaim and utilize later.

She would read this first *Post* tonight, yes tonight she would read this first delicious *Post*. Page on page she would eat it and tomorrow night, if there was going to be a tomorrow night, but maybe there wouldn't be a tomorrow night here, maybe the motor would start and there'd be odors of exhaust and round hum of rubber tire on road and wind riding in the window and pennanting her hair—but, suppose, just suppose there would BE a tomorrow night here, in this room. Well, then, there would be two more *Posts*, one for tomorrow night, and the next for the next night. How neatly she said it to herself with her mind's tongue. She turned the first page.

She turned the second page. Her eyes moved over it and over it and her fingers unknown to her slipped under the next page and flickered it in preparation for turning, and the watch ticked on her wrist, and time passed and she sat turning pages, turning pages, hungrily seeing the framed people in the pictures, people who lived in another land in another world where neons bravely held off the night with crimson bars and the smells were home smells and the people talked good fine words and here she was turning the pages, and all the lines went across and down and the pages flew under her hands, making a fan. She threw down the first *Post*, seized on and riffled through the second in half an hour, threw that down, took up the third, threw that down a good fifteen minutes later and found herself breathing, breathing stiffly and swiftly in her body and out of her mouth. She put her hand up to the back of her neck.

Somewhere, a soft breeze was blowing.

The hairs along the back of her neck slowly stood upright.

She touched them with one pale hand as one touches the nape of a dandelion.

Outside, in the plaza, the street lights rocked like crazy flashlights on a wind. Papers ran through the gutters in sheep flocks. Shadows penciled and slashed under the bucketing lamps now this way, now that, here a shadow one instant, there a shadow next, now no shadows, all cold light, now no light, all cold blue-black shadow. The lamps creaked on their high metal hasps.

In the room her hands began to tremble. She saw them tremble. Her body began to tremble. Under the bright bright print of the brightest, loudest skirt she could find to put on especially for tonight, in which she had whirled and cavorted feverishly before the coffin-sized mirror, beneath the rayon skirt the body was all wire and tendon and excitation. Her teeth chattered and fused and chattered. Her lipstick smeared, one lip crushing another.

Joseph knocked on the door.

They got ready for bed. He had returned with the news that something had been done to the car and it would take time, he'd go watch them tomorrow.

"But don't knock on the door," she said, standing before the mirror as she undressed.

"Leave it unlocked then," he said.

"I want it locked. But don't rap. Call."

"What's wrong with rapping?" he said.

"It sounds funny," she said.

"What do you mean, funny?"

She wouldn't say. She was looking at herself in the mirror and she was naked, with her hands at her sides, and there were her breasts and her hips and her entire body, and it moved, it felt the floor under it and the walls and air around it, and the breasts could know hands if hands were put there, and the stomach would make no hollow echo if touched.

"For God's sake," he said, "don't stand there admiring yourself." He was in bed. "What are you doing?" he said. "What're you putting your hands up that way for, over your face?"

He put the lights out.

She could not speak to him for she knew no words that he knew and he said nothing to her that she understood, and she walked to her bed and slipped into it and he lay with his back to her in his bed and he was like one of these brown-baked people of this far-away town upon the moon, and the real earth was off somewhere where it would take a star-flight to reach it. If only he could speak with her and she to him tonight, how good the night might be, and how easy to breathe and how lax the vessels of blood in her ankles and in her wrists and the under-arms, but there was no speaking and the night was ten thousand tickings and ten thousand twistings of the blankets, and the pillow was like a tiny white warm stove under-cheek, and the blackness of the room was a mosquito netting draped all about so that a turn entangled her in it. If only there was one word, one word between them. But there was no word and the veins did not rest easy in the wrists and the heart was a bellows forever blowing upon a little coal of fear, forever illuminating and making it into a cherry light, again, pulse, and again, an ingrown light which her inner eyes stared upon with unwanting fascination. The lungs did not rest but were exercised as if she were a drowned person and she herself performing artificial respiration to keep the last life going. And all of these things were lubricated by the sweat of her glowing body, and she was glued fast between the heavy blankets like something pressed, smashed, redolently moist between the white pages of a heavy book.

And as she lay this way the long hours of midnight came

when again she was a child. She lay, now and again thumping her heart in tambourine hysteria, then, quieting, the slow sad thoughts of bronze childhood when everything was sun on green trees and sun on water and sun on blond child hair. Faces flowed by on merry-go-rounds of memory, a face rushing to meet her, facing her, and away to the right; another, whirling in from the left, a quick fragment of lost conversation, and out to the right. Around and round. Oh, the night was very long. She consoled herself by thinking of the car starting tomorrow, the throttling sound and the power sound and the road moving under, and she smiled in the dark with pleasure. But then, suppose the car did *not* start? She crumpled in the dark, like a burning, withering paper. All the folds and corners of her clenched in about her and tick tick tick went the wristwatch, tick tick tick and another tick to wither on. . . .

Morning. She looked at her husband lying straight and easy on his bed. She let her hand laze down at the cool space between the beds. All night her hand had hung in that cold empty interval between. Once she had put her hand out toward him, stretching, but the space was just a little too long, she couldn't reach him. She had snapped her hand back, hoping he hadn't heard the movement of her silent reaching.

There he lay now. His eyes gently closed, the lashes softly interlocked like clasped fingers. Breathing so quietly you could scarce see his ribs move. As usual, by this time of morning, he had worked out of his pajamas. His naked chest was revealed from the waist up. The rest of him lay under cover. His head lay on the pillow, in thoughtful profile.

There was a beard stubble on his chin.

The morning light showed the white of her eyes. They

were the only things in the room in motion, in slow starts and stops, tracing the anatomy of the man across from her.

Each little hair was perfect on the chin and cheeks. A tiny hole of sunlight from the window-shade lay on his chin and picked out, like the spikes of a music-box cylinder, each little hair on his face.

His wrists on either side of him had little curly black hairs, each perfect, each separate and shiny and glittering.

The hair on his head was intact, strand by dark strand, down to the roots. The ears were beautifully carved. The teeth were intact behind the lips.

"Joseph!" she screamed.

"Joseph!" she screamed again, flailing up in terror.

Bong! Bong! Bong! went the bell thunder across the street, from the great tiled cathedral!

Pigeons rose in a papery white whirl, like so many magazines fluttered past the window! The pigeons circled the plaza, spiraling up. Bong! went the bells! Honk went a taxi horn! Far away down an alley a music box played "Cielito Lindo."

All these faded into the dripping of the faucet in the bath sink.

Joseph opened his eyes.

His wife sat on her bed, staring at him.

"I thought—" he said. He blinked. "No." He shut his eyes and shook his head. "Just the bells." A sigh. "What time is it?"

"I don't know. Yes, I do. Eight o'clock."

"Good God," he murmured, turning over. "We can sleep three more hours."

"You've got to get up!" she cried.

"Nobody's up. They won't be to work at the garage until

ten, you know that, you can't rush these people; keep quiet now."

"But you've got to get up," she said.

He half-turned. Sunlight prickled black hairs into bronze on his upper lip. "*Why?* Why, in Christ's name, do I *have* to get up?"

"You need a shave!" she almost screamed.

He moaned. "So I have to get up and lather myself at eight in the morning because I need a shave."

"Well, you do need one."

"I'm not shaving again till we reach Texas."

"You can't go around looking like a tramp!"

"I can and will. I've shaved every morning for thirty goddamn mornings and put on a tie and had a crease in my pants. From now on, no pants, no ties, no shaving, no nothing."

He yanked the covers over his ears so violently that he pulled the blankets off one of his naked legs.

The leg hung upon the rim of the bed, warm white in the sunlight, each little black hair—perfect.

Her eyes widened, focused, stared upon it.

She put her hand over her mouth, tight.

He went in and out of the hotel all day. He did not shave. He walked along the plaza tiles below. He walked so slowly she wanted to throw a lightning bolt out of the window and hit him. He paused and talked to the hotel manager below, under a drum-cut tree, shifting his shoes on the pale blue plaza tiles. He looked at birds on trees and saw how the State Theatre statues were dressed in fresh morning gilt, and stood on the corner, watching the traffic carefully. There was no traffic! He was standing there on purpose, taking his time, not looking back at her. Why didn't he run, lope down the alley, down the hill to the garage, pound on the doors, threaten the mechanics, lift them by their pants, shove them into the car motor! He stood instead, watching the ridiculous traffic pass. A hobbled swine, a man on a bike, a 1927 Ford, and three half-nude children. Go, go, go, she screamed silently, and almost smashed the window.

He sauntered across the street. He went around the corner. All the way down to the garage he'd stop at windows, read signs, look at pictures, handle pottery. Maybe he'd stop in for a beer. God, yes, a beer.

She walked in the plaza, took the sun, hunted for more magazines. She cleaned her fingernails, burnished them, took a bath, walked again in the plaza, ate very little, and returned to the room to feed upon her magazines.

She did not lie down. She was afraid to. Each time she did she fell into a half-dream, half-drowse in which all her childhood was revealed in a helpless melancholy. Old friends, children she hadn't seen or thought of in twenty years filled her mind. And she thought of things she wanted to do and had never done. She had meant to call Lila Holdridge for the past eight years since college, but somehow she never had. What friends they had been! Dear Lila! She thought, when lying down, of all the books, the fine new and old books, she had meant to buy and might never buy now and read. How she loved books and the smell of books. She thought of a thousand old sad things. She'd wanted to own the Oz books all her life, yet had never bought them. Why *not?* while yet there was life! The first thing she'd do would be to buy them when she got

back to New York! And she'd call Lila immediately! And she'd
see Bert and Jimmy and Helen and Louise, and go back to Illinois and walk around in her childhood place and see the things
to be seen there. If she got back to the States. If. Her heart beat
painfully in her, paused, held on to itself, and beat again. *If* she
ever got back.

She lay listening to her heart, critically.

Thud and a thud and a thud. Pause. Thud and a thud and
a thud. Pause.

What if it should stop while she was listening?

There!

Silence inside her.

"Joseph!"

She leaped up. She grabbed at her breasts as if to squeeze,
to pump to start the silent heart again!

It opened in her, closed, rattled and beat nervously, twenty
rapid, shot-like times!

She sank on to the bed. What if it should stop again and
not start? What would she think? What would there be to do?
She'd die of fright, that's what. A joke; it was very humorous.
Die of fright if you heard your heart stop. She would have to
listen to it, keep it beating. She wanted to go home and see
Lila and buy the books and dance again and walk in Central
Park and—listen—

Thud and a thud and a thud. Pause.

Joseph knocked on the door. Joseph knocked on the door and
the car was not repaired and there would be another night, and
Joseph did not shave and each little hair was perfect on his
chin, and the magazine shops were closed and there were no

more magazines, and they ate supper, a little bit anyway for her, and he went out in the evening to walk in the town.

She sat once more in the chair and slow erections of hair rose as if a magnet were passed over her neck. She was very weak and could not move from the chair, and she had no body, she was only a heart-beat, a huge pulsation of warmth and ache between four walls of the room. Her eyes were hot and pregnant, swollen with child of terror behind the bellied, tautened lids.

Deeply inside herself, she felt the first little cog slip. Another night, another night, another night, she thought. And this will be longer than the last. The first little cog slipped, the pendulum missed a stroke. Followed by the second and third interrelated cogs. The cogs interlocked, a small with a little larger one, the little larger one with a bit larger one, the bit larger one with a large one, the large one with a huge one, the huge one with an immense one, the immense one with a titanic one. . . .

A red ganglion, no bigger than a scarlet thread, snapped and quivered; a nerve, no greater than a red linen fiber twisted. Deep in her one little mech was gone and the entire machine, imbalanced, was about to steadily shake itself to bits.

She didn't fight it. She let it quake and terrorize her and knock the sweat off her brow and jolt down her spine and flood her mouth with horrible wine. She felt as if a broken gyro tilted now this way, now that and blundered and trembled and whined in her. The color fell from her face like light leaving a clicked-off bulb, the crystal cheeks of the bulb vessel showing veins and filaments all colorless. . . .

Joseph was in the room, he had come in, but she didn't

even hear him. He was in the room but it made no difference, he changed nothing with his coming. He was getting ready for bed and said nothing as he moved about and she said nothing but fell into the bed while he moved around in a smoke-filled space beyond her and once he spoke but she didn't hear him.

She timed it. Every five minutes she looked at her watch and the watch shook and time shook and the five fingers were fifteen moving, reassembling into five. The shaking never stopped. She called for water. She turned and turned upon the bed. The wind blew outside, cocking the lights and spilling bursts of illumination that hit buildings glancing sidelong blows, causing windows to glitter like opened eyes and shut swiftly as the light tilted in yet another direction. Downstairs, all was quiet after the dinner, no sounds came up into their silent room. He handed her a water glass.

"I'm cold, Joseph," she said, lying deep in folds of cover.

"You're all right," he said.

"No, I'm not. I'm not well. I'm afraid."

"There's nothing to be afraid of."

"I want to get on the train for the United States."

"There's a train in Leon, but none here," he said, lighting a new cigarette.

"Let's drive there."

"In these taxis, with these drivers, and leave our car here?"

"Yes. I want to go."

"You'll be all right in the morning."

"I know I won't be. I'm not well."

He said, "It would cost hundreds of dollars to have the car shipped home."

"I don't care. I have two hundred dollars in the bank at home. I'll pay for it. But, please, let's go home."

"When the sun shines tomorrow you'll feel better, it's just that the sun's gone now."

"Yes, the sun's gone and the wind's blowing," she whispered, closing her eyes, turning her head, listening. "Oh, what a lonely wind. Mexico's a strange land. All the jungles and deserts and lonely stretches, and here and there a little town, like this, with a few lights burning you could put out with a snap of your fingers . . ."

"It's a pretty big country," he said.

"Don't these people ever get lonely?"

"They're used to it this way."

"Don't they get afraid, then?"

"They have a religion for that."

"I wish I had a religion."

"The minute you get a religion you stop thinking," he said. "Believe in one thing too much and you have no room for new ideas."

"Tonight," she said, faintly. "I'd like nothing more than to have no more room for new ideas, to stop thinking, to believe in one thing so much it leaves me no time to be afraid."

"You're not afraid," he said.

"If I had a religion," she said, ignoring him, "I'd have a lever with which to lift myself. But I haven't a lever now and I don't know how to lift myself."

"Oh, for God's—" he mumbled to himself, sitting down.

"I used to have a religion," she said.

"Baptist."

"No, that was when I was twelve. I got over that. I mean—later."

"You never told me."

"You should have known," she said.

"What religion? Plaster saints in the sacristy? Any special saint you liked to tell your beads to?"

"Yes."

"And did he answer your prayers?"

"For a little while. Lately, no, never. Never any more. Not for years now. But I keep praying."

"Which saint is this?"

"Saint Joseph."

"Saint Joseph." He got up and poured himself a glass of water from the glass pitcher, and it was a lonely trickling sound in the room. "My name."

"Coincidence," she said.

They looked at one another for a few moments.

He looked away. "Plaster saints," he said, drinking the water down.

After a while she said, "Joseph?" He said, "Yes?" and she said, "Come hold my hand, will you?" "Women," he sighed. He came and held her hand. After a minute she drew her hand away, hid it under the blanket, leaving his hand empty behind. With her eyes closed she trembled the words, "Never mind. It's not as nice as I can imagine it. It's really nice the way I can make you hold my hand in my mind." "Gods," he said, and went into the bathroom. She turned off the light. Only the small crack of light under the bathroom door showed. She listened to her heart. It beat one hundred and fifty times a minute, steadily, and the little whining tremor was still in her marrow, as if each bone of her body had a blue-bottle fly imprisoned in it, hovering, buzzing, shaking, quivering deep, deep, deep. Her eyes reversed into herself, to watch the secret heart of herself pounding itself to pieces against the side of her chest.

Water ran in the bathroom. She heard him washing his teeth.

"Joseph!"

"Yes," he said, behind the shut door.

"Come here."

"What do you want?"

"I want you to promise me something, please, oh, please."

"What is it?"

"Open the door, first."

"What *is* it?" he demanded, behind the closed door.

"Promise me," she said, and stopped.

"Promise you what?" he asked, after a long pause.

"Promise me," she said, and couldn't go on. She lay there. He said nothing. She heard the watch and her heart pounding together. A lantern creaked on the hotel exterior. "Promise me, if anything—happens," she heard herself say, muffled and paralyzed, as if she were on one of the surrounding hills talking at him from the distance, "—if anything happens to me, you won't let me be buried here in the graveyard over those terrible catacombs!"

"Don't be foolish," he said, behind the door.

"Promise me?" she said, eyes wide in the dark.

"Of all the foolish things to talk about."

"Promise, *please* promise?"

"You'll be all right in the morning," he said.

"Promise so I can sleep. I can sleep if only you'd say you wouldn't let me be put there. I don't want to be put there."

"Honestly," he said, out of patience.

"Please," she said.

"Why should I promise anything so ridiculous?" he said. "You'll be fine tomorrow. And besides, if you died, you'd look very pretty in the catacomb standing between Mr. Grimace and Mr. Gape, with a sprig of morning-glory in your hair." And he laughed sincerely.

Silence. She lay there in the dark.

"Don't you think you'll look pretty there?" he asked, laughingly, behind the door.

She said nothing in the dark room.

"*Don't* you?" he said.

Somebody walked down below in the plaza, faintly, fading away.

"Eh?" he asked her, brushing his teeth.

She lay there, staring up at the ceiling, her breast rising and falling faster, faster, faster, the air going in and out, in and out her nostrils, a little trickle of blood coming from her clenched lips. Her eyes were very wide, her hands blindly constricted the bedclothes.

"Eh?" he said again behind the door.

She said nothing.

"Sure," he talked to himself. "Pretty as hell," he murmured, under the flow of tap water. He rinsed his mouth. "Sure," he said.

Nothing from her in the bed.

"Women are funny," he said to himself in the mirror.

She lay in the bed.

"Sure," he said. He gargled with some antiseptic, spat it down the drain. "You'll be all right in the morning," he said.

Not a word from her.

"We'll get the car fixed."

She didn't say anything.

"Be morning before you know it." He was screwing caps on things now, putting freshener on his face. "And the car fixed tomorrow, maybe, at the very latest the next day. You won't mind another night here, will you?"

She didn't answer.

"*Will* you?" he asked.

No reply.

The light blinked out under the bathroom door.

"Marie?"

He opened the door.

"Asleep?"

She lay with eyes wide, breasts moving up and down.

"Asleep," he said. "Well, good night, lady."

He climbed into his bed. "Tired," he said.

No reply.

"Tired," he said.

The wind tossed the lights outside; the room was oblong and black and he was in his bed dozing already.

She lay, eyes wide, the watch ticking on her wrist, breasts moving up and down.

It was a fine day coming through the Tropic of Cancer. The automobile pushed along the turning road leaving the jungle country behind, heading for the United States, roaring between the green hills, taking every turn, leaving behind a faint vanishing trail of exhaust smoke. And inside the shiny automobile sat Joseph with his pink, healthy face and his Panama hat, and a little camera cradled on his lap as he drove; a swathe of black silk pinned around the left upper arm of his tan coat. He watched the country slide by and absent-mindedly made a gesture to the seat beside him, and stopped. He broke into a little sheepish smile and turned once more to the window of his car, humming a tuneless tune, his right hand slowly reaching over to touch the seat beside him . . .

Which was empty.

THE WATCHFUL POKER CHIP
OF H. MATISSE

hen first we meet George Garvey he is nothing at all. Later he'll wear a white poker chip monocle, with a blue eye painted on it by Matisse himself. Later, a golden bird cage might trill within George Garvey's false leg, and his good left hand might possibly be fashioned of shimmering copper and jade.

But at the beginning—gaze upon a terrifyingly ordinary man.

"Financial section, dear?"

The newspapers rattle in his evening apartment.

"Weatherman says 'rain tomorrow.' "

The tiny black hairs in his nostrils breathe in, breathe out, softly, softly, hour after hour.

"Time for bed."

By his look, quite obviously born of several 1907 wax window dummies. And with the trick, much admired by magicians, of sitting in a green velour chair and—vanishing! Turn your head and you forgot his face. Vanilla pudding.

Yet the merest accident made him the nucleus for the wildest avant-garde literary movement in history!

Garvey and his wife had lived enormously alone for twenty

years. She was a lovely carnation, but the hazard of meeting *him* pretty well kept visitors off. Neither husband nor wife suspected Garvey's talent for mummifying people instantaneously. Both claimed they were satisfied sitting alone nights after a brisk day at the office. Both worked at anonymous jobs. And sometimes even they could not recall the name of the colorless company which used them like white paint on white paint.

Enter the avant-garde! Enter The Cellar Septet!

These odd souls had flourished in Parisian basements listening to a rather sluggish variety of jazz, preserved a highly volatile relationship six months or more, and, returning to the United States on the point of clamorous disintegration, stumbled into Mr. George Garvey.

"My God!" cried Alexander Pape, erstwhile potentate of the clique. "I met the most astounding bore. You simply must see him! At Bill Timmins' apartment house last night, a note said he'd return in an hour. In the hall this Garvey chap asked if I'd like to wait in his apartment. There we sat, Garvey, his wife, myself! Incredible! He's a monstrous Ennui, produced by our materialistic society. He knows a billion ways to paralyze you! Absolutely rococo with the talent to induce stupor, deep slumber, or stoppage of the heart. What a case study. Let's *all* go visit!"

They swarmed like vultures! Life flowed to Garvey's door, life sat in his parlor. The Cellar Septet perched on his fringed sofa, eyeing their prey.

Garvey fidgeted.

"Anyone wants to smoke—" He smiled faintly. "Why—go right ahead—*smoke*."

Silence.

The instructions were: "Mum's the word. Put him on the

spot. That's the only way to see what a colossal *norm* he is. American culture at absolute zero!"

After three minutes of unblinking quiet, Mr. Garvey leaned forward. "Eh," he said, "what's *your* business. Mr. . . . ?"

"Crabtree. The poet."

Garvey mused over this.

"How's," he said, "business?"

Not a sound.

Here lay a typical Garvey silence. Here sat the largest manufacturer and deliverer of silences in the world; name one, he could provide it packaged and tied with throat-clearings and whispers. Embarrassed, pained, calm, serene, indifferent, blessed, golden, or nervous silences; Garvey was *in* there.

Well, The Cellar Septet simply wallowed in this particular evening's silence. Later, in their cold-water flat, over a bottle of "adequate little red wine" (they were experiencing a phase which led them to contact *real* reality) they tore this silence to bits and worried it.

"Did you *see* how he fingered his collar! Ho!"

"By God, though, I must admit he's almost 'cool.' Mention Muggsy Spanier and Bix Beiderbecke. Notice his expression. *Very* cool. I wish *I* could look so uncaring, so unemotional."

Ready for bed, George Garvey, reflecting upon this extraordinary evening, realized that when situations got out of hand, when strange books or music were discussed, he panicked, he froze.

This hadn't seemed to cause undue concern among his rather oblique guests. In fact, on the way out, they had shaken his hand vigorously, thanked him for a splendid time!

"What a really expert A-number-1 bore!" cried Alexander Pape, across town.

"Perhaps he's secretly laughing at us," said Smith, the minor poet, who never agreed with Pape if he was awake.

"Let's fetch Minnie and Tom; they'd love Garvey. A rare night. We'll talk of it for months!"

"Did you notice?" asked Smith, the minor poet, eyes closed smugly. "When you turn the taps in their bathroom?" He paused dramatically. "*Hot* water."

Everyone stared irritably at Smith.

They hadn't thought to *try*.

The clique, an incredible yeast, soon burst doors and windows, growing.

"You haven't met the Garveys? My God! lie back down in your coffin! Garvey *must* rehearse. No one's *that* boorish without Stanislavsky!" Here the speaker, Alexander Pape, who depressed the entire group because he did perfect imitations, now aped Garvey's slow, self-conscious delivery:

" '*Ulysses?* Wasn't that the book about the Greek, the ship, and the one-eyed monster! Beg pardon?' " A pause. " 'Oh.' " Another pause. " 'I see.' " A sitting back. " '*Ulysses* was written by *James Joyce?* Odd. I could *swear* I remember, years ago, in school . . .' "

In spite of everyone *hating* Alexander Pape for his brilliant imitations, they roared as he went on:

" 'Tennessee Williams? Is he the man who wrote that hillbilly "Waltz?" ' "

"Quick! What's Garvey's home address?" everyone cried.

———

"My," observed Mr. Garvey to his wife, "life is fun these days."

"It's you," replied his wife. "Notice, they hang on your every word."

"Their attention is rapt," said Mr. Garvey, "to the point of hysteria. The least thing I say absolutely explodes them. Odd. My jokes at the office always met a stony wall. Tonight, for instance, I wasn't trying to be funny at all. I suppose it's an unconscious little stream of wit that flows quietly under everything I do or say. Nice to know I have it in reserve. Ah, there's the bell. Here we go!"

"He's especially rare if you get him out of bed at four A.M.," said Alexander Pape. "The combination of exhaustion and *fin de siècle* morality is a regular salad!"

Everyone was pretty miffed at Pape for being first to think of seeing Garvey at dawn. Nevertheless, interest ran high after midnight in late October.

Mr. Garvey's subconscious told him in utmost secrecy that he was the opener of a theatrical season, his success dependent upon the staying power of the ennui he inspired in others. Enjoying himself, he nevertheless guessed why these lemmings thronged to his private sea. Underneath, Garvey was a surprisingly brilliant man, but his unimaginative parents had crushed him in the Terribly Strange Bed of their environment. From there he had been thrown to a larger lemon-squeezer: his Office, his Factory, his Wife. The result: a man whose potentialities were a time bomb in his own parlor. Garvey's repressed subconscious half recognized that the avant-gardists had never met anyone like him, or rather had met millions like him but had never considered studying one before.

So here he was, the first of autumn's celebrities. Next month it might be some abstractionist from Allentown who worked on a twelve-foot ladder shooting house-paint, in two colors only, blue and cloud-gray, from cake-decorators and insecticide-sprayers on canvas covered with layers of mucilage and coffee grounds, who simply needed appreciation to grow! or a Chicago tin-cutter of mobiles, aged fifteen, already ancient with knowledge. Mr. Garvey's shrewd subconscious grew even more suspicious when he made the terrible mistake of reading the avant-garde's favorite magazine, *Nucleus*.

"This article on Dante, now," said Garvey. "Fascinating. Especially where it discusses the spatial metaphors conveyed in the foothills of the *Antipurgatorio* and the *Paradiso Terrestre* on top of the Mountain. The bit about Cantos XV–XVIII, the so-called 'doctrinal cantos' is brilliant!"

How did the Cellar Septet react?

Stunned, all of them!

There was a noticeable chill.

They departed in short order when instead of being a delightfully mass-minded, keep-up-with-the-Joneses, machine-dominated chap leading a wishy-washy life of quiet desperation, Garvey enraged them with opinions on *Does Existentialism Still Exist?* or *Is Kraft-Ebbing?* They didn't want opinions on alchemy and symbolism given in a piccolo voice, Garvey's subconscious warned him. They only wanted Garvey's good old-fashioned plain white bread and churned country butter, to be chewed on later at a dim bar, exclaiming how priceless!

Garvey retreated.

———————

Next night he was his old precious self. Dale Carnegie? Splendid religious leader! Hart Schaffner & Marx? Better than Bond Street! Member of the After-Shave Club? That was Garvey! Latest Book-of-the-Month? Here on the table! Had they ever tried Elinor Glyn?

The Cellar Septet was horrified, delighted. They let themselves be bludgeoned into watching Milton Berle. Garvey laughed at everything Berle said. It was arranged for neighbors to tape-record various daytime soap operas which Garvey replayed evenings with religious awe, while the Cellar Septet analyzed his face and his complete devotion to *Ma Perkins* and *John's Other Wife.*

Oh, Garvey was getting sly. His inner self observed: You're on top. Stay there! Please your public! Tomorrow, play the Two Black Crows records! Mind your step! Bonnie Baker, now . . . that's it! They'll shudder, incredulous that you really like her singing. What about Guy Lombardo? That's the ticket!

The mob-mind, said his subconscious. You're symbolic of the crowd. They came to study the dreadful vulgarity of this imaginary Mass Man they pretend to hate. But they're fascinated with the snake-pit.

Guessing his thought, his wife objected. "They *like* you."

"In a frightening sort of way," he said. "I've lain awake figuring why they should come see me! Always hated and bored myself. Stupid, tattletale-gray man. Not an original thought in my mind. All I know now is: I love company. I've always wanted to be gregarious, never had the chance. It's been a ball these last months! But their interest is dying. I want company forever! What shall I do?"

His subconscious provided shopping lists.

Beer. It's unimaginative.

Pretzels. Delightfully "passé."

Stop by Mother's. Pick up Maxfield Parrish painting, the fly-specked, sunburnt one. Lecture on same tonight.

By December Mr. Garvey was really frightened.

The Cellar Septet was now quite accustomed to Milton Berle and Guy Lombardo. In fact, they had rationalized themselves into a position where they acclaimed Berle as really too *rare* for the American public, and Lombardo was twenty years ahead of his time; the nastiest people liked him for the commonest reasons.

Garvey's empire trembled.

Suddenly he was just another person, no longer diverting the tastes of friends, but frantically pursuing them as they seized at Nora Bayes, the 1917 Knickerbocker Quartette, Al Jolson singing "Where Did Robinson Crusoe Go With Friday on Saturday Night," and Shep Fields and his Rippling Rhythm. Maxfield Parrish's rediscovery left Mr. Garvey in the north pasture. Overnight, everyone agreed, "Beer's intellectual. What a shame so many *idiots* drink it."

In short, his friends vanished. Alexander Pape, it was rumored, for a lark, was even considering hot water for his cold-water flat. This ugly canard was quashed, but not before Alexander Pape suffered a comedown among the *cognoscenti*.

Garvey sweated to anticipate the shifting taste! He increased the free food output, foresaw the swing back to the Roaring Twenties by wearing hairy knickers and displaying his wife in a tube dress and boyish bob long before anyone else.

But, the vultures came, ate, and ran. Now that this frightful Giant, TV, strode the world, they were busily re-embracing radio. Bootlegged 1935 transcriptions of *Vic and Sade* and *Pepper Young's Family* were fought over at intellectual galas.

At long last, Garvey was forced to turn to a series of miraculous tours de force, conceived and carried out by his panic-stricken inner self.

The first accident was a slammed car door.

Mr. Garvey's little fingertip was neatly cut off!

In the resultant chaos, hopping about, Garvey stepped on, then kicked the fingertip into a street drain. By the time they fished it out, no doctor would bother sewing it back on.

A happy accident! Next day, strolling by an oriental shop, Garvey spied a beautiful *objet d'art*. His peppy old subconscious, considering his steadily declining box office and his poor audience-rating among the avant-garde, forced him into the shop and dragged out his wallet.

"Have you seen Garvey lately!" screamed Alexander Pape on the phone. "My God, go see!"

"What's *that?*"

Everyone stared.

"Mandarin's finger-guard." Garvey waved his hand casually. "Oriental antique. Mandarins used them to protect the five-inch nails they cultivated." He drank his beer, the gold-thimbled little finger cocked. "Everyone hates cripples, the sight of things missing. It was sad losing my finger. But I'm happier with this gold thing-amajig."

"It's a much nicer finger now than any of us can *ever* have."
His wife dished them all a little green salad. "And George has
the *right* to use it."

Garvey was shocked and charmed as his dwindling popu-
larity returned. Ah, art! Ah, life! The pendulum swinging back
and forth, from complex to simple, again to complex. From romantic to realistic, back to romantic. The clever man could
sense intellectual perihelions, and prepare for the violent new
orbits. Garvey's subconscious brilliance sat up, began to eat a
bit, and some days dared to walk about, trying its unused limbs.
It caught fire!

"How unimaginative the world is," his long-neglected
other self said, using his tongue. "If somehow my leg were sev-
ered accidentally I wouldn't wear a wooden leg, no! I'd have a
gold leg crusted with precious stones made, and part of the leg
would be a golden cage in which a bluebird would sing as I
walked or sat talking to friends. And if my arm were cut off I'd
have a new arm made of copper and jade, all hollow inside, a
section for dry ice in it. And five other compartments, one for
each finger. Drink, anyone? I'd cry. Sherry? Brandy? Dubonnet?
Then I'd twist each finger calmly over the glasses. From five
fingers, five cool streams, five liqueurs or wines. I'd tap the
golden faucets shut. 'Bottoms up!' I'd cry.

"But, most of all, one almost wishes that one's eye would
offend one. Pluck it out, the Bible says. It *was* the Bible, wasn't
it? If that happened to me, I'd use no grisly glass eyes, by
God. None of those black, pirate's patches. Know what I'd do?
I'd mail a poker chip to your friend in France, *what's* his
name? *Matisse!* I'd say, 'Enclosed find poker chip, and personal
check. Please paint on this chip one beautiful blue human eye.
Yrs., sincerely. G. Garvey!'"

Well, Garvey had always abhorred his body, found his eyes pale, weak, lacking character. So he was not surprised a month later (when his Gallup ran low again) to see his right eye water, fester, and then pull a complete blank!

Garvey was absolutely bombed!

But—equally—secretly pleased.

With the Cellar Septet smiling like a jury of gargoyles at his elbow, he airmailed the poker chip to France with a check for fifty dollars.

The check returned, uncashed, a week later.

In the next mail came the poker chip.

H. Matisse had painted a rare, beautiful blue eye on it, delicately lashed and browed. H. Matisse had tucked this chip in a green-plush jeweler's box, quite obviously as delighted as was Garvey with the entire enterprise.

Harper's Bazaar published a picture of Garvey, wearing the Matisse poker-chip eye, and yet another of Matisse, himself, painting the monocle after considerable experimentation with three dozen chips!

H. Matisse had had the uncommon good sense to summon a photographer to Leica the affair for posterity. He was quoted. "After I had thrown away twenty-seven eyes, I finally got the very one I wanted. It flies posthaste to Monsieur Garvey!"

Reproduced in six colors, the eye rested balefully in its green-plush box. Duplicates were struck off for sales by the Museum of Modern Art. The Friends of the Cellar Septet played poker, using red chips with blue eyes, white chips with red eyes, and blue chips with white eyes.

But there was only *one* man in New York who wore the original Matisse monocle and that was Mr. Garvey.

"I'm *still* a nerve-wracking bore," he told his wife, "but now they'll never know what a dreadful ox I am underneath the monocle and the Mandarin's finger. And if their interest should happen to dwindle again, one can always arrange to lose an arm or leg. No doubt of it. I've thrown up a wondrous facade; no one will ever find the ancient boor again."

And as his wife put it only the other afternoon: "I hardly think of him as the old George Garvey any more. He's changed his name. Giulio, he wants to be called. Sometimes, at night, I look over at him and call, 'George,' but there's no answer. There he is, that mandarin's thimble on his little finger, the white and blue Matisse Poker-Chip monocle in his eye. I wake up and look at him often. And do you know? Sometimes that incredible Matisse Poker Chip seems to give out with a *monstrous* wink."

SKELETON ||||

I
t was past time for him to see the doctor again. Mr. Harris
turned palely in at the stair well, and on his way up the flight
saw Dr. Burleigh's name gilded over a pointing arrow. Would
Dr. Burleigh sigh when he walked in? After all, this would
make the tenth trip so far this year. But Burleigh shouldn't
complain; he was paid for the examinations!

The nurse looked Mr. Harris over and smiled, a bit amusedly, as she tiptoed to the glazed glass door, opened it, and put
her head in. Harris thought he heard her say, "Guess who's
here, Doctor." And didn't the doctor's voice reply, faintly, "Oh,
my God, *again?*" Harris swallowed uneasily.

When Harris walked in, Dr. Burleigh snorted. "Aches in
your bones again! Ah!!" He scowled and adjusted his glasses.
"My dear Harris, you've been curried with the finest-tooth
combs and bacteria-brushes known to science. You're just nervous. Let's see your fingers. Too many cigarettes. Let's smell
your breath. Too much protein. Let's see your eyes. Not enough
sleep. My response? Go to bed, stop the protein, no smoking.
Ten dollars, please."

Harris stood sulking.

The doctor glanced up from his papers. "*You* still here? You're a hypochondriac! That's *eleven* dollars, now."

"But why should my bones ache?" asked Harris.

Dr. Burleigh spoke as to a child. "You ever had a sore muscle, and kept irritating it, fussing with it, rubbing it? It gets worse, the more you bother it. Then you leave it alone and the pain vanishes. You realize you caused most of the soreness, yourself. Well, son, that's what's with you. Leave yourself alone. Take a dose of salts. Get out of here and take that trip to Phoenix you've stewed about for months. Do you good to travel!"

Five minutes later, Mr. Harris riffled through a classified phone directory at the corner druggist's. A fine lot of sympathy one got from blind fools like Burleigh! He passed his finger down a list of BONE SPECIALISTS, found one named M. Munigant. Munigant lacked an M.D., or any other academic lettering behind his name, but his office was conveniently near. Three blocks down, one block over. . . .

M. Munigant, like his office, was small and dark. Like his office, he smelled of iodoform, iodine, and other odd things. He was a good listener, though, and listened with eager shiny moves of his eyes, and when he talked to Harris, his accent was such that he softly whistled each word; undoubtedly because of imperfect dentures.

Harris told all.

M. Munigant nodded. He had seen cases like this before. The bones of the body. Man was not aware of his bones. Ah, yes, the bones. The skeleton. Most difficult. Something concerning an imbalance, an unsympathetic coordination between soul, flesh, and skeleton. Very complicated, softly whistled

M. Munigant. Harris listened, fascinated. Now, *here* was a doctor who understood his illness! Psychological, said M. Munigant. He moved swiftly, delicately to a dingy wall and slashed down half a dozen X-rays to haunt the room with their look of things found floating in an ancient tide. Here, here! The skeleton surprised! Here luminous portraits of the long, the short, the large, the small bones. Mr. Harris must be aware of his position, his problem! M. Munigant's hand tapped, rattled, whispered, scratched at faint nebulae of flesh in which hung ghosts of cranium, spinal-cord, pelvis, lime, calcium, marrow, here, there, this, that, these, those, and others! Look!

Harris shuddered. The X-rays and the paintings blew in a green and phosphorescent wind from a land peopled by the monsters of Dali and Fuseli.

M. Munigant whistled quietly. Did Mr. Harris wish his bones—treated?

"That depends," said Harris.

Well, M. Munigant could not help Harris unless Harris was in the proper mood. Psychologically, one had to *need* help, or the doctor was useless. But (shrugging) M. Munigant would "try."

Harris lay on a table with his mouth open. The lights were switched off, the shades drawn. M. Munigant approached his patient.

Something touched Harris's tongue.

He felt his jawbones forced out. They creaked and made faint cracking noises. One of those skeleton charts on the dim wall seemed to quiver and jump. A violent shudder seized Harris. Involuntarily, his mouth snapped shut.

M. Munigant shouted. His nose had almost been bitten off! No use, no use! Now was not the time! M. Munigant whispered the shades up, dreadfully disappointed. When Mr. Harris felt he could cooperate psychologically, when Mr. Harris really *needed* help and trusted M. Munigant to help him, then maybe something could be done. M. Munigant held out his little hand. In the meantime, the fee was only two dollars. Mr. Harris must begin to think. Here was a sketch for Mr. Harris to take home and study. It would acquaint him with his body. He must be tremblingly aware of himself. He must be on guard. Skeletons were strange, unwieldy things. M. Munigant's eyes glittered. Good day to Mr. Harris. Oh, and would he care for a breadstick? M. Munigant proffered a jar of long hard salty breadsticks to Harris, taking one himself, saying that chewing breadsticks kept him in—ah—practice. Good day, good day, to Mr. Harris! Mr. Harris went home.

The next day, Sunday, Mr. Harris discovered innumerable fresh aches and pains in his body. He spent the morning, his eyes fixed staring with new interest at the small, anatomically perfect painting of a skeleton M. Munigant had given him.

His wife, Clarisse, startled him at dinner when she cracked her exquisitely thin knuckles, one by one, until he clapped his hands to his ears and cried, "Stop!"

The rest of the afternoon he quarantined himself in his room. Clarisse played bridge in the parlor laughing and chatting with three other ladies while Harris, hidden away, fingered and weighed the limbs of his body with growing curiosity. After an hour he suddenly rose and called:

"Clarisse!"

She had a way of dancing into any room, her body doing all sorts of soft, agreeable things to keep her feet from ever quite touching the nap of a rug. She excused herself from her friends and came to see him now, brightly. She found him re-seated in a far corner and she saw that he was staring at the anatomical sketch. "Are you still brooding, sweet?" she asked. "Please don't." She sat upon his knees.

Her beauty could not distract him now in his absorption. He juggled her lightness, he touched her kneecap, suspiciously. It seemed to move under her pale, glowing skin. "Is it supposed to do that?" he asked, sucking in his breath.

"Is what supposed to do what?" she laughed. "You mean my kneecap?"

"Is it supposed to run around on top of your knee that way?"

She experimented. "So it *does*," she marveled.

"I'm glad yours slithers, too," he sighed. "I was beginning to worry."

"About what?"

He patted his ribs. "My ribs don't go all the way down, they stop *here*. And I found some confounded ones that dangle in mid-air!"

Beneath the curve of her small breasts, Clarisse clasped her hands.

"Of course, silly, everybody's ribs stop at a given point. And those funny short ones are floating ribs."

"I hope they don't float around too much." The joke was most uneasy. Now, above all, he wished to be alone. Further discoveries, newer and stranger archaeological diggings, lay within reach of his trembling hands, and he did not wish to be laughed at.

"Thanks for coming in, dear," he said.

"Any time." She rubbed her small nose softly against his.

"Wait! Here, now . . ." He put his finger to touch his nose and hers. "Did you realize? The nose-bone grows down only *this* far. From there on a lot of gristly tissue fills out the rest!"

She wrinkled hers. "Of course, darling!" And she danced from the room.

Now, sitting alone, he felt the perspiration rise from the pools and hollows of his face, to flow in a thin tide down his cheeks. He licked his lips and shut his eyes. Now . . . now . . . next on the agenda, what . . . ? The spinal cord, yes. Here. Slowly, he examined it, in the same way he operated the many push-buttons in his office, thrusting them to summon secretaries, messengers. But now, in these pushings of his spinal column, fears and terrors answered, rushed from a million doors in his mind to confront and shake him! His spine felt horribly—unfamiliar. Like the brittle shards of a fish, freshly eaten, its bones left strewn on a cold china platter. He seized the little rounded knobbins. "Lord! Lord!"

His teeth began to chatter. God All-Mighty! he thought, why haven't I realized it all these years? All these years I've gone around with a—SKELETON—inside me! How is it we take ourselves for granted? How is it we never question our bodies and our being?

A skeleton. One of those jointed, snowy, hard things, one of those foul, dry brittle, gouge-eyed, skull-faced, shake-fingered, rattling things that sway from neck-chains in abandoned webbed closets, one of those things found on the desert all long and scattered like dice!

He stood upright, because he could not bear to remain seated. Inside me now, he grasped his stomach, his head, inside my head is a—skull. One of those curved carapaces which holds my brain like an electrical jelly, one of those cracked shells with the holes in front like two holes shot through it by a double-barreled shotgun! With its grottoes and caverns of bone, its revetments and placements for my flesh, my smelling, my seeing, my hearing, my thinking! A skull, encompassing my brain, allowing it exit through its brittle windows to see the outside world!

He wanted to dash into the bridge party, upset it, a fox in a chickenyard, the cards fluttering all around like chicken feathers burst upward in clouds! He stopped himself only with a violent, trembling effort. Now, now, man, control yourself. This is a revelation, take it for what it's worth, understand it, savor it. BUT A SKELETON! screamed his subconscious. I won't stand for it. It's vulgar, it's terrible, it's frightening. Skeletons are horrors; they clink and tinkle and rattle in old castles, hung from oaken beams, making long, indolently rustling pendulums on the wind. . . .

"Darling, will you come meet the ladies?" His wife's clear, sweet voice called from far away.

Mr. Harris stood. His SKELETON held him up! This thing inside, this invader, this horror, was supporting his arms, legs, and head! It was like feeling someone just behind you who shouldn't be there. With every step, he realized how dependent he was on this other Thing.

"Darling, I'll be with you in a moment," he called weakly. To himself he said, Come on, brace up! You've got to go back to work tomorrow. Friday you must make that trip to Phoenix. It's a long drive. Hundreds of miles. Must be in shape for that trip or you won't get Mr. Creldon to invest in your ceramics business. Chin up, now!

A moment later he stood among the ladies, being introduced to Mrs. Withers, Mrs. Abblematt, and Miss Kirthy, all of whom had skeletons inside them, but took it very calmly, because nature had carefully clothed the bare nudity of clavicle, tibia, and femur with breasts, thighs, calves, with coiffure and eyebrow satanic, with bee-stung lips and—LORD! shouted Mr. Harris inwardly—when they talk or eat, part of their skeleton shows—their _teeth_! I never thought of that. "Excuse me," he gasped, and ran from the room only in time to drop his lunch among the petunias over the garden balustrade.

That night, seated on the bed as his wife undressed, he pared his toenails and fingernails scrupulously. These parts, too, were where his skeleton was showing, indignantly growing out. He must have muttered part of this theory, because next thing he knew his wife, in negligee, was on the bed, her arms about his neck, yawning, "Oh, my darling, fingernails are _not_ bone, they're only hardened epidermis!"

He threw the scissors down. "Are you certain? I hope so. I'd feel better." He looked at the curve of her body, marveling. "I hope all people are made the same way."

"If you aren't the darndest hypochondriac!" She held him at arm's length. "Come on. What's wrong? Tell mama."

"Something inside me," he said "Something—I ate."

The next morning and all afternoon at his downtown office, Mr. Harris sorted out the sizes, shapes, and construction of various bones in his body with displeasure. At ten A.M. he asked to feel Mr. Smith's elbow one moment. Mr. Smith obliged, but scowled suspiciously. And after lunch Mr. Harris asked to touch Miss Laurel's shoulder blade and she immediately pushed herself back against him, purring like a kitten and shutting her eyes.

"Miss Laurel!" he snapped. "Stop that!"

Alone, he pondered his neuroses. The war was just over, the pressure of his work, the uncertainty of the future, probably had much to do with his mental outlook. He wanted to leave the office, get into business for himself. He had more than a little talent for ceramics and sculpture. As soon as possible he'd head for Arizona, borrow that money from Mr. Creldon, build a kiln and set up shop. It was a worry. What a case he was. But luckily he had contacted M. Munigant, who seemed eager to understand and help him. He would fight it out with himself, not go back to either Munigant or Dr. Burleigh unless he was forced to. The alien feeling would pass. He sat staring into space.

The alien feeling did not pass. It grew.

On Tuesday and Wednesday it bothered him terrifically that his epidermis, hair and other appendages were of a high disorder, while his integumented skeleton of himself was a slick clean structure of efficient organization. Sometimes, in certain lights with his lips drawn morosely down, weighted with melancholy, he imagined he saw his skull grinning at him behind the flesh.

Let go! he cried. Let go of me! My lungs! Stop!

He gasped convulsively, as if his ribs were crushing the breath from him.

My brain—stop squeezing it!

And terrifying headaches burnt his brain to a blind cinder.

My insides, let them be, for God's sake! Stay away from my heart!

His heart cringed from the fanning motion of ribs like pale spiders crouched and fiddling with their prey.

Drenched with sweat, he lay upon the bed one night while Clarisse was out attending a Red Cross meeting. He tried to gather his wits but only grew more aware of the conflict between his dirty exterior and this beautiful cool clean calciumed thing inside.

His complexion: wasn't it oily and lined with worry?

Observe the flawless, snow-white perfection of the skull.

His nose: wasn't it too large?

Then observe the tiny bones of the skull's nose before that monstrous nasal cartilage begins forming the lopsided proboscis.

His body: wasn't it plump?

Well, consider the skeleton; slender, svelte, economical of line and contour. Exquisitely carved oriental ivory! Perfect, thin as a white praying mantis!

His eyes: weren't they protuberant, ordinary, numb-looking?

Be so kind as to note the eye-sockets of the skull; so deep and rounded, somber, quiet pools, all-knowing, eternal. Gaze deep and you never touch the bottom of their dark understanding. All irony, all life, all everything is there in the cupped darkness.

Compare. Compare. Compare.

He raged for hours. And the skeleton, ever the frail and solemn philosopher, hung quietly inside, saying not a word, suspended like a delicate insect within a chrysalis, waiting and waiting.

Harris sat slowly up.

"Wait a minute. Hold on!" he exclaimed. "You're helpless, too. I've got you, too. I can make you do anything I want! You can't prevent it! I say move your carpals, metacarpals, and phalanges and—sswtt—up they go, as I wave to someone!"

He laughed. "I order the fibula and femur to locomote and *Hunn* two three four, *Hunn* two three four—we walk around the block. There!"

Harris grinned.

"It's a fifty-fifty fight. Even-Stephen. And we'll fight it out, we two! After all, I'm the part that *thinks!* Yes, by God! Yes. Even if I didn't have you, I could still think!"

Instantly, a tiger's jaw snapped shut, chewing his brain in half. Harris screamed. The bones of his skull grabbed hold and gave him nightmares. Then slowly, while he shrieked, nuzzled and ate the nightmares one by one, until the last one was gone and the light went out. . . .

At the end of the week he postponed the Phoenix trip because of his health. Weighing himself on a penny scale he saw the slow gliding red arrow point to: 165.

He groaned. Why, I've weighed 175 for years. I can't have lost ten pounds! He examined his cheeks in the fly-dotted mirror. Cold, primitive fear rushed over him in odd little shivers. You, you! I know what you're about, *you!*

He shook his fist at his bony face, particularly addressing his remarks to his superior maxillary, his inferior maxillary, to his cranium and to his cervical vertebrae.

"You damn thing, you! Think you can starve me, make me lose weight, eh? Peel the flesh off, leave nothing, but skin on bone. Trying to ditch me, so you can be supreme, ah? No, no!"

He fled into a cafeteria.

Turkey, dressing, creamed potatoes, four vegetables, three desserts, he could eat none of it, he was sick to his stomach. He forced himself. His teeth began to ache. Bad teeth, is it? He thought angrily. I'll eat in spite of every tooth clanging and banging and rattling so they fall in my gravy.

His head blazed, his breath jerked in and out of a constricted chest, his teeth raged with pain, but he knew one small victory. He was about to drink milk when he stopped and poured it into a vase of nasturtiums. No calcium for you, my boy, no calcium for you. Never again shall I eat foods with calcium or other bone-fortifying minerals. I'll eat for one of us, not both, my lad.

"One hundred and fifty pounds," he said, the following week to his wife. "Do you *see* how I've changed?"

"For the better," said Clarisse. "You were always a little plump for your height, darling." She stroked his chin. "I like your face. "It's so much nicer; the lines of it are so firm and strong now."

"They're not *my* lines, they're his, damn him! You mean to say you like him better than you like me?"

"Him? Who's '*him?*' "

In the parlor mirror, beyond Clarisse, his skull smiled back at him behind his fleshy grimace of hatred and despair.

Fuming, he popped malt tablets into his mouth. This was one way of gaining weight when you couldn't keep other foods down. Clarisse noticed the malt pellets.

"But, darling, really, you don't have to regain the weight for me," she said.

Oh, shut up! he felt like saying.

She made him lie with his head in her lap. "Darling," she said, "I've watched you lately. You're so—badly off. You don't say anything, but you look—hunted. You toss in bed at night. Maybe you should go to a psychiatrist. But I think I can tell you everything he would say. I've put it all together from hints you've let escape you. I can tell you that you and your skeleton are one and the same, 'one nation, indivisible, with liberty and justice for all.' United you stand, divided you fall. If you two fellows can't get along like an old married couple in the future, go back and see Dr. Burleigh. But, first, relax. You're in a vicious circle; the more you worry, the more your bones stick out, the more you worry. After all, who picked this fight—you or that anonymous entity you claim is lurking around behind your alimentary canal?"

He closed his eyes. "I did. I guess I did. Go on Clarisse, keep talking."

"You rest now," she said softly. "Rest and forget."

Mr. Harris felt buoyed up for half a day, then he began to sag. It was all very well to blame his imagination, but this particular skeleton, by God, was fighting back.

Harris set out for M. Munigant's office late in the day. Walking for half an hour until he found the address, he caught sight of the name "M. Munigant" initialed in ancient, flaking gold on a glass plate outside the building. Then, his bones seemed to explode from their moorings, blasted and erupted with pain. Blinded, he staggered away. When he opened his eyes again he had rounded a corner. M. Munigant's office was out of sight.

The pains ceased.

M. Munigant was the man to help him. If the sight of his name could cause so titanic a reaction of course M. Munigant *must* be just the man.

But, not today. Each time he tried to return to that office, the terrible pains took hold. Perspiring, he had to give up and swayed into a cocktail bar.

Moving across the dim lounge, he wondered briefly if a lot of blame couldn't be put on M. Munigant's shoulders. After all, it was Munigant who'd first drawn specific attention to his skeleton, and let the psychological impact of it slam home! Could M. Munigant be using him for some nefarious purpose? But what purpose? Silly to suspect him. Just a little doctor. Trying to be helpful. Munigant and his jar of breadsticks. Ridiculous. M. Munigant was okay, okay . . .

There was a sight within the cocktail lounge to give him hope. A large, fat man, round as a butterball, stood drinking consecutive beers at the bar. Now *there* was a successful man. Harris repressed a desire to go up, clap the fat man's shoulder, and inquire as to how he'd gone about impounding his bones. Yes, the fat man's skeleton was luxuriously closeted. There were pillows of fat here, resilient bulges of it there, with several round chandeliers of fat under his chin. The poor skeleton was lost; it could never fight clear of that blubber. It might have tried once—but not now, overwhelmed, not a bony echo of the fat man's supporter remained.

Not without envy, Harris approached the fat man as one might cut across the bow of an ocean liner. Harris ordered a drink, drank it, and then dared to address the fat man:

"Glands?"

"You talking to me?" asked the fat man.

"Or is there a special diet?" wondered Harris. "I beg your pardon, but, as you see, I'm down. Can't seem to put on any weight. I'd like a stomach like that one of yours. Did you grow it because you were afraid of something?"

"You," announced the fat man, "are drunk. But—I like drunkards." He ordered more drinks. "Listen close, I'll tell you. Layer by layer," said the fat man, "twenty years, man and boy, I built this." He held his vast stomach like a globe of the world, teaching his audience its gastronomical geography. "It was no overnight circus. The tent was not raised before dawn on the wonders installed within. I have cultivated my inner organs as if they were thoroughbred dogs, cats, and other animals. My stomach is a fat pink Persian tom slumbering, rousing at intervals to purr, mew, growl, and cry for chocolate tidbits. I feed it well, it will 'most sit up for me. And, my dear fellow, my intestines are the rarest pure-bred Indian anacondas you ever viewed in the sleekest, coiled, fine and ruddy health. Keep 'em in prime, I do, all my pets. For fear of something? Perhaps."

This called for another drink for everyone.

"Gain weight?" The fat man savored the words on his tongue. "Here's what you do: get yourself a quarreling bird of a wife, a baker's dozen of relatives who can flush a covey of troubles out from behind the veriest molehill. Add to these a sprinkling of business associates whose prime motivation is snatching your last lonely quid, and you are well on your way to getting fat. How so? In no time you'll begin subconsciously building fat betwixt yourself and them. A buffer epidermal state, a cellular wall. You'll soon find that eating is the only fun on earth. But one needs to be bothered by outside sources. Too many people in this world haven't enough to worry about, then they begin picking on themselves, and they lose weight. Meet all of the vile, terrible people you can possibly meet, and pretty soon you'll be adding the good old fat!"

And with that advice, the fat man launched himself out into the dark tide of night, swaying mightily and wheezing.

"That's exactly what Dr. Burleigh told me, slightly changed," said Harris thoughtfully. "Perhaps that trip to Phoenix, now, at this time—"

The trip from Los Angeles to Phoenix was a sweltering one, crossing, as it did, the Mojave desert on a broiling yellow day. Traffic was thin and inconstant, and for long stretches there would not be a car on the road for miles ahead or behind. Harris twitched his fingers on the steering wheel. Whether or not Creldon, in Phoenix, lent him the money he needed to start his business, it was still a good thing to get away, to put distance behind.

The car moved in the hot sluice of desert wind. The one Mr. H. sat inside the other Mr. H. Perhaps both perspired. Perhaps both were miserable.

On a curve, the inside Mr. H. suddenly constricted the outer flesh, causing him to jerk forward on the hot steering wheel.

The car plunged off the road into boiling sand and turned half over.

Night came, a wind rose, the road was lonely and silent. The few cars that passed went swiftly on their way, their view obstructed. Mr. Harris lay unconscious, until very late he heard a wind rising out of the desert, felt the sting of little sand needles on his cheeks, and opened his eyes.

Morning found him gritty-eyed and wandering in thoughtless senseless circles, having, in his delirium, got away from the road. At noon he sprawled in the poor shade of a bush. The sun struck him with a keen sword edge, cutting through to his—bones. A vulture circled.

Harris' parched lips cracked open. "So that's it?" he whispered, red-eyed, bristle-cheeked. "One way or another you'll walk me, starve me, thirst me, kill me." He swallowed dry burrs of dust. "Sun cook off my flesh so you can peek out. Vultures lunch off me, and there you'll lie, grinning. Grinning with victory. Like a bleached xylophone strewn and played by vultures with an ear for odd music. You'd like that. Freedom."

He walked on through a landscape that shivered and bubbled in the direct pour of sunlight; stumbling, falling flat, lying to feed himself little mouths of fire. The air was blue alcohol flame, and vultures roasted and steamed and glittered as they flew in glides and circles. Phoenix. The road. Car. Water. Safety.

"Hey!"

Someone called from way off in the blue alcohol flame.

Mr. Harris propped himself up.

"Hey!"

The call was repeated. A crunching of footsteps, quick.

With a cry of unbelievable relief, Harris rose, only to collapse again into the arms of someone in a uniform with a badge.

The car tediously hauled, repaired, Phoenix reached, Harris found himself in such an unholy state of mind that the business transaction was a numb pantomime. Even when he got the loan and held the money in his hand, it meant nothing. This Thing within him like a hard white sword in a scabbard tainted his business, his eating, colored his love for Clarisse, made it unsafe to trust an automobile; all in all this Thing had to be put in its place. The desert incident had brushed too close. Too near the bone, one might say with an ironic twist of one's mouth. Harris heard himself thanking Mr. Creldon, dimly, for the money. Then he turned his car and motored back across the long miles, this time cutting across to San Diego, so he would miss that desert stretch between El Centro and Beaumont. He drove north along the coast. He didn't trust that desert. But—careful! Salt waves boomed, hissing on the beach outside Laguna. Sand, fish and crustacea would cleanse his bones as swiftly as vultures. Slow down on the curves over the surf.

Damn, he was sick!

Where to turn? Clarisse? Burleigh? Munigant? Bone specialist. Munigant. Well?

"Darling!" Clarisse kissed him. He winced at the solidness of the teeth and jaw behind the passionate exchange.

"Darling," he said, slowly, wiping his lips with his wrist, trembling.

"You look thinner; oh, darling, the business deal—?"

"It went through. I guess. Yes, it did."

She kissed him again. They ate a slow, falsely cheerful dinner, with Clarisse laughing and encouraging him. He studied the phone; several times he picked it up indecisively, then laid it down.

His wife walked in, putting on her coat and hat. "Well, sorry, but I have to leave." She pinched him on the cheek. "Come on now, cheer up! I'll be back from Red Cross in three hours. You lie around and snooze. I simply *have* to go."

When Clarisse was gone, Harris dialed the phone, nervously.

"M. Munigant?"

The explosions and the sickness in his body after he set

the phone down were unbelievable. His bones were racked with every kind of pain, cold and hot, he had ever thought of or experienced in wildest nightmare. He swallowed all the aspirin he could find, in an effort to stave off the assault; but when the doorbell finally rang an hour later, he could not move; he lay weak and exhausted, panting, tears streaming down his cheeks.

"Come in! Come in, for God's sake!"

M. Munigant came in. Thank God the door was unlocked.

Oh, but Mr. Harris looked terrible. M. Munigant stood in the center of the living room, small and dark. Harris nodded. The pains rushed through him, hitting him with large iron hammers and hooks. M. Munigant's eyes glittered as he saw Harris' protuberant bones. Ah, he saw that Mr. Harris was now psychologically prepared for aid. Was it not so? Harris nodded again, feebly, sobbing. M. Munigant still whistled when he talked; something about his tongue and the whistling. No matter. Through his shimmering eyes Harris seemed to see M. Munigant shrink, get smaller. Imagination, of course. Harris sobbed out his story of the Phoenix trip. M. Munigant sympathized. This skeleton was a—a traitor! They would fix him for once and for all!

"Mr. Munigant," sighed Harris, faintly, "I—I never noticed before. Your tongue. Round, tube-like. Hollow? My eyes. Delirious. What do I do?"

M. Munigant whistled softly, appreciatively, coming closer. If Mr. Harris would relax in his chair, and open his mouth? The lights were switched off. M. Munigant peered into Harris' dropped jaw. Wider, please? It had been so hard, that first visit, to help Harris, with both body and bone in revolt. Now, he had cooperation from the flesh of the man, anyway, even if the skeleton protested. In the darkness, M. Munigant's voice got small, small, tiny, tiny. The whistling became high and shrill. Now. Relax, Mr. Harris. NOW!

Harris felt his jaw pressed violently in all directions, his tongue depressed as with a spoon, his throat clogged. He gasped for breath. Whistle. He couldn't breathe! Something squirmed, corkscrewed his cheeks out, bursting his jaws. Like a hot-water douche, something squirted into his sinuses, his ears clanged! "Ahhhh!" shrieked Harris, gagging. His head, its carapaces riven, shattered, hung loose. Agony shot fire through his lungs.

Harris could breathe again, momentarily. His watery eyes sprang wide. He shouted. His ribs, like sticks picked up and bundled, were loosened in him. Pain! He fell to the floor, wheezing out his hot breath.

Lights flickered in his senseless eyeballs, he felt his limbs swiftly cast loose and free. Through streaming eyes he saw the parlor.

The room was empty.

"M. Munigant? In God's name, where are you, M. Munigant? Come help me!"

M. Munigant was gone.

"Help!"

Then he heard it.

Deep down in the subterranean fissures of his body, the minute, unbelievable noises; little smackings and twistings and little dry chippings and grindings and nuzzling sounds—like a tiny hungry mouse down in the red-blooded dimness, gnawing ever so earnestly and expertly at what might have been, but was not, a submerged timber . . . !

———

Clarisse, walking along the sidewalk, held her head high and marched straight toward her house on Saint James Place. She was thinking of the Red Cross as she turned the corner and almost ran into this little dark man who smelled of iodine.

Clarisse would have ignored him if it were not for the fact that as she passed, he took something long, white and oddly familiar from his coat and proceeded to chew on it, as on a peppermint stick. Its end devoured, his extraordinary tongue darted within the white confection, sucking out the filling, making contented noises. He was still crunching his goody as she proceeded up the sidewalk to her house, turned the doorknob and walked in.

"Darling?" she called, smiling around. "Darling, where are you?" She shut the door, walked down the hall and into the living room. "Darling . . ."

She stared at the floor for twenty seconds, trying to understand.

She screamed.

Outside in the sycamore darkness, the little man pierced a long white stick with intermittent holes; then, softly, sighing, his lips puckered, played a little sad tune upon the improvised instrument to accompany the shrill and awful singing of Clarisse's voice as she stood in the living room.

Many times as a little girl Clarisse had run on the beach sands, stepped on a jellyfish and screamed. It was not so bad, finding an intact, gelatin-skinned jellyfish in one's living room. One could step back from it.

It was when the jellyfish *called you by name* . . .

THE JAR

t was one of those things they keep in a jar in the tent of a sideshow on the outskirts of a little, drowsy town. One of those pale things drifting in alcohol plasma, forever dreaming and circling, with its peeled, dead eyes staring out at you and never seeing you. It went with the noiselessness of late night, and only the crickets chirping, the frogs sobbing off in the moist swampland. One of those things in a big jar that makes your stomach jump as it does when you see a preserved arm in a laboratory vat.

Charlie stared back at it for a long time.

A long time, his big, raw hands, hairy on the roofs of them, clenching the rope that kept back curious people. He had paid his dime and now he stared.

It was getting late. The merry-go-round drowsed down to a lazy mechanical tinkle. Tent-peggers back of a canvas smoked and cursed over a poker game. Lights switched out, putting a summer gloom over the carnival. People streamed homeward in cliques and queues. Somewhere, a radio flared up, then cut, leaving the Louisiana sky wide and silent with stars.

There was nothing in the world for Charlie but that pale thing sealed in its universe of serum. Charlie's loose mouth hung open in a pink weal, teeth showing; his eyes were puzzled, admiring, wondering.

Someone walked in the shadows behind him, small beside Charlie's gaunt tallness. "Oh," said the shadow, coming into the light-bulb glare. "You still here, bud?"

"Yeah," said Charlie, like a man in his sleep.

The carny-boss appreciated Charlie's curiosity. He nodded at his old acquaintance in the jar. "Everybody likes it; in a peculiar kinda way, I mean."

Charlie rubbed his long jaw-bone. "You—uh—ever consider selling it?"

The carny-boss's eyes dilated, then closed. He snorted. "Naw. It brings customers. They like seeing stuff like that. Sure."

Charlie made a disappointed "oh."

"Well," considered the carny-boss, "if a guy had money, maybe—"

"How much money?"

"If a guy had—" the carny-boss estimated, counting fingers, watching Charlie as he tacked it out one finger after another. "If a guy had three, four, say, maybe seven or eight—"

Charlie nodded with each motion, expectantly. Seeing this, the carny-boss raised his total, "—maybe ten dollars, or maybe fifteen—"

Charlie scowled, worried. The carny-boss retreated. "Say a guy has *twelve* dollars—" Charlie grinned. "Why he could buy that thing in that jar," concluded the carny-boss.

"Funny thing," said Charlie, "I got just twelve bucks in my denims. And I been reckoning how looked-up-to I'd be back down at Wilder's Hollow if I brung home something like this to set on my shelf over the table. The folks would sure look up to me then, I bet."

"*Well*, now, listen here—" said the carny-boss.

The sale was completed with the jar put on the back seat of Charlie's wagon. The horse skittered his hoofs when he saw the jar, and whinnied.

The carny-boss glanced up with an expression of, almost, relief. "I was tired of seeing that damn thing around, anyway. Don't thank me. Lately I been thinking things about it, funny things—but, hell, I'm a big-mouthed so-and-so. S'long, farmer!"

Charlie drove off. The naked blue light bulbs withdrew like dying stars, the open, dark country night of Louisiana swept in around wagon and horse. There was just Charlie, the horse timing his gray hoofs, and the crickets.

And the jar behind the high seat.

It sloshed back and forth, back and forth. Sloshed wet. And the cold gray thing drowsily slumped against the glass, looking out, looking out, but seeing nothing, nothing.

Charlie leaned back to pet the lid. Smelling of strange liquor his hand returned, changed and cold and trembling, excited. *Yes, sir!* he thought to himself, *Yes, sir!*

Slosh, slosh, slosh. . . .

In the Hollow, numerous grass-green and blood-red lanterns tossed dusty light over men huddled, murmuring, spitting, sitting on General Store property.

They knew the creak-bumble of Charlie's wagon and did not shift their raw, drab-haired skulls as he rocked to a halt. Their cigars were glowworms, their voices were frog mutterings on summer nights.

Charlie leaned down eagerly. "Hi, Clem! Hi, Milt!"

"Lo, Charlie. Lo, Charlie," they murmured. The political conflict continued. Charlie cut it down the seam:

"I got somethin' here. I got somethin' you might wanna see!"

Tom Carmody's eyes glinted, green in the lamplight, from the General Store porch. It seemed to Charlie that Tom Carmody was forever installed under porches in shadow, or under trees in shadow, or if in a room, then in the farthest niche shining his eyes out at you from the dark. You never knew what his face was doing, and his eyes were always funning you. And every time they looked at you they laughed a different way.

"You ain't got nothin' we wants to see, baby-doll."

Charlie made a fist and looked at it. "Somethin' in a jar," he went on. "Looks kine a like a brain, kine a like a pickled jellyfish, kine a like—well, come see yourself!"

Someone snicked a cigar into a fall of pink ash and ambled over to look. Charlie grandly elevated the jar lid, and in the uncertain lantern light the man's face changed. "Hey, now, what in hell *is* this—?"

It was the first thaw of the evening. Others shifted lazily upright, leaned forward; gravity pulled them into walking. They made no effort, except to put one shoe before the other to keep from collapsing upon their unusual faces. They circled the jar and contents. And Charlie for the first time in his life, seized on some hidden strategy and crashed the glass lid shut.

"You want to see more, drop aroun' my house! It'll be there," he declared, generously.

Tom Carmody spat from out his porch eyrie. "Ha!"

"Lemme see that again!" cried Gramps Medknowe. "Is it a octopus?"

Charlie flapped the reins; the horse stumbled into action.

"Come on aroun'! You're welcome!"

"What'll your wife say?"

"She'll kick the tar off'n our heels!"

But Charlie and wagon were gone over the hill. The men stood, all of them, chewing their tongues, squinting up the road in the dark. Tom Carmody swore softly from the porch. . . .

Charlie climbed the steps of his shack and carried the jar to its throne in the living room, thinking that from now on this lean-to would be a palace, with an "emperor"—that was the word! "emperor"—all cold and white and quiet drifting in his private pool, raised, elevated upon a shelf over a ramshackle table.

The jar, as he watched, burnt off the cold mist that hung over this place on the rim of the swamp.

"What you got there?"

Thedy's thin soprano turned him from his awe. She stood in the bedroom door glaring out, her thin body clothed in faded blue gingham, her hair drawn to a drab knot behind red ears. Her eyes were faded like the gingham. "Well," she repeated. "What is it?"

"What's it look like to you, Thedy?"

She took a thin step forward, making a slow, indolent pendulum of hips, her eyes intent upon the jar, her lips drawn back to show feline milk teeth.

The dead pale thing hung in its serum.

Thedy snapped a dull-blue glance at Charlie, then back to the jar, once more at Charlie, once more to the jar, then she whirled quickly.

"It—it looks—looks just like *you*, Charlie!" she cried.

The bedroom door slammed.

The reverberation did not disturb the jar's contents. But Charlie stood there, longing after his wife, heart pounding frantically. Much later, when his heart slowed, he talked to the thing in the jar.

"I work the bottom land to the butt-bone every year, and she grabs the money and runs off down home visitin' her folks nine weeks at a stretch. I can't keep hold of her. Her and the men from the store, they make fun of me. I can't help it if I don't know a way to hold onto her! Damn, but I *try*!"

Philosophically, the contents of the jar gave no advice.

"Charlie?"

Someone stood in the front-yard door.

Charlie turned, startled, then broke out a grin.

It was some of the men from the General Store.

"Uh—Charlie—we—we thought—well—we came up to have a look at that—stuff—you got in that there jar—"

July passed warm and it was August.

For the first time in years, Charlie was happy as tall corn growing after a drought. It was gratifying of an evening to hear boots shushing through the tall grass, the sound of men spitting into the ditch prior to setting foot on the porch, the sound of heavy bodies creaking the boards, and the groan of the house as yet another shoulder leaned against its frame door and another voice said, as a hairy wrist wiped a mouth clean:

"Kin I come in?"

With elaborate casualness, Charlie'd invite the arrivals in. There'd be chairs, soapboxes for all, or at least carpets to squat on. And by the time crickets were itching their legs into a summertime humming and frogs were throat-swollen like ladies with goiters shouting in the great night, the room would be full to bursting with people from all the bottom lands.

At first nobody would say anything. The first half-hour of such an evening, while people came in and got settled, was spent in carefully rolling cigarettes. Putting tobacco neatly into the rut of brown paper, loading it, tamping it, as they loaded and tamped and rolled their thoughts and fears and amazement for the evening. It gave them time to think. You could see their brains working behind their eyes as they fingered the cigarettes into smoking order.

It was kind of a rude church gathering. They sat, squatted, leaned on plaster walls, and one by one, with reverent awe, they stared at the jar upon its shelf.

They wouldn't stare sudden-like. No, they kind of did it slow, casual, as if they were glancing around the room—letting their eyes fumble over just *any* old object that happened into their consciousness.

And—just by accident, of course—the focus of their wandering eyes would occur always at the same place. After a while all eyes in the room would be fastened to it, like pins stuck in some incredible pincushion. And the only sound would be someone sucking a corncob. Or the children's barefooted scurry on the porch planks outside. Maybe some woman's voice would come, "You kids git away, now! Git!" And with a giggle like soft, quick water, the bare feet would rush off to scare the bullfrogs.

Charlie would be up front, naturally, on his rocking chair, a plaid pillow under his lean rump, rocking slow, enjoying the fame and looked-up-to-ness that came with keeping the jar.

Thedy, she'd be seen way back of the room with the womenfolk in a bunch, all gray and quiet, abiding their men.

Thedy looked like she was ripe for jealous screaming. But she said nothing, just watched men tromp into her living room and sit at the feet of Charlie, staring at this here Holy Grail-like thing, and her lips were set cold and hard and she spoke not a civil word to anybody.

After a period of proper silence, someone, maybe old Gramps Medknowe from Crick Road, would clear the phlegm from a deep cave somewhere inside himself, lean forward, blinking, wet his lips, maybe, and there'd be a curious tremble in his calloused fingers.

This would cue everyone to get ready for the talking to come. Ears were primed. People settled like sows in the warm mud after a rain.

Gramps looked a long while, measured his lips with a lizard tongue, then settled back and said, like always, in a high, thin old-man's tenor:

"Wonder what it is? Wonder if it's a he or a she or just a plain old *it?* Sometimes I wake up nights, twist on my corn-matting, think about that jar settin' here in the long dark. Think about it hangin' in liquid, peaceful and pale like an animal oyster. Sometimes I wake Maw and we both think on it. . . ."

While talking, Gramps moved his fingers in a quavering pantomime. Everybody watched his thick thumb weave, and the other heavy-nailed fingers undulate.

". . . we both lay there, thinkin'. And we shivers. Maybe a hot night, trees sweatin', mosquitoes too hot to fly, but we shivers jest the same, and turn over, tryin' to sleep. . . ."

Gramps lapsed back into silence, as if his speech was enough from him, let some other voice talk the wonder, awe, and strangeness.

Juke Marmer, from Willow Sump, wiped sweat off his palms on the round of his knees and softly said:

"I remember when I was a runnel-nosed kid. We had a cat who was all the time makin' kittens. Lordamighty, she'd a litter any time she jumped around and skipped a fence—" Juke spoke in a kind of holy softness, benevolent. "Well, we give the kittens away, but when this one particular litter busted out, everybody within walkin' distance had one-two our cats by gift, already.

"So Ma busied on the back porch with a big two-gallon glass jar, fillin' it to the top with water. Ma said, 'Juke, you drown them kittens!' I 'member I stood there; the kittens mewed, runnin' 'round, blind, small, helpless, and funny—just beginnin' to get their eyes open. I looked at Ma, I said, 'Not me, Ma! You do it!' But Ma turned pale and said it had to be done and I was the only one handy. And she went off to stir gravy and fix chicken. I—I picked up one—kitten. I held it. It was warm. It made a mewin' sound, I felt like runnin' away, not ever comin' back."

Juke nodded his head now, eyes bright, young, seeing into the past, making it new, shaping it with words, smoothing it with his tongue.

"I dropped the kitten in the water. The kitten closed his eyes, opened his mouth, tryin' for air. I 'member how the little white fangs showed, the pink tongue came out, and bubbles with it, in a line to the top of the water!

"I know to this day the way that kitten floated after it was all over, driftin' aroun', slow and not worryin', lookin' out at

me, not condemnin' me for what I done. But not likin' me, neither. Ahhhh. . . ."

Hearts jumped quick. Eyes swiveled from Juke to the
shelved jar, back down, up again apprehensively.

A pause.

Jahdoo, the black man from Heron Swamp, tossed his
ivory eyeballs, like a dusky juggler, in his head. His dark knuckles knotted and flexed—grasshoppers alive.

"You know what that is? You know, you *know*? I tells you.
That be the center of Life, sure 'nuff! Lord believe me, it so!"

Swaying in a tree-like rhythm, Jahdoo was blown by a
swamp wind no one could see, hear or feel, save himself. His
eyeballs went around again, as if cut free to wander. His voice
needled a dark thread pattern, picking up each person by the
lobes of their ears and sewing them into one unbreathing
design:

"From that, lyin' back in the Middibamboo Sump, all sort
o' thing crawl. It put out hand, it put out feet, it put out tongue
an' horn an' it grow. Little bitty amoeba, perhap. Then a frog
with a bulge-throat fit ta bust! Yah!" He cracked knuckles. "It
slobber on up to its gummy joints and it—it AM HUMAN!
That am the center of creation! That am Middibamboo Mama,
from which we all come ten thousand year ago. Believe it!"

"Ten thousand year ago!" whispered Granny Carnation.

"It am old! Looky it! It donn worra no more. It know
betta. It hang like pork chop in fryin' fat. It got eye to see with,
but it donn blink 'em, they donn look fretted, does they? No,
man! It know betta. It know that we done come *from* it, and we
is going' back *to* it."

"What color eyes it got?"

"Gray."

"Naw, *green!*"

"What color hair? Brown?"

"Black!"

"Red!"

"No, *gray!*"

Then, Charlie would give his drawling opinion. Some nights he'd say the same thing, some nights not. It didn't matter. When you said the same thing night after night in the deep summer, it always sounded different. The crickets changed it. The frogs changed it. The thing in the jar changed it. Charlie said:

"What if an old man went back into the swamp, or maybe a young kid, and wandered aroun' for years and years lost in all that drippin', on the trails and gullies, in them old wet ravines in the nights, skin a turnin' pale, and makin' cold and shrivelin' up. Bein' away from the sun he'd keep witherin' away up and up and finally sink into a muck-hole and lay in a kind of—scum—like the maggot 'skeeters sleepin' in sump-water. Why, why—for all we can tell, this might be someone we *know!* Someone we passed words with once on a time. For all we know—"

A hissing from among the womenfolk back in the shadow. One woman standing, eyes shining black, fumbled for words. Her name was Mrs. Tridden, and she murmured:

"Lots of little kids run stark naked to the swamp ever' year. They runs around and never comes back. I almost got lost maself. I—I lost my little boy, Foley, that way. You—you DON'T SUPPOSE!!!"

Breath was snatched through nostrils, constricted, tightened. Mouths turned down at corners, bent by hard, clinching muscle. Heads turned on celery-stalk necks, and eyes read her horror and hope. It was in Mrs. Tridden's body, wire-taut, holding to the wall back of her with straight fingers stiff.

"My baby," she whispered. She breathed it out. "My baby. My Foley. Foley! Foley, is that you? Foley! Foley, tell me, baby, is that YOU!"

Everybody held their breath, turning to see the jar.

The thing in the jar said nothing. It just stared blind-white out upon the multitude. And deep in rawboned bodies a secret fear juice ran like a spring thaw, and their resolute calmness and belief and easy humbleness was gnawed and eaten by that juice and melted away in a torrent! Someone screamed.

"It moved!"

"No, no, it didn' move. Just your eyes playin' tricks!"

"Hones' ta God!" cried Juke. "I saw it shift slow like a dead kitten!"

"Hush up, now. It's been dead a long, long time. Maybe since before you was born!"

"He made a sign!" screamed Mrs. Tridden. "That's my Foley! My baby you got there! Three-year-old he was! My baby lost and gone in the swamp!"

The sobbing broke from her.

"Now, Mrs. Tridden. There now. Set yourself down, stop shakin'. Ain't no more your child'n mine. There, there."

One of the womenfolk held her and faded out the sobbing into jerked breathing and a fluttering of her lips in butterfly quickness as the breath stroked over them, afraid.

When all was quiet again, Granny Carnation, with a withered pink flower in her shoulder-length gray hair, sucked the pipe in her trap mouth and talked around it, shaking her head to make the hair dance in the light:

"All this talkin' and shovin' words. Like as not we'll never find out, never know what it is. Like as not if we found out we wouldn't *want* to know. It's like magic tricks magicians do at shows. Once you find the fake, ain't no more fun'n the innards of a jackbob. We come collectin' around here every ten nights or so, talkin', social-like, with somethin', always somethin', to talk about. Stands to reason if we spied out what the damn thing is there'd be nothin' to chew about, so there!"

"Well, damn it to hell!" rumbled a bull voice. "I don't think it's nothin'!"

Tom Carmody.

Tom Carmody standing, as always, in shadow. Out on the porch, just his eyes staring in, his lips laughing at you dimly, mocking. His laughter got inside Charlie like a hornet sting. Thedy had put him up to it. Thedy was trying to kill Charlie's new life, she was!

"Nothin'," repeated Carmody, harshly, "in that jar but a bunch of old jellyfish from Sea Cove, a rottin' and stinkin' fit to whelp!"

"You mightn't be jealous, Cousin Carmody?" asked Charlie, slow.

"Haw!" snorted Carmody. "I just come aroun' ta watch you dumb fools jaw about nuthin'. You notice I never set foot inside or took part. I'm goin' home right now. Anybody wanna come along with me?"

He got no offer of company. He laughed again, as if this were a bigger joke, how so many people could be so far gone, and Thedy was raking her palms with her fingernails away back in a corner of the room. Charlie saw her mouth twitch and was cold and could not speak.

Carmody, still laughing, rapped off the porch with his high-heeled boots and the sound of crickets took him away.

Granny Carnation gummed her pipe. "Like I was sayin' before the storm: that thing on the shelf, why couldn't it be sort of—all things? Lots of things. All kinds of life—death—I don't know. Mix rain and sun and muck and jelly, all that together. Grass and snakes and children and mist and all the nights and days in the dead canebrake. Why's it have to be *one* thing? Maybe it's *lots*."

And the talking ran soft for another hour, and Thedy slipped away into the night on the track of Tom Carmody, and Charlie began to sweat. They were up to something, those two. They were planning something. Charlie sweated warm all the rest of the evening. . . .

The meeting broke up late, and Charlie bedded down with mixed emotions. The meeting had gone off well, but what about Thedy and Tom?

Very late, with certain star coveys shuttled down the sky marking the time as after midnight, Charlie heard the shushing of the tall grass parted by her penduluming hips. Her heels tacked soft across the porch, into the house, into the bedroom.

She lay soundlessly in bed, cat eyes staring at him. He couldn't see them, but he could feel them staring.

"Charlie?"

He waited.

Then he said, "I'm awake."

Then she waited.

"Charlie?"

"What?"

"Bet you don't know where I been; bet you don't know where I been." It was a faint, derisive singsong in the night.

He waited.

She waited again. She couldn't bear waiting long, though, and continued:

"I been to the carnival over in Cape City. Tom Carmody drove me. We—we talked to the carny-boss, Charlie, we did, we did, we *sure* did!" And she sort of giggled to herself, secretly.

Charlie was ice-cold. He stirred upright on an elbow.

She said, "We found out what it is in your jar, Charlie—" insinuatingly.

Charlie flumped over, hands to ears. "I don't wanna hear!"

"Oh, but you gotta hear, Charlie. It's a good joke. Oh, it's rare, Charlie," she hissed.

"Go away," he said.

"Unh-unh! No, no, sir, Charlie. Why, no, Charlie—Honey. Not until I tell!"

"Git!" he said.

"Let me tell! We talked to that carny-boss, and he—he liked to die laughin'. He said he sold that jar and what was in it to some, some—hick—for twelve bucks. And it ain't worth more'n two bucks at most!"

Laughter bloomed in the dark, right out of her mouth, an awful kind of laughter.

She finished it, quick:

"It's just junk, Charlie! Rubber, papier-mache, silk, cotton, boric-acid! That's all! Got a metal frame inside! That's all it is, Charlie, That's all!" she shrilled.

"No, no!"

He sat up swiftly, ripping sheets apart in big fingers, roaring.

"I don't wanna hear! Don't wanna hear!" he bellowed over and over.

She said, "Wait'll everyone hears how fake it is! Won't they laugh! Won't they flap their lungs!"

He caught her wrists. "You ain't gonna tell them?"

"Wouldn't wan me known as a liar, would you, Charlie?"

He flung her off and away.

"Whyncha leave me alone? You dirty! Dirty jealous mean of ever'thing I do. I took shine off your nose when I brung the jar home. You didn' sleep right 'til you ruined things!"

She laughed. "Then I won't tell anybody," she said.

He stared at her. "You spoiled *my* fun. That's all that counted. It don't matter if you tell the rest. *I* know. And I'll never have no more fun. You and that Tom Carmody. I wish I could stop him laughin'. He's been laughin' for years at me! Well, you just go tell the rest, the other people, now—might as well have your fun—!"

He strode angrily, grabbed the jar so it sloshed, and would have flung it on the floor, but he stopped trembling, and let it down softly on the spindly table. He leaned over it, sobbing. If he lost this, the world was gone. And he was losing Thedy, too. Every month that passed she danced further away, sneering at him, funning him. For too many years her hips had been the pendulum by which he reckoned the time of his living. But other men, Tom Carmody, for one, were reckoning time from the same source.

Thedy stood waiting for him to smash the jar. Instead, he petted and stroked and gradually quieted himself over it. He thought of the long, good evenings in the past month, those rich evenings of friends and talk, moving about the room. That, at least, was good, if nothing else.

He turned slowly to Thedy. She was lost forever to him.

"Thedy, you didn't go to the carnival."

"Yes, I did."

"You're lyin'," he said, quietly.

"No, I'm not!"

"This—this jar *has* to have somethin' in it. Somethin' be-sides the junk you say. Too many people believe there's some-thin' in it, Thedy. You can't change that. The carny-boss, if you talked with him, he lied." Charlie took a deep breath and then said, "Come here, Thedy."

"What you want?" she asked, sullenly.

"Come over here."

He took a step toward her. "Come here."

"Keep away from me, Charlie."

"Just want to show you something, Thedy." His voice was soft, low, and insistent. "Here, kittie. Here, kittie, kittie, kittie—HERE KITTIE!"

It was another night, about a week later. Gramps Medknowe and Granny Carnation came, followed by young Juke and Mrs. Trid-den and Jahdoo, the colored man. Followed by all the others, young and old, sweet and sour, creaking into chairs, each with his or her thought, hope, fear, and wonder in mind. Each not looking at the shrine, but saying hello softly to Charlie.

They waited for the others to gather. From the shine of their eyes one could see that each saw something different in the jar, something of the life and the pale life after life, and the life in death and the death in life, each with his story, his cue, his lines, familiar, old but new.

Charlie sat alone.

"Hello, Charlie." Somebody peered into the empty bedroom. "Your wife gone off again to visit her folks?"

"Yeah, she run for Tennessee. Be back in a couple weeks. She's the darndest one for runnin'. You know Thedy."

"Great one for jumpin' around, that woman."

Soft voices talking, getting settled, and then, quite suddenly, walking on the dark porch and shining his eyes in at the people—Tom Carmody.

Tom Carmody standing outside the door, knees sagging and trembling, arms hanging and shaking at his side, staring into the room. Tom Carmody not daring to enter. Tom Carmody with his mouth open, but not smiling. His lips wet and slack, not smiling. His face pale as chalk, as if it had been sick for a long time.

Gramps looked up at the jar, cleared his throat and said, "Why, I never noticed so definite before. It's got *blue* eyes."

"It always had blue eyes," said Granny Carnation.

"No," whined Gramps. "No, it didn't. They was brown last time we was here." He blinked upward. "And another thing— it's got brown hair. Didn't have brown hair *before!*"

"Yes, yes, it did," sighed Mrs. Tridden.

"No, it didn't!"

"Yes, it did!"

Tom Carmody, shivering in the summer night, staring in at the jar. Charlie, glancing up at it, rolling a cigarette, casually, all peace and calm, very certain of his life and thoughts. Tom Carmody, alone, seeing things about the jar he never saw before. *Everybody* seeing what they wanted to see; all thoughts running in a fall of quick rain:

"My baby. My little baby." thought Mrs. Tridden.

"A brain!" thought Gramps.

The colored man jigged his fingers. "Middibamboo Mama!"

A fisherman pursed his lips. "Jellyfish!"

"Kitten! Here kittie, kittie, kittie!" the thoughts drowned clawing in Juke's eyes. "Kitten!"

"Everything and anything!" shrilled Granny's weazened thought. "The night, the swamp, death, the pale things, the wet things from the sea!"

Silence. And then Gramps whispered, "I wonder. Wonder if it's a he—or a she—or just a plain old *it*?"

Charlie glanced up, satisfied, tamping his cigarette, shaping it to his mouth. Then he looked at Tom Carmody, who would never smile again, in the door. "I reckon we'll never know. Yeah, I reckon we won't." Charlie shook his head slowly and settled down with his guests, looking, looking.

It was just one of those things they keep in a jar in the tent of a sideshow on the outskirts of a little, drowsy town. One of those pale things drifting in alcohol plasma, forever dreaming and circling, with its peeled dead eyes staring out at you and never seeing you. . . .

THE LAKE

The wave shut me off from the world, from the birds in the sky, the children on the beach, my mother on the shore. There was a moment of green silence. Then the wave gave me back to the sky, the sand, the children yelling. I came out of the lake and the world was waiting for me, having hardly moved since I went away.

I ran up on the beach.

Mama swabbed me with a furry towel. "Stand there and dry," she said.

I stood there, watching the sun take away the water beads on my arms. I replaced them with goose-pimples.

"My, there's a wind," said Mama. "Put on your sweater."

"Wait'll I watch my goose-bumps," I said.

"Harold," said Mama.

I put the sweater on and watched the waves come up and fall down on the beach. But not clumsily. On purpose, with a green sort of elegance. Even a drunken man could not collapse with such elegance as those waves.

It was September. In the last days when things are getting sad for no reason. The beach was so long and lonely with only about six people on it. The kids quit bouncing the ball because somehow the wind made them sad, too, whistling the way it did, and the kids sat down and felt autumn come along the endless shore.

All of the hot-dog stands were boarded up with strips of golden planking, sealing in all the mustard, onion, meat odors of the long, joyful summer. It was like nailing summer into a series of coffins. One by one the places slammed their covers down, padlocked their doors, and the wind came and touched the sand, blowing away all of the million footprints of July and August. It got so that now, in September, there was nothing but the mark of my rubber tennis shoes and Donald and Delaus Arnold's feet, down by the water curve.

Sand blew up in curtains on the sidewalks, and the merry-go-round was hidden with canvas, all of the horses frozen in mid-air on their brass poles, showing teeth, galloping on. With only the wind for music, slipping through canvas.

I stood there. Everyone else was in school. I was not. Tomorrow I would be on my way west across the United States on a train. Mom and I had come to the beach for one last brief moment.

There was something about the loneliness that made me want to get away by myself. "Mama, I want to run up the beach a ways," I said.

"All right, but hurry back, and don't go near the water."

I ran. Sand spun under me and the wind lifted me. You know how it is, running, arms out so you feel veils from your fingers, caused by wind. Like wings.

Mama withdrew into the distance, sitting. Soon she was only a brown speck and I was all alone.

Being alone is a newness to a twelve-year-old child. He is so used to people about. The only way he can be alone is in his mind. There are so many real people around, telling children what and how to do, that a boy has to run off down a beach, even if it's only in his head, to get by himself in his own world.

So now I was really alone.

I went down to the water and let it cool up to my stomach. Always before, with the crowd, I hadn't dared to look, to come to this spot and search around in the water and call a certain name. But now—

Water is like a magician. Sawing you in half. It feels as if you were cut in two, part of you, the lower part, sugar, melting, dissolving away. Cool water, and once in a while a very elegantly stumbling wave that fell with a flourish of lace.

I called her name. A dozen times I called it.

"Tally! Tally! Oh, Tally!"

You really expect answers to your calling when you are young. You feel that whatever you may think can be real. And some times maybe that is not so wrong.

I thought of Tally, swimming out into the water last May, with her pigtails trailing, blond. She went laughing, and the sun was on her small twelve-year-old shoulders. I thought of the water settling quiet, of the life guard leaping into it, of Tally's mother screaming, and of how Tally never came out. . . .

The life guard tried to persuade her to come out, but she did not. He came back with only bits of water-weed in his big-knuckled fingers, and Tally was gone. She would not sit across from me at school any longer, or chase indoor balls on the brick streets on summer nights. She had gone too far out, and the lake would not let her return.

And now in the lonely autumn when the sky was huge and the water was huge and the beach was so very long, I had come down for the last time, alone.

I called her name again and again. Tally, oh, Tally!

The wind blew so very softly over my ears, the way wind blows over the mouths of sea-shells to set them whispering. The water rose, embraced my chest, then my knees, up and down, one way and another, sucking under my heels.

"Tally! Come back, Tally!"

I was only twelve. But I know how much I loved her. It was that love that comes before all significance of body and morals. It was that love that is no more bad than wind and sea and sand lying side by side forever. It was made of all the warm long days together at the beach, and the humming quiet days of droning education at the school. All the long autumn days of the years past when I had carried her books home from school.

Tally!

I called her name for the last time. I shivered. I felt water on my face and did not know how it got there. The waves had not splashed that high.

Turning, I retreated to the sand and stood there for half an hour, hoping for one glimpse, one sign, one little bit of Tally to remember. Then, I knelt and built a sand castle, shaping it fine, building it as Tally and I had often built so many of them. But this time, I only built half of it. Then I got up.

"Tally, if you hear me, come in and build the rest."

I walked off toward that far-away speck that was Mama. The water came in, blended the sand-castle circle by circle, mashing it down little by little into the original smoothness.

Silently, I walked along the shore.

Far away, a merry-go-round jangled faintly, but it was only the wind.

The next day, I went away on the train.

A train has a poor memory; it soon puts all behind it. It forgets the cornlands of Illinois, the rivers of childhood, the bridges, the lakes, the valleys, the cottages, the hurts and the joys. It spreads them out behind and they drop back on a horizon.

I lengthened my bones, put flesh on them, changed my young mind for an older one, threw away clothes as they no longer fitted, shifted from grammar to high-school, to college. And then there was a young woman in Sacramento. I knew her for a time, and we were married. By the time I was twenty-two, I had almost forgotten what the East was like.

Margaret suggested that our delayed honeymoon be taken back in that direction.

Like a memory, a train works both ways. A train can bring rushing back all those things you left behind so many years before.

Lake Bluff, population 10,000, came up over the sky. Margaret looked so handsome in her fine new clothes. She watched me as I felt my old world gather me back into its living. She held my arm as the train slid into Bluff Station and our baggage was escorted out.

So many years, and the things they do to people's faces and bodies. When we walked through the town together I saw no one I recognized. There were faces with echoes in them. Echoes of hikes on ravine trails. Faces with small laughter in them from closed grammar schools and swinging on metal-linked swings and going up and down on teeter-totters. But I didn't speak. I walked and looked and filled up inside with all those memories, like leaves stacked for autumn burning.

We stayed on two weeks in all, revisiting all the places

together. The days were happy. I thought I loved Margaret well. At least I thought I did.

It was on one of the last days that we walked down by the shore. It was not quite as late in the year as that day so many years before, but the first evidences of desertion were coming upon the beach. People were thinning out, several of the hot-dog stands had been shuttered and nailed, and the wind, as always, waited there to sing for us.

I almost saw Mama sitting on the sand as she used to sit. I had that feeling again of wanting to be alone. But I could not force myself to speak of this to Margaret. I only held onto her and waited.

It got late in the day. Most of the children had gone home and only a few men and women remained basking in the windy sun.

The life-guard boat pulled up on the shore. The life guard stepped out of it, slowly, with something in his arms.

I froze there. I held my breath and I felt small, only twelve years old, very little, very infinitesimal and afraid. The wind howled. I could not see Margaret. I could see only the beach, the life guard slowly emerging from the boat with a gray sack in his hands, not very heavy, and his face almost as gray and lined.

"Stay here, Margaret," I said. I don't know why I said it.

"But, why?"

"Just stay here, that's all—"

I walked slowly down the sand to where the life guard stood. He looked at me.

"What is it?" I asked.

The life guard kept looking at me for a long time and he

couldn't speak. He put the gray sack on the sand, and water whispered wet up around it and went back.

"What is it?" I insisted.

"Strange," said the life guard, quietly.

I waited.

"Strange," he said, softly. "Strangest thing I ever saw. She's been dead a long time."

I repeated his words.

He nodded. "Ten years, I'd say. There haven't been any children drowned here this year. There were twelve children drowned here since 1933, but we found all of them before a few hours had passed. All except one, I remember. This body here, why it must be ten years in the water. It's not—pleasant."

I stared at the gray sack in his arms. "Open it," I said. I don't know why I said it. The wind was louder.

He fumbled with the sack.

"Hurry, man, open it!" I cried.

"I better not do that," he said. Then perhaps he saw the way my face must have looked. "She was such a *little* girl—"

He opened it only part way. That was enough.

The beach was deserted. There was only the sky and the wind and the water and the autumn coming on lonely. I looked down at her there.

I said something over and over. A name. The life guard looked at me. "Where did you find her?" I asked.

"Down the beach, that way, in the shallow water. It's a long, long time for her, isn't it?"

I shook my head.

"Yes, it is. Oh God, yes it is."

I thought: people grow. I have grown. But she has not

changed. She is still small. She is still young. Death does not permit growth or change. She still has golden hair. She will be forever young and I will love her forever, oh God, I will love her forever.

The life guard tied up the sack again.

Down the beach, a few moments later, I walked by myself. I stopped, and looked down at something. This is where the life guard found her, I said to myself.

There, at the water's edge, lay a sand castle, only half-built. Just like Tally and I used to build them. She half and I half.

I looked at it. I knelt beside the sand castle and saw the small prints of feet coming in from the lake and going back out to the lake again and not returning.

Then—I knew.

"I'll help you finish it," I said.

I did. I built the rest of it up very slowly, then I arose and turned away and walked off, so as not to watch it crumble in the waves, as all things crumble.

I walked back up the beach to where a strange woman named Margaret was waiting for me, smiling. . . .

THE EMISSARY

Martin knew it was autumn again, for Dog ran into the house bringing wind and frost and a smell of apples turned to cider under trees. In dark clock-springs of hair, Dog fetched goldenrod, dust of farewell-summer, acorn-husk, hair of squirrel, feather of departed robin, sawdust from fresh-cut cordwood, and leaves like charcoals shaken from a blaze of maple trees. Dog jumped. Showers of brittle fern, blackberry vine, marsh-grass sprang over the bed where Martin shouted. No doubt, no doubt of it at all, this incredible beast was October!

"Here, boy, here!"

And Dog settled to warm Martin's body with all the bonfires and subtle burnings of the season, to fill the room with soft or heavy, wet or dry odors of far-traveling. In spring, he smelled of lilac, iris, lawn-mowered grass; in summer, ice-cream-mustached, he came pungent with firecracker, Roman candle, pinwheel, baked by the sun. But autumn! Autumn!

"Dog, what's it like outside?"

And lying there, Dog told as he always told. Lying there, Martin found autumn as in the old days before sickness bleached him white on his bed. Here was his contact, his carry-all, the quick-moving part of himself he sent with a yell to run and return, circle and scent, collect and deliver the time and texture of worlds in town, country, by creek, river, lake, downcellar, up-attic, in closet or coal-bin. Ten dozen times a day he was gifted with sunflower seed, cinder-path, milkweed, horsechestnut, or full flame-smell of pumpkin. Through the loomings of the universe Dog shuttled; the design was hid in his pelt. Put out your hand, it was there. . . .

"And where did you go this morning?"

But he knew without hearing where Dog had rattled down hills where autumn lay in cereal crispness, where children lay in funeral pyres, in rustling heaps, the leaf-buried but watchful dead, as Dog and the world blew by. Martin trembled his fingers, searched the thick fur, read the long journey. Through stubbled fields, over glitters of ravine creek, down marbled spread of cemetery yard, into woods. In the great season of spices and rare incense, now Martin ran through his emissary, around, about, and home!

The bedroom door opened.

"That dog of yours is in trouble again."

Mother brought in a tray of fruit salad, cocoa, and toast, her blue eyes snapping.

"Mother . . ."

"Always digging places. Dug a hole in Miss Tarkin's garden this morning. She's spittin' mad. That's the fourth hole he's dug there this week."

"Maybe he's looking for something."

"Fiddlesticks, he's too darned curious. If he doesn't behave he'll be locked up."

Martin looked at this woman as if she were a stranger. "Oh, you wouldn't do that! How would I learn anything? How would I find things out if Dog didn't tell me?"

Mom's voice was quieter. "Is that what he does—tell you things?"

"There's nothing I don't know when he goes out and around and back, *nothing* I can't find out from him!"

They both sat looking at Dog and the dry strewings of mold and seed over the quilt.

"Well, if he'll just stop digging where he shouldn't, he can run all he wants," said Mother.

"Here, boy, here!"

And Martin snapped a tin note to the dog's collar:

MY OWNER IS MARTIN SMITH—TEN YEARS OLD—SICK IN BED—VISITORS WELCOME.

Dog barked. Mother opened the downstairs door and let him out.

Martin sat listening.

Far off and away you could hear Dog run in the quiet autumn rain that was falling now. You could hear the barking-jingling fade, rise, fade again as he cut down alley, over lawn, to fetch back Mr. Holloway and the oiled metallic smell of the delicate snowflake-interiored watches he repaired in his home shop. Or maybe he would bring Mr. Jacobs, the grocer, whose clothes were rich with lettuce, celery, tomatoes, and the secret tinned and hidden smell of the red demons stamped on cans of deviled ham. Mr. Jacobs and his unseen pink-meat devils waved often from the yard below. Or Dog brought Mr. Jackson, Mrs. Gillespie, Mr. Smith, Mrs. Holmes, *any* friend or near-friend, encountered, cornered, begged, worried, and at last shepherded home for lunch, or tea-and-biscuits.

Now, listening, Martin heard Dog below, with footsteps

moving in a light rain behind him. The downstairs bell rang, Mom opened the door, light voices murmured. Martin sat forward, face shining. The stair treads creaked. A young woman's voice laughed quietly. Miss Haight, of course, his teacher from school!

The bedroom door sprang open.

Martin had company.

Morning, afternoon, evening, dawn and dusk, sun and moon circled with Dog, who faithfully reported temperatures of turf and air, color of earth and tree, consistency of mist or rain, but—most important of all—brought back again and again and again—Miss Haight.

On Saturday, Sunday and Monday she baked Martin orange-iced cupcakes, brought him library books about dinosaurs and cavemen. On Tuesday, Wednesday and Thursday somehow he beat her at dominoes, somehow she lost at checkers, and soon, she cried, he'd defeat her handsomely at chess. On Friday, Saturday and Sunday they talked and never stopped talking, and she was so young and laughing and handsome and her hair was a soft, shining brown like the season outside the window, and she walked clear, clean and quick, a heartbeat warm in the bitter afternoon when he heard it. Above all, she had the secret of signs, and could read and interpret Dog and the symbols she searched out and plucked forth from his coat with her miraculous fingers. Eyes shut, softly laughing, in a gypsy's voice, she divined the world from the treasures in her hands.

And on Monday afternoon, Miss Haight was dead.

Martin sat up in bed, slowly.

"Dead?" he whispered.

Dead, said his mother, yes, dead, killed in an auto accident a mile out of town. Dead, yes, dead, which meant cold to
Martin, which meant silence and whiteness and winter come
long before its time. Dead, silent, cold, white. The thoughts
circled round, blew down, and settled in whispers.

Martin held Dog, thinking; turned to the wall. The lady
with the autumn-colored hair. The lady with the laughter that
was very gentle and never made fun and the eyes that watched
your mouth to see everything you ever said. The-other-half-of-
autumn-lady, who told what was left untold by Dog, about the
world. The heartbeat at the still center of gray afternoon. The
heartbeat fading . . .

"Mom? What do they do in the graveyard, Mom, under
the ground? Just lay there?"

"*Lie* there."

"Lie there? Is that *all* they do? It doesn't sound like much
fun."

"For goodness' sake, it's not made out to be fun."

"Why don't they jump up and run around once in a while
if they get tired lying there? God's pretty silly—"

"Martin!"

"Well, you'd think He'd treat people better than to tell
them to lie still for keeps. That's impossible. Nobody can do it!
I tried once. Dog tries. I tell him, 'dead Dog!' He plays dead
awhile, then gets sick and tired and wags his tail or opens one
eye and looks at me, bored. Boy, I bet sometimes those graveyard people do the same, huh, Dog?"

Dog barked.

"Be still with that kind of talk!" said Mother.

Martin looked off into space.

"Bet that's exactly what they do," he said.

Autumn burnt the trees bare and ran Dog still farther around, fording creek, prowling graveyard as was his custom, and back in the dusk to fire off volleys of barking that shook windows wherever he turned.

In the late last days of October, Dog began to act as if the wind had changed and blew from a strange country. He stood quivering on the porch below. He whined, his eyes fixed at the empty land beyond town. He brought no visitors for Martin. He stood for hours each day, as if leashed, trembling, then shot away straight, as if someone had called. Each night he returned later, with no one following. Each night, Martin sank deeper and deeper in his pillow.

"Well, people are busy," said Mother. "They haven't time to notice the tag Dog carries. Or they mean to come visit, but forget."

But there was more to it than that. There was the fevered shining in Dog's eyes, and his whimpering tic late at night, in some private dream. His shivering in the dark, under the bed. The way he sometimes stood half the night, looking at Martin as if some great and impossible secret was his and he knew no way to tell it save by savagely thumping his tail, or turning in endless circles, never to lie down, spinning and spinning again.

On October thirtieth, Dog ran out and didn't come back at all, even when after supper Martin heard his parents call and call. The hour grew late, the streets and sidewalks stood empty, the air moved cold about the house and there was nothing, nothing.

Long after midnight, Martin lay watching the world beyond the cool, clear glass windows. Now there was not even autumn, for there was no Dog to fetch it in. There would be no winter, for who could bring the snow to melt in your hands? Father, Mother? No, not the same. They couldn't play the game with its special secrets and rules, its sounds and pantomimes. No more seasons. No more time. The go-between, the emissary, was lost to the wild throngings of civilization, poisoned, stolen, hit by a car, left somewhere in a culvert. . . .

Sobbing, Martin turned his face to his pillow. The world was a picture under glass, untouchable. The world was dead.

Martin twisted in bed and in three days the last Hallowe'en pumpkins were rotting in trash cans, papier-mache skulls and witches were burnt on bonfires, and ghosts were stacked on shelves with other linens until next year.

To Martin, Hallowe'en had been nothing more than one evening when tin horns cried off in the cold autumn stars, children blew like goblin leaves along the flinty walks, flinging their heads, or cabbages, at porches, soap-writing names or similar magic symbols on icy windows. All of it as distant, unfathomable, and nightmarish as a puppet show seen from so many miles away that there is no sound or meaning.

For three days in November, Martin watched alternate light and shadow sift across his ceiling. The fire-pageant was over forever; autumn lay in cold ashes. Martin sank deeper, yet deeper in white marble layers of bed, motionless, listening always listening. . . .

Friday evening, his parents kissed him good-night and walked out of the house into the hushed cathedral weather toward a motion-picture show. Miss Tarkins from next door stayed on in the parlor below until Martin called down he was sleepy, then took her knitting off home.

In silence, Martin lay following the great move of stars down a clear and moonlit sky, remembering nights such as this when he'd spanned the town with Dog ahead, behind, around about, tracking the green-plush ravine, lapping slumbrous streams gone milky with the fullness of the moon, leaping cemetery tombstones while whispering the marble names; on, quickly on, through shaved meadows where the only motion was the off-on quivering of stars, to streets where shadows would not stand aside for you but crowded all the sidewalks for mile on mile. Run now run! chasing, being chased by bitter smoke, fog, mist, wind, ghost of mind, fright of memory; home, safe, sound, snug-warm, asleep. . . .

Nine o'clock.

Chime. The drowsy clock in the deep stairwell below. Chime.

Dog, come home, and run the world with you. Dog, bring a thistle with frost on it, or bring nothing else but the wind. Dog, where *are* you? Oh, listen, now, I'll call.

Martin held his breath.

Way off somewhere—a sound.

Martin rose up, trembling.

There, again—the sound.

So small a sound, like a sharp needle-point brushing the sky long miles and many miles away.

The dreamy echo of a dog—barking.

The sound of a dog crossing fields and farms, dirt roads and rabbit paths, running, running, letting out great barks of steam, cracking the night. The sound of a circling dog which came and went, lifted and faded, opened up, shut in, moved forward, went back, as if the animal were kept by someone on a fantastically long chain. As if the dog were running and someone whistled under the chestnut trees, in mold-shadow, tar-shadow, moon-shadow, walking, and the dog circled back and sprang out again toward home.

Dog! Martin thought, oh Dog, come home, boy! Listen, oh, listen, where you *been*? Come on, boy, make tracks!

Five, ten, fifteen minutes; near, very near, the bark, the sound. Martin cried out, thrust his feet from the bed, leaned to the window. Dog! Listen, boy! Dog! Dog! He said it over and over. Dog! Dog! Wicked Dog, run off and gone all these days! Bad Dog, good Dog, home, boy, hurry, and bring what you can!

Near now, near, up the street, barking, to knock clapboard housefronts with sound, whirl iron cocks on rooftops in the moon, firing off volleys—Dog! now at the door below. . . .

Martin shivered.

Should he run—let Dog in, or wait for Mom and Dad? Wait? Oh, God, wait? But what if Dog ran off again? No, he'd go down, snatch the door wide, yell, grab Dog in, and run upstairs so fast, laughing, crying, holding tight, that . . .

Dog stopped barking.

Hey! Martin almost broke the window, jerking to it.

Silence. As if someone had told Dog to hush now, hush, hush.

A full minute passed. Martin clenched his fists.

Below, a faint whimpering.

Then, slowly, the downstairs front door opened. Someone was kind enough to have opened the door for Dog. Of course! Dog had brought Mr. Jacobs or Mr. Gillespie or Miss Tarkins, or . . .

The downstairs door shut.

Dog raced upstairs, whining, flung himself on the bed.

"Dog, Dog, where've you *been*, what've you *done*! Dog, Dog!"

And he crushed Dog hard and long to himself, weeping. Dog, Dog. He laughed and shouted. Dog! But after a moment he stopped laughing and crying, suddenly.

He pulled back away. He held the animal and looked at him, eyes widening.

The odor coming from Dog was different.

It was a smell of strange earth. It was a smell of night within night, the smell of digging down deep in shadow through earth that had lain cheek by jowl with things that were long hidden and decayed. A stinking and rancid soil fell away in clods of dissolution from Dog's muzzle and paws. He had dug deep. He had dug very deep indeed. That *was* it, wasn't it? wasn't it? *wasn't* it!

What kind of message was this from Dog? What could such a message mean? The stench—the ripe and awful cemetery earth.

Dog was a bad dog, digging where he shouldn't. Dog was a good dog, always making friends. Dog loved people. Dog brought them home.

And now, moving up the dark hall stairs, at intervals, came the sound of feet, one foot dragged after the other, painfully, slowly, slowly, slowly.

Dog shivered. A rain of strange night earth fell seething on the bed.

Dog turned.

The bedroom door whispered in.

Martin had company.

TOUCHED WITH FIRE

They stood in the blazing sunlight for a long while, looking at the bright faces of their old-fashioned railroad watches, while the shadows tilted beneath them, swaying, and the perspiration ran out under their porous summer hats. When they uncovered their heads to mop their lined and pinkened brows, their hair was white and soaked through, like something that had been out of the light for years. One of the men commented that his shoes felt like two loaves of baked bread and then, sighing warmly, added:

"Are you positive this is the right tenement?"

The second old man, Foxe by name, nodded, as if any quick motion might make him catch fire by friction alone. "I saw this woman every day for three days. She'll show up. If she's still alive, that is. Wait till you *see* her, Shaw. Lord! what a case."

"Such an odd business," said Shaw. "If people knew they'd think us Peeping Toms, doddering old fools. Lord, I feel self-conscious standing here."

Foxe leaned on his cane. "Let me do all the talking if—hold on! There she is!" He lowered his voice. "Take a slow look as she comes out."

The tenement front door slammed viciously. A dumpy woman stood at the top of the thirteen porch steps glancing this way and that with angry jerkings of her eyes. Jamming a plump hand in her purse, she seized some crumpled dollar bills, plunged down the steps brutally, and set off down the street in a charge. Behind her, several heads peered from apartment windows above, summoned by her crashing of the door.

"Come on," whispered Foxe. "Here we go to the butcher's."

The woman flung open a butchershop door, rushed in. The two old men had a glimpse of a mouth sticky with raw lipstick. Her eyebrows were like mustaches over her squinting, always suspicious eyes. Abreast of the butchershop, they heard her voice already screaming inside.

"I want a good cut of meat. Let's see what you got hidden to take home for yourself!"

The butcher stood silently in his bloody-fingerprinted frock, his hands empty. The two old men entered behind the woman and pretended to admire a pink loaf of fresh-ground sirloin.

"Them lambchops look sickly!" cried the woman. "What's the price on brains?"

The butcher told her in a low dry voice.

"Well, weigh me a pound of liver!" said the woman. "Keep your thumbs off!"

The butcher weighed it out, slowly.

"Hurry up!" snapped the woman.

The butcher now stood with his hands out of sight below the counter.

"Look," whispered Foxe. Shaw leaned back a trifle to peer below the case.

In one of the butcher's bloody hands, empty before, a silvery meat ax was now clenched tightly, relaxed, clenched tightly, relaxed. The butcher's eyes were blue and dangerously serene above the white porcelain counter while the woman yelled into those eyes and that pink self-contained face.

"Now do you believe?" whispered Foxe. "She really needs our help."

They stared at the raw red cube-steaks for a long time, noticing all the little dents and marks where it had been hit, ten dozen times, by a steel mallet.

The braying continued at the grocer's and the dime store, with the two old men following at a respectful distance.

"Mrs. Death-Wish," said Mr. Foxe quietly. "It's like watching a two-year-old run out on a battlefield. Any moment, you say, she'll hit a mine; bang! Get the temperature just right, too much humidity, everyone itching, sweating, irritable. Along'll come this fine lady, whining, shrieking. And so good-by. Well, Shaw, do we start business?"

"You mean just walk up to her?" Shaw was stunned by his own suggestion. "Oh, but we're not really going to do this, are we? I thought it was sort of a hobby. People, habits, customs, et cetera. It's been fun. But actually mixing in—? We've better things to do."

"Have we?" Foxe nodded down the street to where the woman ran out in front of cars, making them stop with a great squall of brakes, horn-blowing, and cursing. "Are we Christians? Do we let her feed herself subconsciously to the lions? Or do we convert her?"

"Convert her?"

"To love, to serenity, to a longer life. Look at her. Doesn't want to live any more. Deliberately aggravates people. One day soon, someone'll favor her, with a hammer, or strychnine. She's been going down for the third time a long while now. When you're drowning, you get nasty, grab at people, scream. Let's have lunch and lend a hand, eh? Otherwise, our victim will run on until she finds her murderer."

Shaw stood with the sun driving him into the boiling white sidewalk, and it seemed for a moment the street tilted vertically, became a cliff down which the woman fell toward a blazing sky. At last he shook his head.

"You're right," he said. "I wouldn't want her on my conscience."

The sun burnt the paint from the tenement fronts, bleached the air raw and turned the gutter-waters to vapor by mid-afternoon when the old men, numbed and evaporated, stood in the inner passageways of a house that funneled bakery air from front to back in a searing torrent. When they spoke it was the submerged, muffled talk of men in steam rooms, preposterously tired and remote.

The front door opened. Foxe stopped a boy who carried a well-mangled loaf of bread. "Son, we're looking for the woman who gives the door an *awful* slam when she goes out."

"Oh, *her*?" The boy ran upstairs, calling back. "Mrs. Shrike!"

Foxe grabbed Shaw's arm. "Lord, Lord! It can't be true!"

"I want to go home," said Shaw.

"But there it is!" said Foxe, incredulous, tapping his cane on the room-index in the lobby. "Mr. and Mrs. Alfred Shrike, 331 upstairs! Husband's a longshoreman, big hulking brute, comes home dirty. Saw them out on Sunday, her jabbering, him never speaking, never looking at her. Oh, come *on*, Shaw."

"It's no use," said Shaw. "You can't help people like her unless they want to be helped. That's the first law of mental health. You know it, I know it. If you get in her way, she'll trample you. Don't be a fool."

"But who's to speak for her—and people like her? Her husband? Her friends? The grocer, the butcher? They'd sing at her wake! Will they tell her she needs a psychiatrist? Does she know it? No. Who knows it? We do. Well, then, you don't keep vital information like that from the victim, do you?"

Shaw took off his sopping hat and gazed bleakly into it. "Once, in biology class, long ago, our teacher asked if we thought we could remove a frog's nervous system, intact, with a scalpel. Take out the whole delicate antennalike structure, with all its little pink thistles and half-invisible ganglions. Impossible, of course. The nervous system's so much a part of the frog there's no way to pull it like a hand from a green glove. You'd destroy the frog, doing it. Well, that's Mrs. Shrike. There's no way to operate on a souring ganglion. Bile is in the vitreous humor of her mad little elephant eyes. You might as well try to get all the saliva out of her mouth forever. It's very sad. But I think we've gone too far already."

"True," said Foxe patiently, earnestly, nodding. "But all I want to do is post a warning. Drop a little seed in her subconscious. Tell her, 'You're a murderee, a victim looking for a place to happen.' One tiny seed I want to plant in her head and hope it'll sprout and flower. A very faint, very poor hope that before it's too late, she'll gather her courage and go see a psychiatrist!"

"It's too hot to talk."

"All the more reason to act! More murders are committed

at ninety-two degrees Fahrenheit than any other temperature. Over one hundred, it's too hot to move. Under ninety, cool enough to survive. But right *at* ninety-two degrees lies the apex of irritability, everything is itches and hair and sweat and cooked pork. The brain becomes a rat rushing around a red-hot maze. The least thing, a word, a look, a sound, the drop of a hair and—irritable murder. *Irritable murder*, there's a pretty and terrifying phrase for you. Look at that hall thermometer, eighty-nine degrees. Crawling up toward ninety, itching up toward ninety-one, sweating toward ninety-two an hour, two hours from now. Here's the first flight of stairs. We can rest on each landing. Up we *go!*"

The two old men moved in the third-floor darkness.

"Don't check the numbers," said Foxe. "Let's guess which apartment is hers."

Behind the last door a radio exploded, the ancient paint shuddered and flaked softly onto the worn carpet at their feet. The men watched the entire door jitter with vibration in its grooves.

They looked at each other and nodded grimly.

Another sound cut like an ax through the paneling; a woman, shrieking to someone across town on a telephone.

"No phone necessary. She should just open her window and yell."

Foxe rapped.

The radio blasted out the rest of its song, the voice bellowed. Foxe rapped again, and tested the knob. To his horror the door got free of his grasp and floated swiftly inward, leaving them like actors trapped on-stage when a curtain rises too soon.

"Oh, no!" cried Shaw.

They were buried in a flood of sound. It was like standing in the spillway of a dam and pulling the gate-lever. Instinctively, the old men raised their hands, wincing as if the sound were pure blazing sunlight that burnt their eyes.

The woman (it was indeed Mrs. Shrike!) stood at a wall phone, saliva flying from her mouth at an incredible rate. She showed all of her large white teeth, chunking off her monologue, nostrils flared, a vein in her wet forehead ridged up, pumping, her free hand flexing and unflexing itself. Her eyes were clenched shut as she yelled:

"Tell that damned son-in-law of mine I won't see him, he's a lazy bum!"

Suddenly the woman snapped her eyes wide, some animal instinct having felt rather than heard or seen an intrusion. She continued yelling into the phone, meanwhile piercing her visitors with a glance forged of the coldest steel. She yelled for a full minute longer, then slammed down the receiver and said, without taking a breath: "Well?"

The two men moved together for protection. Their lips moved.

"Speak up!" cried the woman.

"Would you mind," said Foxe, "turning the radio down?"

She caught the word "radio" by lip reading. Still glaring at them out of her sunburnt face, she slapped the radio without looking at it, as one slaps a child that cries all day every day and has become an unseen pattern in life. The radio subsided.

"I'm not buyin' anything!"

She ripped a dog-eared packet of cheap cigarettes like it was a bone with meat on it, snapped one of the cigarettes in her smeared mouth and lit it, sucking greedily on the smoke, jetting it through her thin nostrils until she was a feverish dragon confronting them in a fire-clouded room. "I got work to do. Make your pitch!"

They looked at the magazines spilled like great catches of bright-colored fish on the linoleum floor, the unwashed coffee cup near the broken rocking chair, the tilted, greasy thumb-marked lamps, the smudged windowpanes, the dishes piled in the sink under a steadily dripping, dripping faucet, the cobwebs floating like dead skin in the ceiling corners, and over all of it the thickened smell of life lived too much, too long, with the window down.

They saw the wall thermometer.

Temperature: ninety degrees Fahrenheit.

They gave each other a half-startled look.

"I'm Mr. Foxe, this is Mr. Shaw. We're retired insurance salesmen. We still sell occasionally, to supplement our retirement fund. Most of the time, however, we're taking it easy and—"

"You tryin' to sell me insurance!" She cocked her head at them through the cigarette smoke.

"There's no money connected with this, no."

"Keep talking," she said.

"I hardly know how to begin. May we sit down?" He looked about and decided there wasn't a thing in the room he would trust himself to sit on. "Never mind." He saw she was about to bellow again, so went on swiftly. "We retired after forty years of seeing people from nursery to cemetery gate, you might say. In that time we'd formulated certain opinions. Last year, sitting in the park talking, we put two and two together. We realized that many people didn't have to die so young. With the correct investigation, a new type of Customer's

Information might be provided as a sideline by insurance companies . . ."

"I'm not sick," said the woman.

"Oh, but you *are!*" cried Mr. Foxe, and then put two fingers to his mouth in dismay.

"Don't tell *me* what I am!" she cried.

Foxe plunged headlong. "Let me make it clear. People die every day, psychologically speaking. Some part of them gets tired. And that small part tries to kill off the entire person. For example—" He looked about and seized on his first evidence with what amounted to a vast relief. "There! That light bulb in your bathroom, hung right over the tub on frayed wire. Someday you'll slip, make a grab and—pfft!"

Mrs. Albert J. Shrike squinted at the light bulb in the bathroom. "So?"

"People," Mr. Foxe warmed to his subject, while Mr. Shaw fidgeted, his face now flushed, now dreadfully pale, edged toward the door, "people, like cars, need their brakes checked; their emotional brakes, do you see? Their lights, their batteries, their approaches and responses to life."

Mrs. Shrike snorted. "Your two minutes are up. I haven't learned a damned thing."

Mr. Foxe blinked, first at her, then at the sun burning mercilessly through the dusty windowpanes. Perspiration was running in the soft lines of his face. He chanced a look at the wall thermometer.

"Ninety-one," he said.

"What's eatin' you, pop?" asked Mrs. Shrike.

"I beg your pardon." He stared in fascination at the red-hot line of mercury firing up the small glass vent across the room. "Sometimes—sometimes we all make wrong turnings.

Our choice of marriage partners. A wrong job. No money. Illness. Migraine headaches. Glandular deficiencies. Dozens of little prickly, irritable things. Before you know it, you're taking it out on everyone everywhere."

She was watching his mouth as if he were talking a foreign language; she scowled, she squinted, she tilted her head, her cigarette smoldering in one plump hand.

"We run about screaming, making enemies." Foxe swallowed and glanced away from her. "We make people want to see us—gone—sick—dead, even. People want to hit us, knock us down, shoot us. It's all unconscious, though. You *see?*

God, it's hot in here, he thought. If there were only one window open. Just one. Just one window open.

Mrs. Shrike's eyes were widening, as if to allow in everything he said.

"Some people are not only accident-prones, which means they want to punish themselves physically, for some crime, usually a petty immorality they think they've long forgotten. But their subconscious puts them in dangerous situations, makes them jaywalk, makes them—" He hesitated and the sweat dripped from his chin. "Makes them ignore frayed electric cords over bathtubs— They're potential victims. It is marked on their faces, hidden like—like tattoos, you might say, on the inner rather than the outer skin. A murderer passing one of these accident-prones, these wishers-after-death, would see the invisible markings, turn, and follow them, instinctively, to the nearest alley. With luck, a potential victim might not happen to cross the tracks of a potential murderer for fifty years. Then—one afternoon—fate! These people, these death-prones, touch all the wrong nerves in passing strangers; they brush the murder in all our breasts."

Mrs. Shrike mashed her cigarette in a dirty saucer, very slowly.

Foxe shifted his cane from one trembling hand to the other. "So it was that a year ago we decided to try to find people who needed help. These are always the people who don't even know they need help, who'd never dream of going to a psychiatrist. At first, I said, we'll make dry-runs. Shaw was always against it, save as a hobby, a harmless little quiet thing between ourselves. I suppose you'd say I'm a fool. Well, we've just completed a year of dry-runs. We watched two men, studied their environmental factors, their work, marriages, at a discreet distance. None of our business, you say? But each time, the men came to a bad end. One killed in a bar-room. Another pushed out a window. A woman we studied, run down by a streetcar. Coincidence? What about that old man accidentally poisoned? Didn't turn on the bathroom light one night. What was there in his mind that wouldn't let him turn the light on? What made him move in the dark and drink medicine in the dark and die in the hospital next day, protesting he wanted nothing but to live? Evidence, evidence, we have it, we have it. Two dozen cases. Coffins nailed to a good half of them in that little time. No more dry-runs; it's time for action, preventative use of data. Time to work *with* people, make friends before the undertaker slips in the side door."

Mrs. Shrike stood as if he had struck her on the head, quite suddenly, with a large weight. Then just her blurred lips moved. "And you came *here*?"

"Well—"

"You've been watching *me*?"

"We only—"

"Following *me*?"

"In order to—"

"Get out!" she said.

"We can—"

"Get out!" she said.

"If you'll only listen—"

"Oh, I *said* this would happen," whispered Shaw, shutting his eyes.

"Dirty old men, get out!" she shouted.

"There's no money involved."

"I'll throw you out, I'll throw you out!" she shrieked, clenching her fists, gritting her teeth. Her face colored insanely. "Who are you, dirty old grandmas, coming here, spying, you old cranks!" she yelled. She seized the straw hat from Mr. Foxe's head; he cried out; she tore the lining from it, cursing. "Get out, get out, get out, get out!" She hurled it to the floor. She crunched one heel through the middle. She kicked it. "Get out, get out!"

"Oh, but you *need* us!" Foxe stared in dismay at the hat as she swore at him in a language that turned corners, blazing, that flew in the air like great searing torches. The woman knew every language and every word in every language. She spoke with fire and alcohol and smoke.

"Who do you think you are? God? God and the Holy Ghost, passing on people, snooping, prying, you old jerks, you old dirty-minded grandmas! You, you—" She gave them further names, names that forced them toward the door in shock, recoiling. She gave them a long vile list of names without pausing for breath. Then she stopped, gasped, trembled, heaved in a great suction of air, and started a further list of ten dozen even viler names.

"See here!" said Foxe, stiffening.

Shaw was out the door, pleading with his partner to come along, it was over and done, it was as he expected, they were fools, they were everything she said they were, oh, how embarrassing!

"Old maid!" shouted the woman.

"I'll thank you to keep a civil tongue."

"Old maid, old maid!"

Somehow this was worse than all the really vile names.

Foxe swayed, his mouth clapped open, shut, open, shut.

"Old woman!" she cried. "Woman, woman, woman!"

He was in a blazing yellow jungle. The room was drowned in fire, it clenched upon him, the furniture seemed to shift and whirl about, the sunlight shot through the rammed-shut windows, firing the dust, which leaped up from the rug in angry sparks when a fly buzzed a crazy spiral from nowhere; her mouth, a feral red thing, licked the air with all the obscenities collected just behind it in a lifetime, and beyond her on the baked brown wallpaper the thermometer said ninety-two, and he looked again and it said ninety-two, and still the woman screamed like the wheels of a train scraping around a vast iron curve of track; fingernails down a blackboard, and steel across marble. "Old maid! Old maid! Old maid!"

Foxe drew his arm back, cane clenched in fist, very high, and struck.

"No!" cried Shaw in the doorway.

But the woman had slipped and fallen aside, gibbering, clawing the floor. Foxe stood over her with a look of positive disbelief on his face. He looked at his arm and his wrist and his hand and his fingers, each in turn, through a great invisible glaring hot wall of crystal that enclosed him. He looked at the cane as if it was an easily seen and incredible exclamation point come out of nowhere to the center of the room. His mouth stayed open, the dust fell in silent embers, dead. He felt the blood drop from his face as if a small door had banged wide into his stomach. "I—"

She frothed.

Scrabbling about, every part of her seemed a separate animal. Her arms and legs, her hands, her head, each was a lopped-off bit of some creature wild to return to itself, but blind to the proper way of making that return. Her mouth still gushed out her sickness with words and sounds that were not even faintly words. It had been in her a long time, a long long time. Foxe looked upon her, in a state of shock, himself. Before today, she had spat her venom out, here, there, another place. Now he had loosed the flood of a lifetime and he felt in danger of drowning here. He sensed someone pulling him by his coat. He saw the door sills pass on either side. He heard the cane fall and rattle like a thin bone far away from his hand, which seemed to have been stung by some terrible unseen wasp. And then he was out, walking mechanically, down through the burning tenement, between the scorched walls. Her voice crashed like a guillotine down the stair. "Get out! Get out! Get *out!*"

Fading like the wail of a person dropped down an open well into darkness.

At the bottom of the last flight, near the street door, Foxe turned himself loose from this other man here, and for a long moment leaned against the wall, his eyes wet, able to do nothing but moan. His hands, while he did this, moved in the air to find the lost cane, moved on his head, touched at his moist eyelids, amazed, and fluttered away. They sat on the bottom hall step for ten minutes in silence, drawing sanity into their lungs with every shuddering breath. Finally Mr. Foxe looked over at Mr. Shaw, who had been staring at him in wonder and fright for the full ten minutes.

"Did you *see* what I did? Oh, oh, that was close. Close. Close." He shook his head. "I'm a fool. That poor, poor woman. She was right."

"There's nothing to be done."

"I see that now. It had to fall on me."

"Here, wipe your face. That's better."

"Do you think she'll tell Mr. Shrike about us?"

"No, no."

"Do you think we could—"

"Talk to *him?*"

They considered this and shook their heads. They opened the front door to a gush of furnace heat and were almost knocked down by a huge man who strode between them.

"Look where you're going!" he cried.

They turned and watched the man move ponderously, in fiery darkness, one step at a time, up into the tenement house, a creature with the ribs of a mastodon and the head of an unshorn lion, with great beefed arms, irritably hairy, painfully sunburnt. The face they had seen briefly as he shouldered past was a sweating, raw, sunblistered pork face, salt droplets under the red eyes, dripping from the chin; great smears of perspiration stained the man's armpits, coloring his tee-shirt to the waist.

They shut the tenement door gently.

"That's him," said Mr. Foxe. "That's the husband."

They stood in the little store across from the tenement. It was five-thirty, the sun tilting down the sky, the shadows the color of hot summer grapes under the rare few trees and in the alleys.

"What was it, hanging out of the husband's back pocket?"

"Longshoreman's hook. Steel. Sharp, heavy-looking. Like those claws one-armed men used to wear on the end of their stumps, years ago."

Mr. Foxe did not speak.

"What's the temperature?" asked Mr. Foxe, a minute later, as if he were too tired to turn his head to look.

"Store thermometer still reads ninety-two. Ninety-two right on the nose."

Foxe sat on a packing crate, making the least motion to hold an orange soda bottle in his fingers. "Cool off," he said. "Yes, I need an orange pop very much, right now."

They sat there in the furnace, looking up at one special tenement window for a long time, waiting, waiting . . .

THE SMALL ASSASSIN

Just when the idea occurred to her that she was being murdered she could not tell. There had been little subtle signs, little suspicions for the past month; things as deep as sea tides in her, like looking at a perfectly calm stretch of tropic water, wanting to bathe in it and finding, just as the tide takes your body, that monsters dwell just under the surface, things unseen, bloated, many-armed, sharp-finned, malignant and inescapable.

A room floated around her in an effluvium of hysteria. Sharp instruments hovered and there were voices, and people in sterile white masks.

My name, she thought, what is it?

Alice Leiber. It came to her. David Leiber's wife. But it gave her no comfort. She was alone with these silent, whispering white people and there was great pain and nausea and death-fear in her.

I am being murdered before their eyes. These doctors, these nurses don't realize what hidden thing has happened to me. David doesn't know. Nobody knows except me and—the killer, the little murderer, the small assassin.

I am dying and I can't tell them now. They'd laugh and call me one in delirium. They'll see the murderer and hold him and never think him responsible for my death. But here I am, in front of God and man, dying, no one to believe my story, everyone to doubt me, comfort me with lies, bury me in ignorance, mourn me and salvage my destroyer.

Where is David? she wondered. In the waiting room, smoking one cigarette after another, listening to the long tickings of the very slow clock?

Sweat exploded from all of her body at once, and with it an agonized cry. Now. Now! Try and kill me, she screamed. Try, try, but I won't die! I won't!

There was a hollowness. A vacuum. Suddenly the pain fell away. Exhaustion, and dusk came around. It was over. Oh, God! She plummeted down and struck a black nothingness which gave way to nothingness and nothingness and another and still another. . . .

Footsteps. Gentle, approaching footsteps.

Far away, a voice said, "She's asleep. Don't disturb her."

An odor of tweeds, a pipe, a certain shaving lotion. David was standing over her. And beyond him the immaculate smell of Dr. Jeffers.

She did not open her eyes. "I'm awake," she said, quietly. It was a surprise, a relief to be able to speak, to not be dead.

"Alice," someone said, and it was David beyond her closed eyes, holding her tired hands.

Would you like to meet the murderer, David? she thought. I hear your voice asking to see him, so there's nothing but for me to point him out to you.

David stood over her. She opened her eyes. The room came into focus. Moving a weak hand, she pulled aside a coverlet.

The murderer looked up at David Leiber with a small, red-faced, blue-eyed calm. Its eyes were deep and sparkling.

"Why!" cried David Leiber, smiling. "He's a *fine* baby!"

Dr. Jeffers was waiting for David Leiber the day he came to take his wife and new child home. He motioned Leiber to a chair in his office, gave him a cigar, lit one for himself, sat on the edge of his desk, puffing solemnly for a long moment. Then he cleared his throat, looked David Leiber straight on and said, "Your wife doesn't like her child, Dave."

"What!"

"It's been a hard thing for her. She'll need a lot of love this next year. I didn't say much at the time, but she was hysterical in the delivery room. The strange things she said—I won't repeat them. All I'll say is that she feels alien to the child. Now, this may simply be a thing we can clear up with one or two questions." He sucked on his cigar another moment, then said, "Is this child a 'wanted' child, Dave?"

"Why do you ask?"

"It's vital."

"Yes. Yes, it is a 'wanted' child. We planned it together. Alice was so happy, a year ago, when—"

"Mmmm—That makes it more difficult. Because if the child was unplanned, it would be a simple case of a woman hating the idea of motherhood. That doesn't fit Alice." Dr. Jeffers took his cigar from his lips, rubbed his hand across his jaw. "It must be something else, then. Perhaps something buried in her childhood that's coming out now. Or it might be the simple temporary doubt and distrust of any mother who's gone through the unusual pain and near-death that Alice has. If so, then a little time should heal that. I thought I'd tell you, though, Dave. It'll help you be easy and tolerant with her if she says anything about—well—about wishing the child had been born dead. And if things don't go well, the three of you drop in on me. I'm always glad to see old friends, eh? Here, take another cigar along for—ah—for the baby."

It was a bright spring afternoon. Their car hummed along wide, tree-lined boulevards. Blue sky, flowers, a warm wind. Dave talked a lot, lit his cigar, talked some more. Alice answered directly, softly, relaxing a bit more as the trip progressed. But she held the baby not tightly or warmly or motherly enough to satisfy the queer ache in Dave's mind. She seemed to be merely carrying a porcelain figurine.

"Well," he said, at last, smiling. "What'll we name him?"

Alice Leiber watched green trees slide by. "Let's not decide yet. I'd rather wait until we get an exceptional name for him. Don't blow smoke in his face." Her sentences ran together with no change of tone. The last statement held no motherly reproof, no interest, no irritation. She just mouthed it and it was said.

The husband, disquieted, dropped the cigar from the window. "Sorry," he said.

The baby rested in the crook of his mother's arm, shadows of sun and tree changing his face. His blue eyes opened like fresh blue spring flowers. Moist noises came from the tiny, pink, elastic mouth.

Alice gave her baby a quick glance. Her husband felt her shiver against him.

"Cold?" he asked.

"A chill. Better raise the window, David."

It was more than a chill. He rolled the window slowly up.

Suppertime.

Dave had brought the child from the nursery, propped him at a tiny, bewildered angle, supported by many pillows, in a newly purchased high chair.

Alice watched her knife and fork move. "He's not high-chair size," she said.

"Fun having him here, anyway," said Dave, feeling fine. "Everything's fun. At the office, too. Orders up to my nose. If I don't watch myself I'll make another fifteen thousand this year. Hey, look at Junior, will you? Drooling all down his chin!" He reached over to wipe the baby's mouth with his napkin. From the corner of his eye he realized that Alice wasn't even watching. He finished the job.

"I guess it wasn't very interesting," he said, back again at his food. "But one would think a mother'd take some interest in her own child!"

Alice jerked her chin up. "Don't speak that way! Not in front of him! Later, if you must."

"Later?" he cried. "In front of, in back of, what's the difference?" He quieted suddenly, swallowed, was sorry. "All right. Okay. I know how it is."

After dinner she let him carry the baby upstairs. She didn't tell him to; she *let* him.

Coming down, he found her standing by the radio, listening to music she didn't hear. Her eyes were closed, her whole attitude one of wondering, self-questioning. She started when he appeared.

Suddenly, she was at him, against him, soft, quick; the same. Her lips found him, kept him. He was stunned. Now that the baby was gone, upstairs, out of the room, she began to breathe again, live again. She was free. She was whispering, rapidly, endlessly.

"Thank you, thank you, darling. For being yourself, always. Dependable, so very dependable!"

He had to laugh. "My father told me, 'Son, provide for your family!' "

Wearily, she rested her dark, shining hair against his neck. "You've overdone it. Sometimes I wish we were just the way we were when we were first married. No responsibilities, nothing but ourselves. No—no babies."

She crushed his hand in hers, a supernatural whiteness in her face.

"Oh, Dave, once it was just you and me. We protected each other, and now we protect the baby, but get no protection from it. Do you understand? Lying in the hospital I had time to think a lot of things. The world is evil—"

"Is it?"

"Yes. It is. But laws protect us from it. And when there aren't laws, then love does the protecting. You're protected from my hurting you, by my love. You're vulnerable to me, of all people, but love shields you. I feel no fear of you, because love cushions all your irritations, unnatural instincts, hatreds and immaturities. But—what about the baby? It's too young to know love, or a law of love, or anything, until we teach it. And in the meantime be vulnerable to it."

"Vulnerable to a baby?" He held her away and laughed gently.

"Does a baby know the difference between right and wrong?" she asked.

"No. But it'll learn."

"But a baby is so new, so amoral, so conscience-free." She stopped. Her arms dropped from him and she turned swiftly. "That noise? What was it?"

Leiber looked around the room. "I didn't hear—"

She stared at the library door. "In there," she said, slowly.

Leiber crossed the room, opened the door and switched the library lights on and off. "Not a thing." He came back to her. "You're worn out. To bed with you—right now."

Turning out the lights together, they walked slowly up the soundless hall stairs, not speaking. At the top she apologized. "My wild talk, darling. Forgive me. I'm exhausted."

He understood, and said so.

She paused, undecided, by the nursery door. Then she fingered the brass knob sharply, walked in. He watched her approach the crib much too carefully, look down, and stiffen as if she'd been struck in the face. "David!"

Leiber stepped forward, reached the crib.

The baby's face was bright red and very moist; his small pink mouth opened and shut, opened and shut; his eyes were a fiery blue. His hands leapt about on the air.

"Oh," said Dave, "he's just been crying."

"Has he?" Alice Leiber seized the crib-railing to balance herself. "I didn't hear him."

"The door was closed."

"Is that why he breathes so hard, why his face is red?"

"Sure. Poor little guy. Crying all alone in the dark. He can sleep in our room tonight, just in case he cries."

"You'll spoil him," his wife said.

Leiber felt her eyes follow as he rolled the crib into their bedroom. He undressed silently, sat on the edge of the bed. Suddenly he lifted his head, swore under his breath, snapped his fingers. "Damn it! Forgot to tell you. I must fly to Chicago Friday."

"Oh, David." Her voice was lost in the room.

"I've put this trip off for two months, and now it's so critical I just *have* to go."

"I'm afraid to be alone."

"We'll have the new cook by Friday. She'll be here all the time. I'll only be gone a few days."

"I'm afraid. I don't know of what. You wouldn't believe me if I told you. I guess I'm crazy."

He was in bed now. She darkened the room; he heard her walk around the bed, throw back the cover, slide in. He smelled the warm woman-smell of her next to him. He said, "If you want me to wait a few days, perhaps I could—"

"No," she said, unconvinced. "You go. I know it's important. It's just that I keep thinking about what I told you. Laws and love and protection. Love protects you from me. But, the baby—" She took a breath. "What protects you from him, David?"

Before he could answer, before he could tell her how silly it was, speaking of infants, she switched on the bed light, abruptly.

"Look," she said, pointing.

The baby lay wide-awake in its crib, staring straight at him, with deep, sharp blue eyes.

The lights went out again. She trembled against him.

"It's not nice being afraid of the thing you birthed." Her whisper lowered, became harsh, fierce, swift. "He tried to kill me! He lies there, listens to us talking, waiting for you to go away so he can try to kill me again! I swear it!" Sobs broke from her.

"Please," he kept saying, soothing her. "Stop it, stop it. Please."

She cried in the dark for a long time. Very late she relaxed, shakingly, against him. Her breathing came soft, warm, regular, her body twitched its worn reflexes and she slept.

He drowsed.

And just before his eyes lidded wearily down, sinking him into deeper and yet deeper tides, he heard a strange little sound of awareness and awakeness in the room.

The sound of small, moist, pinkly elastic lips.

The baby.

And then—sleep.

In the morning, the sun blazed. Alice smiled.

David Leiber dangled his watch over the crib. "See, baby? Something bright. Something pretty. Sure. Sure. Something bright. Something pretty."

Alice smiled. She told him to go ahead, fly to Chicago, she'd be very brave, no need to worry. She'd take care of baby. Oh, yes, she'd take care of him, all right.

The airplane went east. There was a lot of sky, a lot of sun and clouds and Chicago running over the horizon. Dave was dropped into the rush of ordering, planning, banqueting, telephoning, arguing in conference. But he wrote letters each day and sent telegrams to Alice and the baby.

On the evening of his sixth day away from home he received the long-distance phone call. Los Angeles.

"Alice?"

"No, Dave. This is Jeffers speaking."

"Doctor!"

"Hold onto yourself, son. Alice is sick. You'd better get the next plane home. It's pneumonia. I'll do everything I can, boy. If only it wasn't so soon after the baby. She needs strength."

Leiber dropped the phone into its cradle. He got up, with no feet under him, and no hands and no body. The hotel room blurred and fell apart.

"Alice," he said, blindly, starting for the door.

The propellers spun about, whirled, fluttered, stopped; time and space were put behind. Under his hand, David felt the doorknob turn; under his feet the floor assumed reality, around him flowed the walls of a bedroom, and in the late-afternoon sunlight Dr. Jeffers stood, turning from a window, as Alice lay waiting in her bed, something carved from a fall of winter snow. Then Dr. Jeffers was talking, talking continuously, gently, the sound rising and falling through the lamplight, a soft flutter, a white murmur of voice.

"Your wife's too good a mother, Dave. She worried more about the baby than herself. . . ."

Somewhere in the paleness of Alice's face, there was a sudden constriction which smoothed itself out before it was realized. Then, slowly, half-smiling, she began to talk and she talked as a mother should about this, that and the other thing, the telling detail, the minute-by-minute and hour-by-hour report of a mother concerned with a dollhouse world and the miniature life of that world. But she could not stop; the spring was wound tight, and her voice rushed on to anger, fear and the faintest touch of revulsion, which did not change Dr. Jeffers' expression, but caused Dave's heart to match the rhythm of this talk that quickened and could not stop:

"The baby wouldn't sleep. I thought he was sick. He just lay, staring, in his crib, and late at night he'd cry. So loud, he'd cry, and he'd cry all night and all night. I couldn't quiet him, and I couldn't rest."

Dr. Jeffers' head nodded slowly, slowly. "Tired herself right into pneumonia. But she's full of sulfa now and on the safe side of the whole damn thing."

David felt ill. "The baby, what about the baby?"

"Fit as a fiddle; cock of the walk!"

"Thanks, Doctor."

The doctor walked off away and down the stairs, opened the front door faintly, and was gone.

"David!"

He turned to her frightened whisper.

"It was the baby again." She clutched his hand. "I try to lie to myself and say that I'm a fool, but the baby knew I was weak from the hospital, so he cried all night every night, and when he wasn't crying he'd be much too quiet. I knew if I switched on the light he'd be there, staring up at me."

David felt his body close in on itself like a fist. He remembered seeing the baby, feeling the baby, awake in the dark, awake very late at night when babies should be asleep. Awake and lying there, silent as thought, not crying, but watching from its crib. He thrust the thought aside. It was insane.

Alice went on. "I was going to kill the baby. Yes, I was.

When you'd been gone only a day on your trip I went to his room and put my hands about his neck; and I stood there, for a long time, thinking, afraid. Then I put the covers up over his face and turned him over on his face and pressed him down and left him that way and ran out of the room."

He tried to stop her.

"No, let me finish," she said, hoarsely, looking at the wall. "When I left his room I thought, It's simple. Babies smother every day. No one'll ever know. But when I came back to see him dead, David, he was alive! Yes, alive, turned over on his back, alive and smiling and breathing. And I couldn't touch him again after that. I left him there and I didn't come back, not to feed him or look at him or do anything. Perhaps the cook tended to him. I don't know. All I know is that his crying kept me awake, and I thought all through the night, and walked around the rooms and now I'm sick." She was almost finished now. "The baby lies there and thinks of ways to kill me. Simple ways. Because he knows I know so much about him. I have no love for him; there is no protection between us; there never will be."

She was through. She collapsed inward on herself and finally slept. David Leiber stood for a long time over her, not able to move. His blood was frozen in his body, not a cell stirred anywhere, anywhere at all.

The next morning there was only one thing to do. He did it. He walked into Dr. Jeffers' office and told him the whole thing, and listened to Jeffers' tolerant replies:

"Let's take this thing slowly, son. It's quite natural for

mothers to hate their children, sometimes. We have a label for it—ambivalence. The ability to hate, while loving. Lovers hate each other, frequently. Children detest their mothers—"

Leiber interrupted. "I never hated my mother."

"You won't admit it, naturally. People don't enjoy admitting hatred for their loved ones."

"So Alice hates her baby."

"Better say she has an obsession. She's gone a step further than plain, ordinary ambivalence. A Caesarian operation brought the child into the world and almost took Alice out of it. She blames the child for her near-death and her pneumonia. She's projecting her troubles, blaming them on the handiest object she can use as a source of blame. We *all* do it. We stumble into a chair and curse the furniture, not our own clumsiness. We miss a golf-stroke and damn the turf or our club, or the make of ball. If our business fails we blame the gods, the weather, our luck. All I can tell you is what I told you before. Love her. Finest medicine in the world. Find little ways of showing your affection, give her security. Find ways of showing her how harmless and innocent the child is. Make her feel that the baby was worth the risk. After a while, she'll settle down, forget about death, and begin to love the child. If she doesn't come around in the next month or so, ask me. I'll recommend a good psychiatrist. Go on along now, and take that look off your face."

When summer came, things seemed to settle, become easier. Dave worked, immersed himself in office detail, but found much time for his wife. She, in turn, took long walks, gained strength, played an occasional light game of badminton. She rarely burst out any more. She seemed to have rid herself of her fears.

Except on one certain midnight when a sudden summer wind swept around the house, warm and swift, shaking the trees like so many shining tambourines. Alice wakened, trembling, and slid over into her husband's arms, and let him console her, and ask her what was wrong.

She said, "Something's here in the room, watching us."

He switched on the light. "Dreaming again," he said. "You're better, though. Haven't been troubled for a long time."

She sighed as he clicked off the light again, and suddenly she slept. He held her, considering what a sweet, weird creature she was, for about half an hour.

He heard the bedroom door sway open a few inches.

There was nobody at the door. No reason for it to come open. The wind had died.

He waited. It seemed like an hour he lay silently, in the dark.

Then, far away, wailing like some small meteor dying in the vast inky gulf of space, the baby began to cry in his nursery.

It was a small, lonely sound in the middle of the stars and the dark and the breathing of this woman in his arms and the wind beginning to sweep through the trees again.

Leiber counted to one hundred, slowly. The crying continued.

Carefully disengaging Alice's arm he slipped from bed, put on his slippers, robe, and moved quietly from the room.

He'd go downstairs, he thought, fix some warm milk, bring it up, and—

The blackness dropped out from under him. His foot

slipped and plunged. Slipped on something soft. Plunged into nothingness.

He thrust his hands out, caught frantically at the railing. His body stopped falling. He held. He cursed.

The "something soft" that had caused his feet to slip, rustled and thumped down a few steps. His head rang. His heart hammered at the base of his throat, thick and shot with pain.

Why do careless people leave things strewn about a house? He groped carefully with his fingers for the object that had almost spilled him headlong down the stairs.

His hand froze, startled. His breath went in. His heart held one or two beats.

The thing he held in his hand was a toy. A large cumbersome, patchwork doll he had bought as a joke, for—

For the baby.

Alice drove him to work the next day.

She slowed the car halfway downtown; pulled to the curb and stopped it. Then she turned on the seat and looked at her husband.

"I want to go away on a vacation. I don't know if you can make it now, darling, but if not, please let me go alone. We can get someone to take care of the baby, I'm sure. But I just have to get away. I thought I was growing out of this—this *feeling*. But I haven't. I can't stand being in the room with him. He looks up at me as if he hates me, too. I can't put my finger on it; all I know is I want to get away before something happens."

He got out on his side of the car, came around, motioned to her to move over, got in. "The only thing you're going to do is see a good psychiatrist. And if he suggests a vacation, well,

okay. But this can't go on; my stomach's in knots all the time."
He started the car. "I'll drive the rest of the way."

Her head was down; she was trying to keep back tears. She
looked up when they reached his office building. "All right.
Make the appointment. I'll go talk to anyone you want, David."

He kissed her. "Now, you're talking sense, lady. Think you
can drive home okay?"

"Of course, silly."

"See you at supper, then. Drive carefully."

"Don't I always? 'Bye."

He stood on the curb, watching her drive off, the wind
taking hold of her long, dark, shining hair. Upstairs, a minute
later, he phoned Jeffers and arranged an appointment with a
reliable neuropsychiatrist.

The day's work went uneasily. Things fogged over; and in
the fog he kept seeing Alice lost and calling his name. So
much of her fear had come over to him. She actually had him
convinced that the child was in some ways not quite natural.

He dictated long, uninspired letters. He checked some
shipments downstairs. Assistants had to be questioned, and
kept going. At the end of the day he was exhausted, his head
throbbed, and he was very glad to go home.

On the way down in the elevator he wondered, What if I
told Alice about the toy—that patchwork doll—I slipped on
on the stairs last night? Lord, wouldn't *that* back her off? No, I
won't ever tell her. Accidents are, after all, accidents.

Daylight lingered in the sky as he drove home in a taxi. In
front of the house he paid the driver and walked slowly up the
cement walk, enjoying the light that was still in the sky and
the trees. The white colonial front of the house looked unnatu-
rally silent and uninhabited, and then, quietly, he remembered

this was Thursday, and the hired help they were able to obtain from time to time were all gone for the day.

He took a deep breath of air. A bird sang behind the house. Traffic moved on the boulevard a block away. He twisted the key in the door. The knob turned under his fingers, oiled, silent.

The door opened. He stepped in, put his hat on the chair with his briefcase, started to shrug out of his coat, when he looked up.

Late sunlight streamed down the stairwell from the window near the top of the hall. Where the sunlight touched it took on the bright color of the patchwork doll sprawled at the bottom of the stairs.

But he paid no attention to the toy.

He could only look, and not move, and look again at Alice.

Alice lay in a broken, grotesque, pallid gesturing and angling of her thin body, at the bottom of the stairs, like a crumpled doll that doesn't want to play any more, ever.

Alice was dead.

The house remained quiet, except for the sound of his heart.

She was dead.

He held her head in his hands, he felt her fingers. He held her body. But she wouldn't live. She wouldn't even try to live. He said her name, out loud, many times, and he tried, once again, by holding her to him, to give her back some of the warmth she had lost, but that didn't help.

He stood up. He must have made a phone call. He didn't remember. He found himself, suddenly, upstairs. He opened the nursery door and walked inside and stared blankly at the crib. His stomach was sick. He couldn't see very well.

The baby's eyes were closed, but his face was red, moist with perspiration, as if he'd been crying long and hard.

"She's dead," said Leiber to the baby. "She's dead."

Then he started laughing low and soft and continuously for a long time until Dr. Jeffers walked in out of the night and slapped him again and again across his face.

"Snap out of it! Pull yourself together!"

"She fell down the stairs, doctor. She tripped on a patchwork doll and fell. I almost slipped on it the other night, myself. And now—"

The doctor shook him.

"Doc, Doc, Doc," said Dave, hazily. "Funny thing. Funny. I—I finally thought of a name for the baby.

The doctor said nothing.

Leiber put his head back in his trembling hands and spoke the words. "I'm going to have him christened next Sunday. Know what name I'm giving him? I'm going to call him Lucifer."

It was eleven at night. A lot of strange people had come and gone through the house, taking the essential flame with them—Alice.

David Leiber sat across from the doctor in the library.

"Alice wasn't crazy," he said, slowly. "She had good reason to fear the baby."

Jeffers exhaled. "Don't follow after her! She blamed the child for her sickness, now you blame it for her death. She stumbled on a toy, remember that. You can't blame the child."

"You mean Lucifer?"

"Stop calling him that!"

Leiber shook his head. "Alice heard things at night, moving in the halls. You want to know what made those noises, Doctor? They were made by the baby. Four months old, moving in the dark, listening to us talk. Listening to every word!" He held to the sides of the chair. "And if I turned the lights on, a baby is so small. It can hide behind furniture, a door, against a wall—below eye-level."

"I want you to stop this!" said Jeffers.

"Let me say what I think or I'll go crazy. When I went to Chicago, who was it kept Alice awake, tiring her into pneumonia? The baby! And when Alice didn't die, then he tried killing me. It was simple; leave a toy on the stairs, cry in the night until your father goes downstairs to fetch your milk, and stumbles. A crude trick, but effective. It didn't get me. But it killed Alice dead."

David Leiber stopped long enough to light a cigarette. "I should have caught on. I'd turn on the lights in the middle of the night, many nights, and the baby'd be lying there, eyes wide. Most babies sleep all the time. Not this one. He stayed awake, thinking."

"Babies don't think."

"He stayed awake doing whatever he *could* do with his brain, then. What in hell do we know about a baby's mind? He had every reason to hate Alice; she suspected him for what he was—certainly not a normal child. Something—different. What do you know of babies, doctor? The general run, yes. You know, of course, how babies kill their mothers at birth. Why? Could it be resentment at being forced into a lousy world like this one?"

Leiber leaned toward the doctor, tiredly. "It all ties up. Suppose that a few babies out of all the millions born are instantaneously able to move, see, hear, think, like many animals and insects can. Insects are born self-sufficient. In a few weeks most mammals and birds adjust. But children take years to speak and learn to stumble around on their weak legs.

"But suppose one child in a billion is—strange? Born perfectly aware, able to think, instinctively. Wouldn't it be a perfect setup, a perfect blind for anything the baby might want to do? He could pretend to be ordinary, weak, crying, ignorant. With just a *little* expenditure of energy he could crawl about a darkened house, listening. And how easy to place obstacles at the top of stairs. How easy to cry all night and tire a mother into pneumonia. How easy, right at birth, to be so close to the mother that *a few deft maneuvers might cause peritonitis!*"

"For God's sake!" Jeffers was on his feet. "That's a repulsive thing to say!"

"It's a repulsive thing I'm speaking of. How many mothers have died at the birth of their children? How many have suckled strange little improbabilities who cause death one way or another? Strange, red little creatures with brains that work in a bloody darkness we can't even guess at. Elemental little brains, aswarm with racial memory, hatred, and raw cruelty, with no more thought than self-preservation. And self-preservation in this case consisted of eliminating a mother who realized what a horror she had birthed. I ask you, doctor, what is there in the world more selfish than a baby? Nothing!"

Jeffers scowled and shook his head, helplessly.

Leiber dropped his cigarette down. "I'm not claiming any great strength for the child. Just enough to crawl around a little, a few months ahead of schedule. Just enough to listen all the time. Just enough to cry late at night. That's enough, more than enough."

Jeffers tried ridicule. "Call it murder, then. But murder must be motivated. What motive had the child?"

Leiber was ready with the answer. "What is more at peace, more dreamfully content, at ease, at rest, fed, comforted, unbothered, than an unborn child? Nothing. It floats in a sleepy, timeless wonder of nourishment and silence. Then, suddenly, it is asked to give up its berth, is forced to vacate, rushed out into a noisy, uncaring, selfish world where it is asked to shift for itself, to hunt, to feed from the hunting, to seek after a vanishing love that once was its unquestionable right, to meet confusion instead of inner silence and conservative slumber! And the child *resents* it! Resents the cold air, the huge spaces, the sudden departure from familiar things. And in the tiny filament of brain the only thing the child knows is selfishness and hatred because the spell has been rudely shattered. Who is responsible for this disenchantment, this rude breaking of the spell? The mother. So here the new child has someone to hate with all its unreasoning mind. The mother has cast it out, rejected it. And the father is no better, kill him, too! He's responsible in *his* way!"

Jeffers interrupted. "If what you say is true, then every woman in the world would have to look on her baby as something to dread, something to wonder about."

"And why not? Hasn't the child a perfect alibi? A thousand years of accepted medical belief protects him. By all natural accounts he is helpless, not responsible. The child is born hating. And things grow worse, instead of better. At first the baby gets a certain amount of attention and mothering. But then as time passes, things change. When very new, a baby has the power to make parents do silly things when it cries or sneezes, jump when it makes a noise. As the years pass, the baby feels even that small power slip rapidly, forever away, never to return. Why shouldn't it grasp all the power it can have? Why shouldn't it jockey for position while it has all the advantages? In later years it would be too late to express its hatred. *Now* would be the time to strike."

Leiber's voice was very soft, very low.

"My little boy baby, lying in his crib nights, his face moist and red and out of breath. From crying? No. From climbing slowly out of his crib, from crawling long distances through darkened hallways. My little boy baby. I want to kill him."

The doctor handed him a water glass and some pills. "You're not killing anyone. You're going to sleep for twenty-four hours. Sleep'll change your mind. Take this."

Leiber drank down the pills and let himself be led upstairs to his bedroom, crying, and felt himself being put to bed. The doctor waited until he was moving deep into sleep, then left the house.

Leiber, alone, drifted down, down.

He heard a noise. "What's—what's *that?*" he demanded, feebly.

Something moved in the hall.

David Leiber slept.

Very early the next morning, Dr. Jeffers drove up to the house. It was a good morning, and he was here to drive Leiber to the country for a rest. Leiber would still be asleep upstairs. Jeffers had given him enough sedative to knock him out for at least fifteen hours.

He rang the doorbell. No answer. The servants were probably not up. Jeffers tried the front door, found it open, stepped in. He put his medical kit on the nearest chair.

Something white moved out of sight at the top of the stairs. Just a suggestion of a movement. Jeffers hardly noticed it.

The smell of gas was in the house.

Jeffers ran upstairs, crashed into Leiber's bedroom.

Leiber lay motionless on the bed, and the room billowed with gas, which hissed from a released jet at the base of the wall near the door. Jeffers twisted it off, then forced up all the windows and ran back to Leiber's body.

The body was cold. It had been dead quite a few hours.

Coughing violently, the doctor hurried from the room, eyes watering. Leiber hadn't turned on the gas himself. He *couldn't* have. Those sedatives had knocked him out, he wouldn't have wakened until noon. It wasn't suicide. Or was there the faintest possibility?

Jeffers stood in the hall for five minutes. Then he walked to the door of the nursery. It was shut. He opened it. He walked inside and to the crib.

The crib was empty.

He stood swaying by the crib for half a minute, then he said something to nobody in particular.

"The nursery door blew shut. You couldn't get back into your crib where it was safe. You didn't plan on the door blowing shut. A little thing like a slammed door can ruin the best of plans. I'll find you somewhere in the house, hiding, pretending to be something you are not." The doctor looked dazed. He put his hand to his head and smiled palely. "Now I'm talking like Alice and David talked. But, I can't take any chances. I'm not sure of anything, but I can't take any chances."

He walked downstairs, opened his medical bag on the chair, took something out of it and held it in his hands.

Something rustled down the hall. Something very small and very quiet. Jeffers turned rapidly.

I had to operate to bring you into this world, he thought. Now I guess I can operate to take you out of it. . . .

He took half-a-dozen slow, sure steps forward into the hall. He raised his hand into the sunlight.

"See, baby! Something bright—something pretty!"

A scalpel.

THE CROWD

Mr. Spallner put his hands over his face.

There was the feeling of movement in space, the beautifully tortured scream, the impact and tumbling of the car with wall, through wall, over and down like a toy, and him hurled out of it. Then—silence.

The crowd came running. Faintly, where he lay, he heard them running. He could tell their ages and their sizes by the sound of their numerous feet over the summer grass and on the lined pavement, and over the asphalt street, and picking through the cluttered bricks to where his car hung half into the night sky, still spinning its wheels with a senseless centrifuge.

Where the crowd came from he didn't know. He struggled to remain aware and then the crowd faces hemmed in upon him, hung over him like the large glowing leaves of down-bent trees. They were a ring of shifting, compressing, changing faces over him, looking down, looking down, reading the time of his life or death by his face, making his face into a moon-dial, where the moon cast a shadow from his nose out upon his cheek to tell the time of breathing or not breathing any more ever.

How swiftly a crowd comes, he thought, like the iris of an eye compressing in out of nowhere.

A siren. A police voice. Movement. Blood trickled from his lips and he was being moved into an ambulance. Someone said, "Is he dead?" And someone else said, "No, he's not dead." And a third person said, "He won't die, he's not going to die." And he saw the faces of the crowd beyond him in the night, and he knew by their expressions that he wouldn't die. And that was strange. He saw a man's face, thin, bright, pale; the man swallowed and bit his lips, very sick. There was a small woman, too, with red hair and too much red on her cheeks and lips. And a little boy with a freckled face. Others' faces. An old man with a wrinkled upper lip, an old woman, with a mole upon her chin. They had all come from—where? Houses, cars, alleys, from the immediate and the accident-shocked world. Out of alleys and out of hotels and out of streetcars and seemingly out of nothing they came.

The crowd looked at him and he looked back at them and did not like them at all. There was a vast wrongness to them. He couldn't put his finger on it. They were far worse than this machine-made thing that happened to him now.

The ambulance doors slammed. Through the windows he saw the crowd looking in, looking in. That crowd that always came so fast, so strangely fast, to form a circle, to peer down, to probe, to gawk, to question, to point, to disturb, to spoil the privacy of a man's agony by their frank curiosity.

The ambulance drove off. He sank back and their faces still stared into his face, even with his eyes shut.

The car wheels spun in his mind for days. One wheel, four wheels, spinning, spinning, and whirring, around and around.

He knew it was wrong. Something wrong with the wheels

and the whole accident and the running of feet and the curiosity. The crowd faces mixed and spun into the wild rotation of the wheels.

He awoke.

Sunlight, a hospital room, a hand taking his pulse.

"How do you feel?" asked the doctor.

The wheels faded away. Mr. Spallner looked around.

"Fine—I guess."

He tried to find words. About the accident. "Doctor?"

"Yes?"

"That crowd—was it last night?"

"Two days ago. You've been here since Thursday. You're all right, though. You're doing fine. Don't try and get up."

"That crowd. Something about wheels, too. Do accidents make people, well, a—little off?"

"Temporarily, sometimes."

He lay staring up at the doctor. "Does it hurt your time sense?"

"Panic sometimes does."

"Makes a minute seem like an hour, or maybe an hour seem like a minute?"

"Yes."

"Let me tell you then." He felt the bed under him, the sunlight on his face. "You'll think I'm crazy. I was driving too fast, I know. I'm sorry now. I jumped the curb and hit that wall. I was hurt and numb, I know, but I still remember things. Mostly—the crowd." He waited a moment and then decided to go on, for he suddenly knew what it was that bothered him. "The crowd got there too quickly. Thirty seconds after the smash they were all standing over me and staring at me . . . it's not right they should run that fast, so late at night. . . ."

181

"You only think it was thirty seconds," said the doctor. "It was probably three or four minutes. Your senses—"

"Yeah, I know—my senses, the accident. But I was conscious! I remember one thing that puts it all together and makes it funny, God, so damned funny. The wheels of my car, upside down. The wheels were still spinning when the crowd got there!"

The doctor smiled.

The man in bed went on. "I'm positive! The wheels were spinning and spinning fast—the front wheels! Wheels don't spin very long, friction cuts them down. And these were really spinning!"

"You're confused," said the doctor.

"I'm not confused. That street was empty. Not a soul in sight. And then the accident and the wheels still spinning and all those faces over me, quick, in no time. And the way they looked down at me, I *knew* I wouldn't die. . . ."

"Simple shock," said the doctor, walking away into the sunlight.

They released him from the hospital two weeks later. He rode home in a taxi. People had come to visit him during his two weeks on his back, and to all of them he had told his story, the accident, the spinning wheels, the crowd. They had all laughed with him concerning it, and passed it off.

He leaned forward and tapped on the taxi window.

"What's wrong?"

The cabbie looked back. "Sorry, boss. This is one helluva town to drive in. Got an accident up ahead. Want me to detour?"

"Yes. No. no! Wait. Go ahead. Let's—let's take a look."

The cab moved forward, honking.

"Funny damn thing," said the cabbie. "Hey, *you!* Get that fleatrap out the way!" Quieter, "Funny thing—more damn people. Nosy people."

Mr. Spallner looked down and watched his fingers tremble on his knee. "You noticed that, too?"

"Sure," said the cabbie. "All the time. There's always a crowd. You'd think it was their own mother got killed."

"They come running awfully fast," said the man in the back of the cab.

"Same way with a fire or an explosion. Nobody around. Boom. Lotsa people around. I dunno."

"Ever seen an accident—at night?"

The cabbie nodded. "Sure. Don't make no difference. There's always a crowd."

The wreck came in view. A body lay on the pavement. You knew there was a body even if you couldn't see it. Because of the crowd. The crowd with its back toward him as he sat in the rear of the cab. With its back toward him. He opened the window and almost started to yell. But he didn't have the nerve. If he yelled they might turn around.

And he was afraid to see their faces.

"I seem to have a penchant for accidents," he said, in his office. It was late afternoon. His friend sat across the desk from him, listening. "I got out of the hospital this morning and first thing on the way home, we detoured around a wreck."

"Things run in cycles," said Morgan.

"Let me tell you about my accident."

"I've heard it. Heard it all."

"But it was funny, you must admit."

"I must admit. Now how about a drink?"

They talked on for half an hour or more. All the while they talked, at the back of Spallner's brain a small watch ticked, a watch that never needed winding. It was the memory of a few little things. Wheels and faces.

At about five-thirty there was a hard metal noise in the street. Morgan nodded and looked out and down. "What'd I tell you? Cycles. A truck and a cream-colored Cadillac. Yes, yes."

Spallner walked to the window. He was very cold and as he stood there, he looked at his watch, at the small minute hand. One two three four five seconds—people running—eight nine ten eleven twelve—from all over, people came running—fifteen sixteen seventeen eighteen seconds—more people, more cars, more horns blowing. Curiously distant, Spallner looked upon the scene as an explosion in reverse, the fragments of the detonation sucked back to the point of impulsion. Nineteen, twenty, twenty-one seconds and the crowd was there. Spallner made a gesture down at them, wordless.

The crowd had gathered so fast.

He saw a woman's body a moment before the crowd swallowed it up.

Morgan said, "You look lousy. Here. Finish your drink."

"I'm all right, I'm all right. Let me alone. I'm all right. Can you see those people? Can you see any of them? I wish we could see them closer."

Morgan cried out, "Where in hell are you going?"

Spallner was out the door, Morgan after him, and down the stairs, as rapidly as possible. "Come along, and hurry."

"Take it easy, you're not a well man!"

They walked out onto the street. Spallner pushed his way forward. He thought he saw a red-haired woman with too much red color on her cheeks and lips.

"There!" He turned wildly to Morgan. "Did you see her?"

"See *who?*"

"Damn it; she's gone. The crowd closed in!"

The crowd was all around, breathing and looking and shuffling and mixing and mumbling and getting in the way when he tried to shove through. Evidently the red-haired woman had seen him coming and run off.

He saw another familiar face! A little freckled boy. But there are many freckled boys in the world. And, anyway, it was no use, before Spallner reached him, this little boy ran away and vanished among the people.

"Is she dead?" a voice asked. "Is she dead?"

"She's dying," someone else replied. "She'll be dead before the ambulance arrives. They shouldn't have moved her. They shouldn't have moved her."

All the crowd faces—familiar, yet unfamiliar, bending over, looking down, looking down.

"Hey, mister, stop pushing."

"Who you shovin', buddy?"

Spallner came back out, and Morgan caught hold of him before he fell. "You damned fool. You're still sick. Why in hell'd you have to come down here?" Morgan demanded.

"I don't know, I really don't. They moved her, Morgan, someone moved her. You should never move a traffic victim. It kills them. It kills them."

"Yeah. That's the way with people. The idiots."

———

Spallner arranged the newspaper clippings carefully.

Morgan looked at them. "What's the idea? Ever since your accident you think every traffic scramble is part of you. What are these?"

"Clippings of motor-car crackups, and photos. Look at them. Not at the cars," said Spallner, "but at the crowds around the cars." He pointed. "Here. Compare this photo of a wreck in the Wilshire District with one in Westwood. No resemblance. But now take this Westwood picture and align it with one taken in the Westwood District ten years ago." Again he motioned. "This woman is in both pictures."

Coincidence. The woman happened to be there once in 1936, again in 1946."

"A coincidence once, maybe. But twelve times over a period of ten years, when the accidents occurred as much as three miles from one another, no. Here." He dealt out a dozen photographs. "She's in *all* of these!"

"Maybe she's perverted."

"She's more than that. How does she *happen* to be there so quickly after each accident? And why does she wear the same clothes in pictures taken over a period of a decade?"

"I'll be damned, so she does."

"And, last of all, why was she standing over *me* the night of my accident, two weeks ago!"

They had a drink. Morgan went over the files. "What'd you do, hire a clipping service while you were in the hospital to go back through the newspapers for you?" Spallner nodded. Morgan sipped his drink. It was getting late. The street lights were coming on in the streets below the office. "What does all this add up to?"

"I don't know," said Spallner, "except that there's a uni-

186

versal law about accidents. *Crowds gather.* They always gather. And like you and me, people have wondered year after year, why they gathered so quickly, and how? I know the answer. Here it is!"

He flung the clippings down. "It frightens me."

"These people—mightn't they be thrill-hunters, perverted sensationalists with a carnal lust for blood and morbidity?"

Spallner shrugged. "Does that explain their being at all the accidents? Notice, they stick to certain territories. A Brentwood accident will bring out one group. A Huntington Park another. But there's a norm for faces, a certain percentage appear at each wreck."

Morgan said, "They're not *all* the same faces, are they?"

"Naturally not. Accidents draw normal people, too, in the course of time. But these, I find, are always the *first* ones there."

"Who are they? What do they want? You keep hinting and never telling. Good Lord, you must have some idea. You've scared yourself and now you've got me jumping."

"I've tried getting to them, but someone always trips me up, I'm always too late. They slip into the crowd and vanish. The crowd seems to offer protection to some of its members. They see me coming."

"Sounds like some sort of clique."

"They have one thing in common, they always show up together. At a fire or an explosion or on the sidelines of a war, at any public demonstration of this thing called death. Vultures, hyenas, or saints, I don't know which they are, I just don't know. But I'm going to the police with it, this evening. It's gone on long enough. One of them shifted that woman's body today. They shouldn't have touched her. It killed her."

He placed the clippings in a briefcase. Morgan got up and

slipped into his coat. Spallner clicked the briefcase shut. "Or, I just happened to think . . ."

"What?"

"Maybe they *wanted* her dead."

"Why?"

"Who knows. Come along?"

"Sorry. It's late. See you tomorrow. Luck." They went out together. "Give my regards to the cops. Think they'll believe you?"

"Oh, they'll believe me all right. Good night."

Spallner took it slow driving downtown.

"I want to get there," he told himself, "alive."

He was rather shocked, but not surprised, somehow, when the truck came rolling out of an alley straight at him. He was just congratulating himself on his keen sense of observation and talking out what he would say to the police in his mind, when the truck smashed into his car. It wasn't really his car, that was the disheartening thing about it. In a preoccupied mood he was tossed first this way and then that way, while he thought, what a shame, Morgan has gone and lent me his extra car for a few days until my other car is fixed, and now here I go again. The windshield hammered back into his face. He was forced back and forth in several lightning jerks. Then all motion stopped and all noise stopped and only pain filled him up.

He heard their feet running and running and running. He fumbled with the car door. It clicked. He fell out upon the pavement drunkenly and lay, ear to the asphalt, listening to them coming. It was like a great rainstorm, with many drops, heavy and light and medium, touching the earth. He waited a few seconds and listened to their coming and their arrival. Then, weakly, expectantly, he rolled his head up and looked.

The crowd was there.

He could smell their breaths, the mingled odors of many people sucking and sucking on the air a man needs to live by. They crowded and jostled and sucked and sucked all the air up from around his gasping face until he tried to tell them to move back, they were making him live in a vacuum. His head was bleeding very badly. He tried to move and he realized something was wrong with his spine. He hadn't felt much at the impact, but his spine was hurt. He didn't dare move.

He couldn't speak. Opening his mouth, nothing came out but a gagging.

Someone said, "Give me a hand. We'll roll him over and lift him into a more comfortable position."

Spallner's brain burst apart.

No! Don't move me!

"We'll move him," said the voice, casually.

You idiots, you'll kill me, don't!

But he could not say any of this out loud. He could only think it.

Hands took hold of him. They started to lift him. He cried out and nausea choked him up. They straightened him out into a ramrod of agony. Two men did it. One of them was thin, bright, pale, alert, a young man. The other man was very old and had a wrinkled upper lip.

He had seen their faces before.

A familiar voice said, "Is—is he dead?"

Another voice, a memorable voice, responded, "No. Not yet. But he will be dead before the ambulance arrives."

It was all a very silly, mad plot. Like every accident. He

squealed hysterically at the solid wall of faces. They were all around him, these judges and jurors with the faces he had seen before. Through his pain he counted their faces.

The freckled boy. The old man with the wrinkled upper lip.

The red-haired, red-cheeked woman. An old woman with a mole on her chin.

I know what you're here for, he thought. You're here just as you're at all accidents. To make certain the right ones live and the right ones die. That's why you lifted me. You knew it would kill. You knew I'd live if you left me alone.

And that's the way it's been since time began, when crowds gather. You murder much easier, this way. Your alibi is very simple; you didn't know it was dangerous to move a hurt man. You didn't mean to hurt him.

He looked at them, above him, and he was curious as a man under deep water looking up at people on a bridge. Who are you? Where do you come from and how do you get here so soon? You're the crowd that's always in the way, using up good air that a dying man's lungs are in need of, using up space he should be using to lie in, alone. Tramping on people to make sure they die, that's you. I know *all* of you.

It was like a polite monologue. They said nothing. Faces. The old man. The red-haired woman.

Someone picked up his briefcase. "Whose is this?"

It's mine! It's evidence against all of you!

Eyes, inverted over him. Shiny eyes under tousled hair or under hats.

Faces.

Somewhere—a siren. The ambulance was coming.

But, looking at the faces, the construction, the cast, the

form of the faces, Spallner saw it was too late. He read it in their faces. They *knew*.

He tried to speak. A little bit got out:

"It—looks like I'll—be joining up with you. I—guess I'll be a member of your—group—now."

He closed his eyes then, and waited for the coroner.

JACK-IN-THE-BOX

H e looked through the cold morning windows with the Jack-in-the-Box in his hands, prying the rusted lid. But no matter how he struggled, the Jack would not jump to the light with a cry, or slap its velvet mittens on the air, or bob in a dozen directions with a wild and painted smile. Crushed under the lid, in its jail, it stayed crammed tight coil on coil. With your ear to the box, you felt pressure beneath, the fear and panic of the trapped toy. It was like holding someone's heart in your hand. Edwin could not tell if the box pulsed or if his own blood beat against the lid.

He threw the box down and looked to the window. Outside the window the trees surrounded the house which surrounded Edwin. He could not see beyond the trees. If he tried to find another World beyond them, the trees wove themselves thick with the wind, to still his curiosity, to stop his eyes.

"Edwin!" Behind him, Mother's waiting, nervous breath as she drank her breakfast coffee. "Stop staring. Come eat."

"No," he whispered.

"What?" A stiffened rustle. She must have turned. "Which is more important, breakfast or that window?"

"The window . . ." he whispered and sent his gaze running

the paths and trails he had tried for thirteen years. Was it true that the trees flowed on ten thousand miles to nothingness? He could not say. His sight returned defeated, to the lawn, the steps, his hands trembling on the pane.

He turned to eat his tasteless apricots, alone with his mother in the vast and echoing breakfast room. Five thousand mornings at this table, this window, and no movement beyond the trees.

The two of them ate silently.

She was the pale woman that no one but the birds saw in old country houses in fourth-floor cupola windows, each morning at six, each afternoon at four, each evening at nine, and also passing by one minute after midnight, there she would be, in her tower, silent and white, high and alone and quiet. It was like passing a deserted greenhouse in which one last wild white blossom lifted its head to the moonlight.

And her child, Edwin, was the thistle that one breath of wind might unpod in a season of thistles. His hair was silken and his eyes were of a constant blue and feverish temperature. He had a haunted look, as if he slept poorly. He might fly apart like a packet of ladyfinger firecrackers if a certain door slammed.

His mother began to talk, slowly and with great caution, then more rapidly, and then angrily, and then almost spitting at him.

"Why must you disobey every morning? I don't like your staring from the window, do you hear? What do you want? Do you want to see them?" she cried, her fingers twitching. She was blazingly lovely, like an angry white flower. "Do you want to see the Beasts that run down paths and crush people like strawberries?"

Yes, he thought, I'd like to see the Beasts, horrible as they are.

"Do you want to go out there," she cried, "like your father did before you were born, and be killed as he was killed, struck down by one of those Terrors on the road, would you like that?"

"No . . ."

"Isn't it enough they murdered your Father? Why should you even think of those Beasts!" She motioned toward the forest. "Well, if you really want to die that much, go ahead!"

She quieted, but her fingers kept opening and closing on the tablecloth. "Edwin, Edwin, your Father built every part of this World, it was beautiful for him, it should be for you. There's nothing, nothing, beyond those trees but death; I won't have you near it! This *is* the World. There's no other worth bothering with."

He nodded miserably.

"Smile now, and finish your toast," she said.

He ate slowly, with the window reflected in secret on his silver spoon.

"Mom . . . ?" He couldn't say it. "What's . . . dying? You talk about it. Is it a feeling?"

"To those who must live on after someone else, a bad feeling, yes." She stood up suddenly. "You're late for school! Run!"

He kissed her as he grabbed his books. "Bye!"

"Say hello to teacher!"

He fled from her like a bullet from gun. Up endless staircases, through passages, halls, past windows that poured down dark gallery panels like white waterfalls. Up, up through the layer-cake Worlds with the thick frostings of Oriental rug between, and bright candles on top.

From the highest stair he gazed down through four intervals of Universe.

Lowlands of kitchen, dining room, parlor. Two Middle Countries of music, games, pictures, and locked, forbidden rooms. And here—he whirled—the Highlands of picnics, adventure, and learning. Here he roamed, idled, or sat singing lonely child songs on the winding journey to school.

This, then, was the Universe. Father (or God, as Mother often called him) had raised its mountains of wallpapered plaster long ago. This was Father-God's creation, in which stars blazed at the flick of a switch. And the sun was Mother, and Mother was the sun, about which all the Worlds swung, turning. And Edwin, a small dark meteor, spun up around through the dark carpets and shimmering tapestries of space. You saw him rise to vanish on vast comet staircases, on hikes and explorations.

Sometimes he and Mother picnicked in the Highlands, spread cool snow linens on red-tuffed, Persian lawns, on crimson meadows in a rarefied plateau at the summit of the Worlds where flaking portraits of sallow strangers looked meanly down on their eating and their revels. They drew water from silver taps in hidden tiled niches, smashed the tumblers on hearthstones, shrieking. Played hide-and-seek in enchanted Upper Countries, in unknown, wild, and hidden lands, where she found him rolled like a mummy in a velvet window drape or under sheeted furniture like a rare plant protected from some wind. Once, lost, he wandered for hours in insane foothills of dust and echoes, where the hooks and hangers in closets were hung only with night. But she found him and carried him weeping down through the leveling Universe to the Parlor where dust motes, exact and familiar, fell in showers of sparks on the sunlit air.

He ran up a stair.

Here he knocked a thousand thousand doors, all locked and forbidden. Here Picasso ladies and Dali gentlemen screamed silently from canvas asylums, their gold eyes burning when he dawdled.

"Those Things live *out there*," his mother had said, pointing to the Dali-Picasso families.

Now running quickly past, he stuck out his tongue at them.

He stopped running.

One of the forbidden doors stood open.

Sunlight slanted warm through it, exciting him.

Beyond the door, a spiral stair screwed around up in sun and silence.

He stood, gasping. Year after year he had tried the doors that were always found locked. What would happen now if he shoved this one full open and climbed the stair? Was some Monster hiding at the top?

"Hello!"

His voice leapt up around the spiraled sunlight. "Hello . . ." whispered a faint, far lazy echo, high, high, and gone.

He moved through the door.

"Please, please, don't hurt me," he whispered to the high sunlit place.

He climbed, pausing with each step to wait for his punishment, eyes shut like a penitent. Faster now, he leapt around and around and up until his knees ached and his breath fountained in and out and his head banged like a bell and at last he reached the terrible summit of the climb and stood in an open, sun-drenched tower.

The sun struck his eyes a blow. Never, never so much sun! He stumbled to the iron rail.

"It's there!" His mouth opened from one direction to another. "It's there!" He ran in a circle. "There!"

He was above the somber tree barrier. For the first time he stood high over the windy chestnuts and elms and as far as he could see was green grass, green trees, and white ribbons on which beetles ran, and the other half of the world was blue and endless, with the sun lost and dropping away in an incredible deep blue room so vast he felt himself fall with it, screamed, and clutched the tower ledge, and beyond the trees, beyond the white ribbons where the beetles ran he saw things like fingers sticking up, but he saw no Dali-Picasso terrors, he saw only some small red-and-white-and-blue handkerchiefs fluttering high on great white poles.

He was suddenly sick; he was sick again.

Turning, he almost fell flat down the stairs.

He slammed the forbidden door, fell against it.

"You'll go blind." He crushed his hands to his eyes. "You shouldn't have seen, you shouldn't, you shouldn't!"

He fell to his knees, he lay on the floor twisted tight, covered up. He need wait but a moment—the blindness would come.

Five minutes later he stood at an ordinary Highlands window, looking out at his own familiar Garden World.

He saw once more the elms and hickory trees and the stone wall, and that forest which he had taken to be an endless wall itself, beyond which lay nothing but nightmare nothingness, mist, rain, and eternal night. Now it was certain, the

Universe did not end with the forest. There were other worlds than those contained in Highland or Lowland.

He tried the forbidden door again. Locked.

Had he really gone up? Had he really discovered those half-green, half-blue vastnesses? Had God seen him? Edwin trembled. God. God, who smoked mysterious black pipes and wielded magical walking sticks. God who might be watching even now!

Edwin murmured, touching his cold face.

"I can still see. Thank you, thank you. I can *still* see!"

At nine-thirty, half an hour late, he rapped on the school door.

"Good morning, Teacher!"

The door swung open. Teacher waited in her tall gray, thick-clothed monk's robe, the cowl hiding her face. She wore her usual silver spectacles. Her gray-gloved hands beckoned.

"You're late."

Beyond her the land of books burned in bright colors from the hearth. There were walls bricked with encyclopedias, and a fireplace in which you could stand without bumping your head. A log blazed fiercely.

The door closed, and there was a warm quiet. Here was the desk, where God had once sat, he'd walked this carpet, stuffing his pipe with rich tobacco, and scowled out that vast, stained-glass window. The room smelled of God, rubbed wood, tobacco, leather, and silver coins. Here, Teacher's voice sang like a solemn harp, telling of God, the old days, and the World when it had shaken with God's determination, trembled at his wit, when the World was abuilding under God's hand, a blueprint, a cry, and timber rising. God's fingerprints still lay like half-melted snowflakes on a dozen sharpened pencils in a locked glass display. They must never never be touched lest they melt away forever.

Here, here in the Highlands, to the soft sound of Teacher's voice running on, Edwin learned what was expected of him and his body. He was to grow into a Presence, he must fit the odors and the trumpet voice of God. He must some day stand tall and burning with pale fire at this high window to shout dust off the beams of the Worlds; he must be God Himself! Nothing must prevent it. Not the sky or the trees or the Things beyond the trees.

Teacher moved like a vapor in the room.

"Why are you late, Edwin?"

"I don't know."

"I'll ask you again. Edwin, why are you late?"

"One—one of the forbidden doors was open. . . ."

He heard the hiss of Teacher's breath. He saw her slowly slide back and sink into the large hand-carved chair, swallowed by darkness, her glasses flashing light before they vanished. He felt her looking out at him from shadow and her voice was numbed and so like a voice he heard at night, his own voice crying just before he woke from some nightmare. "Which door? Where?" she said. "Oh, it must be locked!"

"The door by the Dali-Picasso people," he said, in panic. He and Teacher had always been friends. Was that finished now? Had he spoiled things? "I climbed the stair. I had to, I had to! I'm sorry, I'm sorry. Please, don't tell Mother!"

Teacher sat lost in the hollow chair, in the hollow cowl. Her glasses made faint firefly glitters in the well where she moved alone. "And what did you *see* up there?" she murmured. . . .

"A big blue room!"

"Did you?"

"And a green one, and ribbons with bugs running on them, but I didn't, I didn't stay long, I swear, I swear!"

"Green room, ribbons, yes ribbons, and the little bugs running along them, yes," she said, and her voice made him sad.

He reached out for her hand, but it fell away to her lap and groped back, in darkness, to her breast. "I came right down, I locked the door, I won't go look again, ever!" he cried.

Her voice was so faint he could hardly hear what she said. "But now you've seen, and you'll want to see more, and you'll always be curious now." The cowl moved slowly back and forth. Its deepness turned toward him, questioning. "Did you—*like* what you saw?"

"I was scared. It was big."

"Big, yes, too big. Large, large, so large, Edwin. Not like *our* world. Big, large, uncertain. Oh, why did you do this! You knew it was wrong!"

The fire bloomed and withered on the hearth while she waited for his answer and finally when he could not answer she said, as if her lips were barely moving, "Is it your Mother?"

"I don't know!"

"Is she nervous, is she mean, does she snap at you, does she hold too tight, do you want time alone, is that it, is that it, is that it?"

"Yes, yes!" he sobbed, wildly.

"Is that why you ran off, she demands all your time, all your thoughts?" Lost and sad, her voice. "Tell me . . ."

His hands had gone sticky with tears. "Yes!" He bit his fingers and the backs of his hands. "Yes!" It was wrong to admit such things, but he didn't have to say them now, she said them, she said them, and all he must do is agree, shake his head, bite his knuckles, cry out between sobs.

Teacher was a million years old.

"We learn," she said, wearily. Rousing from her chair, she moved with a slow swaying of gray robes to the desk where her gloved hand searched a long time to find pen and paper. "We learn, oh God, but slowly, and with pain, we learn. We think we do right, but all the time, all the time, we kill the Plan. . . ." She hissed her breath, jerked her head up suddenly. The cowl looked completely empty, shivering.

She wrote words on the paper.

"Give this to your mother. It tells her you must have two full hours every afternoon to yourself, to prowl where you wish. Anywhere. Except *out there*. Are you listening, child?"

"Yes." He dried his face. "But—"

"Go on."

"Did Mother lie to me about *out there*, and the Beasts?"

"Look at me," she said. "I've been your friend, I've never beaten you, as your mother sometimes must. We're both here to help you understand and grow so you won't be destroyed as God was."

She arose, and in rising, turned the cowl such a way that color from the hearth washed over her face. Swiftly, the fire-light erased her many wrinkles.

Edwin gasped. His heart gave a jolting thump. "The fire!"

Teacher froze.

"The fire!" Edwin looked at the fire and back to her face. The cowl jerked away from his gaze, the face vanished in the deep well, gone. "Your face," said Edwin numbly. "You look like Mother!"

She moved swiftly to the books, seized one down. She talked to the shelves in her high, singing, monotonous voice. "Women look alike, you know that! Forget it! Here, here!" And she brought him the book. "Read the first chapter! Read the diary!"

Edwin took the book but did not feel its weight in his hands. The fire rumbled and sucked itself brilliantly up the flue as he began to read and as he read Teacher sank back down and settled and quieted and the more he read the more the gray cowl nodded and became serene, the hidden face like a clapper gone solemn in its bell. Firelight ignited the gold animal lettering of the shelved books as he read and he spoke the words but was really thinking of these books from which pages had been razored, and clipped, certain lines erased, certain pictures torn, the leather jaws of some books glued tight, others like mad dogs, muzzled in hard bronze straps to keep him away. All this he thought while his lips moved through the fire-quiet:

"In the Beginning was God. Who created the Universe, and the Worlds within the Universe, the Continents within the Worlds and the Lands within the Continents, and shaped from His mind and hand His loving wife and a child who in time would be God Himself . . .

Teacher nodded slowly. The fire fell softly away to slumbering coals. Edwin read on.

Down the banister, breathless, he slid into the Parlor. "Mom, Mom!"

She lay in a plump maroon chair, breathless, as if she, too, had run a great way.

"Mom, Mom, you're soaking wet!"

"Am I?" she said, as if it was his fault she'd been rushing about. "So I am, so I am." She took a deep breath and sighed. Then she took his hands and kissed each one. She looked at him steadily, her eyes dilating. "Well now, listen here, I've a surprise! Do you know what's coming tomorrow? You can't guess! Your birthday!"

"But it's only been ten months!"

"Tomorrow it is! Do us wonders, I say. And anything I *say* is so is *really* so, my dear."

She laughed.

"And we open another secret room?" He was dazed.

"The fourteenth room, yes! Fifteenth room next year, sixteenth, seventeenth, and so on and on till your twenty-first birthday, Edwin! Then, oh, then we'll open up the triple-locked doors to the most important room and you'll be Man of the House, Father, God, Ruler of the Universe!"

"Hey," he said. And, "Hey!" He tossed his books straight up in the air. They exploded like a great burst of doves, whistling. He laughed. She laughed. Their laughter flew and fell with the books. He ran to scream down the banister again.

At the bottom of the stairs, she waited, arms wide, to catch him.

Edwin lay on his moonlit bed and his fingers pried at the Jack-in-the-Box, but the lid stayed shut; he turned it in his hands, blindly, but did not look down at it. Tomorrow, his birthday— but why? Was he *that* good? No. Why then, should the birthday come so soon? Well, simply because things had gotten, what word could you use? Nervous? Yes, things had begun to shimmer by day as well as by night. He saw the white tremor, the moonlight sifting down and down of an invisible snow in his mother's face. It would take yet another of his birthdays to quiet her again.

"My birthdays," he said to the ceiling, "will come quicker from now on. I know, I know. Mom laughs so loud, so much, and her eyes are funny. . . ."

Would Teacher be invited to the party? No. Mother and Teacher had never met. "Why not?" "Because," said Mom. "Don't you *want* to meet Mom, Teacher?" "Some day," said Teacher, faintly, blowing off like cobwebs in the hall. "Some . . . day. . . ."

And where did Teacher go at night? Did she drift through all those secret mountain countries high up near the moon where the chandeliers were skinned blind with dust, or did she wander out beyond the trees that lay beyond the trees that lay beyond the trees? No, hardly that!

He twisted the toy in his sweating hands. Last year, when things began to tremble and quiver, hadn't Mother advanced his birthday several months, too? Yes, oh, yes, yes.

Think of something else. God. God building cold midnight cellar, sun-baked attic, and all miracles between. Think of the hour of his death, crushed by some monstrous beetle beyond the wall. Oh, how the worlds must have rocked with His passing!

Edwin moved the Jack-in-the-Box to his face, whispered against the lid. "Hello! Hello! Hello, hello . . ."

No answer save the sprung-tight coiled-in tension there. I'll get you out, thought Edwin. Just wait, just wait. It may hurt, but there's only one way. Here, here . . .

And he moved from bed to window and leaned far out, looking down to the marbled walk in the moonlight. He raised the box high, felt the sweat trickle from his armpit, felt his fingers clench, felt his arm jerk. He flung the box out, shouting. The box tumbled in the cold air, down. It took a long time to strike the marble pavement.

Edwin bent still further over, gasping.

"Well?" he cried. "Well?" and again, "You there!" and "You!"

The echoes faded. The box lay in the forest shadows. He could not see if the crash had broken it wide. He could not see if the Jack had risen, smiling, from its hideous jail or if it bobbed upon the wind now this way, that, this way, that, its silver bells jingling softly. He listened. He stood by the window for an hour staring, listening, and at last went back to bed.

Morning. Bright voices moved near and far, in and out the Kitchen World and Edwin opened his eyes. Whose voices, now whose could they be? Some of God's workmen? The Dali people? But Mother hated them; no. The voices faded in a humming roar. Silence. And from a great distance, a running, running grew louder and still louder until the door burst open.

"Happy Birthday!"

They danced, they ate frosted cookies, they bit lemon ices, they drank pink wines, and there stood his name on a snow-powdered cake as Mother chorded the piano into an avalanche of sound and opened her mouth to sing, then whirled to seize him away to more strawberries, more wines, more laughter that shook chandeliers into trembling rain. Then, a silver key flourished, they raced to unlock the fourteenth forbidden door.

"Ready! Hold on!"

The door whispered into the wall.

"Oh," said Edwin.

For, disappointingly enough, this fourteenth room was noth-ing at all but a dusty dull-brown closet. It promised nothing as had the rooms given him on other anniversaries! His sixth birthday present, now, had been the schoolroom in the High-lands. On his seventh birthday he had opened the playroom in the Lowlands. Eighth, the music room; Ninth, the miraculous hell-fired kitchen! Tenth was the room where phonographs hissed in a continuous exhalation of ghosts singing on a gentle wind. Eleventh was the vast green diamond room of the Gar-den with a carpet that had to be cut instead of swept!

"Oh, don't be disappointed; move!" Mother, laughing, pushed him in the closet. "Wait till you see how magical! Shut the door!"

She thrust a red button flush with the wall.

Edwin shrieked. "No!"

For the room was quivering, working, like a mouth that held them in iron jaws; the room moved, the wall slid away below.

"Oh, hush now, darling," she said. The door drifted down through the floor, and a long insanely vacant wall slithered by like an endlessly rustling snake to bring another door and an-other door with it that did not stop but traveled on while Ed-win screamed and clutched his mother's waist. The room whined and cleared its throat somewhere; the trembling ceased, the room stood still. Edwin stared at a strange new door and heard his mother say go on, open it, there, now, there. And the new door gaped upon still further mystery. Edwin blinked.

"The Highlands! This is the Highlands! How did we get here? Where's the Parlor, mom, where's the Parlor!"

She fetched him out through the door. "We jumped

straight up, and we flew. Once a week, you'll fly to school instead of running the long way around!"

He still could not move, but only stood looking at the mystery of Land exchanged for Land, of Country replaced by higher and further Country.

"Oh, mother, mother . . ." he said.

It was a sweet long time in the deep grass of the garden where they idled most deliciously, sipped huge cupfuls of apple cider with their elbows on crimson silk cushions, their shoes kicked off, their toes bedded in sour dandelions, sweet clover. Mother jumped twice when she heard Monsters roar beyond the forest. Edwin kissed her cheek. "It's all right," he said, "I'll protect you."

"I know you will," she said, but she turned to gaze at the pattern of trees, as if any moment the chaos out there might smash the forest with a blow and stamp its Titan's foot down and grind them to dust.

Late in the long blue afternoon, they saw a chromium bird thing fly through a bright rift in the trees, high and roaring. They ran for the Parlor, heads bent as before a green storm of lightning and rain, feeling the sound pour blinding showers to drench them.

Crackle, crackle—the birthday burnt away to cellophane nothingness. At sunset, in the dim soft Parlor Country, Mother inhaled champagne with her tiny seedling nostrils and her pale summer-rose mouth, then, drowsy wild, herded Edwin off to his room and shut him in.

He undressed in slow-pantomimed wonder, thinking, this year, next year, and which room two years, three years, from today? What about the Beasts, the Monsters? And being mashed and God killed? What was killed? What was Death? Was Death a feeling? Did God enjoy it so much he never came back? Was Death a journey then?

In the hall, on her way downstairs, Mother dropped a champagne bottle. Edwin heard and was cold, for the thought that jumped through his head was, that's how Mother'd sound. If she fell, if she broke, you'd find a million fragments in the morning. Bright crystal and clear wine on the parquet flooring, that's all you'd see at dawn.

Morning was the smell of vines and grapes and moss in his room, a smell of shadowed coolness. Downstairs, breakfast was in all probability, at this instant, manifesting itself in a finger-snap on the wintry tables.

Edwin got up to wash and dress and wait, feeling fine. Now things would be fresh and new for at least a month. To-day, like all days, there'd be breakfast, school, lunch, songs in the music room, an hour or two at the electrical games, then—tea in the Outlands, on the luminous grass. Then up to school again for a late hour or so, where he and Teacher might prowl the censored library together and he'd puzzle with words and thoughts about that world *out there* that had been censored from his eyes.

He had forgotten Teacher's note. Now, he must give it to Mother.

He opened the door. The hall was empty. Down through the deeps of the Worlds, a soft mist floated, through a silence which no footsteps broke; the hills were quiet; the silver fonts did not pulse in the first sunlight, and the banister, coiling up from the mists was a prehistoric monster peering into his room. He pulled away from this creature, looking to find Mother, like a white boat, drifted by the dawn tides and vapors below.

She was not there. He hurried down through the hushed lands, calling, "Mother!"

He found her in the Parlor, collapsed on the floor in her shiny green-gold party dress, a champagne goblet in one hand, the carpet littered with broken glass.

She was obviously asleep, so he sat at the magical breakfast table. He blinked at the empty white cloth and the gleaming plates. There was no food. All his life wondrous foods had awaited him here. But not today.

"Mother, wake up!" He ran to her. "Shall I go to school? Where's the food? Wake up!"

He ran up the stairs.

The Highlands were cold and shadowed, and the white glass suns no longer glowed from the ceilings in this day of sullen fog. Down dark corridors, through dim continents of silence, Edwin rushed. He rapped and rapped at the school door. It drifted in, whining, by itself.

The school lay empty and dark. No fire roared on the hearth to toss shadows on the beamed ceiling. There was not a crackle or a whisper.

"Teacher?"

He poised in the center of the flat, cold room.

"Teacher!" he screamed.

He slashed the drapes aside; a faint shaft of sunlight fell through the stained glass.

Edwin gestured. He commanded the fire to explode like a

popcorn kernel on the hearth. He commanded it to bloom to life! He shut his eyes, to give Teacher time to appear. He opened his eyes and was stupefied at what he saw on her desk.

Neatly folded was the gray cowl and robe, atop which gleamed her silver spectacles, and one gray glove. He touched them. One gray glove was gone. A piece of greasy cosmetic chalk lay on the robe. Testing it, he made dark lines on his hands.

He drew back, staring at Teacher's empty robe, the glasses, the greasy chalk. His hand touched a knob of a door which had always been locked. The door swung slowly wide. He looked into a small brown closet.

"Teacher!"

He ran in, the door crashed shut, he pressed a red button. The room sank down, and with it sank a slow mortal coldness. The World was silent, quiet, and cool. Teacher gone and Mother—sleeping. Down fell the room, with him in its iron jaws.

Machinery clashed. A door slid open. Edwin ran out.

The Parlor!

Behind was not a door, but a tall oak panel from which he had emerged.

Mother lay uncaring, asleep. Folded under her, barely showing as he rolled her over, was one of Teacher's soft gray gloves.

He stood near her, holding the incredible glove, for a long time. Finally, he began to whimper.

He fled back up to the Highlands. The hearth was cold, the room empty. He waited. Teacher did not come. He ran down again to the solemn Lowlands, commanded the table to fill with steaming dishes! Nothing happened. He sat by his

mother, talking and pleading with her and touching her, and her hands were cold.

The clock ticked and the light changed in the sky and still she did not move, and he was hungry and the silent dust dropped down on the air through all the Worlds. He thought of Teacher and knew that if she was in none of the hills and mountains above, then there was only one place she could be. She had wandered, by error, into the Outlands, lost until some-one found her. And so he must go out, call after her, bring her back to wake Mother, or she would lie here forever with the dust falling in the great darkened spaces.

Through the kitchen, out back, he found late afternoon sun and the Beasts hooting faintly beyond the rim of the World. He clung to the garden wall, not daring to let go, and in the shadows, at a distance, saw the shattered box he had flung from the window. Freckles of sunlight quivered on the broken lid and touched tremblingly over and over the face of the Jack jumped out and sprawled with its arms overhead in an eternal gesture of freedom. The doll smiled and did not smile, smiled and did not smile, as the sun winked on the mouth, and Edwin stood, hypnotized, above and beyond it. The doll opened its arms toward the path that led off between the secret trees, the forbidden path smeared with oily droppings of the Beasts. But the path lay silent and the sun warmed Edwin and he heard the wind blow softly in the trees. At last, he let go of the gar-den wall.

"Teacher?"

He edged along the path a few feet.

"Teacher!"

His shoes slipped on the animal droppings and he stared

far down the motionless tunnel, blindly. The path moved under, the trees moved over him.

"Teacher!"

He walked slowly but steadily. He turned. Behind him lay his World and its very new silence. It was diminished, it was small! How strange to see it less than it had been. It had always and forever seemed so large. He felt his heart stop. He stepped back. But then, afraid of that silence in the World, he turned to face the forest path ahead.

Everything before him was new. Odors filled his nostrils, colors, odd shapes, incredible sizes filled his eyes.

If I run beyond the trees I'll die, he thought, for that's what Mother said. You'll die, you'll die.

But what's dying? Another room? A blue room, a green room, far larger than all the rooms that ever were! But where's the key? There, far ahead, a great half-open iron door, a wrought-iron gate. Beyond a room as large as the sky, all colored green with trees and grass! Oh, Mother, Teacher . . .

He rushed, stumbled, fell, got up, ran again, his numb legs under him were left behind as he fell down and down the side of a hill, the path gone, wailing, crying, and then not wailing or crying any more, but making new sounds. He reached the great rusted, screaming iron gate, leapt through; the Universe dwindled behind, he did not look back at his old Worlds, but ran as they withered and vanished.

The policeman stood at the curb, looking down the street.

"These kids. I'll never be able to figure them."

"How's that?" asked the pedestrian.

The policeman thought it over and frowned. "Couple sec-

onds ago a little kid ran by. He was laughing and crying, crying and laughing, both. He was jumping up and down and touching things. Things like lampposts, the telephone poles, fire hydrants, dogs, people. Things like sidewalks, fences, gates, cars, plateglass windows, barber poles. Hell, he even grabbed hold and looked at me, and looked at the sky, you should have seen the tears, and all the time he kept yelling and yelling something funny."

"What did he yell?" asked the pedestrian.

"He kept yelling, 'I'm dead, I'm dead, I'm glad I'm dead, I'm dead, I'm dead, I'm glad I'm dead, I'm dead, I'm dead, it's *good* to be dead!' " The policeman scratched his chin slowly. "One of them new kid games, I guess."

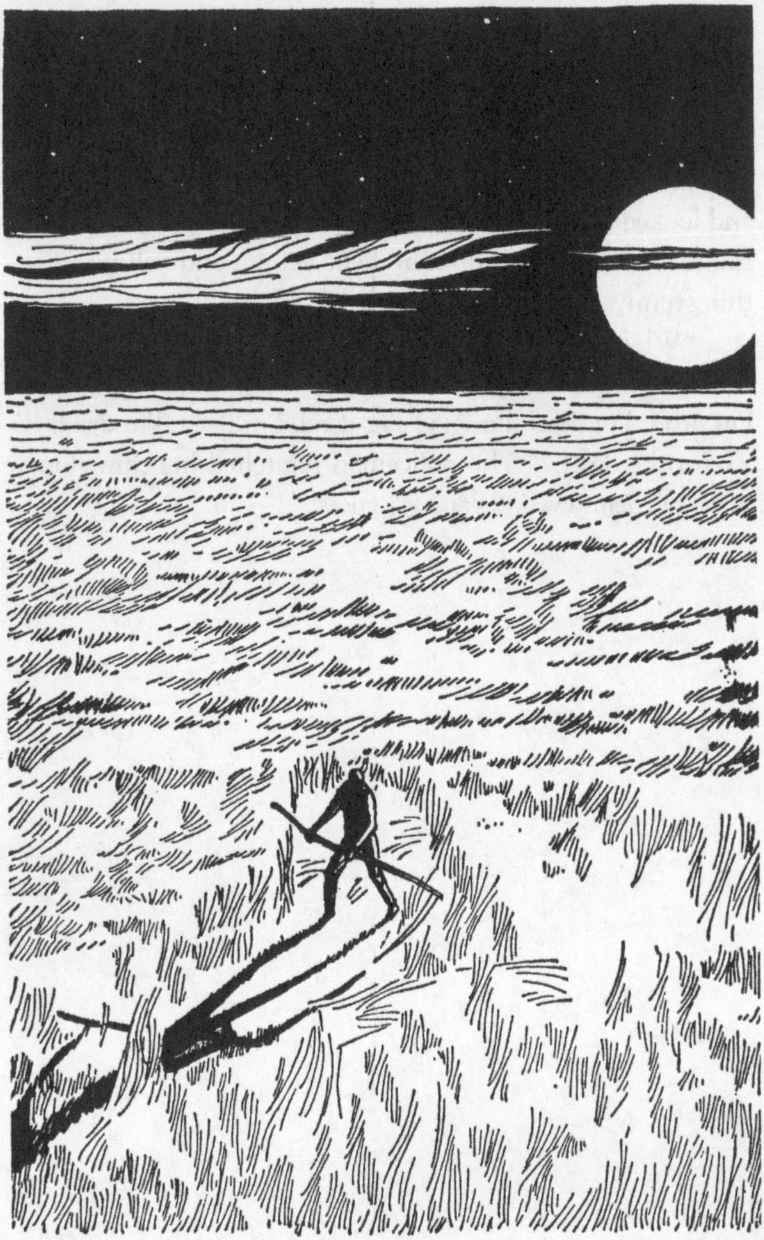

THE SCYTHE

Quite suddenly there was no more road. It ran down the valley like any other road, between slopes of barren, stony ground and live oak trees, and then past a broad field of wheat standing alone in the wilderness. It came up beside the small white house that belonged to the wheat field and then just faded out, as though there was no more use for it.

It didn't matter much, because just there the last of the gas was gone. Drew Erickson braked the ancient car to a stop and sat there, not speaking, staring at his big, rough farmer's hands.

Molly spoke, without moving where she lay in the corner beside him. "We must of took the wrong fork back yonder."

Drew nodded.

Molly's lips were almost as white as her face. Only they were dry, where her skin was damp with sweat. Her voice was flat, with no expression in it.

"Drew," she said. "Drew, what are we a-goin' to do now?"

Drew stared at his hands. A farmer's hands, with the farm blown out from under them by the dry, hungry wind that never got enough good loam to eat.

The kids in the back seat woke up and pried themselves

out of the dusty litter of bundles and bedding. They poked their heads over the back of the seat and said:

"What are we stoppin' for, Pa? Are we gonna eat now, Pa? Pa, we're awful hungry. Can we eat now, Pa?"

Drew closed his eyes. He hated the sight of his hands.

Molly's fingers touched his wrist. Very light, very soft. "Drew, maybe in the house there they'd spare us somethin' to eat?"

A white line showed around his mouth. "Beggin'," he said harshly. "Ain't none of us ever begged before. Ain't none of us ever goin' to."

Molly's hand tightened on his wrist. He turned and saw her eyes. He saw the eyes of Susie and little Drew, looking at him. Slowly all the stiffness went out of his neck and his back. His face got loose and blank, shapeless like a thing that has been beaten too hard and too long. He got out of the car and went up the path to the house. He walked uncertainly, like a man who is sick, or nearly blind.

The door of the house was open. Drew knocked three times. There was nothing inside but silence, and a white window curtain moving in the slow, hot air.

He knew it before he went in. He knew there was death in the house. It was that kind of silence.

He went through a small, clean living room and down a little hall. He wasn't thinking anything. He was past thinking. He was going toward the kitchen, unquestioning, like an animal.

Then he looked through an open door and saw the dead man.

He was an old man, lying out on a clean white bed. He hadn't been dead long; not long enough to lose the last quiet

look of peace. He must have known he was going to die, because he wore his grave clothes—an old black suit, brushed
and neat, and a clean white shirt and a black tie.

A scythe leaned against the wall beside the bed. Between
the old man's hands there was a blade of wheat, still fresh. A
ripe blade, golden and heavy in the tassel.

Drew went into the bedroom, walking soft. There was a
coldness on him. He took off his broken, dusty hat and stood
by the bed, looking down.

The paper lay open on the pillow beside the old man's
head. It was meant to be read. Maybe a request for burial, or to
call a relative. Drew scowled over the words, moving his pale,
dry lips.

> *To him who stands beside me at my death bed:* Being of
> sound mind, and alone in the world as it has been de-
> creed, I, John Buhr, do give and bequeath this farm,
> with all pertaining to it, to the man who is to come.
> Whatever his name or origin shall be, it will not
> matter. The farm is his, and the wheat; the scythe,
> and the task ordained thereto. Let him take them
> freely, and without question—and remember that I,
> John Buhr, am only the giver, not the ordainer. To
> which I set my hand and seal this third day of April,
> 1938. (Signed) John Buhr. *Kyrie eléison!*

Drew walked back through the house and opened the
screen door. He said, "Molly, you come in. Kids, you stay in
the car."

Molly came inside. He took her to the bedroom. She
looked at the will, the scythe, the wheat field moving in a hot

wind outside the window. Her white face tightened up and she bit her lips and held onto him. "It's too good to be true. There must be some trick to it."

Drew said, "Our luck's changin', that's all. We'll have work to do, stuff to eat, somethin' over our heads to keep rain off." He touched the scythe. It gleamed like a half-moon. Words were scratched on its blade: WHO WIELDS ME—WIELDS THE WORLD! It didn't mean much to him, right at that moment.

"Drew," Molly asked, staring at the old man's clasped hands, "why—why's he holdin' that wheat-stalk so hard in his fingers?"

Just then the heavy silence was broken by the sound of the kids scrambling up the front porch. Molly gasped.

They lived in the house. They buried the old man on a hill and said some words over him, and came back down and swept the house and unloaded the car and had something to eat, because there was food, lots of it, in the kitchen; and they did nothing for three days but fix the house and look at the land and lie in the good beds, and then look at one another in surprise that all this was happening this way, and their stomachs were full and there was even a cigar for him to smoke in the evenings.

There was a small barn behind the house and in the barn a bull and three cows; and there was a well-house, a spring-house, under some big trees that kept it cool. And inside the well-house were big sides of beef and bacon and pork and mutton, enough to feed a family five times their size for a year, two years, maybe three. There was a churn and a box of cheese there, and big metal cans for the milk.

On the fourth morning Drew Erickson lay in bed looking at the scythe, and he knew it was time for him to work because there was ripe grain in the long field; he had seen it with his eyes, and he did not want to get soft. Three days sitting were enough for any man. He roused himself in the first fresh smell of dawn and took the scythe and held it before him as he walked out into the field. He held it up in his hands and swung it down.

It was a big field of grain. Too big for one man to tend, and yet one man had tended it.

At the end of the first day of work, he walked in with the scythe riding his shoulder quietly, and there was a look on his face of a puzzled man. It was a wheat field the like of which he had never seen. It ripened only in separate clusters, each set off from the others. Wheat shouldn't do that. He didn't tell Molly. Nor did he tell her the other things about the field. About how, for instance, the wheat rotted within a few hours after he cut it down. Wheat shouldn't do that, either. He was not greatly worried. After all, there was food at hand.

The next morning the wheat he had left rotting, cut down, had taken hold and came up again in little green sprouts, with tiny roots, all born again.

Drew Erickson rubbed his chin, wondered what and why and how it acted that way, and what good it would be to him— he couldn't sell it. A couple of times during the day he walked far up in the hills to where the old man's grave was, just to be sure the old man was there, maybe with some notion he might get an idea there about the field. He looked down and saw how much land he owned. The wheat stretched three miles in one direction toward the mountains, and was about two acres wide, patches of it in seedlings, patches of it golden, patches of it green, patches of it fresh cut by his hand. But the old man said nothing concerning this; there were a lot of stones and dirt in his face now. The grave was in the sun and the wind and silence. So Drew Erickson walked back down to use the scythe, curious, enjoying it because it seemed important. He didn't know just why, but it was. Very, very important.

He couldn't just let the wheat stand. There were always new patches of it ripened, and in his figuring out loud to no one in particular he said, "If I cut the wheat for the next ten years, just as it ripens up, I don't think I'll pass the same spot twice. Such a damn big field." He shook his head. "That wheat ripens just *so*. Never too much of it so I can't cut all the ripe stuff each day. That leaves nothin' but green grain. And the next mornin', sure enough, another patch of ripe stuff. . . ."

It was damned foolish to cut the grain when it rotted as quick as it fell. At the end of the week he decided to let it go a few days.

He lay in bed late, just listening to the silence in the house that wasn't anything like death silence, but a silence of things living well and happily.

He got up, dressed, and ate his breakfast slowly. He wasn't going to work. He went out to milk the cows, stood on the porch smoking a cigarette, walked about the backyard a little and then came back in and asked Molly what he had gone out to do.

"Milk the cows," she said.

"Oh, yes," he said, and went out again. He found the cows waiting and full, and milked them and put the milk cans in the spring-house, but thought of other things. The wheat. The scythe.

All through the morning he sat on the back porch rolling cigarettes. He made a toy boat for little Drew and one for Susie,

and then he churned some of the milk into butter and drew off
the buttermilk, but the sun was in his head, aching. It burned
there. He wasn't hungry for lunch. He kept looking at the
wheat and the wind bending and tipping and ruffling it. His
arms flexed, his fingers, resting on his knee as he sat again on
the porch, made a kind of grip in the empty air, itching. The
pads of his palms itched and burned. He stood up and wiped his
hands on his pants and sat down and tried to roll another cigarette and got mad at the mixings and threw it all away with a
muttering. He had a feeling as if a third arm had been cut off of
him, or he had lost something of himself. It had to do with his
hands and his arms.

He heard the wind whisper in the field.

By one o'clock he was going in and out of the house, getting underfoot, thinking about digging an irrigation ditch, but
all the time really thinking about the wheat and how ripe and
beautiful it was, aching to be cut.

"Damn it to hell!"

He strode into the bedroom, took the scythe down off its
wall-pegs. He stood holding it. He felt cool. His hands stopped
itching. His head didn't ache. The third arm was returned to
him. He was intact again.

It was instinct. Illogical as lightning striking and not hurting. Each day the grain must be cut. It had to be cut. Why?
Well, it just did, that was all. He laughed at the scythe in his big
hands. Then, whistling, he took it out to the ripe and waiting
field and did the work. He thought himself a little mad. Hell, it
was an ordinary-enough wheat field, really, wasn't it? Almost.

_____

The days loped away like gentle horses.

Drew Erickson began to understand his work as a sort of dry ache and hunger and need. Things built in his head.

One noon, Susie and little Drew giggled and played with the scythe while their father lunched in the kitchen. He heard them. He came out and took it away from them. He didn't yell at them. He just looked very concerned and locked the scythe up after that, when it wasn't being used.

He never missed a day, scything.

Up. Down. Up, down, and across. Back and up and down and across. Cutting. Up. Down.

Up.

Think about the old man and the wheat in his hands when he died.

Down.

Think about this dead land, with wheat living on it.

Up.

Think about the crazy patterns of ripe and green wheat, the way it grows!

Down.

Think about . . .

The wheat whirled in a full yellow tide at his ankles. The sky blackened. Drew Erickson dropped the scythe and bent over to hold his stomach, his eyes running blindly. The world reeled.

"I've killed somebody!" he gasped, choking, holding to his chest, falling to his knees beside the blade. "I've killed a lot—"

The sky revolved like a blue merry-go-round at the county fair in Kansas. But no music. Only a ringing in his ears.

Molly was sitting at the blue kitchen table peeling potatoes when he blundered into the kitchen, dragging the scythe behind him.

"Molly!"

She swam around in the wet of his eyes.

She sat there, her hands fallen open, waiting for him to finally get it out.

"Get the things packed!" he said, looking at the floor.

"Why?"

"We're leaving," he said, dully.

"We're leaving?" she said.

"That old man. You know what he did here? It's the wheat, Molly, and this scythe. Every time you use the scythe on the wheat a thousand people die. You cut across them and—"

Molly got up and put the knife down and the potatoes to one side and said, understandingly, "We traveled a lot and haven't eaten good until the last month here, and you been workin' every day and you're tired—"

"I hear voices, sad voices, out there. In the wheat," he said. "Tellin' me to stop. Tellin' me not to kill them!"

"Drew!"

He didn't hear her. "The field grows crooked, wild, like a crazy thing. I didn't tell you. But it's wrong."

She stared at him. His eyes were blue glass, nothing else.

"You think I'm crazy," he said, "but wait 'til I tell you. Oh, God, Molly, help me; I just killed my mother!"

"Stop it!" she said firmly.

"I cut down one stalk of wheat and I killed her. I felt her dyin', that's how I found out just now—"

"Drew!" Her voice was like a crack across the face, angry and afraid now. "Shut up!"

He mumbled. "Oh—Molly—"

The scythe dropped from his hands, clamored on the floor. She picked it up with a snap of anger and set it in one corner. "Ten years I been with you," she said. "Sometimes we had nothin' but dust and prayers in our mouths. Now, all this good luck sudden, and you can't bear up under it!"

She brought the Bible from the living room.

She rustled its pages over. They sounded like the wheat rustling in a small, slow wind. "You sit down and listen," she said.

A sound came in from the sunshine. The kids, laughing in the shade of the large live oak beside the house.

She read from the Bible, looking up now and again to see what was happening to Drew's face.

She read from the Bible each day after that. The following Wednesday, a week later, when Drew walked down to the distant town to see if there was any General Delivery mail, there was a letter.

He came home looking two hundred years old.

He held the letter out to Molly and told her what it said in a cold, uneven voice.

"Mother passed away—one o'clock Tuesday afternoon— her heart—"

All that Drew Erickson had to say was, "Get the kids in the car, load it up with food. We're goin' on to California."

"Drew—" said his wife, holding the letter.

"You know yourself," he said, "this is poor grain land. Yet look how ripe it grows. I ain't told you all the things. It ripens in patches, a little each day. It ain't right. And when I cut it, it rots! And next mornin' it comes up without any help, growin' again! Last Tuesday, a week ago, when I cut the grain it was like rippin' my own flesh. I heard somebody scream. It sounded just like— And now, today, this letter."

She said, "We're stayin' here."

"Molly."

"We're stayin' here, where we're sure of eatin' and sleepin' and livin' decent and livin' long. I'm not starvin' my children down again, ever!"

The sky was blue through the windows. The sun slanted in, touching half of Molly's calm face, shining one eye bright blue. Four or five water drops hung and fell from the kitchen faucet slowly, shining, before Drew sighed. The sigh was husky and resigned and tired. He nodded, looking away. "All right," he said. "We'll stay."

He picked up the scythe weakly. The words on the metal leaped up with a sharp glitter.

WHO WIELDS ME—WIELDS THE WORLD!

"We'll stay. . . ."

Next morning he walked to the old man's grave. There was a single fresh sprout of wheat growing in the center of it. The same sprout, reborn, that the old man had held in his hands weeks before.

He talked to the old man, getting no answers.

"You worked the field all your life because you *had* to, and one day you came across your own life growin' there. You knew it was yours. You cut it. And you went home, put on your grave clothes, and your heart gave out and you died. That's how it was, wasn't it? And you passed the land on to me, and when I die, I'm supposed to hand it over to someone else."

Drew's voice had awe in it. "How long a time has this been goin' on? With nobody knowin' about this field and its use except the man with the scythe . . . ?"

Quite suddenly he felt very old. The valley seemed ancient, mummified, secretive, dried and bent and powerful. When the Indians danced on the prairie it had been here, this field. The same sky, the same wind, the same wheat. And, before the Indians? Some Cro-Magnon, gnarled and shag-haired, wielding a crude wooden scythe, perhaps, prowling down through the living wheat. . . .

Drew returned to work. Up, down. Up, down. Obsessed with the idea of being the wielder of *the* scythe. He, himself! It burst upon him in a mad, wild surge of strength and horror.

Up! WHO WIELDS ME! Down! WIELDS THE WORLD!

He had to accept the job with some sort of philosophy. It was simply his way of getting food and housing for his family. They deserved eating and living decent, he thought, after all these years.

Up and down. Each grain a life he neatly cut into two pieces. If he planned it carefully—he looked at the wheat—why, he and Molly and the kids could live forever!

Once he found the place where the grain grew that was Molly and Susie and little Drew he would never cut it.

And then, like a signal, it came, quietly.

Right there, before him.

Another sweep of the scythe and he'd cut them away.

Molly, Drew, Susie. It was certain. Trembling, he knelt and looked at the few grains of wheat. They glowed at his touch.

He groaned with relief. What if he had cut them down, never guessing? He blew out his breath and got up and took the scythe and stood back away from the wheat and stood for a long while looking down.

Molly thought it awfully strange when he came home early and kissed her on the cheek, for no reason at all.

At dinner, Molly said, "You quit early today? Does—does the wheat still spoil when it falls?"

He nodded and took more meat.

She said, "You ought to write to the Agriculture people and have them come look at it."

"No," he said.

"I was just suggestin'," she said.

His eyes dilated. "I got to stay here all my life. Can't nobody else mess with that wheat; they wouldn't know where to cut and not to cut. They might cut the wrong parts."

"What wrong parts?"

"Nothin'," he said, chewing slowly. "Nothin' at all."

He slapped his fork down, hard. "Who knows *what* they might want to do! Those government men! They might even— might even want to plow the whole field under!"

Molly nodded. "That's just what it needs," she said. "And start all over again, with new seed."

He didn't finish eating. "I'm not writin' any gover'ment, and I'm not handin' this field over to no stranger to cut, and that's that!" he said, and the screen door banged behind him.

He detoured around that place where the lives of his children and his wife grew up in the sun, and used his scythe on the far end of the field where he knew he would make no mistakes.

But he no longer liked the work. At the end of an hour he knew he had brought death to three of his old, loved friends in Missouri. He read their names in the cut grain and couldn't go on.

He locked the scythe in the cellar and put the key away. He was done with the reaping, done for good and all.

He smoked his pipe in the evening, on the front porch, and told the kids stories to hear them laugh. But they didn't laugh much. They seemed withdrawn, tired and funny, like they weren't his children any more.

Molly complained of a headache, dragged around the house a little, went to bed early and fell into a deep sleep. That was funny, too. Molly always stayed up late and was full of vinegar.

The wheat field rippled with moonlight on it, making it into a sea.

It wanted cutting. Certain parts needed cutting *now*. Drew Erickson sat, swallowing quietly, trying not to look at it.

What'd happen to the world if he never went in the field again? What'd happen to people ripe for death, who waited the coming of the scythe?

He'd wait and see.

Molly was breathing softly when he blew out the oil lamp and got to bed. He couldn't sleep. He heard the wind in the wheat, felt the hunger to do the work in his arms and fingers.

In the middle of the night he found himself walking in the field, the scythe in his hands. Walking like a crazy man, walking and afraid, half-awake. He didn't remember unlocking the cellar door, getting the scythe, but here he was in the moon-light, walking in the grain.

Among these grains there were many who were old, weary, wanting so very much to sleep. The long, quiet, moon-less sleep.

The scythe held him, grew into his palms, forced him to walk.

Somehow, struggling, he got free of it. He threw it down, ran off into the wheat, where he stopped and went down on his knees.

"I don't want to kill anymore," he said. "If I work with the scythe I'll have to kill Molly and the kids. Don't ask me to do that!"

The stars only sat in the sky, shining.

Behind him, he heard a dull, thumping sound.

Something shot up over the hill into the sky. It was like a living thing, with arms of red color, licking at the stars. Sparks fell into his face. The thick, hot odor of fire came with it.

The house!

Crying out, he got sluggishly, hopelessly, to his feet, look-ing at the big fire.

The little white house with the live oaks was roaring up in one savage bloom of fire. Heat rolled over the hill and he swam in it and went down in it, stumbling, drowning over his head.

By the time he got down the hill there was not a shingle, bolt or threshold of it that wasn't alive with flame. It made blis-tering, crackling, fumbling noises.

No one screamed inside. No one ran around or shouted.

He yelled in the yard. "Molly! Susie! Drew!"

He got no answer. He ran close in until his eyebrows withered and his skin crawled hot like paper burning, crisping, curling up in tight little curls.

"Molly! Susie!"

The fire settled contentedly down to feed. Drew ran around the house a dozen times, all alone, trying to find a way in. Then he sat where the fire roasted his body and waited until all the walls had sunken down with fluttering crashes, until the last ceilings bent, blanketing the floors with molten plaster and scorched lathing. Until the flames died and smoke coughed up, and the new day came slowly; and there was nothing but embering ashes and an acid smoldering.

Disregarding the heat fanning from the leveled frames, Drew walked into the ruin. It was still too dark to see much. Red light glowed on his sweating throat. He stood like a stranger in a new and different land. Here—the kitchen. Charred tables, chairs, the iron stove, the cupboards. Here—the hall. Here the parlor and then over here was the bedroom where—

Where Molly was still alive.

She slept among fallen timbers and angry-colored pieces of wire spring and metal.

She slept as if nothing had happened. Her small white hands lay at her sides, flaked with sparks. Her calm face slept with a flaming lath across one cheek.

Drew stopped and didn't believe it. In the ruin of her smoking bedroom she lay on a glittering bed of sparks, her skin intact, her breast rising, falling, taking air.

"Molly!"

Alive and sleeping after the fire, after the walls had roared down, after ceilings had collapsed upon her and flame had lived all about her.

His shoes smoked as he pushed through piles of fuming litter. It could have seared his feet off at the ankles, he wouldn't have known.

"Molly . . ."

He bent over her. She didn't move or hear him, and she didn't speak. She wasn't dead. She wasn't alive. She just lay there with the fire surrounding her and not touching her, not harming her in any way. Her cotton nightgown was streaked with ashes, but not burnt. Her brown hair was pillowed on a tumble of red-hot coals.

He touched her cheek, and it was cold, cold in the middle of hell. Tiny breaths trembled her half-smiling lips.

The children were there, too. Behind a veil of smoke he made out two smaller figures huddled in the ashes sleeping.

He carried all three of them out to the edge of the wheat field.

"Molly. Molly, wake up! Kids! Kids, wake up!"

They breathed and didn't move and went on sleeping.

"Kids, wake up! Your mother is—"

Dead? No, not dead. But—

He shook the kids as if they were to blame. They paid no attention; they were busy with their dreams. He put them back down and stood over them, his face cut with lines.

He knew why they'd slept through the fire and continued to sleep now. He knew why Molly just lay there, never wanting to laugh again.

The power of the wheat and the scythe.

Their lives, supposed to end yesterday, May 30th, 1938, had been prolonged simply because he refused to cut the grain. They should have died in the fire. That's the way it was meant to *be*. But since he had not used the scythe, nothing could hurt them. A house had flamed and fallen and still they lived, caught halfway, not dead, not alive. Simply—waiting. And all over the world thousands more just like them, victims of accidents, fires, disease, suicide, waited, slept just like Molly and her children slept. Not able to die, not able to live. All because a man was afraid of harvesting the ripe grain. All because one man thought he could stop working with a scythe and never work with that scythe again.

He looked down upon the children. The job had to be done every day and every day with never a stopping but going on, with never a pause, but always the harvesting, forever and forever and forever.

All right, he thought. All right. I'll use the scythe.

He didn't say good-by to his family. He turned with a slow-feeding anger and found the scythe and walked rapidly, then he began to trot, then he ran with long jolting strides into the field, raving, feeling the hunger in his arms, as the wheat whipped and flailed his legs. He pounded through it, shouting. He stopped.

"Molly!" he cried, and raised the blade and swung it down.

"Susie!" he cried. "Drew!" And swung the blade down again.

Somebody screamed. He didn't turn to look at the fire-ruined house.

And then, sobbing wildly, he rose above the grain again and again and hewed to left and right and to left and to right and to left and to right. Over and over and over! Slicing out huge scars in green wheat and ripe wheat, with no selection and no care, cursing, over and over, swearing, laughing, the blade swinging up in the sun and falling in the sun with a singing whistle! Down!

Bombs shattered London, Moscow, Tokyo.

The blade swung insanely.

And the kilns of Belsen and Buchenwald took fire.

The blade sang, crimson wet.

And mushrooms vomited out blind suns at White Sands, Hiroshima, Bikini, and up, through, and in continental Siberian skies.

The grain wept in a green rain, falling.

Korea, Indo-China, Egypt, India trembled; Asia stirred, Africa woke in the night. . . .

And the blade went on rising, crashing, severing, with the fury and the rage of a man who has lost and lost so much that he no longer cares what he does to the world.

Just a few short miles off the main highway, down a rough dirt road that leads to nowhere, just a few short miles from a highway jammed with traffic bound for California.

Once in a while during the long years a jalopy gets off the main highway, pulls up steaming in front of the charred ruin of a little white house at the end of the dirt road, to ask instructions from the farmer they see just beyond, the one who works insanely, wildly, without ever stopping, night and day, in the endless fields of wheat.

But they get no help and no answer. The farmer in the field is too busy, even after all these years; too busy slashing and chopping the green wheat instead of the ripe.

And Drew Erickson moves on with his scythe, with the light of blind suns and a look of white fire in his never-sleeping eyes, on and on and on. . . .

UNCLE EINAR

"It will take only a minute," said Uncle Einar's sweet wife.

"I refuse," he said. "And that takes but a *second*."

"I've worked all morning," she said, holding to her slender back, "and you won't help? It's drumming for a rain."

"Let it rain," he cried, morosely. "I'll not be pierced by lightning just to air your clothes."

"But you're so quick at it."

"Again, I refuse." His vast tarpaulin wings hummed nervously behind his indignant back.

She gave him a slender rope on which were tied four dozen fresh-washed clothes. He turned it in his fingers with distaste. "So it's come to this," he muttered, bitterly. "To this, to this, to this." He almost wept angry and acid tears.

"Don't cry; you'll wet them down again," she said. "Jump up, now, run them about."

"Run them about." His voice was hollow, deep, and terribly wounded. "I say: let it thunder, let it pour!"

"If it was a nice, sunny day I wouldn't ask," she said, reasonably. "All my washing gone for nothing if you don't. They'll hang about the house—"

That *did* it. Above all, he hated clothes flagged and festooned so a man had to creep under on the way across a room. He jumped up. His vast green wings boomed. "Only so far as the pasture fence!"

Whirl: up he jumped, his wings chewed and loved the cool air. Before you'd say Uncle Einar Has Green Wings he sailed low across his farmland, trailing the clothes in a vast fluttering loop through the pounding concussion and back-wash of his wings!

"Catch!"

Back from the trip, he sailed the clothes, dry as popcorn, down on a series of clean blankets she'd spread for their landing.

"Thank you!" she cried.

"Gahh!" he shouted, and flew off under the apple tree to brood.

Uncle Einar's beautiful silk-like wings hung like sea-green sails behind him, and whirred and whispered from his shoulders when he sneezed or turned swiftly. He was one of the few in the Family whose talent was visible. All his dark cousins and nephews and brothers hid in small towns across the world, did unseen mental things or things with witch-fingers and white teeth, or blew down the sky like fire-leaves, or loped in forests like moon-silvered wolves. They lived comparatively safe from normal humans. Not so a man with great green wings.

Not that he hated his wings. Far from it! In his youth he'd always flown nights, because nights were rare times for winged men! Daylight held dangers, always had, always would; but nights, ah, nights, he had sailed over islands of cloud and seas of summer sky. With no danger to himself. It had been a rich, full soaring, an exhilaration.

But now he could not fly at night.

On his way home to some high mountain pass in Europe after a Homecoming among Family members in Mellin Town, Illinois (some years ago) he had drunk too much rich crimson wine. "I'll be all right," he had told himself, vaguely, as he beat his long way under the morning stars, over the moon-dreaming country hills beyond Mellin Town. And then—crack out of the sky—

A high-tension tower.

Like a netted duck! A great sizzle! His face blown black by a blue sparkler of wire, he fended off the electricity with a terrific back-jumping percussion of his wings, and fell.

His hitting the moonlit meadow under the tower made a noise like a large telephone book dropped from the sky.

Early the next morning, his dew-sodden wings shaking violently, he stood up. It was still dark. There was a faint bandage of dawn stretched across the east. Soon the bandage would stain and all flight would be restricted. There was nothing to do but take refuge in the forest and wait out the day in the deepest thicket until another night gave his wings a hidden motion in the sky.

In this fashion he met his wife.

During the day, which was warm for November first in Illinois country, pretty young Brunilla Wexley was out to udder a lost cow, for she carried a silver pail in one hand as she sidled through thickets and pleaded cleverly to the unseen cow to please return home or burst her gut with unplucked milk. The fact that the cow would have most certainly come home when her teats really needed pulling did not concern Brunilla Wexley. It was a sweet excuse for forest-journeying, thistle-blowing, and flower chewing; all of which Brunilla was doing as she stumbled upon Uncle Einar.

Asleep near a bush, he seemed a man under a green shelter.

"Oh," said Brunilla, with a fever. "A man. In a camp-tent."

Uncle Einar awoke. The camp-tent spread like a large green fan behind him.

"Oh," said Brunilla, the cow-searcher. "A man with wings."

That was how she took it. She was startled, yes, but she had never been hurt in her life, so she wasn't afraid of anyone, and it was a fancy thing to see a winged man and she was proud to meet him. She began to talk. In an hour they were old friends, and in two hours she'd quite forgotten his wings were there. And he somehow confessed how he happened to be in this wood.

"Yes, I noticed you looked banged around," she said. "That right wing looks very bad. You'd best let me take you home and fix it. You won't be able to fly all the way to Europe on it, anyway. And who wants to live in Europe these days?"

He thanked her, but he didn't quite see how he could accept.

"But I live alone," she said. "For, as you see, I'm quite ugly."

He insisted she was not.

"How kind of you," she said. "But I am, there's no fooling myself. My folks are dead, I've a farm, a big one, all to myself, quite far from Mellin Town, and I'm in need of talking company."

But wasn't she afraid of him? he asked.

"Proud and jealous would be more near it," she said. "*May*

I?" And she stroked his large green membraned veils with careful envy. He shuddered at the touch and put his tongue between his teeth.

So there was nothing for it but that he come to her house for medicaments and ointments, and my! what a burn across his face, beneath his eyes! "Lucky you weren't blinded," she said. "How'd it happen?"

"Well . . ." he said, and they were at her farm, hardly noticing they'd walked a mile, looking at each other.

A day passed, and another, and he thanked her at her door and said he must be going, he much appreciated the ointment, the care, the lodging. It was twilight and between now, six o'clock, and five the next morning, he must cross an ocean and a continent. "Thank you; good-by," he said, and started to fly off in the dusk and crashed right into a maple tree.

"Oh!" she screamed, and ran to his unconscious body.

When he waked the next hour he knew he'd fly no more in the dark again ever; his delicate night-perception was gone. The winged telepathy that had warned him where towers, trees, houses and hills stood across his path, the fine clear vision and sensibility that guided him through mazes of forest, cliff, and cloud, all were burnt forever by that strike across his face, that blue electric fry and sizzle.

"How?" he moaned softly. "How can I go to Europe? If I flew by day, I'd be seen and—miserable joke—maybe shot down! Or kept for a zoo perhaps, what a life *that'd* be! Brunilla, tell me, what shall I do?"

"Oh," she whispered, looking at her hands. "We'll think of something. . . ."

They were married.

The Family came for the wedding. In a great autumnal avalanche of maple, sycamore, oak, elm leaf they hissed and rustled, fell in a shower of horse-chestnut, thumped like winter apples on the earth, with an over-all scent of farewell-summer on the wind they made in their rushing. The ceremony? The ceremony was brief as a black candle lit, blown out, and smoke left still on the air. Its briefness, darkness, upside-down and backward quality escaped Brunilla, who only listened to the great tide of Uncle Einar's wings faintly murmuring above them as they finished out the rite. And as for Uncle Einar, the wound across his nose was almost healed and, holding Brunilla's arm, he felt Europe grow faint and melt away in the distance.

He didn't have to see very well to fly straight up, or come straight down. It was only natural that on this night of their wedding he take Brunilla in his arms and fly right up into the sky.

A farmer, five miles over, glanced at a low cloud at midnight, saw faint glows and crackles.

"Heat lightning," he observed, and went to bed.

They didn't come down till morning, with the dew.

The marriage took. She had only to look at him, and it lifted her to think she was the only woman in the world married to a winged man. "Who else could say it?" she asked her mirror. And the answer was: "No one!"

He, on the other hand, found great beauty behind her face, great kindness and understanding. He made some changes in his diet to fit her thinking, and was careful with his wings about the house; knocked porcelains and broken lamps were

239

nerve-scrapers, he stayed away from them. He changed his sleeping habits, since he couldn't fly nights now anyhow. And she in turn fixed chairs so they were comfortable for his wings, put extra padding here or took it out there, and the things she said were the things he loved her for. "We're in our cocoons, all of us. See how ugly I am?" she said. "But one day I'll break out, spread wings as fine and handsome as you."

"You broke out long ago," he said.

She thought it over. "Yes," she had to admit. "I know just which day it was, too. In the woods when I looked for a cow and found a tent!" They laughed, and with him holding her she felt so beautiful she knew their marriage had slipped her from her ugliness, like a bright sword from its case.

They had children. At first there was fear, all on his part, that they'd be winged.

"Nonsense, I'd love it!" she said, "Keep them out from under foot."

"Then," he exclaimed, "they'd be in your *hair*!"

"Ow!" she cried.

Four children were born, three boys and a girl, who, for their energy, seemed to have wings. They popped up like toadstools in a few years, and on hot summer days asked their father to sit under the apple tree and fan them with his cooling wings and tell them wild starlit tales of island clouds and ocean skies and textures of mist and wind and how a star tastes melting in your mouth, and how to drink cold mountain air, and how it feels to be a pebble dropped from Mt. Everest, turning to a green bloom, flowering your wings just before you strike bottom!

This was his marriage.

And today, six years later, here sat Uncle Einar, here he

was, festering under the apple tree, grown impatient and un-kind; not because this was his desire, but because after the long wait, he was still unable to fly the wild night sky; his extra sense had never returned. Here he sat despondently, nothing more than a summer sun-parasol, green and discarded, aban-doned for the season by the reckless vacationers who once sought the refuge of its translucent shadow. Was he to sit here forever, afraid to fly by day because someone might see him? Was his only flight to be as a drier of clothes for his wife, or a fanner of children on hot August noons? His one occupation had *always* been flying Family errands, quicker than storms. A boomerang, he'd whickled over hills and valleys and like a thistle, landed. He had always had money; the Family had good use for their winged man! But now? Bitterness! His wings jit-tered and whisked the air and made a captive thunder.

"Papa," said little Meg.

The children stood looking at his thought-dark face.

"Papa," said Ronald. "Make more thunder!"

"It's a cold March day, there'll soon be rain and plenty of thunder," said Uncle Einar.

"Will you come watch us?" asked Michael.

"Run on, run on! Let papa brood!"

He was shut of love, the children of love, and the love of children. He thought only of heavens, skies, horizons, infini-ties, by night or day, lit by star, moon, or sun, cloudy or clear, but always it was skies and heavens and horizons that ran ahead of you forever when you soared. Yet here he was, sculling the pasture, kept low for fear of being seen.

Misery in a deep well!

"Papa, come watch us; it's March!" cried Meg. "And we're going to the Hill with all the kids from town!"

Uncle Einar grunted. "What hill is that?"

"The Kite Hill, of course!" they all sang together.

Now he looked at them.

Each held a large paper kite, their faces sweating with anticipation and an animal glowing. In their small fingers were balls of white twine. From the kites, colored red and blue and yellow and green, hung caudal appendages of cotton and silk strips.

"We'll fly our kites!" said Ronald. "Won't you come?"

"No," he said, sadly. "I mustn't be seen by anyone or there'd be trouble."

"You could hide and watch from the woods." said Meg. "We made the kites ourselves. Just because we know how."

"How do you know how?"

"You're our father!" was the instant cry. "That's why!"

He looked at his children for a long while. He sighed. "A kite festival, is it?"

"Yes, sir!"

"I'm going to win," said Meg.

"No, *I'm!*" Michael contradicted.

"Me, *me!*" piped Stephen.

"God up the chimney!" roared Uncle Einar, leaping high with a deafening kettledrum of wings. "Children! Children, I love you dearly!"

"Father, what's wrong?" said Michael, backing off.

"Nothing, nothing, nothing!" chanted Einar. He flexed his wings to their greatest propulsion and plundering. Whoom! they slammed like cymbals. The children fell flat in the backwash! "I have it, I *have* it! I'm free again! Fire in the flue! Feather on the wind! Brunilla!" Einar called to the house. His wife appeared. "I'm free!" he called, flushed and tall, on his toes. "Listen, Brunilla, I don't need the night any more! I can fly by day! I don't need the night! I'll fly *every* day and *any* day of the year from now on!—but, God, I waste time, talking. Look!"

And as the worried members of his family watched, he seized the cotton tail from one of the little kites, tied it to his belt behind, grabbed the twine ball, held one end in his teeth, gave the other end to his children, and up, up into the air he flew, away into the March wind!

And across the meadows and over the farms his children ran, letting out string to the daylit sky, bubbling and stumbling, and Brunilla stood back in the farmyard and waved and laughed to see what was happening; and her children marched to the far Kite Hill and stood, the four of them, holding the ball of twine in their eager, proud fingers, each tugging and directing and pulling. And the children from Mellin Town came running with *their* small kites to let up on the wind, and they saw the great green kite leap and hover in the sky and exclaimed:

"Oh, oh, what a kite! What a kite! Oh, I wish I'd a kite like that! Where, where did you *get* it!"

"Our father made it!" cried Meg and Michael and Stephen and Ronald, and gave an exultant pull on the twine and the humming, thundering kite in the sky dipped and soared and made a great and magical exclamation mark across a cloud!

THE WIND

The phone rang at five-thirty that evening. It was December, and long since dark as Thompson picked up the phone.

"Hello."

"Hello, *Herb*?"

"Oh, it's you, Allin."

"Is your wife home, Herb?"

"Sure. Why?"

"Damn it."

Herb Thompson held the receiver quietly. "What's up? You sound funny."

"I wanted you to come over tonight."

"We're having company."

"I wanted you to spend the night. When's your wife going away?"

"That's next week," said Thompson. "She'll be in Ohio for about nine days. Her mother's sick. I'll come over then."

"I wish you could come over tonight."

"Wish I could. Company and all, my wife'd kill me."

"I wish you could come over."

"What's it? The wind again?"

"Oh, no. No."

245

"Is it the wind?" asked Thompson.

The voice on the phone hesitated. "Yeah. Yeah, it's the wind."

"It's a clear night, there's not much wind."

"There's enough. It comes in the window and blows the curtains a little bit. Just enough to tell me."

"Look, why don't you come and spend the night here?" said Herb Thompson looking around the lighted hall.

"Oh, no. It's too late for that. It might catch me on the way over. It's a damned long distance. I wouldn't dare, but thanks, anyway. It's thirty miles, but thanks."

"Take a sleeping-tablet."

"I've been standing in the door for the past hour, Herb. I can see it building up in the west. There are some clouds there and I saw one of them kind of rip apart. There's a wind coming, all right."

"Well, you just take a nice sleeping-tablet. And call me any time you want to call. Later this evening if you want."

"Any time?" said the voice on the phone.

"Sure."

"I'll do that, but I wish you could come out. Yet I wouldn't want you hurt. You're my best friend and I wouldn't want that. Maybe it's best I face this thing alone. I'm sorry I bother you."

"Hell, what's a friend for? Tell you what you do, sit down and get some writing done this evening," said Herb Thompson, shifting from one foot to the other in the hall. "You'll forget about the Himalayas and the Valley of the Winds and this pre-occupation of yours with storms and hurricanes. Get another chapter done on your next travel book."

"I might do that. Maybe I will, I don't know. Maybe I will. I might do that. Thanks a lot for letting me bother you."

"Thanks, hell. Get off the line, now, you. My wife's calling me to dinner."

Herb Thompson hung up.

He went and sat down at the supper table and his wife sat across from him. "Was that Allin?" she asked. He nodded. "Him and his winds that blow up and winds that blow down and winds that blow hot and blow cold," she said, handing him his plate heaped with food.

"He did have a time in the Himalayas, during the war," said Herb Thompson.

"You don't believe what he said about that valley, do you?"

"It makes a good story."

"Climbing around, climbing up things. Why do men climb mountains and scare themselves?"

"It was snowing," said Herb Thompson.

"Was it?"

"And raining and hailing and blowing all at once, in that valley. Allin's told me a dozen times. He tells it well. He was up pretty high. Clouds, and all. The valley made a noise."

"I *bet* it did," she said.

"Like a lot of winds instead of just one. Winds from all over the world." He took a bite. "So says Allin."

"He shouldn't have gone there and looked, in the first place," she said. "You go poking around and first thing you know you get ideas. Winds start getting angry at you for intruding, and they follow you."

"Don't joke, he's my best friend," snapped Herb Thompson.

"It's all so silly!"

"Nevertheless he's been through a lot. That storm in Bombay, later, and the typhoon off New Guinea two months after that. And that time, in Cornwall."

"I have no sympathy for a man who continually runs into wind storms and hurricanes, and then gets a persecution complex because of it."

The phone rang just then.

"Don't answer it," she said.

"Maybe it's important."

"It's only Allin, again."

They sat there and the phone rang nine times and they didn't answer. Finally, it quieted. They finished dinner. Out in the kitchen, the window curtains gently moved in the small breeze from a slightly opened window.

The phone rang again.

"I can't let it ring," he said, and answered it. "Oh, hello, Allin."

"Herb! It's here! It got here!"

"You're too near the phone, back up a little."

"I stood in the open door and waited for it. I saw it coming down the highway, shaking all the trees, one by one, until it shook the trees just outside the house and it dived down toward the door and I slammed the door in its face!"

Thompson didn't say anything. He couldn't think of anything to say, his wife was watching him in the hall door.

"How interesting," he said, at last.

"It's all around the house, Herb. I can't get out now, I can't do anything. But I fooled it, I let it think it had me, and just as it came down to get me I slammed and locked the door! I was ready for it, I've been getting ready for weeks."

"Have you, now; tell me about it, Allin, old man." Herb Thompson played it jovially into the phone, while his wife looked on and his neck began to sweat.

"It began six weeks ago. . . ."

"Oh, yes? Well, well."

". . . I thought I had it licked. I thought it had given up following and trying to get me. But it was just waiting. Six weeks ago I heard the wind laughing and whispering around the corners of my house, out here. Just for an hour or so, not very long, not very loud. Then it went away."

Thompson nodded into the phone. "Glad to hear it, glad to hear it." His wife stared at him.

"It came back, the next night. It slammed the shutters and kicked sparks out of the chimney. It came back five nights in a row, a little stronger each time. When I opened the front door, it came in at me and tried to pull me out, but it wasn't strong enough. Tonight it *is*."

"Glad to hear you're feeling better," said Thompson.

"I'm not better, what's wrong with you? Is your wife listening to us?"

"Yes."

"Oh, I see. I know I sound like a fool."

"Not at all. Go on."

Thompson's wife went back into the kitchen. He relaxed. He sat down on a little chair near the phone. "Go on, Allin, get it out of you, you'll sleep better."

"It's all around the house now, like a great big vacuum machine nuzzling at all the gables. It's knocking the trees around."

"That's funny, there's no wind *here*. Allin."

"Of course not, it doesn't care about you, only about me."

"I guess that's one way to explain it."

"It's a killer, Herb, the biggest damnedest prehistoric killer that ever hunted prey. A big sniffling hound, trying to smell me out, find me. It pushed its big cold nose up to the house, taking air, and when it finds me in the parlor it drives its pressure there, and when I'm in the kitchen it goes there. It's trying to get in the windows, now, but I had them reinforced and I put new hinges on the doors, and bolts. It's a strong house. They built them strong in the old days. I've got all the lights in the house on, now. The house is all lighted up, bright. The wind followed me from room to room, looking through all the windows, when I switched them on. Oh!"

"What's wrong?"

"It just snatched off the front screen door!"

"I wish you'd come over here and spend the night, Allin."

"I can't! God, I can't leave the house. I can't do anything. I know this wind. Lord, it's big and it's clever. I tried to light a cigarette a moment ago, and a little draft sucked the match out. The wind likes to play games, it likes to taunt me, it's taking its time with me; it's got all night. And now! God, right now, one of my old travel books, on the library table, I wish you could see it. A little breeze from God knows what small hole in the house, the little breeze is—blowing the pages one by one. I wish you could see it. There's my introduction. Do you remember the introduction to my book on Tibet, Herb?"

"Yes."

"*This book is dedicated to those who lost the game of elements, written by one who has seen, but who has always escaped.*"

"Yes, I remember."

"The lights have gone out!"

The phone crackled.

"The power lines just went down. Are you there, Herb?"

"I still hear you."

"The wind doesn't like all that light in my house, it tore

the power lines down. The telephone will probably go next. Oh, it's a real party, me and the wind, I tell you! Just a second."

"Allin?" A silence. Herb leaned against the mouthpiece. His wife glanced in from the kitchen. Herb Thompson waited. "Allin?"

"I'm back," said the voice on the phone. "There was a draft from the door and I shoved some wadding under it to keep it from blowing on my feet. I'm glad you didn't come out after all, Herb, I wouldn't want you in this mess. There! It just broke one of the living-room windows and a regular gale is in the house, knocking pictures off the wall! Do you hear it?"

Herb Thompson listened. There was a wild sirening on the phone and a whistling and banging. Allin shouted over it. "Do you hear it?"

Herb Thompson swallowed drily. "I hear it."

"It wants me alive, Herb. It doesn't dare knock the house down in one fell blow. That'd kill me. It wants me alive, so it can pull me apart, finger by finger. It wants what's inside me. My mind, my brain. It wants my life-power, my psychic force, my ego. It wants intellect."

"My wife's calling me, Allin. I have to go wipe the dishes."

"It's a big cloud of vapors, winds from all over the world. The same wind that ripped the Celebes a year ago, the same pampero that killed in Argentina, the typhoon that fed on Hawaii, the hurricane that knocked the coast of Africa early this year. It's part of all those storms I escaped. It followed me from the Himalayas because it didn't want me to know what I know about the Valley of the Winds where it gathers and plans its destruction. Something, a long time ago, gave it a start in the direction of life. I know its feeding grounds, I know where it is born and where parts of it expire. For that reason, it hates me; and my books that tell how to defeat it. It doesn't want me preaching any more. It wants to incorporate me into its huge body, to give it knowledge. It wants me on its own side!"

"I have to hang up, Allin, my wife—"

"What?" A pause, the blowing of the wind in the phone, distantly. "What did you say?"

"Call me back in about an hour, Allin."

He hung up.

He went out to wipe the dishes. His wife looked at him and he looked at the dishes, rubbing them with a towel.

"What's it like out tonight?" he said.

"Nice. Not very chilly. Stars," she said. "Why?"

"Nothing."

The phone rang three times in the next hour. At eight o'clock the company arrived, Stoddard and his wife. They sat around until eight-thirty talking and then got out and set up the card table and began to play Gin.

Herb Thompson shuffled the cards over and over, with a clittering, shuttering effect and clapped them out, one at a time before the three other players. Talk went back and forth. He lit a cigar and made it into a fine gray ash at the tip, and adjusted his cards in his hand and on occasion lifted his head and listened. There was no sound outside the house. His wife saw him do this, and he cut it out immediately, and discarded a Jack of Clubs.

He puffed slowly on his cigar and they all talked quietly with occasional small eruptions of laughter, and the clock in the hall sweetly chimed nine o'clock.

"Here we all are," said Herb Thompson, taking his cigar out and looking at it reflectively. "And life is sure funny."

"Eh?" said Mr. Stoddard.

"Nothing, except here we are, living our lives, and some place else on earth a billion other people live their lives."

"That's a rather obvious statement."

"Life," he put his cigar back in his lips, "is a lonely thing. Even with married people. Sometimes when you're in a person's arms you feel a million miles away from them."

"I like *that*," said his wife.

"I didn't mean it that way," he explained, not with haste; because he felt no guilt, he took his time. "I mean we all believe what we believe and live our own little lives while other people live entirely different ones. I mean, we sit here in this room while a thousand people are dying. Some of cancer, some of pneumonia, some of tuberculosis. I imagine someone in the United States is dying right now in a wrecked car."

"This isn't very stimulating conversation," said his wife.

"I mean to say, we all live and don't think about how other people think or live their lives or die. We wait until death comes *to* us. What I mean is here we sit, on our self-assured butt-bones, while, thirty miles away, in a big old house, completely surrounded by night and God-knows-what, one of the finest guys who ever lived is—"

"Herb!"

He puffed and chewed on his cigar and stared blindly at his cards. "Sorry." He blinked rapidly and bit his cigar. "Is it my turn?"

"It's your turn."

The playing went around the table, with a flittering of cards, murmurs, conversation. Herb Thompson sank lower into his chair and began to look ill.

The phone rang. Thompson jumped and ran to it and jerked it off the hook.

"Herb! I've been calling and calling. What's it like at your house, Herb?"

"What do you mean, what's it like?"

"Has the company come?"

"Hell, yes, it has—"

"Are you talking and laughing and playing cards?"

"Christ, yes, but what has that got to do with—"

"Are you smoking your ten-cent cigar?"

"God damn it, yes, but . . ."

"Swell," said the voice on the phone. "That sure is swell. I wish I could be there. I wish I didn't know the things I know. I wish lots of things."

"Are you all right?"

"So far, so good. I'm locked in the kitchen now. Part of the front wall of the house blew in. But I planned my retreat. When the kitchen door gives, I'm heading for the cellar. If I'm lucky I may hold out there until morning. It'll have to tear the whole damned house down to get to me, and the cellar floor is pretty solid. I have a shovel and I may dig—deeper. . . ."

It sounded like a lot of other voices on the phone.

"What's *that?*" Herb Thompson demanded, cold, shivering.

"That?" asked the voice on the phone. "Those are the voices of twelve thousand killed in a typhoon, seven thousand killed by a hurricane, three thousand buried by a cyclone. Am I boring you? That's what the wind is. It's a lot of people dead. The wind killed them, took their minds to give itself intelligence. It took all their voices and made them into one voice. All those millions of people killed in the past ten thousand years, tortured and run from continent to continent on the backs and in the bellies of monsoons and whirlwinds. Oh Christ, what a poem you could write about it!"

The phone echoed and rang with voices and shouts and whinings.

"Come on back, Herb," called his wife from the card table.

"That's how the wind gets more intelligent each year, it adds to itself, body by body, life by life, death by death."

"We're waiting for you, Herb," called his wife.

"Damn it!" He turned, almost snarling. "Wait just a moment, won't you!" Back to the phone. "Allin, if you want me to come out there now, I will! I should have come earlier . . ."

"Wouldn't think of it. This is a grudge fight, wouldn't do to have you in it now. I'd better hang up. The kitchen door looks bad; I'll have to get in the cellar."

"Call me back, later?"

"Maybe, if I'm lucky. I don't think I'll make it. I slipped away and escaped so many times, but I think it has me now. I hope I haven't bothered you too much, Herb."

"You haven't bothered anyone, damn it. Call me back."

"I'll try. . . ."

Herb Thompson went back to the card game. His wife glared at him. "How's Allin, your friend?" she asked, "Is he sober?"

"He's never taken a drink in his life," said Thompson, sullenly, sitting down. "I should have gone out there hours ago."

"But he's called every night for six weeks and you've been out there at least ten nights to stay with him and nothing was wrong."

"He needs help. He might hurt himself."

"You were just out there, two nights ago, you can't always be running after him."

"First thing in the morning I'll move him into a sanatorium. Didn't want to. He seems so reasonable otherwise."

At ten-thirty coffee was served. Herb Thompson drank his slowly, looking at the phone. I wonder if he's in the cellar now, he thought.

Herb Thompson walked to the phone, called long-distance, gave the number.

"I'm sorry," said the operator. "The lines are down in that district. When the lines are repaired, we will put your call through."

"Then the telephone lines *are* down!" cried Thompson. He let the phone drop. Turning, he slammed open the closet door, pulled out his coat. "Oh Lord," he said. "Oh, Lord, Lord," he said, to his amazed guests and his wife with the coffee urn in her hand. "Herb!" she cried. "I've got to get out there!" he said, slipping into his coat.

There was a soft, faint stirring at the door.

Everybody in the room tensed and straightened up.

"Who could that be?" asked his wife.

The soft stirring was repeated, very quietly.

Thompson hurried down the hall where he stopped, alert.

Outside, faintly, he heard laughter.

"I'll be damned," said Thompson. He put his hand on the doorknob, pleasantly shocked and relieved. "I'd know that laugh anywhere. It's Allin. He came on over in his car, after all. Couldn't wait until morning to tell me his confounded stories." Thompson smiled weakly. "Probably brought some friends with him. Sounds like a lot of other . . ."

He opened the front door.

The porch was empty.

Thompson showed no surprise; his face grew amused and sly. He laughed. "Allin? None of your tricks now! Come on."

He switched on the porch-light and peered out and around. "Where are you, Allin? Come on, now."

A breeze blew into his face.

Thompson waited a moment, suddenly chilled to his marrow. He stepped out on the porch and looked uneasily, and very carefully, about.

A sudden wind caught and whipped his coat flaps, disheveled his hair. He thought he heard laughter again. The wind rounded the house and was a pressure everywhere at once, and then, storming for a full minute, passed on.

The wind died down, sad, mourning in the high trees, passing away; going back out to the sea, to the Celebes, to the Ivory Coast, to Sumatra and Cape Horn, to Cornwall and the Philippines. Fading, fading, fading.

Thompson stood there, cold. He went in and closed the door and leaned against it, and didn't move, eyes closed.

"What's wrong . . . ?" asked his wife.

THE MAN UPSTAIRS

He remembered how carefully and expertly Grandmother would fondle the cold cut guts of the chicken and withdraw the marvels therein; the wet shining loops of meat-smelling intestine, the muscled lump of heart, the gizzard with the collection of seeds in it. How neatly and nicely Grandma would slit the chicken and push her fat little hand in to deprive it of its medals. These would be segregated, some in pans of water, others in paper to be thrown to the dog later, perhaps. And then the ritual of taxidermy, stuffing the bird with watered, seasoned bread, and performing surgery with a swift, bright needle, stitch after pulled-tight stitch.

This was one of the prime thrills of Douglas's eleven-year-old life span.

Altogether, he counted twenty knives in the various squeaking drawers of the magic kitchen table from which Grandma, a kindly, gentle-faced, white-haired old witch, drew paraphernalia for her miracles.

Douglas was to be quiet. He could stand across the table from Grandmama, his freckled nose tucked over the edge, watching, but any loose boy-talk might interfere with the spell. It was a wonder when Grandma brandished silver shakers over the bird, supposedly sprinkling showers of mummy-dust and pulverized Indian bones, muttering mystical verses under her toothless breath.

"Grammy," said Douglas at last, breaking the silence, "Am I like that inside?" He pointed at the chicken.

"Yes," said Grandma. "A little more orderly and presentable, but just about the same. . . ."

"And more *of* it!" added Douglas, proud of his guts.

"Yes," said Grandma. "More of it."

"Grandpa has lots more'n me. His sticks out in front so he can rest his elbows on it."

Grandma laughed and shook her head.

Douglas said, "And Lucie Williams, down the street, she . . ."

"Hush, child!" cried Grandma.

"But she's got . . ."

"Never you mind what she's got! That's different."

"But why is *she* different?"

"A darning-needle dragon-fly is coming by some day and sew up your mouth," said Grandma firmly.

Douglas waited, then asked, "How do you know I've got insides like that, Grandma?"

"Oh, go 'way, now!"

The front doorbell rang.

Through the front-door glass as he ran down the hall, Douglas saw a straw hat. The bell jangled again and again. Douglas opened the door.

"Good morning, child, is the landlady at home?"

Cold gray eyes in a long, smooth, walnut-colored face gazed upon Douglas. The man was tall, thin, and carried a suitcase, a brief case, an umbrella under one bent arm, gloves rich and thick and gray on his thin fingers, and wore a horribly new straw hat.

Douglas backed up. "She's busy."

"I wish to rent her upstairs room, as advertised."

"We've got ten boarders, and it's already rented; go away!"

"Douglas!" Grandma was behind him suddenly. "How do you do?" she said to the stranger. "Never mind this child."

Unsmiling, the man stepped stiffly in. Douglas watched them ascend out of sight up the stairs, heard Grandma detailing the conveniences of the upstairs room. Soon she hurried down to pile linens from the linen closet on Douglas and send him scooting up with them.

Douglas paused at the room's threshold. The room was changed oddly, simply because the stranger had been in it a moment. The straw hat lay brittle and terrible upon the bed, the umbrella leaned stiff against one wall like a dead bat with dark moist wings folded.

Douglas blinked at the umbrella.

The stranger stood in the center of the changed room, tall, tall.

"Here!" Douglas littered the bed with supplies. "We eat at noon sharp, and if you're late coming down the soup'll get cold. Grandma fixes it so it will, every time!"

The tall strange man counted out ten new copper pennies and tinkled them in Douglas' blouse pocket. "We shall be friends," he said, grimly.

It was funny, the man having nothing but pennies. Lots of them. No silver at all, no dimes, no quarters. Just new copper pennies.

Douglas thanked him glumly. "I'll drop these in my dime bank when I get them changed into a dime. I got six dollars and fifty cents in dimes all ready for my camp trip in August."

"I must wash now," said the tall strange man.

Once, at midnight, Douglas had wakened to hear a storm rumbling outside—the cold hard wind shaking the house, the rain driving against the window. And then a lightning bolt had landed outside the window with a silent, terrific concussion. He remembered that fear of looking about at his room, seeing it strange and awful in the instantaneous light.

So it was, now, in this room. He stood looking up at the stranger. This room was no longer the same, but changed inde-finably because this man, quick as a lightning bolt, had shed his light about it. Douglas backed up slowly as the stranger advanced.

The door closed in his face.

The wooden fork went up with mashed potatoes, came down empty. Mr. Koberman, for that was his name, had brought the wooden fork and wooden knife and spoon with him when Grandma called lunch.

"Mrs. Spaulding," he had said, quietly, "my own cutlery; please use it. I will have lunch today, but from tomorrow on, only breakfast and supper."

Grandma bustled in and out, bearing steaming tureens of soup and beans and mashed potatoes to impress her new boarder, while Douglas sat rattling his silverware on his plate, because he had discovered it irritated Mr. Koberman.

"I know a trick," said Douglas. "Watch." He picked a fork-tine with his fingernail. He pointed at various sectors of the table, like a magician. Wherever he pointed, the sound of the vibrating fork-tine emerged, like a metal elfin voice. Simply done, of course. He pressed the fork handle on the table-top, secretly. The vibration came from the wood like a sounding board. It looked quite magical. "There, there, and *there!*" exclaimed Douglas, happily plucking the fork again. He pointed at Mr. Koberman's soup and the noise came from it.

Mr. Koberman's walnut-colored face became hard and firm and awful. He pushed the soup bowl away violently, his lips twisting. He fell back in his chair.

Grandma appeared. "Why, what's wrong, Mr. Koberman?"

"I cannot eat this soup."

"Why?"

"Because I am full and can eat no more. Thank you."

Mr. Koberman left the room, glaring.

"What did you do, just then?" asked Grandma at Douglas, sharply.

"Nothing. Grandma, why does he eat with *wooden* spoons?"

"Yours not to question! When do you go back to school, anyway?"

"Seven weeks."

"Oh, my land!" said Grandma.

Mr. Koberman worked nights. Each morning at eight he arrived mysteriously home, devoured a very small breakfast, and then slept soundlessly in his room all through the dreaming hot daytime, until the huge supper with all the other boarders at night.

Mr. Koberman's sleeping habits made it necessary for Douglas to be quiet. This was unbearable. So, whenever Grandma visited down the street, Douglas stomped up and down stairs beating a drum, bouncing golf balls, or just screaming for three minutes outside Mr. Koberman's door, or flushing the toilet seven times in succession.

Mr. Koberman never moved. His room was silent, dark. He did not complain. There was no sound. He slept on and on. It was very strange.

Douglas felt a pure white flame of hatred burn inside himself with a steady, unflickering beauty. Now that room was Koberman Land. Once it had been flowery bright when Miss Sadlowe lived there. Now it was stark, bare, cold, clean, everything in its place, alien and brittle.

Douglas climbed upstairs on the fourth morning.

Halfway to the second floor was a large sun-filled window, framed by six-inch panes of orange, purple, blue, red and burgundy glass. In the enchanted early mornings when the sun fell through to strike the landing and slide down the stair banister, Douglas stood entranced at this window peering at the world through the multicolored windows.

Now a blue world, a blue sky, blue people, blue streetcars and blue trotting dogs.

He shifted panes. Now—an amber world! Two lemonish women glided by, resembling the daughters of Fu Manchu! Douglas giggled. This pane made even the sunlight more purely golden.

It was eight A.M. Mr. Koberman strolled by below, on the sidewalk, returning from his night's work, his cane looped over his elbow, straw hat glued to his head with patent oil.

Douglas shifted panes again. Mr. Koberman was a red man walking through a red world with red trees and red flowers and—something else.

Something about—Mr. Koberman.

Douglas squinted.

The red glass *did* things to Mr. Koberman. His face, his suit, his hands. The clothes seemed to melt away. Douglas almost believed, for one terrible instant, that he could see *inside* Mr. Koberman. And what he saw made him lean wildly against the small red pane, blinking.

Mr. Koberman glanced up just then, saw Douglas, and raised his cane-umbrella angrily, as if to strike. He ran swiftly across the red lawn to the front door.

"Young man!" he cried, running up the stairs. "What were you doing?"

"Just looking," said Douglas, numbly.

"That's all, is it?" cried Mr. Koberman.

"Yes, sir. I look through all the glasses. All kinds of worlds. Blue ones, red ones, yellow ones. All different."

"All kinds of worlds, is it!" Mr. Koberman glanced at the little panes of glass, his face pale. He got hold of himself. He wiped his face with a handkerchief and pretended to laugh. "Yes. All kinds of worlds. All different." He walked to the door of his room. "Go right ahead; play," he said.

The door closed. The hall was empty. Mr. Koberman had gone in.

Douglas shrugged and found a new pane.

"Oh, everything's violet!"

Half an hour later, while playing in his sandbox behind the house, Douglas heard the crash and the shattering tinkle. He leaped up.

A moment later, Grandma appeared on the back porch, the old razor strop trembling in her hand.

"Douglas! I told you time and again never fling your basketball against the house! Oh, I could just cry!"

"I been sitting right here," he protested.

"Come see what you've done, you nasty boy!"

The great colored window panes lay shattered in a rainbow chaos on the upstairs landing. His basketball lay in the ruins.

Before he could even begin telling his innocence, Douglas was struck a dozen stinging blows upon his rump. Wherever he landed, screaming, the razor strop struck again.

Later, hiding his mind in the sandpile like an ostrich, Douglas nursed his dreadful pains. He knew who'd thrown that basketball. A man with a straw hat and a stiff umbrella and a cold, gray room. Yeah, yeah, yeah. He dribbled tears. Just wait. Just *wait*.

He heard Grandma sweeping up the broken glass. She brought it out and threw it in the trash bin. Blue, pink, yellow meteors of glass dropped brightly down.

When she was gone, Douglas dragged himself, whimpering, over to save out three pieces of the incredible glass. Mr. Koberman disliked the colored windows. These—he clinked them in his fingers—would be worth saving.

Grandfather arrived from his newspaper office each night, shortly ahead of the other boarders, at five o'clock. When a slow, heavy tread filled the hall, and a thick, mahogany cane thumped in the cane-rack, Douglas ran to embrace the large stomach and sit on Grandpa's knee while he read the evening paper.

"Hi, Grampa!"

"Hello, down there!"

"Grandma cut chickens again today, It's fun watching," said Douglas.

Grandpa kept reading. "That's twice this week, chickens. She's the chickenist woman. You like to watch her cut 'em, eh? Cold-blooded little pepper! Ha!"

"I'm just curious."

"You are," rumbled Grandpa, scowling. "Remember that day when that young lady was killed at the rail station. You just walked over and looked at her, blood and all." He laughed. "Queer duck. Stay that way. Fear nothing, ever in your life. I guess you get it from your father, him being a military man and all, and you so close to him before you came here to live last year." Grandpa returned to his paper.

A long pause. "Gramps?"

"Yes?"

"What if a man didn't have a heart or lungs or stomach but still walked around, alive?"

"That," rumbled Gramps, "would be a miracle."

"I don't mean a—a miracle. I mean, what if he was all *different* inside. Not like me."

"Well, he wouldn't be quite human then, would he, boy?"

"Guess not, Gramps. Gramps, you got a heart and lungs?"

Gramps chuckled. "Well, tell the truth, I don't *know*. Never seen them. Never had an X-ray, never been to a doctor. Might as well be potato-solid for all I know."

"Have *I* got a stomach?"

"You certainly have!" cried Grandma from the parlor entry. " 'Cause I feed it! And you've lungs, you scream loud enough to wake the crumblees. And you've dirty hands, go wash them! Dinner's ready. Grandpa, come on. Douglas, git!"

In the rush of boarders streaming downstairs, Grandpa, if he intended questioning Douglas further about the weird conversation, lost his opportunity. If dinner delayed an instant more, Grandma and the potatoes would develop simultaneous lumps.

The boarders, laughing and talking at the table—Mr. Koberman silent and sullen among them—were silenced when Grandfather cleared his throat. He talked politics a few minutes and then shifted over into the intriguing topic of the recent peculiar deaths in the town.

"It's enough to make an old newspaper editor prick up his ears," he said, eying them all. "That young Miss Larsson, lived across the ravine, now. Found her dead three days ago for no reason, just funny kinds of tattoos all over her, and a facial expression that would make Dante cringe. And that other young lady, what was her name? Whitely? She disappeared and *never did* come back."

"Them things happen alla time," said Mr. Britz, the garage mechanic, chewing. "Ever peek inna Missing Peoples Bureau file? It's *that* long." He illustrated. "Can't tell *what* happens to most of 'em."

"Anyone want more dressing?" Grandma ladled liberal portions from the chicken's interior. Douglas watched, thinking about how that chicken had had two kinds of guts—God-made and Man-made.

Well, how about *three* kinds of guts?

Eh?

Why not?

Conversation continued about the mysterious death of so-

268

and-so, and, oh, yes, remember a week ago, Marion Barsumian died of heart failure, but maybe that didn't connect up? or did it? you're crazy! forget it, why talk about it at the dinner table? So.

"Never can tell," said Mr. Britz. "Maybe we got a vampire in town."

Mr. Koberman stopped eating.

"In the year 1927?" said Grandma. "A vampire? Oh, go on, now."

"Sure," said Mr. Britz. "Kill 'em with silver bullets. Anything silver for that matter. Vampires *hate* silver. I read it in a book somewhere, once. Sure, I did."

Douglas looked at Mr. Koberman who ate with wooden knives and forks and carried only new copper pennies in his pocket.

"It's poor judgment," said Grandpa, "to call anything by a name. We don't know what a hobgoblin or a vampire or a troll is. Could be lots of things. You can't heave them into categories with labels and say they'll act one way or another. That'd be silly. They're people. People who do things. Yes, that's the way to put it: people who *do* things."

"Excuse me," said Mr. Koberman, who got up and went out for his evening walk to work.

The stars, the moon, the wind, the clock ticking, and the chiming of the hours into dawn, the sun rising, and here it was another morning, another day, and Mr. Koberman coming along the sidewalk from his night's work. Douglas stood off like a small mechanism whirring and watching with carefully microscopic eyes.

At noon, Grandma went to the store to buy groceries.

As was his custom every day when Grandma was gone, Douglas yelled outside Mr. Koberman's door for a full three minutes. As usual, there was no response. The silence was horrible.

He ran downstairs, got the pass-key, a silver fork, and the three pieces of colored glass he had saved from the shattered window. He fitted the key to the lock and swung the door slowly open.

The room was in half light, the shades drawn. Mr. Koberman lay atop his bedcovers, in slumber clothes, breathing gently, up and down. He didn't move. His face was motionless.

"Hello, Mr. Koberman!"

The colorless walls echoed the man's regular breathing.

"Mr. Koberman, hello!"

Bouncing a golf ball, Douglas advanced. He yelled. Still no answer. "Mr. Koberman!"

Bending over Mr. Koberman, Douglas picked the tines of the silver fork in the sleeping man's face.

Mr. Koberman winced. He twisted. He groaned bitterly.

Response. Good. Swell.

Douglas drew a piece of blue glass from his pocket. Looking through the blue glass fragment he found himself in a blue room, in a blue world different from the world he knew. As different as was the red world. Blue furniture, blue bed, blue ceiling and walls, blue wooden eating utensils atop the blue bureau, and the sullen dark blue of Mr. Koberman's face and arms and his blue chest rising, falling. Also . . .

Mr. Koberman's eyes were wide, staring at him with a hungry darkness.

Douglas fell back, pulled the blue glass from his eyes.

Mr. Koberman's eyes were shut.

Blue glass again—open. Blue glass away—shut. Blue glass again—open. Away—shut. Funny. Douglas experimented, trembling. Through the glass the eyes seemed to peer hungrily, avidly through Mr. Koberman's closed lids. Without the blue glass they seemed tightly shut.

But it was the rest of Mr. Koberman's body. . . .

Mr. Koberman's bedclothes dissolved off him. The blue glass had something to do with it. Or perhaps it was the clothes themselves, just being *on* Mr. Koberman. Douglas cried out.

He was looking through the wall of Mr. Koberman's stomach, right *inside* him!

Mr. Koberman was solid.

Or, nearly so, anyway.

There were strange shapes and sizes within him.

Douglas must have stood amazed for five minutes, thinking about the blue worlds, the red worlds, the yellow worlds side by side, living together like glass panes around the big white stair window. Side by side, the colored panes, the different worlds; Mr. Koberman had said so himself.

So this was why the colored window had been broken.

"Mr. Koberman, wake up!"

No answer.

"Mr. Koberman, where do you work at night? Mr. Koberman, where do you work?"

A little breeze stirred the blue window shade.

"In a red world or a green world or a yellow one, Mr. Koberman?"

Over everything was a blue glass silence.

"Wait there," said Douglas.

He walked down to the kitchen, pulled open the great squeaking drawer and picked out the sharpest, biggest knife.

Very calmly he walked into the hall, climbed back up the stairs again, opened the door to Mr. Koberman's room, went in, and closed it, holding the sharp knife in one hand.

Grandma was busy fingering a piecrust into a pan when Douglas entered the kitchen to place something on the table.

"Grandma, what's this?"

She glanced up briefly, over her glasses. "I don't know."

It was square, like a box, and elastic. It was bright orange in color. It had four square tubes, colored blue, attached to it. It smelled funny.

"Ever see anything like it, Grandma?"

"No."

"That's what *I* thought."

Douglas left it there, went from the kitchen. Five minutes later he returned with something else. "How about *this*?"

He laid down a bright pink linked chain with a purple triangle at one end.

"Don't bother me," said Grandma. "It's only a chain."

Next time he turned with two hands full. A ring, a square, a triangle, a pyramid, a rectangle, and—other shapes. All of them were pliable, resilient, and looked as if they were made of gelatin. "This isn't all," said Douglas, putting them down. "There's more where this came from."

Grandma said, "Yes, yes," in a far-off tone, very busy.

"You were wrong, Grandma."

"About what?"

"About all people being the same inside."

"Stop talking nonsense."

"Where's my piggy-bank?"

"On the mantel, where you left it."

"Thanks."

He tromped into the parlor, reached up for his piggy-bank.
Grandpa came home from the office at five.

"Grandpa, come upstairs."

"Sure, son. Why?"

"Something to show you. It's not nice; but it's interesting."

Grandpa chuckled, following his grandson's feet up to Mr.
Koberman's room.

"Grandma mustn't know about this; she wouldn't like it,"
said Douglas. He pushed the door wide open. "There."

Grandfather gasped.

Douglas remembered the next few hours all the rest of his life.
Standing over Mr. Koberman's naked body, the coroner and his
assistants. Grandma, downstairs, asking somebody, "What's going on up there?" and Grandpa saying, shakily, "I'll take Douglas away on a long vacation so he can forget this whole ghastly
affair. Ghastly, ghastly affair!"

Douglas said, "Why should it be bad? I don't see anything
bad. I don't feel bad."

The coroner shivered and said, "Koberman's dead, all
right."

His assistant sweated. "Did you see those *things* in the pans
of water and in the wrapping paper?"

"Oh, my God, my God, yes, I saw them."

"Christ."

The coroner bent over Mr. Koberman's body again. "This
better be kept secret, boys. It wasn't murder. It was a mercy the
boy acted. God knows what might have happened if he hadn't."

"What was Koberman? A vampire? A monster?"

"Maybe. I don't know. Something—not human." The coroner moved his hands deftly over the suture.

Douglas was proud of his work. He'd gone to much trouble. He had watched Grandmother carefully and remembered. Needle and thread and all. All in all, Mr. Koberman was as neat a job as any chicken ever popped into hell by Grandma.

"I heard the boy say that Koberman lived even after all those *things* were taken out of him." The coroner looked at the triangles and chains and pyramids floating in the pans of water. "Kept on *living*. God."

"Did the boy say that?"

"He did."

"Then, what *did* kill Koberman?"

The coroner drew a few strands of sewing thread from their bedding.

"This. . . ." he said.

Sunlight blinked coldly off a half-revealed treasure trove; six dollars and seventy cents' worth of silver dimes inside Mr. Koberman's chest.

"I think Douglas made a wise investment," said the coroner, sewing the flesh back up over the "dressing" quickly.

THERE WAS AN OLD WOMAN

"**N**o, there's no lief arguin'. I got my mind fixed. Run along with your silly wicker basket. Land, where you ever get notions like that? You just skit out of here; don't bother me, I got my tattin' and knittin' to do, and no never minds about tall, dark gentlemen with fangled ideas."

The tall, dark young man stood quietly, not moving. Aunt Tildy hurried on with her talk.

"You *heard* what I said! If you got a mind to talk to me, well, you can talk, but meantime I hope you don't mind if I pour myself coffee. There. If you'd been more polite, I'd offer you some, but you jump in here high and mighty and you never rapped on the door or nothin'. You think you *own* the place."

Aunt Tildy fussed with her lap. "Now, you made me lose count! I'm makin' myself a comforter. These winters get on mighty chill, and it ain't fittin' for a lady with bones like rice-paper to be settin' in a drafty old house without warmin' herself."

The tall, dark man sat down.

"That's an antique chair, so be gentle," warned Aunt Tildy. "Start again, tell me things you got to tell, I'll listen respectful. But keep your voice in your shoes and stop starin' at me with funny lights in your eyes. Land, it gives me the collywobbles."

The bone-porcelain, flowered clock on the mantel finished chiming three. Out in the hall, grouped around the wicker basket, four men waited, quietly, as if they were frozen.

"Now, about that wicker basket," said Aunt Tildy. "It's past six feet long, and by the look, it ain't laundry. And those four men you walked in with, you don't need them to carry that basket—why, it's light as thistles. Eh?"

The dark young man was leaning forward on the antique chair. Something in his face suggested the basket wouldn't be so light after a while.

"Pshaw," Aunt Tildy mused. "Where've I seen a wicker like that before? Seems it was only a couple years ago. Seems to me—oh! Now I remember. It was when Mrs. Dwyer passed away next door."

Aunt Tildy set her coffee cup down, sternly. "So *that's* what you're up to? I thought you were workin' to sell me somethin'. You just set there until my little Emily trounces home from college this afternoon! I wrote her a note last week. Not admittin', of course, that I wasn't feelin' quite ripe and pert, but sort of hintin' I want to see her again, it's been a good many weeks. Her livin' in New York and all. Almost like my own daughter, Emily is.

"Now, she'll take care of you, young man. She'll shoo you out'n this parlor so quick it'll—"

The dark young man looked at Aunt Tildy as if she were tired.

"No, I'm *not*!" she snapped.

He weaved back and forth on the chair, half-shutting his eyes, resting himself. O, wouldn't she like to rest, too? he seemed to murmur. Rest, rest, nice rest. . . .

"Great sons of Goshen on the Gilberry Dike! I got a hunderd comforters, two hunderd sweaters and six hunderd potholders in these fingers, no matter they're skinny! You run off, come back when I'm done, maybe I'll talk to you." Aunt Tildy shifted subjects. "Let me tell you about Emily, my sweet, fair child."

Aunt Tildy nodded thoughtfully. Emily, with hair like yellow corn tassels, just as soft and fine.

"I well remember the day her mother died, twenty years ago, leavin' Emily to my house. That's why I'm mad at you and your wickers and such goings-on. Who ever heard of people dyin' for any good cause? Young man, I don't *like* it. Why, I remember—"

Aunt Tildy paused; a brief pain of memory touched her heart. Twenty-five years back, her father's voice trembled in the late afternoon:

"Tildy," he whispered, "what you goin' to *do* in life? The way you act, men don't walk much with you. You kiss and skedaddle. Why won't you settle down, marry, raise children?"

"Papa," Tildy shouted back at him, "I like laughin' and playin' and singin'. I'm not the marryin' kind. I can't find a man with my philosophy, Papa."

"What 'philosophy's' that?"

"That death is ridiculous! It run off with Mama when we needed her most. You call *that* intelligent?"

Papa's eyes got wet and gray and bleak. "You're always right, Tildy. But what can we do? Death comes to everybody."

"Fight!" she cried. "Strike it below the belt! Don't *believe* in it!"

"Can't be done," said Papa sadly. "We all stand alone in the world."

"There's got to be a change sometime, Papa. I'm startin'

my own philosophy here and now! Why, it's silly people live a couple years and are shoved like wet seeds in a hole; but nothin' sprouts. What good do they do? Lay there a million years, helpin' no one. Most of them fine, nice, neat people, or at least tryin'."

But Papa wasn't listening. He bleached out, faded away, like a photo left lying in the sun. She tried to talk him out of it, but he passed on, anyway. She spun about and ran. She couldn't stay on once he was cold, for his coldness denied her philosophy. She didn't attend his burial. She didn't do anything but set up this antique shop on the front of an old house and live alone for years, that is, until Emily came. Tildy didn't want to take the girl in. Why? Because Emily believed in dying. But her mother was an old friend and Tildy had promised help.

"Emily," continued Aunt Tildy, to the man in black, "was the first to live in this house with me in all the years. I never got married. I feared the idea of livin' with a man twenty-thirty years and then have him up and die on me. It'd shake my convictions like a house of cards. I shied off from the world. I screamed at people if they so much as mentioned death."

The young man listened patiently, politely. Then he lifted his hand. He seemed to know everything, with the dark, cold shining of his eyes, before she opened her mouth. He knew about her and World War II, when she shut off her radio forever and stopped the newspapers and beat a man's head with an umbrella, driving him from her shop when he insisted on describing the invasion beaches and the long, slow tides of the dead drifting under the silent urgings of the moon.

Yes, the dark young man smiled from the antique rocker, he knew how Aunt Tildy had stuck to her nice old phonograph records. Harry Lauder singing "Roamin' in the Gloamin'," Madame Schumann-Heink and lullabies. With no interruptions, no foreign calamities, murders, poisonings, auto accidents, suicides. Music stayed the same each day, every day. So the years ran, while Aunt Tildy tried to teach Emily her philosophy. But Emily's mind was fixed on mortality. She respected Aunt Tildy's way of thinking, however, and never mentioned—eternity.

All this the young man knew.

Aunt Tildy sniffed. "How do you know all those things? Well, if you think you can talk me into that silly wicker basket, you're way off the trestle. You lay hands on me, I'll spit right *in* your face!"

The young man smiled. Aunt Tildy sniffed again.

"Don't simper like a sick dog. I'm too old to be made love at. That's all twisted dry, like an old tube of paint, and left behind in the years."

There was a noise. The mantel clock chimed three. Aunt Tildy flashed her eyes to it. Strange. Hadn't it chimed three o'clock just five minutes ago? She liked the bone-white clock with gold angels dangling naked about its numeraled face and its tone like cathedral bells, soft and far away.

"Are you just goin' to *sit* there, young man?"

He was.

"Then, you won't mind if I take a little cat nap. Now, don't you stir off that chair. Don't come creepin' around me. Just goin' to close my eyes for a spell. That's right. That's right. . . ."

Nice and quiet and restful time of day. Silence. Just the clock ticking away, busy as termites in wood. Just the old room smelling of polished mahogany and oiled leather in the morris chair, and books sitting stiff on the shelves. So nice. Nice. . . .

"You aren't getting' up from the chair, are you, mister? Better not. I got one eye open for you. Yes, indeed I have. Yes, I have. Oh. Ah, hmmmm."

So feathery. So drowsy. So deep. Under water, almost. Oh, so nice.

Who's that movin' around in the dark with my eyes closed?

Who's that kissin' my cheek? You, Emily? No. No. Guess it was my thoughts. Only—dreamin'. Land, yes, that's it. Driftin' off, off, off. . . .

AH? WHAT SAY? OH!

"Wait while I put on my glasses. There!"

The clock chimed three again. Shame, old clock, now, shame. Have to have you fixed.

The young man in the dark suit stood near the door. Aunt Tildy nodded.

"You leavin' so soon, young man? Had to give up, didn't you? Couldn't convince me; no, I'm mule-stubborn. Never get me free of this house, so don't bother comin' back to try!"

The young man bowed with slow dignity.

He had no intention of coming again, ever.

"Fine," declared Aunt Tildy. "I always told Papa I'd win! Why, I'll knit in this window the next thousand years. They'll have to chew the boards down around me to get me out."

The dark young man twinkled his eyes.

"Quit lookin' like the cat that ate the bird," cried Aunt Tildy. "Get that old fool wicker away!"

The four men trod heavily out the front door. Tildy studied the way they handled an empty basket, yet staggered with its weight.

"Here, now!" She rose in tremulous indignation. "Did you steal my antiques? My books? The clocks? What you got in that wicker?"

The dark young man whistled jauntily, turning his back to her, walking along behind the four staggering men. At the door he pointed to the wicker, offered its lid to Aunt Tildy. In pantomime he wondered if she would like to open it and gaze inside.

"Curious? Me? Pshaw, no. Get out!" cried Aunt Tildy.

The dark young man tapped a hat onto his head, saluted her crisply.

"Good-by!" Aunt Tildy slammed the door.

There, there. That was better. Gone. Darned fool men with their maggoty ideas. No never minds about the wicker. If they stole something, she didn't care, long as they let her alone.

"Look." Aunt Tildy smiled. "Here comes Emily, home from college. About time. Lovely girl. See how she walks. But, land, she looks pale and funny today, walkin' so slow. I wonder why. Looks worried, she does. Poor girl. I'll just fix some coffee and a tray of cakes."

Emily tapped up the front steps. Aunt Tildy, rustling around, could hear the slow, deliberate steps. What *ailed* the girl? Didn't sound like she had no more spunk than a flue-lizard. The front door swung wide. Emily stood in the hall, holding to the brass doorknob.

"Emily?" called Aunt Tildy.

Emily shuffled into the parlor, head down.

"Emily! I been waitin' for you! There was the darndest fool men here with a wicker. Tryin' to sell me something I didn't want. Glad you're home. Makes it right cozy—"

Aunt Tildy realized that for a full minute Emily had been staring.

"Emily, what's wrong? Stop starin'. Here, I'll bring you a cup of coffee. There!

"Emily, why you backin' away from me?

"Emily, stop screamin', child. Don't scream, Emily! Don't! You keep screamin' that way, you go crazy. Emily, get up off the floor, get away from that wall! Emily! Stop cringin', child. I won't hurt you!

"Land, if it ain't one thing it's another.

"Emily, what's *wrong*, child . . ."

Emily groaned through her hands over her face.

"Child, child," whispered Aunt Tildy. "Here, sip this water. Sip it, Emily, that's it."

Emily widened her eyes, saw something, then shut them, quivering, pulling into herself. "Aunt Tildy, Aunt Tildy, Aunt—"

"Stop that!" Tildy slapped her. "What *ails* you?"

Emily forced herself to look up again.

She thrust her fingers out. They vanished inside Aunt Tildy.

"What fool notion!" cried Tildy. "Take your hand away! Take it, I say!"

Emily dropped aside, jerked her head, the golden hair shaking into shiny temblors. "You're not here, Aunt Tildy. I'm dreaming. You're dead!"

"Hush, baby."

"You *can't* be here."

"Land of Goshen, Emily—"

She took Emily's hand. It passed clean through her. Instantly, Aunt Tildy raised straight up, stomping her foot.

"Why, why!" she cried angrily. "That—fibber! That sneak-thief!" Her thin hands knotted to wiry, hard, pale fists. "That dark, dark fiend! He stole it! He toted it away, he did, oh he did, he did! Why, I—" Wrath steamed in her. Her pale blue eyes were fire. She sputtered into an indignant silence. Then she turned to Emily. "Child, get up! I need you!"

Emily lay, quivering.

"Part of me's here!" declared Aunt Tildy. "By the Lord Harry, what's left will have to do, for a bit. Fetch my bonnet!"

Emily confessed. "I'm scared."

"Certainly, oh, certainly not of *me?*"

"Yes."

"Why, I'm no spook! You known me most of your life! Now's no time to snivel-sop. Fetch up on your heels or I'll slap you crack across your nose!"

Emily rose, in sobs, stood like something cornered, trying to decide which direction to bolt in.

"Where's your car, Emily?"

"Down at the garage—ma'am."

"Good!" Aunt Tildy hustled her through the front door. "Now—" Her sharp eyes poked up and down the streets. "Which way's the mortuary?"

Emily held to the step rail, fumbling down. "What're you going to do, Aunt Tildy?"

"Do?" cried Aunt Tildy, tottering after her, jowls shaking in a thin, pale fury. "Why, get my body back, of course! Get my body back! Go on!"

The car roared, Emily clenched to the steering wheel, staring straight ahead at the curved, rain-wet streets. Aunt Tildy shook her parasol.

"Hurry, child, hurry, before they squirt juices in my body

and dice and cube it the way them persnickety morticians have a habit of doin'. They cut and sew it so it ain't no good to no one!"

"Oh, Auntie, Auntie, let me go, don't make me drive! It won't do any good, no good at all," sighed the girl.

"Here we are." Emily pulled to the curb, and collapsed over the wheel, but Aunt Tildy had already popped from the car and trotted with mincing skirt up the mortuary drive, around behind to where the shiny black hearse was unloading a wicker basket.

"You!" she directed her attack at one of the four men with the wicker. "Put that down!"

The four men looked up.

One said, "Step aside, lady. We're doing our job."

"That's my body tucked in there!" She brandished the parasol.

"That I wouldn't know anything about," said a second man. "Please don't block traffic, madam. This thing is heavy."

"Sir!" she cried, wounded. "I'll have you know I weigh only one hundred and ten pounds."

He looked at her casually. "I'm not interested in your heft, lady. I'm due home for supper. My wife'll kill me if I'm late."

The four of them moved on, Aunt Tildy in pursuit, down a hall, into a preparations room.

A white-smocked man awaited the wicker's arrival with a rather pleased smile on his long, eager-looking face. Aunt Tildy didn't care for the avidity of that face, or the entire personality of the man. The basket was deposited, the four men wandered off.

The man in the white smock glanced at Auntie and said:

"Madam, this is no fit place for a gentlewoman."

"Well," she said, gratified, "glad you feel that way. It's exactly what I tried to tell that dark-clothed young man!"

The mortician puzzled. "What dark-clothed young man is that?"

"The one that came puddlin' around my house, that's who."

"No one of that description works for us."

"No matter. As you just so intelligently stated, this is no place for a lady. I don't want me here. I want me home cookin' ham for Sunday visitors, it's near Easter. I got Emily to feed, sweaters to knit, clocks to wind—"

"You are quite philosophical, and philanthropical, no doubt of it, madam, but I have work. A body has arrived." This last, he said with apparent relish, and a winnowing of his knives, tubes, jars, and instruments.

Tildy bristled. "You put so much as a fingerprint on that body, and I'll—"

He laid her aside like a little old moth. "George," he called with a suave gentleness, "escort this lady out, please."

Aunt Tildy glared at the approaching George.

"Show me your backside, goin' the other way!"

George took her wrists. "This way, please."

Tildy extricated herself. Easily. Her flesh sort of—slipped. It even amazed Tildy. Such an unexpected talent to develop at this late day.

"See?" she said, pleased with her ability. "You can't budge me. I want my body back!"

The mortician opened the wicker lid casually. Then, in a recurrent series of scrutinies he realized the body inside was . . .

it seemed . . . could it be? . . . maybe . . . yes . . . no . . . no . . . it just *couldn't* be, but . . . "Ah," he exhaled, abruptly. He turned. His eyes were wide, then they narrowed.

"Madam," he said, cautiously. "This lady here is—a—relative—of yours?"

"A very dear relation. Be careful of her."

"A sister, perhaps?" He grasped at a straw of dwindling logic, hopefully.

"No, you fool. Me, do you hear? *Me!*"

The mortician considered the idea. "No," he said. "Things like this don't happen." He fumbled with his tools. "George, get help from the others. I can't work with a crank present."

The four men returned. Aunt Tildy crossed her arms in defiance. "Won't budge!" she cried, as she was moved like a pawn on a chessboard, from preparations room to slumber room, to hall, to waiting chamber, to funeral parlor, where she threw herself down on a chair in the very center of the vestibule. There were pews going back into gray silence, and a smell of flowers.

"Please, ma'am," said one of the men. "That's where the body rests for the service tomorrow."

"I'm sittin' right plumb here until I get what I want."

She sat, pale fingers fussing with the lace at her throat, jaw set, one high-buttoned shoe tapping with irritation. If a man got in whopping distance, she gave him a parasol whop. And when they touched her, now, she remembered to—slip away.

Mr. Carrington, Mortuary President, heard the disturbance in his office and came toddling down the aisle to investigate. "Here, here," he whispered to everyone, finger to mouth.

"More respect, more respect. What is this? Oh, madam, may I help you?"

She looked him up and down. "You may."

"How may I be of service, please?"

"Go in that room back there," directed Aunt Tildy.

"Yee-ess."

"And tell that eager young investigator to quit fiddlin' with my body. I'm a maiden lady. My moles, birthmarks, scars, and other bric-a-brac, including the turn of my ankle, are my own secret. I don't want him pryin' and probin', cuttin', or hurtin' it any way."

This was vague to Mr. Carrington, who hadn't correlated bodies yet. He looked at her in blank helplessness.

"He's got me in there on his table, like a pigeon ready to be drawn and stuffed!" she told him.

Mr. Carrington hustled off to check. After fifteen minutes of waiting silence and horrified arguing, comparing notes with the mortician behind closed doors, Carrington returned, three shades whiter.

Carrington dropped his glasses, picked them up. "You're making it difficult for us."

"*I* am?" raged Aunt Tildy. "Saint Vitus in the mornin'! Looky here, Mister Blood and Bones or whatever, you tell that—"

"We're already draining the blood from the—"

"What!"

"Yes, yes, I assure you, yes. So, you just go away, now; there's nothing to be done." He laughed nervously. "Our mortician is also performing a brief autopsy to determine cause of death."

Auntie jumped to her feet, burning.

"He can't do that! Only coroners are allowed to do that!"

"Well, we sometimes allow a little—"

"March straight in and tell that Cut-'em-up to pump all that fine New England blue blood right back into that fine-skinned body, and if he's taken anything out, for him to attach it back in so it'll function proper, and then turn that body, fresh as paint, into my keepin'. You hear!"

"There's nothing I can do. Nothing."

"Tell you *what*. I'm settin' here for the next two hunderd years. You listenin'? And every time any of your customers come by, I'll spit ectoplasm right squirt up their nostrils!"

Carrington groped that thought around his weakening mind and emitted a groan. "You'd ruin our business. You wouldn't do that."

Auntie smiled. "*Wouldn't I?*"

Carrington ran up the dark aisle. In the distance you could hear him dialing a phone over and over again. Half an hour later cars roared up in front of the mortuary. Three vice-presidents of the mortuary came down the aisle with their hysterical president.

"What seems to be the trouble?"

Auntie told them with a few well-chosen infernalities.

They held a conference, meanwhile notifying the mortician to discontinue his homework, at least until such time as an agreement was reached. . . . The mortician walked from his chamber and stood smiling amiably, smoking a big black cigar.

Auntie stared at the cigar.

"Where'd you put the *ashes*?" she cried, in horror.

The mortician only grinned imperturbably and puffed.

The conference broke up.

"Madam, in all fairness, you wouldn't force us out on the street to continue our services, would you?"

Auntie scanned the vultures. "Oh, I wouldn't mind at all."

Carrington wiped sweat from his jowls. "You can have your body back."

"Ha!" shouted Auntie. Then, with caution: "Intact?"

"Intact."

"No formaldehyde?"

"No formaldehyde."

"Blood in it?"

"Blood, my God, yes, blood, if only you'll take it and go!"

A prim nod. "Fair enough. Fix 'er up. It's a deal."

Carrington snapped his fingers at the mortician. "Don't *stand* there, you mental incompetent. Fix it up!"

"And be careful with that cigar!" said the old woman.

"Easy, easy," said Aunt Tildy. "Put the wicker on the floor where I can step in it."

She didn't look at the body much. Her only comment was, "Natural-lookin'." She let herself fall back into the wicker.

A biting sensation of arctic coldness gripped her, followed by an unlikely nausea and a giddy whorling. She was two drops of matter fusing, water trying to seep into concrete. Slow to do. Hard. Like a butterfly trying to squirm back into a discarded husk of flinty chrysalis!

The vice-presidents watched Aunt Tildy with apprehension. Mr. Carrington wrung his fingers and tried to assist with boosting and pushing moves of his hands and arms. The mortician, frankly skeptical, watched with idle, amused eyes.

Seeping into cold, long granite. Seeping into a frozen and ancient statue. Squeezing all the way.

"Come alive, damn ye!" shouted Aunt Tildy to herself. "Raise up a bit."

The body half-rose, rustling in the dry wicker.

"Fold your legs, woman!"

The body grabbled up, blindly groping.

"See!" shouted Aunt Tildy.

Light entered the webbed blind eyes.

"Feel!" urged Aunt Tildy.

The body felt the warmth of the room, the sudden reality of the preparations table on which to lean, panting.

"Move!"

The body took a creaking, slow step.

"Hear!" she snapped.

The noises of the place came into the dull ears. The harsh, expectant breath of the mortician, shaken; the whimpering Mr. Carrington; her own crackling voice.

"Walk!" she said.

The body walked.

"Think!" she said.

The old brain thought.

"Speak!" she said.

The body spoke, bowing to the morticians:

"Much obliged. Thank you."

"Now," she said, finally, "cry!"

And she began to cry tears of utter happiness.

And now, any afternoon about four, if you want to visit Aunt Tildy, you just walk around to her antique shop and rap.

There's a big, black funeral wreath on the door. Don't mind that! Aunt Tildy left it there; that's how her humor runs. You rap on the door. It's double-barred and triple-locked, and when you rap her voice shrills out at you.

"Is that the man in black?"

And you laugh and say no, no, it's only me, Aunt Tildy.

And she laughs and says, "Come on in, quick!" and she whips the door open and slams it shut behind, so no man in black can ever slip in with you. Then she sets you down and pours your coffee and shows you her latest knitted sweater. She's not as fast as she used to be, and can't see as good, but she gets on.

"And if you're 'specially good," Aunt Tildy declares, setting her coffee cup to one side, "I'll give you a little treat."

"What's that?" visitors will ask.

"This," says Auntie, pleased with her little uniqueness, her little joke.

Then with modest moves of her fingers she will unfasten the white lace at her neck and chest and for a brief moment show what lies beneath.

The long blue scar where the autopsy was neatly sewn together.

"Not bad sewin' for a man," she allows. "Oh, some more coffee? *There!*"

THE CISTERN

t was an afternoon of rain, and lamps lighted against the gray. For a long while the two sisters had been in the dining-room. One of them, Juliet, embroidered tablecloths; the younger, Anna, sat quietly on the window seat, staring out at the dark street and the dark sky.

Anna kept her brow pressed against the pane, but her lips moved and after reflecting a long moment, she said, "I never thought of that before."

"Of what?" asked Juliet.

"It just came to me. There's actually a city under a city. A dead city, right here, right under our feet."

Juliet poked her needle in and out the white cloth. "Come away from the window. That rain's done something to you."

"No, really. Didn't you ever think of the cisterns before? They're all through the town, there's one for every street, and you can walk in them without bumping your head, and they go everywhere and finally go down to the sea," said Anna, fascinated with the rain on the asphalt pavement out there and the rain falling from the sky and vanishing down the gratings at each corner of the distant intersection. "Wouldn't you like to live in a cistern?"

293

"I would not!"

"But wouldn't it be fun—I mean, very secret? To live in the cistern and peek up at people through the slots and see them and them not see you? Like when you were a child and played hide-and-seek and nobody found you, and there you were in their midst all the time, all sheltered and hidden and warm and excited. I'd like that. That's what it must be like to live in the cistern."

Juliet looked slowly up from her work. "You *are* my sister, aren't you, Anna? You *were* born, weren't you? Sometimes, the way you talk, I think Mother found you under a tree one day and brought you home and planted you in a pot and grew you to this size and there you are, and you'll never change."

Anna didn't reply, so Juliet went back to her needle. There was no color in the room; neither of the two sisters added any color to it. Anna held her head to the window for five minutes. Then she looked way off into the distance and said, "I guess you'd call it a dream. While I've been here, the last hour, I mean. Thinking. Yes, Juliet, it was a dream."

Now it was Juliet's turn not to answer.

Anna whispered. "All this water put me to sleep awhile, I guess, and then I began to think about the rain and where it came from and where it went and how it went down those little slots in the curb, and then I thought about deep under, and suddenly there *they* were. A man . . . and a woman. Down in that cistern, under the road."

"What would they be doing there?" asked Juliet.

Anna said, "Must they have a reason?"

"No, not if they're insane, no," said Juliet. "In that case no reasons are necessary. There they are in their cistern, and let them stay."

"But they aren't just in the cistern," said Anna, knowingly, her head to one side, her eyes moving under the half-down lids. "No, they're in love, these two."

"For heaven's sake," said Juliet, "did love make them crawl down there?"

"No, they've been there for years and years," said Anna.

"You can't tell me they've been in that cistern for years, living together," protested Juliet.

"Did I say they were alive?" asked Anna, surprised. "Oh, but no. They're dead."

The rain scrambled in wild, pushing pellets down the window. Drops came and joined with others and made streaks.

"Oh," said Juliet.

"Yes," said Anna, pleasantly. "Dead. He's dead and she's dead." This seemed to satisfy her; it was a nice discovery, and she was proud of it. "He looks like a very lonely man who never traveled in all his life."

"How do you know?"

"He looks like the kind of man who never traveled but wanted to. You know by his eyes."

"You know what he looks like, then?"

"Yes. Very ill and very handsome. You know how it is with a man made handsome by illness? Illness brings out the bones in the face."

"And he's dead?" asked the older sister.

"For five years." Anna talked softly, with her eyelids rising and falling, as if she were about to tell a long story and knew it and wanted to work into it slowly, and then faster and then faster, until the very momentum of the story would carry her on, with her eyes wide and her lips parted. But now it was slowly, with only a slight fever to the telling. "Five years ago this man was walking along a street and he knew he'd been walking the same street on many nights and he'd go on walking it, so he came to a manhole cover, one of those big iron waffles in the center of the street, and he heard the river rushing under his feet, under the metal cover, rushing toward the sea." Anna put out her right hand. "And he bent slowly and lifted up the cistern lid and looked down at the rushing foam and the water, and he thought of someone he wanted to love and couldn't, and then he swung himself onto the iron rungs and walked down them until he was all gone. . . ."

"And what about her?" asked Juliet, busy. "When'd she die?"

"I'm not sure. She's new. She's just dead, now. But she *is* dead. Beautifully, beautifully dead." Anna admired the image she had in her mind. "It takes death to make a woman really beautiful, and it takes death by drowning to make her most beautiful of all. Then all the stiffness is taken out of her, and her hair hangs up on the water like a drift of smoke." She nodded her head, amusedly. "All the schools and etiquettes and teachings in the world can't make a woman move with this dreamy ease, supple and ripply and fine." Anna tried to show how fine, how ripply, how graceful, with her broad, coarse hand.

"He'd been waiting for her, for five years. But she hadn't known where he was till now. So there they are, and will be, from now on. . . . In the rainy season they'll live. But in the dry seasons—that's sometimes months—they'll have long rest periods, they'll lie in little hidden niches, like those Japanese water flowers, all dry and compact and old and quiet."

Juliet got up and turned on yet another little lamp in the corner of the dining-room. "I wish you wouldn't talk about it."

Anna laughed. "But let me tell you about how it starts,

how they come back to life. I've got it all worked out." She bent forward, held onto her knees, staring at the street and the rain and the cistern mouths. "There they are, down under, dry and quiet, and up above the sky gets electrical and powdery." She threw back her dull, graying hair with one hand. "At first all the upper world is pellets. Then there's lightning and then thunder and the dry season is over, and the little pellets run along the gutters and get big and fall into the drains. They take gum wrappers and theatre tickets with them, and bus transfers!"

"Come away from that window, now."

Anna made a square with her hands and imagined things. "I know just what it's like under the pavement, in the big square cistern. It's huge. It's all empty from the weeks with nothing but sunshine. It echoes if you talk. The only sound you can hear standing down there is an auto passing above. Far up above. The whole cistern is like a dry, hollow camel bone in a desert, waiting."

She lifted her hand, pointing, as if she herself were down in the cistern, waiting. "Now, a little trickle. It comes down on the floor. It's like something was hurt and bleeding up in the outer world. There's some thunder! Or was it a truck going by?"

She spoke a little more rapidly now, but held her body relaxed against the window, breathing out, and in the next words: "It seeps down. Then, into all the other hollows come other seepages. Little twines and snakes. Tobacco-stained water. Then it moves. It joins others. It makes snakes and then one big constrictor which rolls along on the flat, papered floor. From everywhere, from the north and south, from other streets, other streams come and they join and make one hissing and shining coil. And the water writhes into those two little dry niches I told you about. It rises slowly around those two, the man and the woman, lying there like Japanese flowers."

She clasped her hands, slowly, working finger into finger, interlacing.

"The water soaks into them. First, it lifts the woman's hand. In a little move. Her hand's the only live part of her. Then her arm lifts and one foot. And her hair . . ." she touched her own hair as it hung about her shoulders, ". . . unloosens and opens out like a flower in the water. Her shut eyelids are blue. . . ."

The room got darker, Juliet sewed on, and Anna talked and told all she saw in her mind. She told how the water rose and took the woman with it, unfolding her out and loosening her and standing her full upright in the cistern. "The water is interested in the woman, and she lets it have its way. After a long time of lying still, she's ready to live again, any life the water wants her to have."

Somewhere else, the man stood up in the water also. And Anna told of that, and how the water carried him slowly, drifting, and her, drifting, until they met each other. "The water opens their eyes. Now they can see but not see each other. They circle, not touching yet." Anna made a little move of her head, eyes closed. "They watch each other. They glow with some kind of phosphorus. They smile. . . . They—touch hands."

At last Juliet, stiffening, put down her sewing and stared at her sister, across the gray, rain-silent room.

"Anna!"

"The tide—makes them touch. The tide comes and puts them together. It's a perfect kind of love, with no ego to it, only two bodies, moved by the water, which makes it clean and all right. It's not wicked, this way."

"It's bad you're saying it!" cried her sister.

"No, it's all right," insisted Anna, turning for an instant. "They're not thinking, are they? They're just so deep down and quiet and not caring."

She took her right hand and held it over her left hand very slowly and gently, quavering and interweaving them. The rainy window, with the pale spring light penetrating, put a movement of light and running water on her fingers, made them seem submerged, fathoms deep in gray water, running one about the other as she finished her little dream:

"Him, tall and quiet, his hands open." She showed with a gesture how tall and how easy he was in the water. "Her, small and quiet and relaxed." She looked at her sister, leaving her hands just that way. "They're dead, with no place to go, and no one to tell them. So there they are, with nothing applying to them and no worries, very secret and hidden under the earth in the cistern waters. They touch their hands and lips and when they come into a cross-street outlet of the cistern, the tide rushes them together. Then, later . . ." she disengaged her hands, ". . . maybe they travel together, hand in hand, bobbling and floating, down all the streets, doing little crazy upright dances when they're caught in sudden swirls." She whirled her hands about, a drenching of rain spatted the window. "And they go down to the sea, all across the town, past cross drain and cross drain, street and street. Genesee Avenue, Crenshaw, Edmond Place, Washington, Motor City, Ocean Side and then the ocean. They go anywhere the water wants them, all over the earth, and come back later to the cistern inlet and float back up under the town, under a dozen tobacco shops and four dozen liquor stores, and six dozen groceries and ten theatres, a rail junction, Highway 101, under the walking feet of thirty thousand people who don't even know or think of the cistern."

Anna's voice drifted and dreamed and grew quiet again.

"And then—the day passes and the thunder goes away up on the street. The rain stops. The rain season's over. The tunnels drip and stop. The tide goes down." She seemed disappointed, sad it was over. "The river runs out to the ocean. The man and woman feel the water leave them slowly to the floor. They settle." She lowered her hands in little bobblings to her lap, watching them fixedly, longingly. "Their feet lose the life the water has given them from outside. Now the water lays them down, side by side, and drains away, and the tunnels are drying. And there they lie. Up above, in the world, the sun comes out. There they lie, in the darkness, sleeping, until the next time. Until the next rain."

Her hands were now upon her lap, palms up and open. "Nice man, nice woman," she murmured. She bowed her head over them and shut her eyes tight.

Suddenly Anna sat up and glared at her sister. "Do you know who the man is?" she shouted, bitterly.

Juliet did not reply; she had watched, stricken, for the past five minutes while this thing went on. Her mouth was twisted and pale. Anna almost screamed:

"The man is Frank, that's who he is! And *I'm* the woman!"

"Anna!"

"Yes, it's Frank, down there!"

"But Frank's been gone for years, and certainly not down there, Anna!"

Now, Anna was talking to nobody, and to everybody, to Juliet, to the window, the wall, the street. "Poor Frank," she cried. "I know that's where he went. He couldn't stay anywhere in the world. His mother spoiled him for all the world! So he saw the cistern and saw how secret and fine it was. Oh, poor Frank. And poor Anna, poor me, with only a sister. Oh, Julie, why didn't I hold onto Frank when he was here? Why didn't I fight to win him from his mother?"

"Stop it, this minute, do you hear, this minute!"

Anna slumped down into the corner, by the window, one hand up on it, and wept silently. A few minutes later she heard her sister say, "Are you finished?"

"What?"

"If you're done, come help me finish this, I'll be forever at it."

Anna raised her head and glided over to her sister. "What do you want me to do?" she sighed.

"This and this," said Juliet, showing her.

"All right," said Anna, and took it and sat by the window looking at the rain, moving her hands with the needle and thread, but watching how dark the street was now, and the room, and how hard it was to see the round metal top of the cistern now—there were just little midnight gleams and glitters out there in the black black late afternoon. Lightning crackled over the sky in a web.

Half an hour passed. Juliet drowsed in her chair across the room, removed her glasses, placed them down with her work and for a moment rested her head back and dozed. Perhaps thirty seconds later she heard the front door open violently, heard the wind come in, heard the footsteps run down the walk, turn, and hurry along the black street.

"What?" asked Juliet, sitting up, fumbling for her glasses. "Who's there? Anna, did someone come in the door?" She stared at the empty window seat where Anna had been. "Anna!" she cried. She sprang up and ran out into the hall.

The front door stood open, rain fell through it in a fine mist.

"She's only gone out for a moment," said Juliet, standing there, trying to peer into the wet blackness. "She'll be right back. *Won't* you be right back, Anna dear? Anna, answer me, you *will* be right back, won't you, sister?"

Outside, the cistern lid rose and slammed down.

The rain whispered on the street and fell upon the closed lid all the rest of the night.

HOMECOMING

"Here they come," said Cecy, lying there flat in her bed.

"Where are they?" cried Timothy from the doorway.

"Some of them are over Europe, some over Asia, some of them over the Islands, some over South America!" said Cecy, her eyes closed, the lashes long, brown, and quivering.

Timothy came forward upon the bare plankings of the upstairs room. "Who are they?"

"Uncle Einar and Uncle Fry, and there's Cousin William, and I see Frulda and Helgar and Aunt Morgiana and Cousin Vivian, and I see Uncle Johann! They're all coming fast!"

"Are they up in the sky?" cried Timothy, his little gray eyes flashing. Standing by the bed, he looked no more than his fourteen years. The wind blew outside, the house was dark and lit only by starlight.

"They're coming through the air and traveling along the ground, in many forms," said Cecy, in her sleeping. She did not move on the bed; she thought inward on herself and told what she saw. "I see a wolflike thing coming over a dark river—at the shallows—just above a waterfall, the starlight shining up his pelt. I see a brown oak leaf blowing far up in the sky. I see a small bat flying. I see many other things, running through the forest trees and slipping through the highest branches; and they're *all* coming this way!"

"Will they be here by tomorrow night?" Timothy clutched the bedclothes. The spider on his lapel swung like a black pendulum, excitedly dancing. He leaned over his sister. "Will they all be here in time for the Homecoming?"

"Yes, yes, Timothy, yes," sighed Cecy. She stiffened. "Ask no more of me. Go away now. Let me travel in the places I like best."

"Thanks, Cecy," he said. Out in the hall, he ran to his room. He hurriedly made his bed. He had just awakened a few minutes ago, at sunset, and as the first stars had risen, he had gone to let his excitement about the party run with Cecy. Now she slept so quietly there was not a sound. The spider hung on a silvery lasso about Timothy's slender neck as he washed his face. "Just think, Spid, tomorrow night is Allhallows Eve!"

He lifted his face and looked into the mirror. His was the only mirror allowed in the house. It was his mother's concession to his illness. Oh, if only he were not so afflicted! He opened his mouth, surveyed the poor, inadequate teeth nature had given him. No more than so many corn kernels—round, soft and pale in his jaws. Some of the high spirit died in him.

It was now totally dark and he lit a candle to see by. He felt exhausted. This past week the whole family had lived in the fashion of the old country. Sleeping by day, rousing at sunset to move about. There were blue hollows under his eyes. "Spid, I'm no good," he said, quietly, to the little creature. "I can't even get used to sleeping days like the others."

He took up the candleholder. Oh, to have strong teeth, with incisors like steel spikes. Or strong hands, even, or a strong mind. Even to have the power to send one's mind out,

free, as Cecy did. But, no, he was the imperfect one, the sick one. He was even—he shivered and drew the candle flame closer—afraid of the dark. His brothers snorted at him. Bion and Leonard and Sam. They laughed at him because he slept in a bed. With Cecy it was different; her bed was part of her comfort for the composure necessary to send her mind abroad to hunt. But Timothy, did he sleep in the wonderful polished boxes like the others? He did not! Mother let him have his own bed, his own room, his own mirror. No wonder the family skirted him like a holy man's crucifix. If only the wings would sprout from his shoulder blades. He bared his back, stared at it. And sighed again. No chance. Never.

Downstairs were exciting and mysterious sounds, the slithering black crape going up in all the halls and on the ceilings and doors. The sputter of burning black tapers in the banistered stair well. Mother's voice, high and firm. Father's voice, echoing from the damp cellar. Bion walking from outside the old country house lugging vast two-gallon jugs.

"I've just got to go to the party, Spid," said Timothy. The spider whirled at the end of its silk, and Timothy felt alone. He would polish cases, fetch toadstools and spiders, hang crape, but when the party started he'd be ignored. The less seen or said of the imperfect son the better.

All through the house below, Laura ran.

"The Homecoming!" she shouted gaily. "The Homecoming!" Her footsteps everywhere at once.

Timothy passed Cecy's room again, and she was sleeping quietly. Once a month she went belowstairs. Always she stayed in bed. Lovely Cecy. He felt like asking her, "Where are you

now, Cecy? And *in* who? And what's happening? Are you beyond the hills? And what goes on there?" But he went on to
Ellen's room instead.

Ellen sat at her desk, sorting out many kinds of blond, red
and black hair and little scimitars of fingernail gathered from
her manicurist job at the Mellin Village beauty parlor fifteen
miles over. A sturdy mahogany case lay in one corner with her
name on it.

"Go away," she said, not even looking at him. "I can't
work with you gawking."

"Allhallows Eve, Ellen; just think!" he said, trying to be
friendly.

"Hunh!" She put some fingernail clippings in a small
white sack, labeled them. "What can it mean to you? What do
you know of it? It'll scare the hell out of you. Go back to bed."

His cheeks burned. "I'm needed to polish and work and
help serve."

"If you don't go, you'll find a dozen raw oysters in your bed
tomorrow," said Ellen, matter-of-factly. "Good-by, Timothy."

In his anger, rushing downstairs, he bumped into Laura.

"Watch where you're going!" she shrieked from clenched
teeth.

She swept away. He ran to the open cellar door, smelled
the channel of moist earthy air rising from below. "Father?"

"It's about time," Father shouted up the steps. "Hurry
down, or they'll be here before we're ready!"

Timothy hesitated only long enough to hear the million
other sounds in the house. Brothers came and went like trains
in a station, talking and arguing. If you stood in one spot long
enough the entire household passed with their pale hands full
of things. Leonard with his little black medical case, Samuel

with his large, dusty ebon-bound book under his arm, bearing more black crape, and Bion excursioning to the car outside and bringing in many more gallons of liquid.

Father stopped polishing to give Timothy a rag and a scowl. He thumped the huge mahogany box. "Come on, shine this up, so we can start on another. Sleep your life away."

While waxing the surface, Timothy looked inside.

"Uncle Einar's a big man, isn't he, Papa?"

"Unh."

"How big is he?"

"The size of the box'll tell you."

"I was only asking. Seven feet tall?"

"You talk a lot."

About nine o'clock Timothy went out into the October weather. For two hours in the now-warm, now-cold wind he walked the meadows collecting toadstools and spiders. His heart began to beat with anticipation again. How many relatives had Mother said would come? Seventy? One hundred? He passed a farmhouse. If only you knew what was happening at our house, he said to the glowing windows. He climbed a hill and looked at the town, miles away, settling into sleep, the town-hall clock high and round white in the distance. The town did not know, either. He brought home many jars of toadstools and spiders.

In the little chapel belowstairs a brief ceremony was celebrated. It was like all the other rituals over the years, with Father chanting the dark lines, Mother's beautiful white ivory hands moving in the reverse blessings, and all the children gathered except Cecy, who lay upstairs in bed. But Cecy was present. You saw her peering, now from Bion's eyes, now

Samuel's, now Mother's, and you felt a movement and now she was in you, fleetingly and gone.

Timothy prayed to the Dark One with a tightened stomach. "Please, please, help me grow up, help me be like my sisters and brothers. Don't let me be different. If only I could put the hair in the plastic images as Ellen does, or make people fall in love with me as Laura does with people, or read strange books as Sam does, or work in a respected job like Leonard and Bion do. Or even raise a family one day, as Mother and Father have done. . . ."

At midnight a storm hammered the house. Lightning struck outside in amazing, snow-white bolts. There was a sound of an approaching, probing, sucking tornado, funneling and nuzzling the moist night earth. Then the front door, blasted half off its hinges, hung stiff and discarded, and in trooped Grandmama and Grandpapa, all the way from the old country!

From then on people arrived each hour. There was a flutter at the side window, a rap on the front porch, a knock at the back. There were fey noises from the cellar; autumn wind piped down the chimney throat, chanting. Mother filled the large crystal punch bowl with a scarlet fluid poured from the jugs Bion had carried home. Father swept from room to room lighting more tapers. Laura and Ellen hammered up more wolfsbane. And Timothy stood amidst this wild excitement, no expression to his face, his hands trembling at his sides, gazing now here, now there. Banging of doors, laughter, the sound of liquid pouring, darkness, sound of wind, the webbed thunder of wings, the padding of feet, the welcoming bursts of talk at the entrances, the transparent rattlings of casements, the shadows passing, coming, going, wavering.

"Well, well, and *this* must be Timothy!"

"What?"

A chilly hand took his hand. A long hairy face leaned down over him. "A good lad, a fine lad," said the stranger.

"Timothy," said his mother. "This is Uncle Jason."

"Hello, Uncle Jason."

"And over here—" Mother drifted Uncle Jason away. Uncle Jason peered back at Timothy over his caped shoulder, and winked.

Timothy stood alone.

From off a thousand miles in the candled darkness, he heard a high fluting voice; that was Ellen. "And my brothers, they *are* clever. Can you guess their occupations, Aunt Morgiana?"

"I have no idea."

"They operate the undertaking establishment in town."

"What!" A gasp.

"Yes!" Shrill laughter. "Isn't that priceless!"

Timothy stood very still.

A pause in the laughter. "They bring home sustenance for Mama, Papa and all of us," said Laura. "Except, of course, Timothy. . . ."

An uneasy silence. Uncle Jason's voice demanded. "Well, come now. What about Timothy?"

"Oh, Laura, your tongue," said Mother.

Laura went on with it. Timothy shut his eyes. "Timothy doesn't—well—doesn't *like* blood. He's delicate."

"He'll learn," said Mother. "He'll learn," she said very firmly. "He's my son, and he'll learn. He's only fourteen."

"But I was raised on the stuff," said Uncle Jason, his voice passing from one room on into another. The wind played the trees outside like harps. A little rain spatted on the windows— "raised on the stuff," passing away into faintness.

Timothy bit his lips and opened his eyes.

"Well, it was all my fault." Mother was showing them into the kitchen now. "I tried forcing him. You can't force children, you only make them sick, and then they never get a taste for things. Look at Bion, now, he was thirteen before he . . ."

"I understand," murmured Uncle Jason. "Timothy will come around."

"I'm sure he will," said Mother, defiantly.

Candle flames quivered as shadows crossed and recrossed the dozen musty rooms. Timothy was cold. He smelled the hot tallow in his nostrils and instinctively he grabbed at a candle and walked with it around and about the house, pretending to straighten the crape.

"*Timothy*," someone whispered behind a patterned wall, hissing and sizzling and sighing the words, "*Timothy is afraid of the dark.*"

Leonard's voice. Hateful Leonard!

"I like the candle, that's all," said Timothy in a reproachful whisper.

More lightning, more thunder. Cascades of roaring laughter. Bangings and clickings and shouts and rustles of clothing. Clammy fog swept through the front door. Out of the fog, settling his wings, stalked a tall man.

"Uncle Einar!"

Timothy propelled himself on his thin legs, straight through the fog, under the green webbing shadows. He threw himself across Einar's arms. Einar lifted him.

"You've wings, Timothy!" He tossed the boy light as thistles. "Wings, Timothy: fly!" Faces wheeled under. Darkness rotated. The house blew away. Timothy felt breezelike. He flapped his arms. Einar's fingers caught and threw him once more to the ceiling. The ceiling rushed down like a charred wall. "Fly, Timothy!" shouted Einar, loud and deep. "Fly with wings! Wings!"

He felt an exquisite ecstasy in his shoulder blades, as if roots grew, burst to explode and blossom into new, moist membrane. He babbled wild stuff; again Einar hurled him high.

The autumn wind broke in a tide on the house, rain crashed down, shaking the beams, causing chandeliers to tilt their enraged candle lights. And the one hundred relatives peered out from every black, enchanted room, circling inward, all shapes and sizes, to where Einar balanced the child like a baton in the roaring spaces.

"Enough!" shouted Einar, at last.

Timothy, deposited on the floor timbers, exaltedly, exhaustedly fell against Uncle Einar, sobbing happily. "Uncle, uncle, uncle!"

"Was it good, flying? Eh, Timothy?" said Uncle Einar, bending down, patting Timothy's head. "Good, good."

It was coming toward dawn. Most had arrived and were ready to bed down for the daylight, sleep motionlessly with no sound until the following sunset, when they would shout out of their mahogany boxes for the revelry.

Uncle Einar, followed by dozens of others, moved toward the cellar. Mother directed them downward to the crowded row on row of highly polished boxes. Einar, his wings like seagreen tarpaulins tented behind him, moved with a curious whistling down the passageway; where his wings touched they made a sound of drumheads gently beaten.

Upstairs, Timothy lay wearily thinking, trying to like the

darkness. There was so much you could do in darkness that people couldn't criticize you for, because they never saw you. He *did* like the night, but it was a qualified liking: sometimes there was so much night he cried out in rebellion.

In the cellar, mahogany doors sealed downward, drawn in by pale hands. In corners, certain relatives circled three times to lie, heads on paws, eyelids shut. The sun rose. There was a sleeping.

Sunset. The revel exploded like a bat nest struck full, shrieking out, fluttering, spreading. Box doors banged wide. Steps rushed up from cellar damp. More late guests, kicking on front and back portals, were admitted.

It rained, and sodden visitors laid their capes, their water-pelleted hats, their sprinkled veils upon Timothy who bore them to a closet. The rooms were crowd-packed. The laughter of one cousin, shot from one room, angled off the wall of another, ricocheted, banked and returned to Timothy's ears from a fourth room, accurate and cynical.

A mouse ran across the floor.

"I know you, Niece Leibersrouter!" exclaimed Father, around him but not to him. The dozens of towering people pressed in against him, elbowed him, ignored him.

Finally, he turned and slipped away up the stairs.

He called softly. "Cecy. Where are you now, Cecy?"

She waited a long while before answering. "In the Imperial Valley," she murmured faintly. "Beside the Salton Sea, near the mud pots and the steam and the quiet. I'm inside a farmer's wife. I'm sitting on a front porch. I can make her move if I want, or do anything or think anything. The sun's going down."

"What's it like, Cecy?"

"You can hear the mud pots hissing," she said, slowly, as if speaking in a church. "Little gray heads of steam push up the mud like bald men rising in the thick syrup, head first, out in the broiling channels. The gray heads rip like rubber fabric, collapse with noises like wet lips moving. And feathery plumes of steam escape from the ripped tissue. And there is a smell of deep sulphurous burning and old time. The dinosaur has been abroiling here ten million years."

"Is he done yet, Cecy?"

The mouse spiraled three women's feet and vanished into a corner. Moments later a beautiful woman rose up out of nothing and stood in the corner, smiling her white smile at them all.

Something huddled against the flooded pane of the kitchen window. It sighed and wept and tapped continually, pressed against the glass, but Timothy could make nothing of it, he saw nothing. In imagination he was outside staring in. The rain was on him, the wind at him, and the taper-dotted darkness inside was inviting. Waltzes were being danced; tall thin figures pirouetted to outlandish music. Stars of light flickered off lifted bottles; small clods of earth crumbled from casques, and a spider fell and went silently legging over the floor.

Timothy shivered. He was inside the house again. Mother was calling him to run here, run there, help, serve, out to the kitchen now, fetch this, fetch that, bring the plates, heap the food—on and on—the party happened.

"Yes, he's done. Quite done." Cecy's calm sleeper's lips turned up. The languid words fell slowly from her shaping mouth. "Inside this woman's skull I am, looking out, watching the sea that does not move, and is so quiet it makes you afraid. I sit on the porch and wait for my husband to come home. Occasionally, a fish leaps, falls back, starlight edging it. The valley, the sea, the few cars, the wooden porch, my rocking chair, myself, the silence."

"What now, Cecy?"

"I'm getting up from my rocking chair," she said.

"Yes?"

"I'm walking off the porch, toward the mud pots. Planes fly over, like primordial birds. Then it is quiet, so quiet."

"How long will you stay inside her, Cecy?"

"Until I've listened and looked and felt enough: until I've changed her life some way. I'm walking off the porch and along the wooden boards. My feet knock on the planks, tiredly, slowly."

"And now?"

"Now the sulphur fumes are all around me. I stare at the bubbles as they break and smooth. A bird darts by my temple, shrieking. Suddenly I am in the bird and fly away! And as I fly, inside my new small glass-bead eyes I see a woman below me, on a boardwalk, take one two three steps forward into the mud pots. I hear a sound as of a boulder plunged into molten depths. I keep flying, circle back. I see a white hand, like a spider, wriggle and disappear into the gray lava pool. The lava seals over. Now I'm flying home, swift, swift, swift!"

Something clapped hard against the window. Timothy started.

Cecy flicked her eyes wide, bright, full, happy, exhilarated.

"Now I'm *home!*" she said.

After a pause, Timothy ventured, "The Homecoming's on. And everybody's here."

"Then why are you upstairs?" She took his hand. "Well, ask me." She smiled slyly. "Ask me what you came to ask."

"I didn't come to ask anything," he said. "Well, almost nothing. Well—oh, Cecy!" It came from him in one long rapid flow. "I want to do something at the party to make them look at me, something to make me good as them, something to make me belong, but there's nothing I can do and I feel funny and, well, I thought you might . . ."

"I might," she said, closing her eyes, smiling inwardly. "Stand up straight. Stand very still." He obeyed. "Now, shut your eyes and blank out your thought."

He stood very straight and thought of nothing, or at least thought of thinking nothing.

She sighed. "Shall we go downstairs now, Timothy?" Like a hand into a glove, Cecy was within him.

"Look everybody!" Timothy held the glass of warm red liquid. He held up the glass so that the whole house turned to watch him. Aunts, uncles, cousins, brothers, sisters!

He drank it straight down.

He jerked a hand at his sister Laura. He held her gaze, whispering to her in a subtle voice that kept her silent, frozen. He felt tall as the trees as he walked to her. The party now slowed. It waited on all sides of him, watching. From all the room doors the faces peered. They were not laughing. Mother's face was astonished. Dad looked bewildered, but pleased and getting prouder every instant.

He nipped Laura, gently, over the neck vein. The candle flames swayed drunkenly. The wind climbed around on the roof outside. The relatives stared from all the doors. He popped toadstools into his mouth, swallowed, then beat his arms against his flanks and circled. "Look, Uncle Einar! I can fly, at last!" Beat went his hands. Up and down pumped his feet. The faces flashed past him.

At the top of the stairs flapping, he heard his mother cry, "Stop, Timothy!" far below. "Hey!" shouted Timothy, and leaped off the top of the well, thrashing.

Halfway down, the wings he thought he owned dissolved. He screamed. Uncle Einar caught him.

Timothy flailed whitely in the receiving arms. A voice burst out of his lips, unbidden. "This is Cecy! This is Cecy! Come see me, all of you, upstairs, first room on the left!" Followed by a long trill of high laughter. Timothy tried to cut if off with his tongue.

Everybody was laughing. Einar set him down. Running through the crowding blackness as the relatives flowed upstairs toward Cecy's room to congratulate her, Timothy banged the front door open.

"Cecy, I hate you, I hate you!"

By the sycamore tree, in deep shadow, Timothy spewed out his dinner, sobbed bitterly and threshed in a pile of autumn leaves. Then he lay still. From his blouse pocket, from the protection of the matchbox he used for his retreat, the spider crawled forth. Spid walked along Timothy's arm. Spid explored up his neck to his ear and climbed in the ear to tickle it. Timothy shook his head. "Don't, Spid. Don't."

The feathery touch of a tentative feeler probing his eardrum set Timothy shivering. "Don't, Spid!" He sobbed somewhat less.

The spider traveled down his cheek, took a station under the boy's nose, looked up into the nostrils as if to seek the brain, and then clambered softly up over the rim of the nose to sit, to squat there peering at Timothy with green gem eyes until Timothy filled with ridiculous laughter. "Go away, Spid!"

Timothy sat up, rustling the leaves. The land was very

bright with the moon. In the house he could hear the faint ribaldry as Mirror, Mirror was played. Celebrants shouted, dimly muffled, as they tried to identify those of themselves whose reflections did not, had not ever appeared in a glass.

"Timothy." Uncle Einar's wings spread and twitched and came in with a sound like kettledrums. Timothy felt himself plucked up like a thimble and set upon Einar's shoulder. "Don't feel badly, Nephew Timothy. Each to his own, each in his own way. How much better things are for you. How rich. The world's dead for us. We've seen so much of it, believe me. Life's best to those who live the least of it. It's worth more per ounce, Timothy, remember that."

The rest of the black morning, from midnight on, Uncle Einar led him about the house, from room to room, weaving and singing. A horde of late arrivals set the entire hilarity off afresh. Great-great-great-great and a thousand more great-greats Grandmother was there, wrapped in Egyptian cerements. She said not a word, but lay straight as a burnt ironing board against the wall, her eye hollows cupping a distant, wise, silent glimmering. At the breakfast, at four in the morning, one-thousand-odd-greats Grandmama was stiffly seated at the head of the longest table.

The numerous young cousins caroused at the crystal punch bowl. Their shiny olive-pit eyes, their conical, devilish faces and curly bronze hair hovered over the drinking table, their hard-soft, half-girl half-boy bodies wrestling against each other as they got unpleasantly, sullenly drunk. The wind got higher, the stars burned with fiery intensity, the noises redoubled, the dances quickened, the drinking became more positive. To

Timothy there were thousands of things to hear and watch. The many darknesses roiled, bubbled, the many faces passed and repassed. . . .

"Listen!"

The party held its breath. Far away the town clock struck its chimes, saying six o'clock. The party was ending. As if at a cue, in time to the rhythm of the clock striking, their one hundred voices began to sing songs that were four hundred years old, songs Timothy could not know. They twined their arms around one another, circling slowly, and sang, and somewhere in the cold distance of morning the town clock finished out its chimes and quieted.

Good-bys were said, there was a great rustling. Mother and Father and the brothers and sisters lined up at the door to shake hands and kiss each departing relative in turn. The sky beyond the open door colored and shone in the east. A cold wind entered.

The shouting and the laughing bit by bit faded and went away. Dawn grew more apparent. Everybody was embracing and crying and thinking how the world was becoming less a place for them. There had been a time when they had met every year, but now decades passed with no reconciliation. "Don't forget, we meet in Salem in 1970!" someone cried.

Salem. Timothy's numbed mind turned the word over. Salem, 1970. And there would be Uncle Fry and Grandma and Grandfather and a thousand-times-great Grandmother in her withered cerements. And Mother and Father and Ellen and Laura and Cecy and Leonard and Bion and Sam and all the rest. But would he be there? Would he be alive that long? Could he be certain of living until then?

With one last withering wind blast, away they all went, so

many scarves, so many fluttery mammals, so many sere leaves, so many wolves loping, so many whinings and clustering noises, so many midnights and ideas and insanities.

Mother shut the door. Laura picked up a broom.

"No," said Mother, "we'll clean tonight. We need sleep first."

Father walked down into the cellar, followed by Laura and Bion and Sam. Ellen walked upstairs, as did Leonard.

Timothy walked across the crape-littered hall. His head was down, and in passing a party mirror he saw himself, the pale mortality of his face all cold and trembling.

"Timothy," said Mother.

He stopped at the stair well. She came to him, laid a hand on his face. "Son," she said. "We love you. Remember that. We all love you. No matter how different you are, no matter if you leave us one day," she said. She kissed his cheek. "And if and when you die, your bones will lie undisturbed, we'll see to that. You'll lie at ease forever, and I'll come see you every Allhallows Eve and tuck you in the more secure."

The house was silent. Far away the wind went over a hill with its last cargo of small dark bats, echoing, chittering.

He walked up the steps, one by one, crying to himself all the way.

THE WONDERFUL DEATH
OF DUDLEY STONE

"**A**live!"

"Dead!"

"Alive in New England, damn it."

"Died twenty years ago!"

"Pass the hat, I'll go myself and bring back his head!"

That's how the talk went that night. A stranger set it off with his mouthings about Dudley Stone dead. Alive! we cried. And shouldn't we know? Weren't we the last frail remnants of those who had burnt incense and read his books by the light of blazing intellectual votives in the twenties?

The Dudley Stone. That magnificent stylist, that proudest of literary lions. Surely you recall the head-pounding, the cliff-jumping, the whistlings of doom that followed on his writing his publishers this note:

Sirs: Today, aged 30, I retire from the field, renounce writing, burn all my effects, toss my latest manuscript on the dump, cry hail and fare thee well. Yrs., affect.

Dudley Stone

Earthquakes and avalanches, in that order.

"*Why?*" we asked ourselves, meeting down the years.

In fine soap-opera fashion we debated if it was women caused him to hurl his literary future away. Was it the Bottle. Or Horses that outran him and stopped a fine pacer in his prime?

We freely admitted to one and all, that were Stone writing now, Faulkner, Hemingway, and Steinbeck would be buried in his lava. All the sadder that Stone, on the brink of his greatest work, turned one day and went off to live in a town we shall call Obscurity by the sea best named The Past.

"*Why?*"

That question forever lived with those of us who had seen the glints of genius in his piebald works.

One night a few weeks ago, musing off the erosion of the years, finding each others' faces somewhat more pouched and our hairs more conspicuously in absence, we became enraged over the typical citizen's ignorance of Dudley Stone.

At least, we muttered, Thomas Wolfe had had a full measure of success before he seized his nose and jumped off the rim of Eternity. At least the critics gathered to stare after his plunge into darkness as after a meteor that made much fire in its passing. But who now remembered Dudley Stone, his coteries, his frenzied followers of the twenties?

"Pass the hat," I said. "I'll travel three hundred miles, grab Dudley Stone by the pants and say: 'Look here, Mr. Stone, why did you let us down so badly? Why haven't you written a book in twenty-five years?' "

The hat was lined with cash; I sent a telegram and took a train.

———

I do not know what I expected. Perhaps to find a doddering and frail praying mantis, whisping about the station, blown by seawinds, a chalk-white ghost who would husk at me with the voices of grass and reeds blown in the night. I clenched my knees in agony as my train chuffed into the station. I let myself down into a lonely country-side, a mile from the sea, like a man foolishly insane, wondering why I had come so far.

On a bulletin board in front of the boarded-up ticket office I found a cluster of announcements, inches thick, pasted and nailed one upon another for uncountable years. Leafing under, peeling away anthropological layers of printed tissue I found what I wanted. Dudley Stone for Alderman, Dudley Stone for Sheriff, Dudley Stone for Mayor! On up through the years his photograph, bleached by sun and rain, faintly recognizable, asked for ever more responsible positions in the life of this world near the sea. I stood reading them.

"Hey!"

And Dudley Stone plunged across the station platform behind me suddenly. "Is that you, Mr. Douglas!" I whirled to confront this great architecture of a man, big but not in the least fat, his legs huge pistons thrusting him on, a bright flower in his lapel, a bright tie at his neck. He crushed my hand, looked down upon me like Michelangelo's God creating Adam with a mighty touch. His face was the face of those illustrated North Winds and South Winds that blow hot and cold in ancient mariners' charts. It was the face that symbolizes the sun in Egyptian carvings, ablaze with life!

My God! I thought. And this is the man who hasn't written in twenty-odd years. Impossible. He's so alive it's sinful. I can hear his *heartbeat*!

I must have stood with my eyes very wide to let the look of him cram in upon my startled senses.

"You thought you'd find Marley's Ghost," he laughed. "Admit it."

"I—"

"My wife's waiting with a New England boiled dinner, we've plenty of ale and stout. I like the ring of those words. To *ale* is not to sicken, but to revive the flagging spirit. A tricky word, that. And *stout*? There's a nice ruddy sound to it. Stout!" A great golden watch bounced on his vestfront, hung in bright chains. He vised my elbow and charmed me along, a magician well on his way back to his cave with a luckless rabbit. "Glad to see you! I suppose you've come, as the others came, to ask the same question, eh! Well, this time I'll tell everything!"

My heart jumped. "Wonderful!"

Behind the empty station sat an open-top 1927-vintage Model-T Ford. "Fresh air. Drive at twilight like this, you get all the fields, the grass, the flowers, coming at you in the wind. I hope you're not one of those who tiptoe around shutting windows! Our house is like the top of a mesa. We let the weather do our broom-work. Hop in!"

Ten minutes later we swung off the highway onto a drive that had not been leveled or filled in years. Stone drove straight on over the pits and bumps, smiling steadily. Bang! We shuddered the last few yards to a wild, unpainted two-story house. The car was allowed to gasp itself away into mortal silence.

"Do you want the truth?" Stone turned to look me in the face and hold my shoulder with an earnest hand. "I was murdered by a man with a gun twenty-five years ago almost to this very day."

I sat staring after him as he leapt from the car. He was solid as a ton of rock, no ghost to him, but yet I knew that somehow the truth was in what he had told me before firing himself like a cannon at the house.

"This is my wife, and this is the house, and that is our supper waiting for us! Look at our view. Windows on three sides of the living room, a view of the sea, the shore, the meadows. We nail the windows open three out of four seasons. I swear you get a smell of limes here midsummer, and something from Antarctica, ammonia and ice cream, come December. Sit down! Lena, isn't it *nice* having him here?"

"I hope you like New England boiled dinner," said Lena, now here, now there, a tall, firmly-built woman, the sun in the East, Father Christmas' daughter, a bright lamp of a face that lit our table as she dealt out the heavy useful dishes made to stand the pound of giants' fists. The cutlery was solid enough to take a lion's teeth. A great whiff of steam rose up, through which we gladly descended, sinners into Hell. I saw the seconds-plate skim by three times and felt the ballast gather in my chest, my throat, and at last my ears. Dudley Stone poured me a brew he had made from wild Concords that had cried for mercy, he said. The wine bottle, empty, had its green glass mouth blown softly by Stone, who summoned out a rhythmic one-note tune that was quickly done.

"Well, I've kept you waiting long enough," he said, peering at me from that distance which drinking adds between people and which, at odd turns in the evening, seems closeness it-self. "I'll tell you about my murder. I've never told anyone be-fore; believe me. Do you know John Oatis Kendall?"

"A minor writer in the twenties, wasn't he?" I said. "A few books. Burnt out by '31. Died last week."

"God rest him." Mr. Stone lapsed into a special brief mel-ancholy from which he revived as he began to speak again.

"Yes. John Oatis Kendall, burnt out by the year 1931, a writer of great potentialities."

"Not as great as yours," I said, quickly.

"Well, just wait. We were boys together, John Oatis and I, born where the shade of an oak tree touched my house in the morning and his house at night, swam every creek in the world together, got sick on sour apples and cigarettes together, saw the same lights in the same blonde hair of the same young girl to-gether, and in our late teens went out to kick Fate in the stomach and get beat on the head together. We both did fair, and then *I* better and still better as the years ran. If his first book got one good notice, mine got six, if I got one bad notice, he got a dozen. We were like two friends on a train which the public has uncou-pled. There went John Oatis on the caboose, left behind, crying out, 'Save me! You're leaving me in Tank Town, Ohio; we're on the same track!' And the conductor saying, 'Yes, but not the same *train!*' And myself yelling, '*I* believe in you, John, be of good heart, I'll come back for you!' And the caboose dwindling behind with its red and green lamps like cherry and lime pops shining in the dark and we yelling our friendship to each other: 'John, old man!' 'Dudley, old pal!' while John Oatis went out on a dark sid-ing behind a tin baling-shed at midnight and my engine, with all the flag-wavers and brass bands, boiled on toward dawn."

Dudley Stone paused and noticed my look of general confusion.

"All this to lead up to my murder," he said. "For it was John Oatis Kendall who, in 1930, traded a few old clothes and some remaindered copies of his books for a gun and came out to this house and this room."

"He really meant to kill you?"

"Meant to, hell! He did! Bang! Have some more wine? That's better."

A strawberry shortcake was set upon the table by Mrs. Stone, while he enjoyed my gibbering suspense. Stone sliced it into three huge chunks and served it around, fixing me with his kindly approximation of the Wedding Guest's eye.

"There he sat, John Oatis, in that chair where you sit now. Behind him, outside, in the smokehouse, seventeen hams; in our wine cellars, five hundred bottles of the best; beyond the window open country, the elegant sea in full lace; overhead a moon like a dish of cool cream, everywhere the full panoply of spring, and Lena across the table, too, a willow tree in the wind, laughing at everything I said or did not choose to say, both of us thirty, mind you, thirty years old, life our magnificent carousel, our fingers playing full chords, my books selling well, fan mail pouring upon us in crisp white founts, horses in the stables for moonlight rides to coves where either we or the sea might whisper all we wished in the night. And John Oatis seated there where you sit now, quietly taking the little blue gun from his pocket."

"I laughed, thinking it was a cigar lighter of some sort," said his wife.

"But John Oatis said quite seriously: 'I'm going to kill you, Mr. Stone.'"

"What did you do?"

"Do? I sat there, stunned, riven; I heard a terrible slam! the coffin lid in my face! I heard coal down a black chute; dirt on my buried door. They say all your *past* hurtles by at such times. Nonsense. The *future* does. You see your face a bloody porridge. You sit there until your fumbling mouth can say, 'But why, John, what have I *done* to you?'

" 'Done!' he cried.

"And his eye skimmed along the vast bookshelf and the handsome brigade of books drawn stiffly to attention there with my name on each blazing like a panther's eye in the Moroccan blackness. 'Done!' he cried, mortally. And his hand itched the revolver in a sweat. 'Now, John,' I cautioned. 'What do you want?'

" 'One thing more than anything else in the world,' he said, 'to kill you and be famous. Get my name in headlines. Be famous as you are famous. Be known for a lifetime and beyond as the man who killed Dudley Stone!'

" 'You can't mean that!'

" 'I do. I'll be very famous. Far more famous than I am today, in your shadow. Oh, listen here, no one in the world knows how to hate like a writer does. God, how I love your work and God, how I hate you because you write so well. Amazing ambivalence. But I can't take it any more, not being able to write as you do, so I'll take my fame the easy way. I'll cut you off before you reach your prime. They say your next book will be your very finest, your most brilliant!'

" 'They exaggerate.'

" 'My guess is they're right!' he said.

"I looked beyond him to Lena who sat in her chair, frightened, but not frightened enough to scream or run and spoil the scene so it might end inadvertently.

" 'Calm,' I said. 'Calmness. Sit there, John. I ask only one minute. Then pull the trigger.'

" 'No!' Lena whispered.

" 'Calmness,' I said to her, to myself, to John Oatis.

"I gazed out the open windows, I felt the wind, I thought of the wine in the cellar, the coves at the beach, the sea, the night moon like a disc of menthol cooling the summer heavens, drawing clouds of flaming salt, the stars, after it in a wheel toward morning. I thought of myself only thirty, Lena thirty, our whole lives ahead. I thought of all the flesh of life hung high and waiting for me to really *start* banqueting! I had never climbed a mountain, I had never sailed an ocean, I had never run for Mayor, I had never dived for pearls, I had never owned a telescope, I had never acted on a stage or built a house or read all the classics I had so *wished* to read. All the *actions* waiting to be done!

"So in that almost instantaneous sixty seconds, I thought at last of my career. The books I had written, the books I *was* writing, the books I intended to write. The reviews, the sales, our huge balance in the bank. And, believe or disbelieve me, for the first time in my life I got free of it all. I became, in one moment, a critic. I cleared the scales. On one hand I put all the boats I hadn't taken, the flowers I hadn't planted, the children I hadn't raised, all the hills I hadn't looked at, with Lena there, goddess of the harvest. In the middle I put John Oatis Kendall with his gun—the upright that held the balances. And on the empty scale a dozen books. I made some minor adjustments. The sixty opposite I laid my pen, my ink, my empty paper, my seconds were ticking by. The sweet night wind blew across the table. It touched a curl of hair on Lena's neck, oh Lord, how softly, softly it touched . . .

"The gun pointed at me. I have seen the moon craters in photographs, and that hole in space called the Great Coal Sack Nebula, but neither was as big, take my word, as the mouth of that gun across the room from me.

" 'John,' I said at last, 'do you hate me *that* much? Because I've been lucky and you not?'

" 'Yes, damn it!' he cried.

"It was almost funny he should envy me. I was not that much better a writer than he. A flick of the wrist made the difference.

" 'John,' I said quietly to him, 'if you want me dead, I'll *be* dead. Would you like for me to never write again?'

"'I'd like nothing better!' he cried. 'Get ready!' He aimed at my heart!

" 'All right,' I said. 'I'll never write again.'

" 'What?' he said.

" 'We're old old friends, we've never lied to each other, have we? Then take my word, from this night on I'll never put pen to paper.'

" 'Oh *God*,' he said, and laughed with contempt and disbelief.

" 'There,' I said, nodding my head at the desk near him, 'are the only original copies of the two books I've been working on for the last three years. I'll burn one in front of you now. The other you yourself may throw in the sea. Clean out the house, take everything faintly resembling literature, burn my published books, too. Here.' I got up. He could have shot me then, but I had him fascinated. I tossed one manuscript on the hearth and touched a match to it.

" 'No!' Lena said. I turned. 'I know what I'm doing,' I said. She began to cry. John Oatis Kendall simply stared at me, bewitched. I brought him the other unpublished manuscript. 'Here,' I said, tucking it under his right shoe so his foot was a paper weight. I went back and sat down. The wind was blowing and the night was warm and Lena was white as apple-blossoms there across the table.

"I said, 'From this day forward I will not write ever again.'

"At last John Oatis managed to say, 'How can you do this?'

" 'To make everyone happy,' I said. 'To make you happy because we'll be friends again, eventually. To make Lena happy because I'll be just her husband again and no agent's performing seal. And myself happy because I'd rather be a live man than a dead author. A dying man will do anything, John. Now take my last novel and get along with you.'

"We sat there, the three of us, just as we three are sitting tonight. There was a smell of lemons and limes and camellias. The ocean roared on the stony coastland below; God, what a lovely moonlit sound. And at last, picking up the manuscripts, John Oatis took them, like my body, out of the room. He paused at the door and said, 'I believe you.' And then he was gone. I heard him drive away. I put Lena to bed. That was one of the few nights in my life I ever walked down by the shore, but walk I did, taking deep breaths and feeling my arms and legs and my face with my hands, crying like a child, walking and wading in the surf to feel the cold salt water foaming about me in a million suds."

Dudley Stone paused. Time had made a stop in the room. Time was in another year, the three of us sitting there, enchanted with his telling of the murder.

"And did he destroy your last novel?" I asked.

Dudley Stone nodded. "A week later one of the pages

drifted up on the shore. He must have thrown them over the cliff, a thousand pages, I see it in my mind's eye, a flock of white sea-gulls it might seem, flying down to the water and going out with the tide at four in the black morning. Lena ran up the beach with that single page in her hand, crying, 'Look, look!' And when I saw what she handed me, I tossed it back in the ocean."

"Don't tell me you honored your promise!"

Dudley Stone looked at me steadily. "What would *you* have done in a similar position? Look at it this way: John Oatis did me a favor. He didn't kill me. He didn't shoot me. He took my word. He honored my word. He let me live. He let me go on eating and sleeping and breathing. Quite suddenly he had broadened my horizons. I was so grateful that standing on the beach hip-deep in water that night, I cried. I was grateful. Do you really understand that word? Grateful he had let me live when he had had it in his hand to annihilate me forever."

Mrs. Stone rose up, the dinner was ended. She cleared the dishes, we lit cigars; and Dudley Stone strolled me over to his office-at-home, a rolltop desk, its jaws propped wide with parcels and papers and ink bottles, a typewriter, documents, ledgers, indexes.

"It was all rolling to a boil in me. John Oatis simply spooned the froth off the top so I could see the brew. It was very clear," said Dudley Stone. "Writing was always so much mustard and gallweed to me; fidgeting words on paper, experiencing vast depressions of heart and soul. Watching the greedy critics graph me up, chart me down, slice me like sausage, eat me at midnight breakfasts. Work of the worst sort. I was *ready* to fling the pack. My trigger was set. Boom! There was John Oatis! Look here."

He rummaged in the desk and brought forth hand-bills and posters. "I had been *writing* about living. Now I wanted to live. *Do* things instead of tell about things. I ran for the board of education. I won. I ran for alderman. I won. I ran for mayor. I won! Sheriff! Town librarian! Sewage disposal official. I shook a lot of hands, saw a lot of life, did a lot of things. We've lived every way there is to live, with our eyes and noses and mouths, with our ears and hands. We've climbed hills and painted pictures, there are some on the wall! We've been three times around the world! I even delivered our baby son, unexpectedly. He's grown and married now—lives in New York! We've done and done again." Stone paused and smiled. "Come on out in the yard; we've set up a telescope, would you like to see the rings of Saturn?"

We stood in the yard, and the wind blew from a thousand miles at sea and while we were standing there, looking at the stars through the telescope, Mrs. Stone went down into the midnight cellar after a rare Spanish wine.

It was noon the next day when we reached the lonely station after a hurricane trip across the jouncing meadows from the sea. Mr. Dudley Stone let the car have its head, while he talked to me, laughing, smiling, pointing to this or that outcrop of Neolithic stone, this or that wild flower, falling silent again only as we parked and waited for the train to come and take me away.

"I suppose," he said, looking at the sky, "you think I'm quite insane."

"No, I'd never say that."

"Well," said Dudley Stone, "John Oatis Kendall did me one other favor."

"What was that?"

Stone hitched around conversationally in the patched leather seat.

"He helped me get out when the going was good. Deep down inside I must have guessed that my literary success was something that would melt when they turned off the cooling system. My subconscious had a pretty fair picture of my future. I knew what none of my critics knew, that I was headed nowhere but down. The two books John Oatis destroyed were very bad. They would have killed me deader than Oatis possibly could. So he helped me decide, unwittingly, what I might not have had the courage to decide myself, to bow gracefully out while the cotillion was still on, while the Chinese lanterns still cast flattering pink lights on my Harvard complexion. I had seen too many writers up, down, and out, hurt, unhappy, suicidal. The combination of circumstance, coincidence, subconscious knowledge, relief, and gratitude to John Oatis Kendall to just *be alive*, were fortuitous, to say the least."

We sat in the warm sunlight another minute.

"And then I had the pleasure of seeing myself compared to all the greats when I announced my departure from the literary scene. Few authors in recent history have bowed out to such publicity. It was a lovely funeral. I looked, as they say, natural. And the echoes lingered. 'His *next* book!' the critics cried, 'would have been *it*! A masterpiece!' I had them panting, waiting. Little did they know. Even now, a quarter-century later, my readers who were college boys then, make sooty excursions on drafty kerosene-stinking shortline trains to solve the mystery of why I've made them wait so long for my 'masterpiece.' And thanks to John Oatis Kendall I still have a little reputation; it has receded slowly, painlessly. The next year I might have died by my own writing hand. How much better to cut your own caboose off the train, before others do it for you.

"My friendship with John Oatis Kendall? It came back. It took time, of course. But he was out here to see me in 1947; it was a nice day, all around, like old times. And now he's dead and at last I've told someone everything. What will you tell your friends in the city? They won't believe a word of this. But it *is* true, I swear it, as I sit here and breathe God's good air and look at the calluses on my hands and begin to resemble the faded handbills I used when I ran for county treasurer."

We stood on the station platform.

"Good-by, and thanks for coming and opening your ears and letting my world crash in on you. God bless to all your curious friends. Here comes the train! I've got to run; Lena and I are going to a Red Cross drive down the coast this afternoon! Good-by!"

I watched the dead man stomp and leap across the platform, felt the plankings shudder, saw him jump into his Model-T, heard it lurch under his bulk, saw him bang the floor-boards with a big foot, idle the motor, roar it, turn, smile, wave to me, and then roar off and away toward that suddenly brilliant town called Obscurity by a dazzling seashore called The Past.

ABOUT THE AUTHOR

RAY BRADBURY has published some five hundred short stories, novels, plays, and poems since his first story appeared in *Weird Tales* when he was twenty years old. For several years he wrote for *Alfred Hitchcock Presents* and *The Twilight Zone* and in 1953 did the screenplay for John Huston's *Moby Dick*. He has produced two of his own plays, written two musicals, two space-age cantatas with Lalo Schifrin and Jerry Goldsmith, and collaborated on an animated film, *Icarus Montgolfer Wright*, which was nominated for an Academy Award in 1962.

Mr. Bradbury was Idea Consultant for the United States Pavilion at the New York World's Fair in 1963, has helped design a ride for Disney World, and is doing consultant work on city engineering and rapid transit. When one of the Apollo astronaut teams landed on the moon, they named Dandelion Crater there to honor Bradbury's novel *Dandelion Wine*. His novel *Something Wicked This Way Comes* was made into a major release feature film, and his own cable television show, called *The Ray Bradbury Theater*, received nineteen cable award nominations and won seven.